The Fearless Flag Thrower of Lucca

To: Rob & Sue
thanks to my
good friends!
[illegible]
9/29/12

The Fearless Flag Thrower of Lucca

Nine Stories of 1990s Tuscany

Cover Photo by Nancy Irons-Murray: A typical flag thrower at a festival in Tuscany.

PAUL SALSINI

THE FEARLESS FLAG THROWER OF LUCCA
NINE STORIES OF 1990S TUSCANY

The author gratefully acknowledges the film "La nave dolce," ("The Human Cargo"), a 2012 film directed by Daniele Vicari that used spectacular footage and interviews to recount the dramatic voyage of thousands of Albanians to Bari, Italy, in 1991.

iUniverse books may be ordered through booksellers or by contacting:

iUniverse
1663 Liberty Drive
Bloomington, IN 47403
www.iuniverse.com
1-800-Authors (1-800-288-4677)

ISBN: 978-1-4917-9526-2 (sc)
ISBN: 978-1-4917-9527-9 (e)

Library of Congress Control Number: 2016906265

Print information available on the last page.

iUniverse rev. date: 04/20/2016

For Barbara,
Jim, Laura and Jack

Also by Paul Salsini

Fiction:

A Piazza for Sant'Antonio: Five Novellas of 1980s Tuscany

The Temptation of Father Lorenzo: Ten Stories of 1970s Tuscany

Dino's Story: A Novel of 1960s Tuscany

Sparrow's Revenge: A Novel of Postwar Tuscany

The Cielo: A Novel of Wartime Tuscany

Nonfiction:

Second Start

For Children:

Stefano and the Christmas Miracles

Introduction

AS I'VE WRITTEN BEFORE, the inspiration for the first novel in this Tuscan series came from the stories my cousin Fosca told me about her experiences in World War II. She and others from her small village near Lucca were forced to flee to a farmhouse in the hills and were captive there for three months.

I was fascinated by her stories and decided to write a fictional account. The result was *The Cielo: A Novel of Wartime Tuscany,* combining what was happening in the farmhouse with the terrifying war outside and the real massacre of almost an entire village a few miles away.

Knowing very little about the war, I needed to do a considerable amount of research but, as a journalist, I found this to be one of the most satisfying parts of this whole adventure. For that first book, I learned about the war, the rise of the Resistance movement, the Nazi occupation, the Allied intervention and, most of all, the heroism of the Italian citizens. When that first book was followed by others over the years, I learned about postwar conflicts between Fascists and Communists in the 1950s, about the devastating flood in Florence in 1966, about the women's movement in the 1970s, about the "Monster of Florence" in the 1980s and about the influx of Albanians in the 1990s. And so much more.

It was a master's degree in Italian history.

The research helped inform the stories, which were set in a village not unlike Fosca's, and in a farmhouse in the hills, not unlike a real farmhouse where my grandfather once lived. I named the place The Cielo, which means "heaven" or "sky."

But the characters illuminated the stories. And that was the fun part.

I don't even like to call them "characters." I don't know how other authors "create" characters, but for me, the people just seemed to emerge from the page, or more correctly, my computer. At the risk of being accused of having imaginary friends, I often felt as though I was simply writing down what they were doing, what they were saying. They became real to me in the course of the writing and they created their stories.

While Fosca was the inspiration for Rosa and Fosca's husband, Renato, for Marco, all the other people are entirely fictional. In the farmhouse, the assorted group also consisted of Rosa's bitter enemy and the woman's husband; two crotchety elderly sisters; two cousins who tease them; a "contessa" who isn't a contessa; an obstinate woman who turns out to be a Nazi sympathizer; a Dante scholar who carries a secret to his grave and a woman with five children ranging from a three-month-old baby to a sixteen-year-old girl.

Outside, there was the priest in the village, assassinated while trying to send a message to the partisans; two young SS soldiers; an escaped British prisoner of war, and, notably, a Resistance fighter who leads his motley band and falls in love with a woman in that doomed village.

Where did all these people come from? I have no idea. I had trouble with only two of them, the Nazi soldiers. I didn't want them to be stereotypical bad guys, so they turned out to be young, idealistic and foolish.

After *The Cielo* was published in 2006, these people had become so real to me that they would not let me go. They wanted—demanded—a sequel. One seemed obvious. If Ezio, that Resistance fighter, had witnessed the massacre at that nearby village, and if he knew that his lover was among the victims, wouldn't he feel an awful lot of hatred and guilt and wouldn't he want to take revenge?

The result was *Sparrow's Revenge: A Novel of Postwar Tuscany.* In it, Ezio (code name: Sparrow) finds the man he believes was the Fascist collaborator for the Nazis, but, as it turns out, the man has his own story and was an unwilling accomplice. His story ends in the waters under a Devil's Bridge, but Ezio has found a new love, the indomitable Donna, who works in a marble factor in Pietrasanta.

Another book was completed, but these people were still in my head. Having written about the 1940s during the war and the postwar 1950s, I decided to write about the 1960s. I vaguely remembered that Florence had experienced a disastrous flood of the Arno River in 1966 and began researching that. Suddenly, Dino, who was born at the end of the first book and was ten years old in the second, told me that he wanted to study art in Florence.

So his coming-of-age story, set during that flood, became *Dino's Story: A Novel of 1960s Tuscany.* Among the other people who frequented Florence at that time were a young Franciscan friar, Father Lorenzo, who ran a soup kitchen, and Sofia, a young woman from "the South," then and now a place looked upon with disdain by many people in the North of Italy.

Father Lorenzo would become Dino's lifelong friend and Sofia would become Dino's wife.

(Sometimes, people ask how these people got their names. In a few cases, I've used family names: Luigi was my father's name, Giuseppina my mother's, Roberto my brother's and Amabilia my grandmother's. All the rest just sounded right.)

Rather than be confined to another novel, the people asked that I write separate stories about them for the next decade. The result was *The Temptation of Father Lorenzo: Ten Stories of 1970s Tuscany,* with the centerpiece about the priest having a short but intense infatuation with a beautiful shopkeeper in Rimini.

Another story describes the "miracle" that occurs at the Christmas crèche in the village church and a third how Ezio and Donna turn the Cielo into a bread-and-breakfast. Of course, while new people are arriving in these stories, and young people are growing up, the older ones are advancing in years. Some leave us forever.

But life goes on, and so *A Piazza for Sant'Antonio: Five Novellas of 1980s Tuscany* not only describes how the village acquired a new town square but also how Donna wrote a best-selling cookbook and how the villagers reacted when an entire family from "the South" moved to Sant'Antonio. In another story, Dino finds his roots in the rugged Garfagnana area of Tuscany, a place where there's a "ghost village."

In researching this decade in Italy, I discovered that Florence was terrorized at this time by a serial killer who murdered young couples in lovers' lanes. Father Lorenzo told me he would help console the survivors.

The Fearless Flag Thrower of Lucca: Nine Stories of 1990s Tuscany is the final volume of A Tuscan Series, and the people are nearing the end of the millennium. A shipload of Albanians tries to find refuge in Italy, Dino's aunt begins a relationship with a "television priest," a nearby supermarket threatens Sant'Antonio's only two shops, a girl surprises a flag-throwing team, Father Lorenzo meets the woman he once cared for, and Frances Mayes' best-selling memoir *Under the Tuscan Sun* impacts a tourist business.

Also, Ezio finishes the novel he's been writing for decades. Oddly, it's about a group of terrified people who flee to a farmhouse in the hills and have to remain there for three months while the war goes on all around them. It also features a valiant Resistance fighter.

We've all gotten older since *The Cielo* was published. The people have grown and changed. Lucia and Paolo have been married for fifty years, Dino and Sofia are in their fifties, Father Lorenzo in his sixties and Ezio and Donna in their seventies. It's time for them and the dozens of others who populate the books to move on and live their lives without me.

I'll miss them.

Contents

The Main Characters

Dino Sporenza, a middle-aged professional in Florence

Sofia, his wife, a nurse

Lucia Sporenza, his mother, who lives in Sant'Antonio

Paolo Ricci, her husband

Anna, a former nun who is Dino's aunt and Lucia's sister

Father Lorenzo, a Franciscan priest in Florence

Father Giancarlo Moretti, a popular television priest in Florence

Ezio Maffini, a former partisan and retired teacher who lives in The Cielo

Donna Fazzini, his wife, who owns a restaurant in Sant'Antonio

Bernadetto Magnimassimo, a wealthy retiree who lives in a villa near Sant'Antonio

Clara Marincola, the daughter of a family from Calabria who now lives in Sant'Antonio

Mario Leoni, the owner of a *bottega* in Sant'Antonio

Anita Manconi, his wife, the owner of a meat market in Sant'Antonio

Bruno Pezzino, Dino's cousin, who is a tour guide in Cortona

A Safe Haven

Florence

EVEN THOUGH their weekend excursion wasn't until August, Dino and Sofia started making plans in May. It had been three years, not since 1988, since they'd been able to get away together for even a few days. Something had always come up, and they didn't want anything to prevent it this time.

Dino told his uncles, who also worked at *Gli Angeli della Casa,* that he wanted five days off over a weekend in August.

"We can't plan that far in advance," Roberto said. "There may be people who need a house repair right away."

"Wait until July and we'll know better," Adolfo said.

"Well," Dino said, "I'm putting it on the calendar. Just so you know I won't be here."

Sofia had no easier time scheduling time off at the hospital. "We don't know if there will be emergencies." "Maybe another nurse will get sick and we'll have to call you in." "Just wait until July so we can know better."

"Well," Sofia said, "I'm putting it on the calendar so you know I won't be here."

After frequent reminders, their co-workers finally agreed that it would be all right for them to have the Saturday to Wednesday off. Sofia looked at the scale and decided she'd better lose five pounds if she was going to fit into her bathing suit. Dino bought a big new straw hat to replace the one that blew away the last time they were at the beach.

Sofia collected a half dozen travel books.

"Dino, some day I want to go to Sicily. And Paris. And London."

Dino chose some about the Medici and the history of Florence. They bought suntan oil and insect spray.

"You'd think we were going for a month," Dino said as he inspected the pile of things on their dining room table ready to be packed.

"I can't wait," Sofia said. "Solento was so beautiful the last time we were there. The white beaches, the beautiful caves."

"And remember the water? I've never seen water so clean and warm."

They had been told about the Solento region by friends fifteen years earlier and had fallen in love with the region the first time they visited. It was a long drive from Florence, down the eastern coast of Italy to the very foot of the boot, going past Ancona, Pescara and Bari before getting to their destination.

"People are discovering it, though," Sofia warned. "I hope we get there before the crowds come."

For many in Italy, August, the hottest month, was a time to escape to the sea. Dino and Sofia knew they were taking a chance that there would be a heavy influx of tourists, but they also knew that Solento in August was especially beautiful.

Friday, August 9, finally arrived, and they packed and were ready to go. Dino washed the breakfast dishes and Sofia straightened up the living room, keeping the television on in the background. She was singing softly to herself until she caught sight of something on the television screen.

"Oh my God," she cried. "Dino, come here, come here quick!"

Wiping his hands on a towel, Dino rushed in. "What happened? Are you OK?"

"It's not me. Look at the TV."

They could hardly believe their eyes. A cargo ship was so laden down with people that the ship itself could barely be seen. Passengers filled the deck and hung from the masts and derricks. They were everywhere. The ship looked like an anthill. And the people were yelling something.

"Who are these people and what are they crying?" Dino wondered.

The sounds became clearer. *"Italia! Italia!"*

"Shhh. Listen," Sofia said. They settled back on the couch.

"These are live pictures," the announcer said. "You are seeing the ship Vlora at the port of Bari. A few days ago it returned from Cuba with ten thousand tons of sugar and arrived at the port of Durres in

Albania. Yesterday, it was being unloaded when hundreds of men, women and children began storming aboard. They said they wanted to get out of Albania. More than ten thousand people, maybe as many as twenty thousand, are on board. They ordered the captain to take them to Italy, and so the ship was forced to head due west through the Strait of Otranto. It tried to stop at Brindisi but the officials there refused, so it sailed up the coast and now it has come to Bari."

"Bari!" Sofia said. "That's where we're going."

"Oh, my God!"

The television cameras continued to focus on the ship and the refugees. Many, mostly young men, began diving into the Adriatic Sea and swimming to the dock.

"Oh no! They're going to drown," Sofia whispered.

Soon there seemed to be hundreds in the swirling waters. Rescue ships marked *Guardia Finanza* picked up some of them.

"This is incredible," Dino said. "Those poor people."

Then the television switched to an office where a man with flowing white hair and wearing a dark suit was seated at a desk. He held papers in his hand and looked over rimless glasses. A scroll at the bottom of the screen identified him as Professor Franco Mantini.

"This is part of what we now call the Albanian exodus to Italy," he said into the camera. "The economic situation in that country has been so bad for years that many Albanians have been trying to leave. Since last year many have gone to Greece and now they are attempting to come to Italy. Remember in March of this year? More than twenty-four thousand of them docked in Apulia at that time. They started in small groups, in fishing boats. Then the boats got bigger and bigger and more people came.

"What did Italy do? Italy welcomed them. In fact, Prime Minister Giulio Andreotti suggested that families 'adopt' Albanians. The Italian politicians claimed that Italy and Albania were part of a common Adriatic culture, and so we had special bonds and obligations to them. The government started a program designed to integrate these people into Italian life, and they even got work permits. They had to get a job in four months or go back home. Many, many of them found jobs. Will this happen again with this group of people? I'm afraid things have gotten even worse in Albania, but attitudes have changed in Italy in just a few months. There is now a lot of suspicion and resentment towards Albanians. And there are so many on this ship! No, I don't believe these people will be welcomed."

Now the cameras, obviously from a helicopter, showed the ship being tied to the dock and a flood of people pouring out. Some of them jumped into the water to get there faster.

Soon hundreds, even thousands, of people milled around or stretched out on the concrete, exhausted.

The announcer came on again. "Police officers don't seem to know what to do. They are giving out a few bottles of water but there isn't nearly enough. These people left Albania last night and haven't had anything to eat or drink since then."

The refugees held up their arms to the cameras in victory signs.

"They think they're safe now," Dino said. "I wonder. Look, there's a man in a suit watching. Must be the mayor or somebody. That doesn't look good."

"Oh, and over there," Sofia said, "there's a young man limping. Something's wrong with his foot. How on earth did he get on the ship and then get off?"

"But there are so many still on the ship. Look, some guys are sliding down a rope to get to the water."

"Now even more are climbing up on the dock. Oh, my God, Dino. It's filled. There's not room for another human being there. And I don't see anyone helping them. Some of them look sick. They're carrying that boy. He's practically naked. And there's another boy stretched out. Who's helping them?"

"Nobody. There aren't any medical people. The heat must be terrible. Most of the guys don't have shirts on. Oh now, finally, somebody is bringing bottles of water."

Sofia turned the volume up. "There's another man carrying a young boy."

"Finally, here comes an ambulance. It says *Mater Dei* on the side. They're putting the boy inside."

"The dock looks so dirty, Dino. It looks like there are piles of coal dust."

"I can't believe we're watching this as it happens. The television crews must be all over."

"There are more people stretched out. Looks like they're passed out. That man won't even take water. Oh my God, these people need help!"

"Sofia, what do you think?"

"Dino, we have to go. Now."

SOFIA HAD BEGUN HER NURSING CAREER LATE, after she married Dino in 1979, and immediately upon graduation she got on the staff of the Ospedale di Santa Maria Nuova. Founded in 1288, it was the oldest hospital in Florence and, with its location in the center of the city, known for its service to the poor.

Sofia excelled in her job. She had a soft and comforting manner with patients and became skilled in a variety of nursing specialties. For the last four years she had been assigned to the I.C.U., a position she requested because she loved to treat emergency patients.

"You should have been a doctor," Dino often told her.

"No, this is just fine."

Turning off the television set, she went into the bedroom and put on her white uniform and even added her cap. Dino changed into a dark green shirt and pants because "it looks sort of like a uniform."

They emptied their refrigerator and took cans and packaged foods from their shelves.

"It didn't look like those people had any food at all," Sofia said, "but what we really need are some medical supplies. We'll have to stop at the hospital."

Dino parked illegally at the Ospedale di Santa Maria Nuova while Sofia ran in and found the supply room. She came back with three big shopping bags filled with bandages, antibiotics, painkillers and other supplies. She had four blankets draped around her shoulders.

"One of the guards tried to stop me," she said as she tossed everything into the back seat, "but I told him there was an emergency."

With everyone escaping to the sea on this Saturday, traffic was heavy going out of Florence, but they were soon on A1 headed past Perugia and Assisi. They crossed the mountains to the Adriatic coastal highway and headed south.

After relinquishing the driving to Dino, Sofia wanted to know more about the political and economic climate of Albania. "I have to confess that I haven't been following the news from Albania very well," she said.

"I don't know that much either," Dino said. "But remember that family that *Gli Angeli della Casa* helped when they came here in March? They had come from Albania."

"I remember they had two kids."

"Edona and Genti. Nice kids. The father Mergim is a carpenter. He's working for us over near Santa Croce now."

"They weren't all that lucky, Dino. I don't think there's a church in Florence that doesn't have an Albanian beggar on the steps. I know I'm not supposed to, but I give them something anyway."

"I do, too. And there's a lot of resentment against Albanians now. I hear a lot of talk about how they should go home."

"So tell me all about Albania in twenty-five words or less."

"It will take more than that," Dino said, "but since I've gotten to know Mergim and his family, I've read more about it. Well, for decades, starting in 1944, there was a Communist dictator in Albania named Enver Hoxha. He was ruthless. He had a secret police force, and found out who the 'enemies of the people' were. The borders were sealed and people couldn't leave. They watched Italian television in secret. And the economy was in shambles. There were food shortages. He died in 1985, I think."

"With a big sigh of relief from the people, I'm sure," Sofia said.

"Students tore down a big statue of him in the square at Tirana. Well, a guy named Ramiz Alia succeeded him. He had been Hoxha's right-hand man. And so there were still lots of crackdowns, purges and executions. It was like Russia under Stalin. My God, he even buried enemies alive."

"Nice guy."

"Well, naturally the country continued to be in turmoil."

"I can see why."

"So finally Alia introduced some reforms. He even eased restrictions on religion and on civil liberties. But the government began to crumble a couple of years ago when the Soviet and Eastern European Communist governments began to collapse. Alia tried to cling to power. He granted amnesty to political prisoners and promised some democratic reforms."

"Sounds like an about-face," Sofia said.

"It was. Sort of. But it didn't work. Everyone knew that Albania was the most backward, the poorest country in Europe. There was one crisis after another. The economy was dying. There were violent protests, and people fled. That's what caused all those people to flee to Greece and Italy earlier this year, as that professor said on television."

"And that's why all these people are fleeing today."

"Exactly."

"Well," Sofia said, "that was more than twenty-five words, but I learned a lot. And I feel so bad for those people. Having to live under those conditions and then to be crammed on a ship for hours and hours and who knows what's going to happen to them now."

"I've noticed that Italy's mood has changed in the last months," Dino said. "I hear comments about Albanians all the time. They're still called strangers, *gli stranieri*. I don't think these people are going to be welcomed with open arms. Who knows what's going to happen. They may even be sent home somehow."

Sofia thought about this, but she also thought about the people lying on the dock.

"Dino, I think we should bring water. Those people are dehydrated."

"There's an *Autogrill* in a few miles. We can stop there."

Paying more *lire* than they expected at the crowded shop, they bought as many cases of bottled water as they could carry and stuff into the car. On the way out, they saw people gathered in front of a television set. It showed more scenes of desperate people on the dock at Bari.

"Stupid people," one onlooker said. "They think they can come here and take our jobs."

"Foreigners!" another man yelled. "Go back home."

"There's enough of your kind here," a third muttered.

Dino and Sofia rushed back to their car.

"Well, now we know what kind of welcome they're going to get," Dino said.

As they neared Bari they were able to get reception from a local station on their radio. The commentator was taking calls about the "invasion" of the immigrants.

"...more than in March or any other time," one caller was saying. "It's true. There must be a half million of them on that ship."

"I don't think the ship would hold a half million," the commentator said.

"Well, there are a lot. Where are they going to go? I'll tell you where they're going to go. They're going to spread all over Italy like a plague."

"Thank you for your comments. Now, another caller?"

"Hello? I just want to say that I have relatives in Albania and it's been terrible there. Maybe they shouldn't come here, but they are having a terrible time there. Thank you."

"And thank you for your comments."

Dino turned the dial. "Maybe we can find out what's happening now."

"...and now the police have moved in. They're forcing the crowds to get together. A few young men are resisting and the police have pushed them back. Now they've stopped resisting. There's a big tanker truck backing into the crowd. Maybe it's water. Now there's another ambulance from *Mater Dei* and two men are carrying another one into it. There's a man stretched out on the concrete. He looks unconscious. I don't know if he's even alive. People are just walking past him as if he wasn't even there. There are more young men stretched out. There's a policeman with a boy over his shoulder like a sack of potatoes. There are still people swimming from the ship to the dock. Now the police are herding the people into one area but this dock isn't big enough for everyone. And it's so hot here. The sun is beating down. And the smell. All these people sweating. And the sea! And besides that, there aren't any bathrooms. They're using pails or going in the water. I think I'm getting sick. I have to say, this seems like something out of Dante's *Inferno.*"

"Oh, my God," Sofia said. "Can you drive faster?"

"Not with all this traffic."

The streets near the port were dense with cars, and it took Dino almost an hour to find a parking place. "We'd better walk from here. We can use that cart in the trunk to carry the water and stuff. Are you ready?"

"I'll have to be."

THERE WERE SO MANY PEOPLE in the streets that it took another hour for Dino and Sofia, pushing the cart filled with supplies, to make it to the dock.

"These aren't Albanians," Sofia said, looking at all the other people around them.

"No, they're Italians who just want to see what's going on."

"And maybe prevent the Albanians from going any farther?"

"Maybe. I hope this doesn't get ugly."

Barricades were set up at the docks, perhaps to keep the immigrants in, perhaps to keep the Italians out. Sofia found a young guard at a locked gate.

"Hello," she said. "As you can see, I'm a nurse. We're here to provide water and some assistance to these people. May we come in?"

The guard looked them over and reluctantly unlocked the gate. Immediately upon seeing Sofia's white uniform, dozens of immigrants, talking loudly in a language she didn't recognize, surrounded them. Then one spoke in Italian.

"Please. My name Rezar. You have water?"

"Yes!" Dino dug into the cart, pulled out a case and began distributing bottles. Without being asked, everyone shared.

Sofia noticed a woman with white hair who had a deep cut on her arm. Rezar translated.

"She says she fell on ship. She used handkerchief but bleeding won't stop."

"I have bandages," Sofia said, dipping into the cart for Mercurochrome and long strips of white cloth. The woman winced as the antiseptic was applied but smiled broadly when Sofia had completed her work. Her two front teeth were missing.

"No food," Rezar said. "Run out of food."

Sofia distributed packages of chips from the cart. She broke off pieces of bread and handed out apples and grapes.

"I'm sorry, but this is all we had on hand."

Again, the people shared.

Dino, meanwhile, was talking to more people. He had learned a few words from his Albanian friend in Florence.

"Why did you come here?" he asked a few of them.

"Freedom! We want freedom!"

"We want out of Albania."

"Italy is beautiful!"

Rezar touched Sofia's arm. "Come."

He led her to a space where a young man had apparently passed out. He had no shirt and his arms and chest were covered with mud. His face was flushed and his forehead felt like a hot iron.

"Dino! More water!" she cried.

She washed the man's face and after many attempts got him to suck on the wet cloth. He was then able to sip from the bottle.

"There," Sofia said. "You'll be fine. Sit up, but don't move. God, I wish there was some shade."

Rezar took Sofia's hand. "Come."

A man about fifty years old was bent over, vomiting into a pail. A woman held him.

"She say her husband has terrible headache," Rezar said. "She say he gets them often. They no have medicine left. He very sick."

Recognizing a migraine, Sofia dug into her medicine bag and found her strongest painkiller. "He needs to rest in a dark place, too. Take off his shirt and put it over his head."

One after another. A man with a broken wrist. A woman with a sprained ankle. A boy cut around his arms. Two men overcome with the heat. A delirious old woman. An old man holding his head and moaning. She made the rounds, and then made the rounds again.

After coaxing a woman into eating an orange, Sofia saw a young couple and a small boy behind her. The young man was shaking the boy and yelling at him. The girl was yelling, too, and the boy was sobbing.

The man's head was shaved and sweat glistened on his bare chest. The girl had red-dyed hair and a heart tattoo on her left arm. Neither looked older than eighteen. The little boy wore a tattered plaid shirt and tan shorts. He had a thin scar running from his right ear to his chin and a big brown bruise on his left arm. He had the blackest eyes and the whitest teeth Dino and Sofia had ever seen. Uncharacteristically, Sofia suddenly wanted to pick him up and hug him.

"Excuse me," Dino said. "Is something wrong?"

"Tarik says he wants some water," the man said. "Well, tough shit. We don't have any water."

"Here," Sofia said, taking a bottle out of the cart and giving it to the boy. "Drink this."

"*Grazie,*" the man said, grabbing the bottle and drinking from it before giving it to the boy. "Oh, my name is Loran and this is my girlfriend Marsela. Oh, and this is Tarik."

Tarik grinned and shook Dino's and Sofia's hands. "I'm from Albania!" he said.

They began to talk, and Dino and Sofia learned that the couple hadn't finished high school and couldn't find any jobs in Albania. They had secretly watched programs from Italy and when they heard friends saying they were going on the Vlora they decided to join them. They had no idea that there would be thousands of people on the ship also seeking refuge in Italy.

"We want to live here," Loran said. "That is our hope. We don't want to live in Albania."

Tarik made a contribution. "I watch cartoons on television. They are funny. Signor Dino, want to hear a joke?"

Loran pushed the boy aside. "Tarik, don't bother the man. Go stand over there."

"I don't mind," Dino said. "Sure, Tarik, tell me your joke."

Tarik grinned again. "Knock, knock."

"Who's there?"

"Iva."

"Iva who?"

"Iva sore hand from knocking! Get it? Iva sore hand from knocking!"

The boy collapsed in laughter and Dino patted him on the head.

"That's great, Tarik," Sofia said. "How old are you?"

"I'm eight. My birthday is the day before Christmas! I'm going to stay in Italy!"

"Well," Sofia said, "I hope you do."

Loran pulled the boy away. "Let's go. I think something may be happening over there."

After they had moved to another part of the dock, Sofia whispered to Dino. "Such a strange young couple. I don't think they're even twenty. That can't be their kid."

"They don't seem to be treating him very well."

"Poor kid."

They would have thought about it more, but Rezar poked Sofia's arm and summoned her to another case of heat exhaustion. It was now nearly 6 o'clock, and they could only hope that the sun would set soon.

"What's going to happen tonight?" Sofia wondered. "Are they all going to sleep here? There's hardly room to stand. How will they all lie down?"

Although police cars moved in and out of the area, forcing the people to scatter, the officers themselves didn't have answers. They mainly talked to one another as if awaiting orders.

Dino went up to one of them. "What do you think will happen to these people when it gets dark? Will they have to stay here?"

The policeman shrugged.

"Are there any plans to bring them some food or water?"

The policeman shrugged again.

"Are more medical people expected?"

The policeman looked away and began talking to another officer.

At the edge of the dock, Dino saw a sudden flurry of people talking excitedly to one another. "What's going on?" he asked one of them.

"We heard some reports," the man replied. "We must go to an office in the morning and get permits to stay here."

"Really?"

"And then we can go anywhere in Italy and find work."

"Really?"

"You don't think this is true?" the man asked.

"Well," Dino said, "I just can't say. Who can predict what the Italian government is going to do?"

"I'm going to believe it. My cousin came in March. Everyone welcomed him. A man and his wife gave him a room. He got a work permit. Now he is working on a farm near Modena. He told me to come, so here I am. I will get a permit and I will get a job. Then I will tell my wife to come. Italy will be paradise."

"Good luck," Dino said.

The man next to him added, "My neighbor came in March, too. Big guy. Strong as an ox. He was walking on the street in Caserta. A car stopped. 'You want a job?' the man asked him. My neighbor said yes. The man brought him home, fed him for two weeks. Now he drives truck for a big company. I'm going to get a job like that."

Another man spoke. "My brother come and found job washing dishes in restaurant. Then he found another job and then another. Lots of jobs in Italy."

Dino reported the conversations to Sofia, who was bandaging a young man with a deep wound on his scalp.

"I'll believe it when I see it," she said. "Meanwhile, we've got thousands of tired, hungry people who have just endured a terrible boat ride and now are suffering intolerable conditions here. These people need help now, and nobody seems to be doing anything. Where are the medical people? I've seen only about a dozen nurses here. And not many ambulances. Where are the people bringing food and water? Where are the officials taking charge? I'm so tired I could lie down myself and go to sleep."

Dino put his arm around her. "Hold on, Sofia. Something's going to happen soon."

"Right."

With nightfall, the putrid smells from the pails increased. There was still no sign of movement. The few policemen told people to stay where they were for the night. Tomorrow, they said, maybe there will be answers.

"Tomorrow?" Sofia cried. "How can these people last until tomorrow? No food, no water, babies crying, people sick. What are we going to do, Dino?"

"We need a miracle. Someone who can multiply loaves and fishes."

"Except that we don't have any loaves or fishes.

STRETCHED OUT on the concrete, jammed among so many smelly bodies, Dino and Sofia hardly slept all night. Shortly after 1 o'clock a man about fifty feet away began yelling.

"My wife! My wife!"

Sofia scrambled over bodies to reach him. The woman was retching.

"She sick," the man said. "She going to have baby in two months."

"Oh dear."

Sofia had no medicine or other remedy for this condition and just hoped that the baby wouldn't decide to come early. She gave the woman some water and sat on the concrete to let the woman rest her head on her lap. Eventually, the woman fell asleep. Sofia crawled back to her space and dozed off next to Dino.

An hour later, they were both awakened by someone screaming nearby and got up to look. A man about thirty years old was doubled up, holding his side.

"Pain, pain," he kept saying.

Sofia gently rubbed his abdomen.

"Have you had this long?"

"No. Since I got here."

"It is sharp or dull?"

"Sharp," the man moaned.

"Is it steady or does it come and go?"

"Steady. Ohhhh."

"You may have something like gallstones. I'll see if I can get an ambulance to get you to a hospital."

One had just returned from Ospedale Generale, and Dino flagged it down. They helped the attendants move the man into the ambulance, which swiftly drove away.

"How many more of these people are going to get so sick?" Sofia wondered.

Eventually, the sun rose to another scorching day. Dino wandered around, trying to pick up information. Around 8 o'clock, he returned and took Sofia aside. She had been making an inventory of the few bandages and painkillers she had left.

"Sofia, I just heard something," he whispered. "They're not going to take these people to get permits. They're going to take them to the Vittoria Stadium. It's not far away. It can hold twenty thousand people."

"Why?"

"Because then they're going to be put on ships and airplanes and sent back to Albania."

"Oh, my God. Are you sure?"

"One of the policemen told me."

"And these people are so excited about staying here. What will happen to them?"

"They'll have to go back to their miserable conditions, I guess. I wonder if we can find Loran and Marsela and Tarik again."

"Why?"

"Sofia, I'm worried about them, especially Tarik. They seem so young and innocent."

"Well, young at least."

"I keep thinking of what will happen to them when they get back, especially that little boy. What's it going to be like living with those two? What's it going to be like growing up there?"

"I can't imagine, Dino."

They looked at each other hard, and each knew what the other was thinking.

"Sofia, what would you think about taking them back to Florence with us? I could see if I could find some sort of job for Loran."

"I don't know. They're going to be illegal, Dino."

"Lots of people are illegal."

"And we might get in trouble, harboring illegals."

"We can face that when it happens. If it happens."

Sofia put her hand on her husband's arm. "Well, we can't leave them here, can we? Let's find them."

A line of buses had arrived and people were pushing and shoving to get on. Policemen tried to keep order but mainly just pushed the Albanians onto the buses. Dino saw the young couple and boy in the middle of the crush. He grabbed them and pushed them to the side.

"Listen," Dino told them. "Come with us."

"But we have to get on the bus!" Loran said.

"Please come. It's important."

Loran and Marsela, holding Tarik's hands, followed Dino and Sofia to the end of the dock.

"Please don't get on the bus," Dino said. "It's not true. They're not going to take you to get permits. They're going to take you to the stadium and then they'll put you on ships and airplanes and send everyone back to Albania."

"No!" Loran cried. "They told us! They promised us!"

"Don't believe them," Sofia said. "The fact is, the Italian government doesn't want you here."

"But they promised!" Marsela gripped Loran's hand. "We don't want to go home. We can't go home!"

Tarik began to cry, and Sofia bent down and hugged him.

"Look," Dino said, putting his hand on Loran's shoulder, "why don't you come with us to Florence? We can find you a place to stay and I can try to find you a job. Then let's see what happens."

Now both Marsela and Tarik were crying.

"You would do that?" Loran said.

"Yes," Sofia said. "We would."

Loran put his arm around Marsela. "All right. We go. Come on, Tarik."

Tarik grabbed Dino's hand.

"Are you taking us to your house, Signor Dino?" the boy asked.

"Yes. I think you'll like it there."

"Will I have my own bed?"

"I don't know," Sofia said. "Would you like to sleep on pillows?"

"Pillows! Can I? I love pillows!"

The boy chatted all the way to the car.

"Signor Dino! I have a joke."

"What's the joke, Tarik?"

"Why do birds fly south in the winter?"

"Hmm. That's a hard one. I don't know."

"Because it's too far to walk! You like that, Signor Dino?"

"I like it a lot, Tarik. Let's go."

WITHOUT THE SUPPLIES they had distributed on the dock, there was room for Marsela and Sofia to sit in the back of the Fiat with Tarik on Sofia's lap. Loran sat in front with Dino.

Marsela was so exhausted she fell asleep right away, and Loran was absorbed in the scenery. Tarik talked nonstop.

"Signora Sofia, do you know why the boy brought the ladder to school?"

"No, why?"

"He wanted to go to high school!"

Sofia laughed.

"Signora Sofia, what has a face and two hands but no arms or legs?"

"Let me guess. Well, I give up."

"It's a clock! Get it, a clock!"

"Oh, of course. A clock. I'm so dumb."

"You not dumb, Signora Sofia. You smart."

"Well, not as smart as you, Tarik. Now, should we look at the scenery for a while?"

"OK."

But soon the boy was back with his riddles and jokes. "What has to be broken before you can use it?" "What has a neck but no head?"

Dino offered to let Sofia drive, but she declared that she was actually enjoying Tarik's chatter. He really was a sweet boy, and very smart. She almost envied Loran and Marsela. She wondered, though, why such a young couple had an eight-year-old boy with them.

It was late when they arrived in Florence, but Tarik was wide awake and ready to explore every nook of Dino and Sofia's apartment.

"Look out this window! You can see the cars down there!" "Come see this closet! It's huge!" "This television is so big!"

"He's such a cute kid," Sofia told Marsela.

"He gets on my nerves," Marsela said. "Talk, talk, talk. He won't stop talking. Drives me crazy."

Meanwhile, Dino and Loran removed boxes and furniture from the guest room, made up a bed for Loran and Marsela, and threw down some pillows for Tarik. Then it was time for baths, which Tarik resisted. Fortunately, Loran and Marsela were about the same size as Dino and Sofia, so clothes were put out for both of them.

For Tarik, Dino would see if his uncle Adolfo had some old clothes from the boy he and Mila had adopted thirteen years ago.

"Leonardo is almost 20 now, but Adolfo never throws anything away, so they must have some around."

Since they had taken all their food with them, there was almost nothing to offer their guests.

"Here's a bag of chips if you want them," Sofia said. "It's been opened so they're probably stale."

"I love chips!" Tarik said.

When their guests had retired, Sofia collapsed on the living room sofa, and Dino brought them both a beer.

"Well, so much for our vacation in Solento," Sofia said.

"There's always next year."

"Or the year after that."

They paused to sip their beers, the only sounds the honking of horns and the revving of motorcycles on the street below.

"Dino, do you think we did the right thing, bringing them back here? We're really taking chances with their lives."

"I don't know. I hope so. I guess it could only be better than what they had."

"Think you'll be able to find Loran a job?"

"I'll ask my uncles. They may have ideas."

"And where will they stay? They can't stay cooped up in here forever."

"I'll have to ask my uncles that, too."

An ambulance screeched by, siren wailing.

"Poor Tarik," Sofia said. "What a cute kid. I wish we knew his story. That scar? And that big bruise? Where did those come from?"

"I suppose a lot of stories will start to come out. Want to find out what's going on in Bari?"

He clicked on the remote.

"I don't know if I want to find out," Sofia said.

The television screen showed thousands of people milling around in the darkened stadium, and the announcer was saying, "…from earlier today and you can see how many people are here. The police brought in some bread but the people were so hungry they practically rioted trying to get some. The police ran off."

Now a woman was being interviewed. "On the ship we had a lot of solidarity. Even on the dock. But now that's all disappeared. Now we all seem at war." She began to cry and crumpled to the ground.

Now a man was answering questions. "Most people on the ship were decent, but there were some criminals, too. People said they were from Tirana and Durres. Now they're here. Some helicopters dropped food into the stadium and these people had sticks and they formed a circle. They caught the food and they beat other people who tried to get close. They kept the food for themselves. We are starving, and these people won't even let us have some food! We had to fight to get some food! And they won't let us out of this goddamn stadium! There's not even a place to shit here."

"Oh, my God," Sofia said. "It's even worse than we thought. Now they're fighting among themselves. Thank God we got out of there."

"And got Loran and Marsela and Tarik out," Dino said.

The scenes now were of young men throwing rocks and debris at the policemen in the stadium. The police had their guns drawn and were forcing the men off to the side.

While more scenes of the rioting were shown, the announcer was commenting. "And we know that there are also fights among the people still on the dock. Not all of them have been brought to the stadium."

"Fight, fight, fight," Sofia said.

The announcer continued. "We have an exclusive report that the mayor of Bari didn't want the people to be brought to the stadium. This was Rome's idea, not the government of Bari, and we hear there's a lot of tension. We heard that President Cossiga is on his way to inspect everything."

"Good grief," Sofia said. "That's all these poor people need, for this to turn into a political battle."

"I'm turning the TV off," Dino said. "I can't watch any more of this."

TARIK WOKE UP first in the morning, ready to tell anyone more jokes. Dino said he would take Loran to *Gli Angeli della Casa* and introduce him to his uncles. Maybe they'd have ideas about employment.

"And maybe a place for them to live," Sofia said.

Alone with Marsela in their apartment, Sofia avoided the news programs on television but found cartoons for Tarik and began washing the breakfast dishes.

"You've had a hard life," she told Marsela.

"Yes. Terrible. Thank God we're out of there."

"What did you do in Durres?"

"Nothing. I hated school, so I quit. Loran had a part-time job working in construction, but then he got laid off."

"So it was just you two and Tarik."

"Yes."

"Such a nice boy."

"If you think so."

"Is he…is he a relative?"

"Well, you should know this stuff, I guess."

"Come sit down."

They sat at the kitchen table, and Sofia poured more coffee. It was Marsela's third cup that morning.

Marsela began her story, recounting it without emotion, as if it had happened to someone else. She began picking off the bright red nail polish on the fingers of her left hand.

"When our mother died, it was just me and my sister and her husband and Tarik in the house," she said. "We never knew where our father was, he was drunk all the time anyway. We were getting along OK, but then my sister and her husband were in this accident. They were driving back from Elbason. That's where the Chinese built a steel mill. You may have heard about it."

"Vaguely."

"Anyway, Drita and Faton, that was my sister and her husband, were driving back when they missed a curve and hit another car. Faton was killed on the spot, Drita lived for a few more days."

"Oh, how terrible. I'm so sorry. Was Tarik hurt?"

"He wasn't with them. He was home with me."

"Poor little kid."

"As I said, Drita lived for a few more days. I went to the hospital every day. The last thing she said to me was, 'Take care of Tarik.'"

"Oh, Marsela, how sad."

"That was almost two years ago. He was six. So then I met Loran and he moved in with me and we've been taking care of him."

"The poor kid must have been traumatized, his parents killed like that."

"He woke up screaming sometimes after the accident. He doesn't scream now, but he whimpers and calls for his mama and I have to go in and stay with him and he squirms and bounces and I don't get any sleep. I'm so tired in the morning."

"He seems so happy."

"Loran says he hides what's really going on in his little head. Maybe that's why he talks so much."

"What a responsibility for you, and you're so young!"

"It's hard work sometimes. Really hard work."

"But you like the little boy, don't you?"

"He's my sister's son, what can I say? But we can't go out, we can't do anything. We always have to stay home with him. All our friends go out all the time, dancing and movies. I get so mad I could scream."

"I'm so sorry."

"Look, we brought him along because we couldn't very well leave him behind."

"No, of course not."

Marsela was now scraping off nail polish on her right hand.

"OK, I need to tell you this. The real reason we brought him is we hope we can find a family here who will take him. It's just too much for us. We tried to find someone in Albania but no one would take him. So we're stuck."

"You'd give him up?"

"Well, he's not my child, you know. I shouldn't have promised my sister. I'll regret that till the day I die."

"He seems to like you two."

"He's afraid of Loran."

"I guess that's natural. Loran isn't his father."

"Loran has some problems. He gets really mad sometimes, he can't control his temper and he thrashes about. He's never hurt me though."

"That scar on Tarik's face, and the bruise?"

"Tarik got scared about a month ago when Loran was having one of his outbursts. He ran and he stumbled down the stairs and hurt his face."

"Oh my. And the bruise?"

"That was just last week. Loran grabbed him too hard."

"Oh, my God. Has that sort of thing happened before?"

"A few times."

"Marsela, I'm so very sorry."

Marsela had now finished with her nails. "I'm going into that room and lie down. I didn't sleep very well last night."

She turned around at the door. "And if we can't find a family, do you think you could find an orphanage where we could put him?"

"Oh, my God," Sofia whispered. She joined Tarik on the couch as he watched *Candy Candy*.

"That's a funny show, isn't it, Tarik?"

"I love this show."

Sofia put her arm around the boy's shoulders and he rested his head on her side. She wondered why she was crying.

When Dino returned home with Loran that afternoon, he had good news from his uncles. Adolfo and Roberto said a maintenance man was needed at one of the apartment buildings they had refurbished, and there actually was an apartment available there.

"It's very small, though. Tarik will have to sleep on the couch."

"Dino," Sofia said, "I want to talk to you about something, but let's wait until tonight."

Dino had brought supplies for supper, and afterwards they all gathered around the television set to find out what was happening in Bari today. Tarik sat between Dino and Sofia on the couch.

"Today," the announcer said against a scene of more people milling around in the stadium, "the president of Italy, Francisco Cossiga, came to Bari and had a press conference. He was clearly upset that the mayor of Bari had objected to moving the refugees to the stadium. The mayor wanted to erect a tent city on the dock instead."

The president, wearing a dark suit, was shown surrounded by his aides.

"I am not here," Cossiga said, "to thank Bari, let alone the mayor of Bari who has made statements that are incredibly irresponsible. I'm sorry that such a generous city like Bari has a mayor of this sort. I hope he will apologize to government authorities. Otherwise I will ask the government to suspend him from his official duties."

"Good God," Sofia said, "now they're fighting over jurisdiction when they should be worrying about those people."

"Well," the announcer said, "it really doesn't matter what the president or the mayor thinks. All those Albanians are on the way back home. And maybe after the way they've been treated at the dock and the stadium, they'll be glad to go back."

"No!" Marsela and Loran shouted.

The cameras showed people lined up in front of a ship, being searched by policemen, and then shuffling on board.

"Look," Marsela said, "that man in the green shirt. He was next to us on the boat. He said he wanted to get a job in Italy and then send for his wife. He said he has two kids. Now he has to go back."

The cameras switched to a scene showing people boarding a military airplane.

"And there," Loran said, "that woman in the brown dress with the funny hair. She was crying on the boat because she was so happy to leave Albania. Bora, I think her name was. Looks like she's crying again."

Tarik piped up. "Why are those people getting on that airplane, Signor Dino?"

"They have to go back home."

"Why?"

"Because Italy doesn't want them to stay."

"Why?"

"I don't know, Tarik. I don't know."

"Do we have to go back?"

"No," Sofia said. "You are going to stay in Italy."

"Can I stay with you?"

"Here, with us?"

"Yes."

"I don't know, Tarik. I just don't know."

"I want to stay here."

AGAIN, after their guests had gone to bed, Dino and Sofia sat on the couch, but they didn't turn the television on.

"Dino," Sofia said, "I'm really upset. I talked to Marsela today."

The whole story about Marsela and Loren and Tarik came out, and by the end of it Sofia was wiping tears away. She rarely cried.

"They want to get rid of that little boy?" Dino said. "How could they do that? He's such a good little kid."

"I'm trying to think what I would have done if I was sixteen years old and suddenly I had to take care of my sister's little boy, if I had a sister. I don't know what I'd do."

Dino threw his newspaper down. "Well, you wouldn't put him in an orphanage, I know that. Sofia, the more I think about this, the madder I'm getting. They can't do that! They can't give that boy away! Goddammit! It's criminal! Maybe there are laws against this."

"What are we going to do, Dino?"

"We can't talk them out of this?"

"No, I don't think so."

"We can't tell them to get some help, somebody to look after the boy?"

"They could never afford that."

Dino began to shout as he paced the floor. "Well, something's got to be done! We can't let this happen!"

Sofia had never seen her husband so angry. "Dino, don't shout. You'll wake the others."

"OK, OK."

He paced some more, picked up the newspaper and threw it at the wall, and then stared out the window.

"Do we know anyone? We must know someone."

"I've been thinking all day, and I can't think of anyone. All of our friends are as old as we are. They're not going to want to raise a little boy."

"What about…what's her name…Flora, that woman at the flower shop? She's young, and she's married, isn't she?"

"I think her husband just dumped her."

They thought for a long while, Dino still pacing the floor.

"What about that young nurse at the hospital?" he said. "You've talked about her. Does she have kids?"

"Anita? I don't know. The way she talks about her husband, I don't think they get along very well. What about you? What about that Albanian family you know? That would be a logical match, wouldn't it?"

"Mergim and his family? I think they're barely making it. I don't know if they'd want another mouth to feed."

"Well, maybe they'd know somebody. You can ask, right?"

"And you can ask that nurse?"

Sofia was on the early shift the following day, so she was home early to find Marsela waiting at the door.

"Sofia, I'm going crazy in here. I've got to get out for a while. Tarik's watching TV. OK?"

"Well, sure. Of course. Why don't you walk down toward Ponte Vecchio. There are a lot of shops you can browse in. Here, take some money. Buy something for yourself, something nice."

She gave her a handful of *lire.* "Take your time. Tarik and I will be fine."

Sofia found the boy engrossed in another cartoon, but he jumped up when he saw her. "Signora Sofia! You're home!"

He ran into her arms and kissed her cheek.

"Oh, Tarik, what a nice greeting. Look, let me change, and then we can do something together, OK?"

"OK!"

Now in an old shirt and jeans, Sofia brought the boy into the kitchen. "How would you like to make some cookies?"

"Really? I've never made cookies. Can I?"

"Sure. Let's see what we have."

She found a box of gingerbread cookie mix and wiped off the kitchen table. She brought out a big bowl and a mixer, and eggs from the refrigerator.

"Have you ever cracked an egg, Tarik?"

"Me? No! Can I?"

Some of the shell got in the bowl, but otherwise he got a "Good job!"

For the next hour, Tarik, with a towel tied around his neck for an apron, chatted nonstop as he helped Sofia mix the dough, roll it out and make seventeen gingerbread men with a cookie cutter. Their little candy eyes and belly buttons weren't quite where they belonged, but Tarik was pleased, especially when Sofia let him lick the spoons.

After sliding the cookies into the oven, he talked about his teacher in Albania and his friend Pieter and Pieter's dog Leka. He talked about what he hoped to get for his birthday. "Some candy!" He talked about the two boys he met on the ship.

"They weren't very nice. They were fighting."

"Tarik," Sofia said, "do you miss your mother and dad?"

The boy grew quiet. "Sometimes. Sometimes I see my mother in my dreams. She is always smiling at me."

"And your father?"

"Sometimes he's there, too. He's watching the soccer games on television. He lets me sit with him."

"Tarik, I'm sorry you don't have them anymore."

"I know. I'm sorry, too."

Sofia feared that he was going to cry, and she hugged him.

"You know, Signora Sofia, you kind of look like my mama."

"Really? How?"

"You have short hair like her. Marsela has long hair. I don't like it. And you don't put paint on your face and your fingers. My mama never put paint on her face and her fingers."

Sofia hugged him again. "Tarik, Tarik. What a funny boy. Well, let's put these men on the counter and let them cool. Then you can have one, and Signor Dino will be home soon."

Dino did arrive an hour later, with bad news. The Albanian family wouldn't be able to take Tarik and they didn't know anybody who would. Sofia reported that Anita also declined to take the little boy, "not with all the stuff going on in our house now."

Dino had another idea: "My aunt. Anna. She runs a place for new mothers over at Santa Croce."

"But it's for new mothers," Sofia said. "Why would a new mother want another kid?"

"I don't know, but we can ask her. Maybe she knows somebody. And maybe my uncles do. I'll get the three of them together. Tomorrow!"

They met at *Casa di Maria,* the home for unmarried girls who were about to have babies that Anna Sporenza had founded after she'd left the convent. Never a close family, and with divergent interests, Anna and her brothers didn't get together often even though they all lived in Florence and were close in age. Anna was now fifty-seven, Roberto fifty-nine and Adolfo fifty-five.

It was a rather awkward meeting, with the brothers and sister and nephew exchanging perfunctory kisses and only brief accounts of what was happening in their lives. Anna said she was challenged by, but enjoying, the work at *Casa di Maria.* Roberto, Adolfo and Dino said they worked long hours at *Gli Angeli della Casa.*

They thought a lot about Dino's dilemma, and they tossed some possible names around, but none of them could think of a couple that would be willing to adopt little Tarik.

"Well, an orphanage isn't an option," Roberto said. "And anyway, I don't think there are any orphanages in Florence anymore."

"Thank God," Anna said. "Remember when we were told about the *Ospedale degli Innocenti* for abandoned children? Built in the fourteen hundreds?"

"I remember the nuns telling us," Adolfo said. "It had a wheel in the wall and a child could be left in it and a nurse would turn the wheel around and pick the baby up. I think they were trying to scare us."

"That sounds pretty barbaric," Dino said. "Abandoning your baby in a wheel."

"Well, at least some children were saved," Anna said. "Anyway, the place closed in the 1800s, so now Florence doesn't have such a place."

Dino was getting more and more upset. "Then what is supposed to happen to a little boy like Tarik? Leave him on the street? Throw him into the Arno?"

"There must be somebody," Adolfo said. "Maybe the government can help?"

"The government?" Dino laughed. "What do you think the government could do?"

"Remember, Adolfo," Anna said, "when we matched you and Mila with Leonardo and little Clara? Leonardo was only seven and Clara was a baby. You didn't want to adopt children, but look how much they've meant to you."

"The best thing we ever did," Adolfo said. "Now Leonardo is almost twenty and Clara is going to be thirteen. Leonardo is the nicest kid you'd ever want to meet. And smart! He's getting such good marks at the university. And Clara is so sweet. She's Mila's best friend. I can't believe it. Those kids changed our lives."

"How old were you when you adopted those kids, Adolfo?" Dino asked.

"Thirty."

"We need to find somebody that young for Tarik."

"How old are you, Dino?" Roberto asked.

"Forty-five."

"Not so old."

HAVING GONE THROUGH the lists of their relatives and work acquaintances, Dino and Sofia decided to talk to the person in Florence they knew they could rely on the most to discuss Tarik's future.

Father Lorenzo was in his tiny room at Santa Croce that night. He had finished washing pots and pans at *cucina popolare*, the famous soup kitchen that had been feeding thousands of Florence's poor for decades, and was about to reread an old novel by Vasco Pratolini.

"Don't mind the soup stains on my sleeves," he said as he told his visitors to sit down. "Fortunately, these Franciscan robes hide stains pretty well. I don't know when I've had this thing cleaned last."

Dino and Sofia had helped out at the soup kitchen for years, and had, in fact, met there during the terrible flood of 1966. Father Lorenzo had married them and had always been their friend and confidante. Now there was a new story to hear, and he listened thoughtfully.

"So that's it," Dino concluded after telling the priest the story about Bari and Loran and Marsela. "Tarik's such a sweet and lovely child…"

"…and smart," Sofia added.

"…and we don't know what's going to happen to him. Even if there were orphanages, we wouldn't let him go to one. We just don't know what to do, Father. Don't you know anyone? There must be couples in this big parish that are just longing to adopt a child. Surely? Anyone?"

"I can't think of any off the top of my head, but let's see."

Father Lorenzo pulled out a dusty, leather-bound book from a shelf behind him.

"Here's a list of our parishioners," he said. "I know it's not complete. It's only those who have signed up, those who put some *lire* in the collection basket, and it's out of date. There are a lot of others who just come to Mass sometimes. Santa Croce's always filled, but mostly with tourists who come to see Michelangelo's tomb."

He began running his finger down the page.

"Accorsi. They're kind of young. He's trying to be an actor, though, and she's working in a restaurant part time, so they don't have much money and they probably need to get settled. Let's see who else."

He ran his finger down another page, mumbling to himself. More pages.

"Buffone…Buffone…why do I know that name? Oh, right. He was just sent off to prison for robbing that bank. I know he took the rap, though. It was really his cousin Pietro."

More pages.

"Filippi. Hmmm. Possible. Francesca and Tommaso. They're such a great young couple, so in love. They've been together for years. They really want to have a baby and are trying hard. So far, no luck. I'll mark them down."

He wrote their name and phone number on a piece of paper and continued his search.

"Let's see. Locatelli. I don't know them too well, but I remember Veronica saying that she wished she could have a child for years but there had been problems. She was going to see a doctor."

He wrote their name and phone number down.

More pages, more pages, more pages. And more mumbling. Dino and Sofia tried to stay calm, but Dino noted that his wife's hands were shaking.

"Palmissaro....Palmissaro. No, no, no. What was I thinking?"

More pages.

"Santini. Luigi and Giuseppina. That's possible. They come to church every Sunday and even put a little in the basket. They have three or four children, I think. They're not that young."

He took down their information.

More pages, more pages. He closed the book.

"OK. Three names. Filippi, Locatelli and Santini. I'll contact them. If that doesn't work, I'll go through the book again. Give me a day, OK?"

"Father, we are so grateful," Dino said as he shook the priest's hand. "You don't know how relieved we are."

"Well, don't count your blessings yet. I haven't talked to these people."

"One of them will surely be interested, right?" Sofia said.

"Pray to Saint Jude," the priest said. "He's the saint of lost causes."

Although they rarely prayed, Dino and Sofia said they would.

Prayers didn't do any good. Father Lorenzo had distressing news the next night when Dino and Sofia again visited. Francesca and Tommaso had told the priest they were moving to England ("England!" Father Lorenzo said. "Why would anyone want to leave Italy? And for England?") to work for an automobile factory; Veronica Locatelli was so excited because she was going to have a baby! And Luigi and Giuseppina Santini were going to have their fourth child.

"I went though the book two more times and I tried some other people, too," Father Lorenzo said, "but no luck. They all had reasons not to do this."

"Well, that's that," Dino said. "You tried. We appreciate your efforts. Let's go, Sofia. Thanks again, Father."

"Wait, don't go yet."

He opened a folder on his desk.

"I've been involved in a number of adoptions over the years. Remember when I helped your uncle Adolfo and Mila get Leonardo and Clara? And there have been four or five others, too. So I've kept a file of what the rules are because, you know, this is Italy, so there are lots of rules."

The priest explained that, as in other countries in Europe, adoption had traditionally been used by childless persons who wanted someone to inherit their estates. But in 1967, he said, Italy passed a law that opened up the modern concept of adoption for children. It was still very complicated. Adoption was under the control of the *tribunale per il minorenni,* the juvenile court. A prosecutor investigates the child's background and reports to the court whether the child is adoptable.

"Well," Dino said, "Tarik is about to be thrown out on the streets. That should mean he's adoptable."

"Then," the priest said, "a social service agency will investigate the couple to make sure they will be good parents. It has 120 days to do that. And if approval is given by that agency, it may take a year or longer for a court to approve."

"Sounds very complicated," Sofia said. "That's going to turn off any couple who might be interested. And we haven't found anyone who's interested."

"Oh, one more thing," Father Lorenzo said. "Regarding the age of the couple. It says here that the adopting parents must be at least eighteen years of age and may not be more than forty-five years older than the child. How old is Tarik?"

"He's eight," Sofia said.

"So someone could be as old as fifty-three," Dino said. "Interesting. We've been thinking about younger couples, but maybe we should look for older couples."

"Yes, well, you could do that, I suppose."

"What are you saying, Father?"

"How old are you, Dino?"

"Forty-five."

"And you, Sofia?"

"Forty-seven."

The priest put the papers back in the folder. "And Tarik is eight. Hmmm. Interesting."

"What?" Dino shouted. "What? What are you trying to say?"

"Nothing, Dino. I was just asking a question. Just asking a question."

"Well, don't even think about it. No! Come on, Sofia."

SOFIA ALWAYS KNEW when Dino was angry or upset. He walked fast. He kept his hands in his pockets. He looked straight ahead and sometimes bumped into people.

"Dino, wait. I can't keep up with you."

They had left Santa Croce and were walking on Via Verdi. Dino finally stopped at the Piazza dei Ciompi and they found a bench outside the flea market.

"Dino, I know what you're thinking, and I agree. We can't adopt Tarik. It would be impossible. We're too old. We both have jobs. We have no idea how to raise a child."

"Right."

"We would have to be committed to him all the time. We wouldn't have a life of our own."

"Right."

"We would have no idea how to help him with his homework."

"Right."

"And we wouldn't be able to play soccer with him, or any other sport."

"Right."

"None of our friends have little kids so who would he play with?"

"Right."

"And imagine watching cartoons all the time."

"Right. Let's go home."

Sofia still had trouble keeping up with Dino, who was walking really fast with his fists in his pockets.

At home, they could hear Loran and Marsela making obvious noises in the bedroom while Tarik sat absorbed in another cartoon on the television set.

"Signor Dino! Signora Sofia!"

He plunged into their arms and wouldn't let go.

"Did you have a good day, Tarik?" Sofia asked.

"It was OK. I watched cartoons."

"All day?"

"They were funny. Want to hear a joke they said?"

"Of course."

"Knock, knock."

"Who's there?"

"Stopwatch!"

"Stopwatch who?"

"Stopwatch you're doing and open this door!"

Tarik jumped up and down. "Stopwatch you're doing and open this door! Get it! Get it!"

"That's very funny, Tarik," Sofia said. "Well, I think Signor Dino has a headache so he's going to lie down for a little while. Let's just sit here and I'll read *Pinocchio* again."

Sofia read from the book, but her mind wasn't on Geppetto and his wooden puppet. She finished two chapters and put the book down.

"I think I have a headache, too, Tarik. We'll read some more tomorrow night, OK? I think I'll lie down, too."

Tarik put his hand on her forehead. "Are you sick, Signora Sofia? Can I get you a glass of water? Or a glass of milk? I can get you a glass of milk from the refrigerator."

"Thank you, Tarik, that's very sweet, but I'll be fine. You can watch more cartoons if you want."

"That's OK. I think I'll just look at this book."

Before Sofia got up, Tarik hugged her tight and kissed her. "I like your hair, Signora Sofia."

"Thanks, Tarik. I'll come back later to put you to bed."

Sofia found Dino lying on the bed and staring at the ceiling.

"Tarik OK?" he asked.

"He's fine."

Sofia busied herself folding sheets and towels from the laundry.

"We can't do it, of course," she finally said.

"No, of course not. It's out of the question."

"And it's not as if he's our responsibility. It was all an accident. We just happened to see Loran and Marsela on the dock and he was with them. It's their responsibility. She told her sister that she would take care of him."

"I know that," Dino said.

He got up and blew his nose. Hard.

She turned her back and looked out the window. "Then why are we both crying?"

"Sofia, I've been going round and round and round. I think one way and then I think the other way."

"Yeah. Me, too."

"Come sit here."

They sat on the side of the bed, holding hands.

"Dino, we can't let them take him with them. It would be terrible for him. I'm scared to think what they might do."

"We've tried, Sofia, we've tried. We couldn't find someone else. No one. Even Father Lorenzo tried."

"I know."

They were so lost in thought they couldn't hear Loran and Marsela still making the obvious noises. Then Dino started to laugh.

"What's so funny?"

"I was just thinking. My mother would be absolutely delirious if we did this."

"Lucia has always wanted a grandchild. I think she blames me for not having a baby."

"That would not be a reason for doing this, of course."

"Of course."

"Look," Dino said, "we know all the arguments against this. Sofia, let's think about the arguments for it."

Against the backdrop of noise from the next room and traffic from the street below, they tried to think of all the reasons why—for heaven's sake—it might be possible for them to actually adopt Tarik. It didn't take long.

"There's really only one reason," Sofia said. "It's because he is the sweetest boy who ever lived."

"And he loves us and we love him."

"What other reasons do we need?"

"None that I know of!" Dino kissed Sofia and they went hand in hand into the living room.

"Guess what, Tarik! You're going to stay with us! You're going to be our son!"

"Really?"

He leaped into their waiting arms.

"Yes!"

"And I can stay here forever?"

"Yes!"

"Really? I love you, Signora Sofia."

"I love you, Tarik."

"I love you, Signor Dino."

"I love you, Tarik."

"Can we stay up late tonight? Want to read a book? Want to hear a joke?"

The Fearless Flag Thrower of Lucca

Sant'Antonio/Lucca

"CLARA!" HER MOTHER CALLED from the bottom of the staircase. "We're waiting. Your father and brothers are ready to come up there to get you. The pasta's getting cold!"

"Coming!"

Using cleanser and a scrubbing brush, Clara Marincola tried to get the last remaining grease off her hands.

"Damn! There goes another nail." She now had three good fingernails on one hand and two on the other. And grease still lurked in the crevices of her fingers and hands.

"Well, I'll finish later."

She pulled off her grease-lined sweatshirt, her grease-stained jeans and her grease-soaked shoes and socks and kicked them into the corner. Wearing only underwear, she looked into her closet for something to wear and finally grabbed her old flannel robe and went barefoot downstairs.

"Well," Francesco said, "I'm glad you decided to dress for dinner. Now the rest of us feel overdressed. Guess I'll take my pants off."

"Stop it right there," Serafina said. "Clara, sit down."

"And let's pray," her husband, Salvo, said.

Their heads bowed, they mumbled the traditional phrases. "Bless us oh Lord…food and family…and all the poor people."

"OK, let's eat," Serafina said. "Pasquale, stop playing with Bruno and pass the pasta. Another hard day, Clara?"

"Two Vespas and a Ducati Paso 750. The guy who owned the Ducati wanted to wait for it."

"Is that so bad?" Francesco asked, filling his plate with linguini.

"He waited while I fixed it. Just stood there watching everything I did. And I had to change the air filter and a sprocket."

"Weren't you nervous?"

"Hell, I just stared back at him."

"Clara, watch your language," her father said.

For a while, the only sounds were forks on plates.

"The problem," Serafina said, getting up to transfer a plate of sliced veal and a bowl of vegetables to the table, "is that Giorgio won't hire more people for his shop. He shouldn't expect you to work on every motorcycle that comes in looking to be fixed."

"Rocco works part time," Clara said, helping herself to three slices of veal and a mound of broccoli.

"Well, part time isn't enough," her mother said. "But there's no telling that to Giorgo. He'd put you on part time, too, if he could get away with it. Anyway, it's Friday. Let's forget about Giorgio for a while. What are you kids planning to do this weekend?"

"I'm going to a movie in Lucca with Farid tonight," Francesco said. "In fact, right now. Can we have the dessert now, please?"

"We'll have it when it's time," Salvo said. "If you're in such a rush, maybe you could leave without dessert?"

"Francesco," Serafina said, "why don't you take your sister to the movies, too?"

"Mother!" Francesco and Clara both shouted. "What are you thinking?"

"Mother, we don't want a girl with us," Francesco said.

"Mother, I don't want to go with those boys," Clara said.

"And what are you going to do after the movies, Francesco?" his father asked.

"I don't know. Drive around, I guess."

"What do you mean drive around? With some of those other guys I see you with?"

"Papa, I'm twenty years old."

"So?"

"So I know not to drink too much and not to take that stuff."

Serafina sighed. "And you, Pasquale? What are you going to do?"

The boy, who as usual hadn't said a word all during dinner but had secretly slipped bits of veal to his dog under the table, said he thought he might go looking for old bullet shells in the hills tomorrow.

"There's tons of them, Mama! Those guys hunting for birds every weekend, they leave shells all over. Bruno and me found hundreds last Saturday."

"Well, don't go up there when they're shooting. Now don't you think Bruno has had enough veal?"

Pasquale put both of his hands on the table. Bruno slunk into a corner.

"What's a fourteen-year-old boy going to do with all those bullet shells?" Francesco asked.

"I dunno. I've got boxes and boxes under my bed. I'll figure something out."

"And you, Clara?" her mother asked.

"Tomorrow morning I'm going to sleep, sleep, sleep," Clara said. "Then in the afternoon I've got a soccer game. At night I'm going to Renata's. She's trying on her wedding dress and I'm going to be a bridesmaid."

"I can't believe she's getting married," Serafina said. "She's too young."

"Mama," Clara said, "she's nineteen, as old as I am."

"It's still too young. Don't you think of getting married at nineteen. Or twenty. Or twenty-one."

"Ha!" Francesco said, "she's lucky if she finds a man when she's forty!"

Clara threw her fork at her brother, who threw a spoon back at her, and soon dinner was a shambles and Serafina declared that there wouldn't be any dessert.

"Before everyone leaves," Salvo said, "I want to say something. You kids have all said what you're going to do this weekend. But I didn't hear anyone say what they were going to do to help around this house."

Silence.

"What needs to be done?" Pasquale finally asked.

"Well, to begin with, the lawn needs raking. The leaves have been piling up all week."

"I can do that," Pasquale said.

"And the lumber from the old shed needs to be cut up," Salvo continued. "We can use it for firewood this winter."

"I can do that," Francesco said, "but I have to have that saw sharpened. Last time, it wouldn't cut anything."

"And I need help," Serafina said, "getting the house in order before we leave next weekend."

"Leave?" the children asked. "Where are you going?"

"Haven't you been listening all these weeks? Your father and I are going to Lucca for our twenty-fifth wedding anniversary."

"Oh."

"Is that next weekend?"

"Yes."

"Your twenty-fifth anniversary?" Francesco said. "You must be awfully old."

"I'm going to ignore that," Serafina said. "You'll be fine. I'll have something in the fridge. If something happens you can go see Paolo and Lucia."

"What are you going to do in Lucca all weekend?" Pasquale asked.

"We'll be staying at a nice hotel," Salvo said. "We'll leave the number."

"You're going to stay at a hotel?" Pasquale asked. "What will you be doing?"

Francesco and Clara rolled their eyes.

"Pasquale," Clara whispered, "don't ask."

"Oh."

AFTER DINNER, when Francesco had gone off with his friends and Pasquale took Bruno up on the tree house next to his room and Salvo vacuumed the dining and living room rugs, Clara helped her mother with the dishes.

"Do you have to play in the game tomorrow, Clara?" her mother asked. "You look awfully tired. Why don't you skip it for once? They can get along without you for once, can't they?"

"Mama, I can't just not go. I'm a member of the team. I'll be fine by tomorrow. You know how I love it. Since I've been playing striker I've been scoring more goals. Coach says I'm the best player on the team. In fact, he said last week that I'm one of the best players he's ever had."

"Papa and I will go to one of your matches."

"Don't. You'd make me nervous."

"I doubt that. You don't get nervous about anything."

Serafina put a soapy hand on her daughter's cheek. "We're proud of you, Clara. Who would have thought we'd have such an athlete for a daughter. You're even better than Francesco."

"Francesco! He's not even interested in sports."

"And you! You play soccer, you swim, you've won tennis matches.

"And that's why they call me a tomboy."

"Don't listen to them. Just because Italy doesn't encourage women in sports doesn't mean you shouldn't go out for them. I just worry that you're going to wear yourself out. Even before you're twenty years old."

"Don't worry, Mama. I know my limits. I just wish there was something new to do. I've been doing these same things since grade school. I wish somebody would invent a new sport."

"Why don't you?"

"Right."

"Well, think about it. Say, how many bridesmaids do you think Renata is going to have?"

"Not many. Maybe three. I mean, this is not going to be a big wedding considering her condition."

"Her condition?"

"Didn't you know? She's starting to show."

"I haven't seen her for a few weeks. Oh my God. How does Filippo feel about this?"

"How do you think? But he's going through with it. He doesn't have a choice. Renata's father is seeing to that."

"Well, don't you ever get into that condition."

"Don't worry, Mama. As Francesco said, I'm lucky if I find a man by the time I'm forty."

"Don't say that." Serafina wiped her hands on the dish towel and took her daughter in her arms. "You're a very beautiful girl."

"Even if I can lift two hundred pounds." She flexed a bicep.

The following afternoon, Clara drove off in her battered Vespa to the soccer field at Camaiore and was again the star of the ragtag *Vendicatori* team, scoring three points and preventing the *Tigri* from scoring any.

"Great job, Clara," the coach said as he slapped her on the back. "Continue like that and you're on the way to the World Cup."

"Right."

Sometimes, she thought this was all too easy.

After a shower, she drove back home, made a thick ham sandwich and drove over to Renata's. The bride-to-be was in the midst of trying on her wedding gown and the place was in a tizzy. She stood on a rickety table while her aunt sat on a folding chair pinning up the hem of her gown. Her mother ran back and forth with swaths of lace for the veil, and her little sister Dorothea was wrapping almonds into bits of lace as favors for the wedding dinner.

"Eighty-six, eighty-seven, eighty-eight," Dorothea said. "Only a hundred and twelve more to go."

"What can I do?" Clara said.

"You can help me," Dorothea said.

Clara sat at the dining room table and began assembling. It took only another hour.

Finally, Clara and Renata escaped to the kitchen and made some coffee. Renata broke down in tears.

"Renata! What's the matter?"

"What's the matter? Can't you see? I'm huge. I'm really huge. Everyone is going to laugh."

"No, they're not." Clara did wonder, though, how Renata's condition could possibly be concealed since the wedding was still four weeks away.

"Yes, they are." She blew her nose loudly into a piece of leftover lace. "And you know what Filippo said? He said I'd better look good or else."

"Or else what?"

"He didn't say. But I can imagine."

Clara moved her coffee cup and grabbed Renata's hand. "*Cara,* do you really want to go through with this? You don't have to, you know."

"Of course I have to. It's too late for…you know. And I've done that already, you know."

Clara did know.

"I want the baby this time. I really do. So I'm going through with this. We're going to have a beautiful wedding, with lots of food. Mama is making most of it. And we're having Davido and the Druidi for the music. It's going to be fun. Really."

She wiped her eyes and managed a grim smile.

"It will be, Renata. I know it will be. I'm looking forward to it so much. When do you think you'll have my dress?"

"Your dress?"

"My dress for the wedding. Didn't you say I'd be a bridesmaid?"

Renata stirred her coffee, now icy cold, and looked away. "Um. I don't think so, Clara. I don't remember that at all."

"Renata, don't you remember? We went to the store in Lucca and we looked at wedding dresses and you said, I'm sure you said this, 'Oh, Clara, you're my very best friend. I want you to be in my wedding.' I remember it like yesterday."

"That's strange. I don't remember that at all. Well, anyway, I've already asked Gabriela and Simona and Pippa and I can't have any more. Papa won't let me."

"Well, OK. It's just that I know you asked me."

Renata's face was suddenly flushed and she began to cry again. "Clara, OK. Here's what happened. I told Filippo that you were going to be a bridesmaid and all hell broke loose. I'd never seen him that way."

"Why, for God's sake? I hardly know Filippo. What's he got against me?"

"He said…he said…he wanted everyone in the wedding party to look…well…to look alike. He's thinking of the wedding photographs. That's what he said, I swear."

Renata's makeshift lace handkerchief was now soaked.

"I don't know what that means," Clara said. "I don't look like the other bridesmaids? I'm not tall. I'm not, well, fat. Some people think I'm rather pretty."

"It's not that, Clara."

"Because my arms are kind of muscled? And my legs? The bridesmaid's dress would hide that."

"No, that's not it."

"Because I'm not, well, as voluptuous as some other girls? My mother says I'm sort of flat. Is that why?"

"No, no."

"Because my hair is long and everyone else has short hair? I can pin it up."

"No, your hair is fine."

"Well, what is it then?"

"Filippo thinks…he thinks…he thinks everyone else in the wedding party will be light-skinned and, well, you know…"

"What?"

"That's what he said."

Clara was angry now. "So this jerk of a guy you're going to marry, this jerk of a guy you're going to spend your life with, this jerk of a guy who is the father of your baby, this jerk of a guy who will probably beat you up every night…"

"Clara, stop!"

"No! I won't stop. This asshole doesn't want me in the wedding party because my skin is dark? Because I'm from Calabria and not from your whitey whitey Tuscany?"

"Clara…"

"Well, Renata, I wouldn't be in your wedding if you were the last person on earth. And you can tell your beloved Filippo he can take his wedding and shove it! And you know where!"

And she was out the door.

SERAFINA WAS MENDING Pasquale's jeans and Salvo was reading *La Repubblica* when Clara stormed through the door and ran up to her room.

"What the…?" Salvo said.

"I'd better go up," Serafina said. "Something terrible must have happened. Maybe she was in an accident. I wish she'd trade in that old motorcycle. It's dangerous."

She found Clara sprawled face down on her bed, her head in the pillow.

"Clara, what's wrong?" Serafina sat at the edge of the bed, her hand on Clara's back.

"Leave me alone."

"Clara, what happened? Something happened. Were you in an accident?"

"No. I wasn't in an accident. I don't want to talk about it. Please go."

"Are you sure?"

"Yes, I'm sure."

"OK, if you say so." Serafina left the room, walked down the hall, stopped and turned back.

"Clara, I think you should tell me what happened."

"Please go away, Mama. It's not your fault."

"My fault? What are you talking about? What's not my fault?"

Clara turned over on her back and wiped her nose on her sleeve. "That we're from Calabria."

"Oh my, Calabria again. I thought we were through with that stuff."

When Salvo and Serafina Marincola and their three young children moved to Sant'Antonio from Corigliano in Calabria in the late 1970s, everyone was so pleased that the old, dilapidated Sanfilippo house was again occupied. It had been abandoned for decades. Neighbors even helped the family paint walls, repair the porch and fix the plumbing. To be sure, there were some condescending comments about how the family would have to get used to life in northern Italy, and there were snide remarks about the family's darker skin.

In the early 1980s, as the parents became more visible in the village and the children began playing with other children, attitudes appeared to change. Many of the villagers seemed more conscious of the differences in dialect, in customs and especially in their skin color. Serafina sometimes found herself ignored by other customers at the village's two shops, Leoni's and Manconi's, and even in church. Little Pasquale, small at seven years and the darkest of the family, became the target of a bully at school.

This upset Serafina so much that she wanted to move back to Corigliano. Salvo had to continually convince her that they had a better life in the north.

Then Pasquale fell off the roof of Signora Cardineli's house while trying to rescue her cat, and during the critical weeks when he was hospitalized, even the most prejudiced of the villagers realized that the color of one's skin really didn't matter when a little boy's life was at stake.

There had been a few other instances over the years—when Francesco didn't make the soccer team until the third try, when Salvo was passed over for a promotion, when Serafina was ignored by a clerk—but generally, the family felt accepted.

Until now.

Clara told her mother what happened more in anger than in sadness. How dare Renata, or really Filippo, make a decision like that? Why didn't Renata object? Why didn't the other bridesmaids?

All her mother could say was, "I don't know."

She tried to assure her daughter that not everyone in Sant'Antonio, in fact very few people, felt the way Filippo did. She pointed out how loving and accepting other villagers were, Mario and Anita, Donna and Ezio, Paolo and even Lucia, who had made such patronizing remarks at the start.

Clara sniffled. Even though she was nineteen years old, an accomplished mechanic in a motorcycle shop and an award-winning athlete, she sometimes needed her mother for comfort.

Salvo appeared at the door. "Clara, are you OK? Anything I can do?"

"I'll be OK, Papa."

"OK, let me know."

Clara blew her nose in a Kleenex and sat in the little rocking chair that she'd had since childhood. Her mother sat on the bed.

"Do you agree, Clara," she said, "that most people accept you for who you are?"

"I guess so."

"I know it's been hard. I don't think I'll ever forget that bully who tormented Pasquale in *Seconda Classe.* He'd come home with his shirt all soiled and his homework all marked up. And then that kid called him that terrible name."

"I remember that."

"And then the kid's father came to apologize. Remember that, too, Clara. People may do awful things, but they recognize what they've done and they apologize."

"Well, the father did, not the son."

"I think the son realizes what he did now. Let's hope so."

Clara stood at the window. Lightning had started in the north, illuminating the church steeple.

"Clara, I think we should talk about something," her mother said.

"I thought we already had that talk."

"Not that one. Clara, ever since you were a little girl you've been so active in sports."

"Maybe because I was never very good at reading and writing. Not to mention math."

"Even though the school didn't offer anything—I wish schools in Italy would have teams like they do in America—you found places where you could swim, where you could play tennis, and even teams where you could play soccer. And they weren't easy to find for girls."

"I found them."

"Your Papa and I keep telling you. You don't have to do all these things. You didn't have to play soccer and tennis, too, but you did. And you got to the semifinals in tennis." Serafina picked up the trophy from Clara's dressing table.

"Why are you telling me all this now, Mama?"

"Clara, I'm not a psychologist. I never even graduated from high school. But it seems to me, and your Papa, that you're doing all these things for a reason."

"What? What reason, Mama?"

Clara was beginning to feel that her anger was returning.

"Clara, do you think—just maybe—that you are trying to prove something?"

"Mama! What could I possibly be trying to prove?"

"Well, as I said, I'm not a psychologist, but maybe that even though you are, well, from Calabria and have sort of a dark skin, that you are just as good as a lot of girls with lighter skin?"

Clara picked up the Kleenex box and threw it on the floor. "Mama, that's ridiculous! That's bull...baloney! That's rubbish! I do these things because I want to do them. And I'm good at them, you know that. I'm not trying to prove anything to anybody."

"Think about it, Clara."

IF SALVO AND SERAFINA had to rank their children in order of intelligence, it would not take them long. Clearly, Pasquale, the youngest, was the brightest of the kids, easily scoring 100s in all of his classes, taking no time at all in the examinations and barely needing to prepare for oral presentations.

He didn't take part in sports because of his small size, but he was an excellent flute player. He had only a few friends, and mostly he liked to go off alone with Bruno and find treasures in the hills.

If not spectacularly, Clara had done well enough in school, getting 85s or so in writing and history and social studies, and lesser grades in science and mathematics. She was in the second tier of her class.

Francesco… Francesco managed to get through school after much prodding by his teachers and many threats by his parents. He may have been good at math, but he failed a few other classes, and Salvo and Serafina were convinced that the school finally just pushed him out the door.

While it was assumed that Pasquale would go on to university when he finished high school, neither Francesco nor Clara had even thought of continuing their education.

Clara, taught by her father to fix things around the house and even small engines, became the first female to work at Giorgio's motorcycle repair shop in nearby Sant'Agostino, probably because no male would consent to work for such low wages. She quickly knew more about fixing the machines than Giorgio.

Francesco had taken his time in looking for a job after graduation. It was too much fun hanging out with his friends, driving into the mountains and swimming at the sea. His parents became more and more worried, especially after two visits from the local *carabinieri,* once for having an expired driver's license but, more significantly, once for becoming too boisterous at a tavern in Lucca.

In October, he finally found a job at a pizza place in Lucca. The pay was low, but enough for gasoline, movies, rock concerts and some other things that his parents didn't want to think about.

"What's going to happen to Francesco and Clara?" Salvo said one night. "Is Clara going to be a motorcycle mechanic all her life? Is Francesco going to be flipping pizzas when he's eighty years old?"

"I don't know, Salvo," Serafina said. "They're still young. They'll find something. I wish they'd find some other interests, something that they could do that would be fun but where they'd make some new friends. There aren't many young people in Sant'Antonio, you know."

Because Francesco was only thirteen months older than Clara, they had been each other's best friend since childhood. They squabbled as little kids, but they made up. As they grew older, they had long talks and confided their secrets. When Clara had troubles with a boyfriend, Francesco held her hand. When Francesco was jilted by his latest girlfriend, Clara told him he'd find another.

Perhaps because of Clara's strong build from all her athletic endeavors, they even looked like one another. People often asked them if they were twins, especially when Clara wore one of Francesco's old jeans jackets.

When Francesco's two friends Farid and Roberto both decided to go to university, he thought he'd better think about his future, too.

"Don't tell Mama and Papa," he told Clara one night when he was losing badly at a game of checkers, "but I think I'll go to university next year."

"Why don't you want Mama and Papa to know?"

"Because they'll just get all excited and ask all these questions, and I don't even know what I want to study. I'll just wait. I'll figure it out. It's just that I'm not much interested in anything."

"What do you like to do?" his sister asked.

"Play video games."

"Besides that?"

Long pause. "Can't think of anything."

"Well, why do you like video games?"

"The action. The competition. The colors. Mostly, the daring."

"Maybe you should join a circus."

"Really? That would be fun! I could walk on the tightrope. I could get shot out of a cannon. I could be a clown!"

"I think you already are."

"What about you? Aren't you interested in something?"

"I don't know. I wish I had something that I could get excited about. Swimming doesn't start for months, and tennis not until spring. So there's only soccer now, and that isn't a challenge anymore. Francesco, you know what? I'm bored."

"Really? So am I. There's nothing to do in this little village. Now my friends are off to college and I don't know what to do with myself. I know one thing. I'm never going to date a girl again. Never. Not after what Regina told me. I hate that woman!"

"Maybe she was just kidding."

"Not on your life."

"Well, I'm not having much of a love life either, you know. Savino keeps asking me out but I know what he wants, and I'm not willing to give it to him. You know what, he smells!"

They collapsed laughing, stopping only when their mother called them to dinner.

It was two weeks after Salvo and Serafino had spent their weekend in Lucca. While Francesco and Clara were lost in their own thoughts, Salvo mentioned to Serafina something he'd heard at the *tabacchi* shop in Lucca.

"...they hope to get organized before the end of the year so they'll be ready next summer," Salvo said.

"That doesn't seem like enough time," Serafina said. "Pasquale, pass the potatoes."

"I didn't think so either, and apparently they're still looking for money. It's going to cost a lot."

"Where will they raise it?" Serafina asked.

"I don't know. They're still looking to find people, I guess."

Hearing the topic of money discussed, Francesco became interested. "What are you guys talking about?"

"Haven't you been listening?" Salvo said.

"Well, some of it."

"We're talking about something that's going to happen in Lucca."

"Which is?" Clara asked.

"The *sbandieratori*," Salvo said.

Serafina began to clear away the dishes. "Someone," she said, "is going to organize a group of flag throwers in Lucca like there is in Florence."

"You're kidding!"

SEVEN YEARS EARLIER, after Pasquale had fully recovered from his terrible accident, their neighbors in Sant'Antonio had presented Salvo and Serafina with a large check.

"You've been through so much," they said. "Get away from here for a few days. Take a vacation."

The family could have returned to Calabria, but Salvo and Serafina feared that would raise old issues and be too depressing. They could have gone to Rome, but that seemed overwhelming. Instead, they decided to go to Florence.

"If we're going to live in Tuscany, we should know something about its history, its art, its culture," Salvo told the children. "Obviously, we have to start in Florence."

So they loaded Francesco, then thirteen, Clara, twelve, and Pasquale, eight, into their twelve-year-old Fiat and headed for Florence. They found a hotel at the end of Ponte Vecchio and set off to explore the city.

"Wait! Wait!" either Salvo or Serafina called as the children ran ahead. "We can't keep up."

"There's too much to see," Clara cried. "We won't have time to see it all."

For the next three days they did try to see it all. They walked all over, from one side of the Arno to the other. They were so overwhelmed by Michelangelo's statue of David in the Accadamia that they spent an hour just walking around and gazing at it.

"He's so big!" Francesco said.

"And beautiful," Clara said.

Pasquale stood frozen, eyes as big as saucers. Serafina was so overcome that she couldn't move from a bench.

After that, it was time for a gelato and a ride on the carousel in the Piazza della Repubblica. All three kids climbed to the top of the Duomo despite Serafina's worries that they would fall, and they all stood to have Polaroid pictures taken in front of what was called Dante's House. Francesco and Clara were vaguely familiar with the poet, but Salvo had to explain *The Divine Comedy* to Pasquale.

Every night they found a *trattoria* for pasta, and every night someone said, "This is not as good as Sarafina/Mama makes." Every morning they had the lavish American-style buffet on the hotel's sixth floor with a panoramic view of tile rooftops and the Duomo. This was a big treat for the children since most Italian breakfasts, including theirs, consisted only of juice, hard bread and coffee.

They walked along the Arno, saw the majestic tombs of famous people in Santa Croce, and shopped—but bought very little—at the public markets. They admired the Botticellis in the Uffizi and the statues in

Loggia dei Lanzi in the Piazza della Signoria. The boys were especially intrigued by the huge Rape of the Sabine Women.

Salvo told them about the friar Girolama Savonarola's bombastic preaching that led to his execution right there in the piazza. Francesco and Pasquale took turns standing on the bronze plaque that marked the spot, and Clara took pictures.

Filled with history, art and culture—and pasta—the family was ready to return to Sant'Antonio on the afternoon of the third day. They were strolling down Via de Pandolfini having one last gelato when they heard the distant sounds of drums. Gradually, the sounds became louder and they noticed that people were moving down Via del Proconsolo.

"What's going on?" Salvo asked a fruit seller who was closing his shop so he could join the crowd.

"It's the *Bandierai Uffizi.* They're going to be in Piazza della Signoria."

"The what?" Francesco asked. "Where is everyone going?"

"It's the flag throwers of Florence," his father said. "I think they're going to have a performance in the Piazza della Signoria."

"People throw flags?" Francesco cried. "Why? Are they trying to hit someone? This is weird."

"No," Salvo said, "they throw the flags high in the air and catch them and do all sorts of other maneuvers. Just wait! It's a magnificent show. I saw it on television once."

"Oh, look!" Clara cried. "Here they come!"

First came a band of about twenty young boys in red velvet caps and white-and-red tunics and tights straight out of the Middle Ages and pounding loudly on their drums. A red fleur-de-lis was emblazoned on each chest. Next came a dozen or so rather elderly men, also in white-and-red doublets and tights and with elaborate feathered hats. They escorted women in elegant low-cut brocade and bejeweled gowns that swept the pavement.

"I can't believe this," Clara said. "This is like the pictures in my history books."

But there was more. Some twenty men, also dressed in white-and-red tunics and tights, carried huge flags that they waved in the air as they strode past. The cheering crowd followed them as they turned onto Via del Condotta and then toward the piazza.

The crowd surged forward, and Francesco, Clara and Pasquale managed to get in front. Then a guard moved everyone back because the performance was about to begin. Suddenly, centuries faded away. It was 1585 and Lorenzo de Medici was ruling Florence. Francesco, Clara and Pasquale were almost jumping up and down with excitement.

To the delight of the crowd, a man with a short trimmed beard and flag held high ran into the piazza followed by his troupe. With the statues of David, Neptune and Perseus looking on, and with the ghost of Girolama Savonarola hovering nearby, the flag throwers arranged themselves in formation. The drummers continued to beat their instruments as each man now threw his flag high in the air, forty, fifty, sixty feet, and easily caught it when it came down.

Again and again, the men, many of them young but a few older members as well, threw the flags in the air. Sometimes they performed in pairs, then in threes, then in fours, throwing the flags expertly to each other. Every flag was skillfully caught, as easily as if it were a pencil thrown across a desk. Not a one fell to the ground.

Then there were more formations. Some of the men maneuvered two and even three flags. The drummers pounded even more loudly. *"Bravo!"* the crowd yelled again and again. And finally all the performers held their flags aloft and bowed to the crowd, which went wild. In formation, the flag throwers ran from the piazza.

Briefly, Pasquale was swallowed up by the crowd, only to be found chatting with one of the young drummers.

"What did he say?" Salvo wanted to know.

"He asked where we were from. I told him Sant'Antonio. He said he would like to visit sometime."

"Right. OK, kids, let's find our way to the car through this mob."

Luckily, they found their car and managed to drive through the heavy traffic. There was no stopping the kids on the way home.

"Did you see that tall guy? He threw it higher than anyone."

"I liked the guy with the crew cut."

"He was showing off."

"No, he wasn't."

"I wonder why they were all men," Clara said.

"Oh, Clara," Francesco said. "You're just being paranoid."

"I saw two girls in the drummers," Pasquale said.

"Sure, as drummers," Clara said. "But not as flag throwers."

"I wonder," Pasquale said, "where they learn that stuff."

"There must be a school in Florence."

"Papa, can we go to the flag throwers school? That was so cool!"

FOR MONTHS AFTER THAT TRIP, Francesco, Clara and Pasquale became obsessed with the *sbandieratori.* They found books and articles about them, and all three wrote papers about their origins for their Italian history classes, getting extra credit.

Although there were sometimes conflicting accounts, they generally found that the beginnings of these flag throwers stretched back to the Renaissance and even medieval times when flag bearers and drummers led military troop movements. The flags were raised on high to lead the soldiers into battle, and it was considered a disgrace if a bearer somehow lost his flag.

"Sometimes, these guys even died trying to save the flags," Clara told her brothers as they wrote their papers at the kitchen table.

In peacetime, the flag bearers became flag jugglers, performing elaborate demonstrations in exhibitions and competitions. There were even manuals on how to carry and throw the flags. Realizing that these exhibitions of flag throwing not only kept a little history alive but also were good for the tourist business, city after city formed the groups and promoted them at festivals. In recent years, a few groups had toured Europe and even the United States.

While Pasquale and Bruno sat on a bench and watched, Francesco and Clara tried to become flag throwers and jugglers themselves in their backyard. They started by throwing cardboard rolls from paper towels to one another. Then they used rulers and then yardsticks. Finally, Francesco took two old broomsticks and tied pieces of curtains on them. They tried throwing them to one another, and at first managed only a few successful tries. Mostly, they wound up with cuts and bruises on their hands.

Then Francesco, and especially Clara, became more adept. She could throw the makeshift flag high, maybe ten or twenty feet into the air, and almost always caught it.

"Clara," Francesco said, "do you have to beat me at everything?"

"Of course!"

Since Francesco and Clara were teenagers and Pasquale was only eight, they gradually became interested in other things, Francesco in girls, Clara in boys and Pasquale in birds. They didn't think about the flag throwers of Florence unless they picked up the photo album that their mother had put together with the Polaroid shots of their trip.

Then, years after their trip to Florence, when Salvo and Serafina told them about the new *sbandieratori* to be formed in Lucca, their interest was aroused again. But Salvo didn't know any more details.

"No," Salvo said, "we don't know who's in charge, we don't know where they're located, we don't know if they have a school, we don't know if they have uniforms, no, no, no."

It was up to Francesco, who worked in Lucca, to find out.

The manager of the pizza place wasn't any help, and none of Francesco's co-workers even seemed interested in the subject.

"Men in tights?" they said. "Sounds a little, well, you know…"

On his lunch break, Francesco went down a street called Corte Campana and found the Lucca Chamber of Commerce and Industry. Surely they would know something.

They did. Signor Raffaelo Mignano was the man to see.

"He lives near Chiesa di San Michele."

"Street address?"

"Just ask someone. They'll know."

Francesco found the church, with its wedding-cake front, and asked a man about to enter.

"Signor Mignano? What do you want him for?"

"I hear he is organizing a *sbandieratori."*

"He is? Well, good luck." The man walked up the stairs and Francesco called after him.

"Why do you say that?"

"Well, there was that dog track that he tried to get started, but the dogs died. He started a record company, but the records wouldn't play. He's opened at least three restaurants and they all failed. Who wants to go to Best Italian Chinese Cuisine"?

"Thanks. But where does he live?"

"Down that street, third door on the left. Upstairs. Number 42."

"Thanks again."

After a dozen rings on the bell, Francesco heard a voice on the intercom and the door clicked to be opened. The wooden stairs, some of them splintered, creaked. Upstairs, down a very dark hall with a frayed rug and a single ceiling light, he found Number 42.

"Come in!"

The room wasn't much brighter than the hall, illuminated mainly by a shaft of sunlight through a dirty window. It might not have been cleaned in months. The pictures on the walls hung at crooked angles. Stacks of books and magazines surrounded a torn brown leather chair in the middle of the room. Francesco noticed that several photography books about flag throwers were opened on the floor.

"Wonder where the guy is," Francesco thought.

The guy suddenly appeared from a room on the left.

Just what Francesco expected after seeing the room. Round face. Stringy white hair falling on his shoulders. Small eyeglasses. Rotund body in a brown three-piece suit, the vest unbuttoned, the necktie askew. A gold chain over his belly. Tobacco stains on his fingers and stubby beard.

He held out a fleshy hand. "I am Raffaelo Mignano. And you are?"

Francesco introduced himself and told the signor that he heard a *sbandieratori* was being established and that his family had been very much interested in flag throwing since they saw a group in Florence years ago.

"And I was told you were the person who would know about this," he concluded.

Signor Mignano went to his desk and picked up a very fragile book.

"You see this? It is *The Flag* by Franz Ferdinand Alfieri, the weapon master of the Academy Delia, and it was published in 1638. Imagine, 1638! Thirty years ago, I was in a little bookshop in Rome and I happened to pick this up. I didn't know much about flag throwing then, but this book inspired me."

He opened the book. "Look at all these illustrations. Don't they want to make you run out and throw a flag in the air?"

Francesco had to agree. He and Clara and Pasquale had heard about the book when they were writing their papers but had been unable to find it.

Signor Mignano went on to explain that he was determined to begin a *sbandieratori* in Lucca and had begun interviewing young men even now for places.

"I have twelve, maybe thirteen, young men now. I need a few more."

Francesco said that he lived in Sant'Antonio, so maybe he couldn't join.

"The name will be Lucca, but I will be taking young men from all over," the signor said.

"I don't know if I'm strong enough."

"We will have to see."

"I have a brother, but he's only fourteen."

"Maybe he could be in the drum corps."

"My sister is nineteen."

"Sister? No! No girls!"

IT TOOK MORE THAN AN HOUR for Clara to quiet down. Her family had expected yelling and screaming after Francesco told her that no girls would be allowed in the *sbandieratori,* but they didn't imagine the foot stomping and the throwing of breakable objects. Poor Bruno fled to the next room when a book narrowly missed his head. Pasquale ran after him and hugged the whimpering dog.

"Clara, settle down," her father said.

"Just forget about it," her mother said.

"I can't."

Pasquale, returning with Bruno in his arms, suggested an alternative.

"I know I'm not so good at flag throwing, but I could play the drums," he said. "I can play the flute, so how much harder is it to play the drums? Anyway, Clara, you could play the drums, too. Remember we saw those two girls in Florence?"

"No."

"It would be fun. We would be together."

"No."

"And we'd still be a part of the *sbandieratori."*

"No. I'm not going to be a little drummer boy."

When Francesco suggested that perhaps Clara could wear a fancy dress and walk in the procession like those medieval women in Florence, Clara's icy stare forced everyone to cringe.

"You people don't understand," she said. "This is 1992! Women are everywhere. I play soccer, I swim, I play tennis. My arms are as strong as any boy's. But they won't allow a woman in the *sbandieratori?* That's insane!"

"I know," Serafina said. "It's terrible."

"You know you're just as good as any man," Salvo said. "And we know that, too."

"I know that, but Signor Mignano doesn't. Asshole."

"Clara!" Salvo said.

Clara slid deeper into the couch, her arms folded, her eyes clenched. She stayed that way for hours, even after everyone else had gone to bed. Bruno followed Pasquale and hid under his bed.

"Sometimes," Serafina told Salvo as they were getting ready for bed, "I think Clara is five years old the way she acts."

"She sure knows what she wants."

"And she always gets it."

The next day, Salvo had an idea.

"Clara, why don't you go to see Signor Mignano and tell him how much you want to become a flag thrower and about all the sports you've been in. Tell him you are just as strong as Francesco."

"No, I'm not going to grovel," Clara said.

"That's not groveling, it's just making things plain. It's not going to hurt."

Clara was about to reject the idea but had second thoughts. "OK, but I don't think it will do any good."

Francesco drove his sister to Lucca, found Number 42 again, and introduced Clara to Signor Mignano.

"Signor," she began, "I know it is not traditional for a woman to be part of the *sbandieratori,* but I would really like to join yours. Ever since my family saw the demonstration in Florence, we have been so thrilled about flag throwing, and when we heard you were going to establish one here, we became even more excited. We can hardly wait until you put this demonstration on because we know that if anyone can make a success of this, we are sure you can."

Clara almost choked on the feigned flattery, but continued.

"I would love to be a part of your team, so I hope you will consider me when you have your tryouts."

Signor Mignano looked at Clara, from her long brown hair to her running shoes.

"No."

"I'm really very strong, Signor. I have won medals for swimming and tennis, and my coach says I'm one of the best soccer players he's ever had."

"No."

"Francesco can tell you that all of this is true."

"It is," Francesco said. "Clara's actually stronger than me."

"No."

"Signor Mignano," Clara said, "may I ask why?"

The signor put his cigar in a tray on his desk and sighed.

"Because, little girl," he said, "there has never been a girl in a *sbandieratori* in all of Italy. Ever. We have always had *ragazzi*, not *ragazze.*"

"Boys but not girls. May I ask if that is your only reason?"

"Do I need another?"

"Couldn't there be a first time? Think of how proud all of Lucca would be knowing that you have allowed a woman to join the flag throwers. You'd make history. You'd be famous."

"No."

"Would you like to think this over? I can come back."

"No. Now, please, I am very busy. Good-bye."

Francesco had to hold on to his sister all the way home, fearing that she would jump out of the car.

A week later, he learned that tryouts for the *sbandieratori* were going to be held on a soccer field outside of Lucca on Thursday nights. He arranged to get the night off from work, and on the next Thursday he and Pasquale drove to the site. Their parents knew where they were going, but both boys had wisely not disclosed their destination at dinner. They simply said they had to meet someone.

Clara knew, of course, but didn't respond. She did, however, throw her plate against the wall before she stormed upstairs.

When they returned, and Clara was nowhere to be seen, Francesco and Pasquale told their parents what had happened.

"There were about fourteen older boys and ten younger ones," Francesco said. "Signor Mignano told the younger ones they could probably be in the drum corps."

"He pointed at me," Pasquale said. "That's OK. I can be a drummer. I just want to be part of it."

"He had the older boys do some calisthenics," Francesco said. "Running, jumping up and down. I wasn't the best, but I wasn't the worst, either."

"Mama, Francesco was really good," Pasquale said.

"That's all we did. So I guess we all made it. He said the next time, he would give us poles to practice on. But we won't get real flags for a while."

In the following weeks, Francesco and Pasquale quietly slipped out the door at 6:30 on Thursday nights, pretending they were going to see someone and Clara pretending that they were. She then went to her room and slammed the door.

The sessions were never discussed at dinner.

But Francesco and Pasquale came home each Thursday night more and more excited.

"This is really fun," Francesco said. "I can throw that pole almost as high as everyone else."

"And he can catch it, too," Pasquale said. "He hardly ever lets it drop."

Pasquale spent Thursday nights practicing on a drum, which took little musical talent.

"I just keep pounding like everyone else," he said, "but it's kind of fun."

After four weeks, Francesco was thrilled when the older boys were allowed to bring their wooden poles home to practice. Then he realized the problem.

"Papa, when can I practice? Clara is always here. She's going to get mad if she sees me."

"Just practice," Salvo said. "Clara can't be ruling this house or what everybody does. If she sees you, fine. Just go do it."

And Francesco did. At first, he did it late in the evening when he knew Clara was either in her room reading or watching television with everyone else. He knew she did not have many dates.

Weeks later, he was surprised when Clara came out and sat on the porch when he was practicing. It was one of his good nights. He deftly caught the pole every time, and Clara applauded. A little.

Encouraged, he began doing a few tricks, turning around and catching it from behind or grabbing it between his legs.

Clara applauded a little more.

Francesco ran around the yard with the pole in the air and when he got to Clara he bowed deeply, pretending to take off a cap.

"Bravo!" she cried.

"Grazie molto, signorina! Io sono al vostro servizio."

Clara made a little curtsy. Salvo and Serafina watched all this from their window and Pasquale giggled on the bench.

Francesco hesitated, and then held the wooden pole out to Clara.

"Vorrebbe che le insegnassi?"

Clara fluttered her eyes. "You would like to teach me? Well, that would be so nice, my gallant hero."

Francesco helped her down the steps and stood behind her as she maneuvered the pole from one side to the other.

"Just go slow," Francesco said. "Just get the feeling of it."

Clara ran her hands across the surface."

"Now put it over your shoulder and run with it like I just did."

She did.

"Now try to use one hand over the other and sort of twirl it."

After several tries, she did. After several more, she was doing it quite expertly.

"Clara, that's good! I'm impressed."

"Brava!" Pasquale cried.

"Tennis arms," Clara said.

"OK, think you could throw it up and catch it? Not too far, just a little."

Clara threw it up, only a couple of feet, but it promptly fell to the ground.

"That's OK. Just reach out a little faster when it comes down."

After two more failed attempts, she caught it with both hands.

"Good! That's good, Clara."

"Brava!" Pasquale cried.

"Swimmer's arms," Clara said.

"OK, try a little higher this time."

No problem.

And for another forty-five minutes, Clara learned the art of flag throwing.

"You know what?" Francesco said. "You're better than me."

"Soccer legs," Clara said.

"Brava!" Pasquale cried and hugged Bruno.

From their window, Salvo said, "Looks like Francesco and Clara have something to do that they like."

"It's a shame Clara can't be in the group," Serafina said. "She'd do so well. She'd be the star!"

"You know, Serafina, I wonder if Clara has something up her sleeve."

CLARA HELPED FRANCESCO practice in the backyard through the cold all winter, even though their hands grew red and stiff. Signor Mignano had given the team members, now numbering sixteen, pieces of cloth the size of the regular flags, and also two poles apiece. Francesco became more adept, but Clara had now exceeded her brother's ability in sending the poles into the air, catching them and doing backhanded and under-the-leg tricks.

"I can't keep up with you," Francesco said.

"Ha! Just try a little harder," Clara said as she sent her pole forty feet into the air.

Signor Mignano canceled a team practice only once, and that was because there were eight inches of snow on the frozen ground of the soccer field.

On February 22, he kept the shivering boys after their practice with two important announcements.

"First, I have gotten permission from the bishop to hold the very first exhibition of the *Sbandieratori di Lucca* on September 13. You of course know what day that is."

"The *Luminara di Santa Croce!"* two young men shouted together.

The *Luminara di Santa Croce* had taken place in Lucca on that date for centuries, and people came from all over to watch pilgrims carrying candles, or *luminari,* and accompany the holy cross, the *Volto Santo,* that was kept in the Duomo through the historic district.

Even if they did not believe it, everyone knew the legend surrounding the cross that inspired the ceremony. It went all the way back to the time of Christ. According to word passed down from mouth to mouth, when Jesus died on the cross, his disciple Joseph of Arimathea was assisted by a man named Nicodemus in placing Christ's body into the tomb.

Although Nicodemus was a Pharisee, the experience inspired him to sculpt a wooden carving of Jesus' body on the cross. But he was unable to carve the face and fell asleep. When he awoke, he found that the face was carved, and he believed it to be the work of an angel.

The Lucca connection was even more miraculous—or speculative. Again according to legend, Nicodemus' wooden sculpture was hidden in a cave in the Holy Land until it was discovered by a Bishop Gualfredo of Siena, who had the work carried to the port of Luni on the Tuscan coast. It was brought, people said, in a boat without sails or a crew. Then the sculpture was rolled to Lucca on a cart driven by oxen. The cart, they also said, had no driver but it somehow found its way to the Basilica of San Frediano. Later, it was relocated to the nearby Cathedral of San Martino.

Over the years, a religious festival developed around the sculpture in the middle of September, even though the *Volto Santo* in the cathedral was actually a thirteenth-century copy of the original.

Some people, notably Clara, scoffed at all of this. An angel carved the face of the sculpture? A boat with no sails or a crew carried the sculpture from the Holy Land to Tuscany? A cart with no driver brought it to Lucca?

That, however, didn't prevent her from joining the rest of her family in going to Lucca in the middle of September every year to watch the procession and, mostly, enjoy the produce, gifts and candy in the markets set up on the streets.

Now the *Sbandieratori di Lucca* would be part of the celebration.

After the team members settled down after hearing the news, Signor Mignano made his second announcement. Each member would wear a costume inspired by the clothing men would have worn to a fancy ball in Venice in the eighteenth century.

"Venice?" one team member yelled. "We're in Tuscany! All the *sbandieratori* in other cities wear medieval costumes from Tuscany!"

"That's exactly the reason," Signor Mignano said. "Everyone else wears those costumes, so we're going to be different."

He did not explain that he went to the famous *Carnivale* in Venice every year and had a fine costume with a dark blue doublet, light blue leggings, white stockings, black patent leather shoes, an elaborate cap with a feather, and a silver mask. Even if it was sweltering in September, he was determined to wear the whole damn thing.

Signor Mignano said he had raised enough money to supply the stockings, caps, shoes and masks for the troupe. But he could supply only the fabrics for the doublets and leggings. The team members would be responsible for having them made.

"What?" one young man cried. "Who's going to make a doublet and leggings for me?"

"How about your mother?"

The flag throwers and drummers went away grumbling. Francesco and Pasquale thought their mother would be perfectly able to sew the costumes, but it would take a lot of work and they were afraid to ask.

"Of course I'll make them," Serafina said when the subject was broached. "It'll be fun!"

Two weeks later, Francesco and Pasquale came home with bolts of fine wool in midnight blue for the doublets and sky blue for the leggings. Serafina measured her sons and set about cutting the material, pinning pieces together and then sewing them together. Signor Mignano had also supplied Lucca's coat of arms to be sewed on the front—a red-and-white shield enclosed by a wreath and topped by a jeweled crown. The emblem would also be on their flags.

He also sent along the silver masks each boy would wear. "These *maschera* are priceless, so be careful. In Venice, these are worn all during *Carnivale* so people can go disguised."

Like most *maschera,* the masks were silver and decorated with (fake) jewels. They covered almost the entire face, with openings for the eyes and mouth.

"Signor Mignano said they're called *larva,* which means ghost," Francesco said.

"I can't even see your face," Pasquale said when his brother tried his on.

"Right," Clara said. "Do you think, dear brother, that Signor Mignano did this on purpose, so that no one would know that he had someone from Calabria in his group? Of course, I for one would not ever believe such a thing. I am absolutely certain he just wanted everyone to look the same."

"Now, Clara," Serafina said, "you're being paranoid again."

"Me? Paranoid?"

"It's Venice at Carnival time," Salvo said. "Everyone wears masks."

"I'm sure you are right," Clara said, trying on the mask herself. "Look, you can't see my face."

When Serafina finished the outfits, she needed Francesco and Pasquale to try them on for adjustments. Pasquale was compliant, but Francesco kept fidgeting.

"You know you're hurting me with those pins, Mama."

"Just keep still."

"Ouch!"

"Oh, all right," Serafina said. "Take it off and I'll do the best I can."

She still wasn't satisfied the following night, but Francesco had left for work.

"Clara, come here. You're the same size as Francesco. Try this on."

"Happy to. It'll be nice to try it on since I'll never wear one myself."

HAVING FINISHED THE COSTUMES for Francesco and Pasquale, Serafina was surprised when her sons came home with more bolts of fabric.

"Look, Mama," Francesco said. "Signor Mignano says you can make yourself a dress and be in the procession."

The cloth was amazing, emerald green brocade with gold bands and pearls, and weighing, Serafina insisted, half a ton.

"Oh, my God," she said. "I've never seen anything so beautiful."

"Are you going to do it?" her son asked.

"Of course I'm going to do it. I wouldn't miss that procession for anything."

Working nonstop morning to night, Serafina needed almost two weeks to finish the gown since her sewing machine surrendered after the first piece of thick cloth tried to go through. She had to do the whole thing by hand.

Serafina modeled the finished result for her husband and children.

"Oh, my!" Salvo said. "What can I say? You look ten years younger. And beautiful!"

The children agreed. Francesco thought the neckline might be a little too low, but Clara disagreed. "Mama's got them, so let her show them."

"Well," Serafina said, "obviously, I can't walk in the procession alone. I need a strong man. Salvo?"

Salvo pretended to object, but he was actually pleased to go to a costume shop in Lucca the next day. The brown doublet and leggings might have looked more like a peasant than a member of a court, but Serafina thought the outfit was just fine. They couldn't wait until September 13.

Francesco took nights off from work now so that Clara could help him practice.

"I'll never be as good as you," he said as they rolled up their flags one night. "I'm not even as good as the others."

"Yes, you are. I know you are."

"You haven't seen the others. How would you know?"

"I can guess."

They sat in sullen silence. Salvo and Serafina watched them from the window.

"They're good kids, aren't they, Serafina."

"I think we can be proud."

"I like the way they're always talking to each other, as if they're sharing some secrets."

"Maybe Clara has a boyfriend. Or Francesco a girlfriend," Serafina said.

"Or maybe they're planning something. They sure have been at it a long time."

After three weeks of beastly weather, September 13 was sunny and actually cool. Salvo, his woolen leggings itchy, drove the family in a large car he rented. Their own Fiat was much too small to accommodate Serafina's gown. For the first time in her life she had gone to a beauty shop and had her long hair done up in a swirl. Clara wound a pearl necklace through it.

"This isn't me," Serafina complained as she gathered her skirts around her. "I'm really just a fat housewife."

"No, no," Clara said. "You are the Countess Serafina Rosa Maria Elizabetha di Sant'Antonio di Lucca di Toscano. And that's your count who's driving."

Serafina sat with Clara in the backseat, and Salvo and the boys squeezed together in front.

They parked as close as they could to the Piazza della Anfiteatro in the north-central part of the city. The ancient Roman amphitheater that once saw gladiators fight to the death would now be the scene of more civilized competitions.

Crowds had already gathered. Merchants hawked miniature flags of the *sbandieratori*. Street performers stood immobile, like statues. At one end, Signor Mignano greeted his team, carefully, since his costume had apparently shrunk since the last time he wore it.

There were other performances first. Acrobats swung on wires. A motley lion snarled as it was carted around in a cage. A military band played marches at the end of the piazza.

Then it was time. First to enter were the costumed royalty. Dozens of women, obviously the mothers of team members, were escorted by their husbands. Clara, in a crowd near the entrance, waved to her mother and father.

"You both look lovely!" she cried.

The couples walked around the piazza twice, then took their places on the reviewing stand, and Clara joined them. Next came the drummers, who could be heard long before they entered.

"There's Pasquale!" Salvo shouted.

"How can you tell?" Serafina asked. "They all look alike with those masks on."

"He's the smallest. Don't you think I know my own son?"

"And he's pounding the hardest," Clara said. "And his cap is too big."

There was a break, apparently to let the vendors sell more little flags, souvenirs and gelato.

On a signal, the drummers, now at the end of the piazza, suddenly began to pound again. Louder and louder. And then, flags held high, the *sbandieratori* roared in. The crowd rose to its feet cheering. In a blur of blue and white, the sixteen flag bearers ran around the piazza, once, twice, three times. Then they settled into a formation, four rows of four each.

Even with the masks hiding their faces, all of the flag throwers appeared to be, like Francesco, barely in their twenties.

"Where's Francesco?" Salvo cried. "I don't see him."

"Second row, third to the left," Serafina said. "I sewed a red stripe under his neck so we could find him. He looks a little nervous."

"He'll do fine," Clara said.

On cue, each boy threw his flag in the air. Miraculously, all reached the same height and all were flawlessly caught. They did it again. And again. And again.

They formed a circle and ran around the piazza, flags high. Then another formation, this time, two rows of eight each. Again the flags were tossed and caught. Not a single error.

"They're amazing," Clara said.

Then four of the boys formed a circle and began tossing their flags to one another. The crowd cheered. Higher and higher. More cheers. Then those on the outer circle tossed flags to the inner circle and each of those boys had two flags to maneuver. High in the air, over to a partner, behind the back, under the legs. Over and over again.

"Francesco is wonderful," Serafina said.

"Bravo, Francesco!" Salvo cried.

The crowd could not get enough of this. The four boys in the middle now had four flags each, tossing them back and forth with incredible ability. It went on for more than forty-five minutes. Then all the boys formed a line and held their flags high in the air as they circled the piazza three times. And then they ran off.

"That's it?" Serafina said. "Aren't they going to take bows?"

"I don't think it's over," Salvo said. "I bet they come back. I think there's more."

Clara stood up. "Well, I hate to miss this, but I really have to pee."

"Clara! You're going to miss the ending? Can't you wait?"

"No, afraid not. Be back in a minute."

Clara got up and ran through the crowd to the exit.

"I think the toilets are on the other side," Salvo said. "Well, she'll find them."

The drummers now took over the piazza, marching in twos around and around.

"Oh, look at Pasquale," Serafina said. "Doesn't he look cute?"

"Serafina, he just turned fifteen. I don't think he wants to be called cute."

After about fifteen minutes, the drummers returned to their places but continued to beat on their drums. Then the line of flag throwers suddenly burst through the entrance again and ran around and around the edge of the piazza holding their flags aloft. They formed a circle, and one by one, each began a solo performance.

There was no doubt that these boys had trained exceedingly well. Not once did a flag touch the ground and only once or twice was it caught a little too late. The crowd cheered each boy until it seemed it could cheer no more.

Twelve, thirteen, fourteen, fifteen. Finally the last boy stepped to the center.

"It's Francesco!" Serafina cried.

"Are you sure?"

"Yes, it is. See the red band just under his neck? *Bravo,* Francesco!"

If the other flag throwers had thrilled the spectators beyond expectations, Francesco had every one of them applauding until their hands were sore. He had two flags, then three, then four. Higher than anyone else. Gracefully twirled around and around, never near the ground.

"He never seemed so good at home," Salvo said.

"Oh, I'm so upset that Clara isn't seeing this," Serafina said. "*Bravo,* Francesco!"

"*Bravo,* Francesco!" Salvo shouted.

The crowd took up the chant. "*Bravo,* Francesco!" Even Pasquale started to yell, and soon the other drummer boys joined in. The entire piazza reverberated with "*Bravo,* Francesco!"

Serafina whispered to her husband. "You know, I'm not sure now if that's really Francesco. He looks, well, a little different."

Salvo looked hard and shook his head. "No, no, that's him. See the red stripe. Who else could it be?"

As the drummers drummed, Francesco took the four flags, put two on each shoulder, and ran around the piazza, waving to the crowd. He stopped in front of the wife of Signor Mignano and, as is customary, bowed low before her. She threw her handkerchief down to him.

Francesco picked it up and kissed it. With a broad gesture, he pulled off his cap. Hair fell to the shoulders. Next, in a dramatic gesture, off came the *maschera.*

The cheers that had filled the piazza moments before now devolved into a loud gasp.

"It's a girl! It's a girl! A girl with dark skin!"

"It's Clara!" Salvo and Serafina shouted together.

No one could understand how this amazingly strong and agile boy had suddenly turned into an amazingly strong and agile girl, and the crowd fell silent. Salvo and Serafina held on to each other, fearing that the mass of people would swoop down and attack their daughter. Out of the corner of his eye Salvo saw Signor Mignano standing up and clenching his fists at the figure on the piazza below.

Then, from the end of the piazza, someone started clapping. Quickly, the applause spread from one side to the other until everyone was laughing and cheering.

"It's a girl! A girl with dark skin! And she was the best one of all!"

They stomped and yelled and waited for Clara to respond. She tossed her cap in the air, caught it, and then twirled around, blowing a kiss to everyone.

"*Brava,* Francesca!" a fat man in front yelled. "Is that your name?"

"No, it's Clara!" she yelled back.

The crowd took up that chant. "*Brava,* Clara! *Brava,* Clara!"

Clara bowed, grabbed two flags and tossed them in the air. Then she ran to one corner of the piazza, bowed to the crowd, and threw the flags in the air again. Then she went to a second corner and did the same thing. Then the third. Then the fourth. She let her long hair blow in the wind.

"*Brava,* Clara! *Brava,* Clara!"

Red-faced and shaking, Signor Mignano started to storm down to Clara but his wife held him back.

Clara approached the couple, bowed low and shook her hair. "*Brava!*" the crowd yelled.

"Well, Raffaelo," his wife said, "it looks like the *sbandieratori* has had its first girl. I hope she's not the last."

IT SEEMED LIKE FOREVER, but Clara finally found Francesco shivering in his underwear in a doorway outside the piazza. He clutched her shirt and jeans in front of him.

"I thought you'd never come," he said. "I thought you'd leave me here forever."

"Quick, give me those clothes," his sister said.

In minutes, Francesco was back in his *sbandieratori* costume and Clara was in her shirt and jeans.

"I don't want to go back in there," she said. "Let's wait until the folks find us."

Eventually, Salvo and Serafina, soon joined by Pasquale who was holding Clara's *maschera,* found the brother and sister leaning against a back doorway to one of the piazza's shops.

"Clara!" Salvo said. "I can't believe it. You were just wonderful."

Serafina hugged her daughter. "You were the best. Amazing! Incredible! Now let's see what Signor Mignano has to say about girls being in the *sbandieratori."*

They didn't have to wait long. Rushing up to the family, with his wife trotting along behind him, Signor Mignano had to wait a few minutes to say anything because he was out of breath.

"You...what's your name again?"

"Clara."

"Clara. Well, Clara, I don't know what to say."

"You could say that you want her to join the *sbandieratori,"* his wife said.

"Well, yes, I guess I could say that."

"Thanks, Signor Mignano," Clara said. "But I did what I wanted to do. I proved I could do it." She looked at her mother, who smiled. "Now maybe some other girl will want to join. I hope so."

She grabbed her mother's hand. "Let's go home."

Anna and the Television Priest

Florence

IN ROME, no one climbed the Spanish Steps, and traffic became so light that cars could drive around the Colosseum without stopping. In Milan, Piazza del Duomo was virtually empty except for the pigeons. In Venice, waiters ceased serving in the restaurants in Saint Mark's Square. Even in Naples, peddlers stopped shouting and you could hear underwear flapping on clotheslines outside upstairs windows.

Every Tuesday night at 8 o'clock, in cities and villages, hamlets and farms, Italians would slow down for a half hour to watch the man universally known as *"il sacerdote dolce,"* The Gentle Priest. They switched their television sets to RAI Uno and waited for the announcer to say, "Welcome to 'Living Life Day by Day' with Father Giancarlo Moretti."

The priest, handsome and silver-haired but still youthful looking in his 50s, walked onto the set, smiled into the camera and started to speak. His voice was soft and comforting, and when he smiled he showed an expanse of white teeth. He sat in a comfortable chair and talked for a half hour. Then he stopped and said good night. That was it.

Sometimes he read from a Gospel and then talked about it. Sometimes he read parables and explained their meaning. Sometimes he told personal stories. Sometimes he used props. Once a month he had a guest.

No one could quite explain the program's popularity, but it had become a sensation, a *sensazione*, as the Italians liked to call it, or a phenomenon, a *fenomeno*, as the newspapers preferred. Father Giancarlo—everyone called him by his first name—was featured in adoring articles in newspapers and magazines, and more than a few women expressed sorrow that he had entered the seminary.

"Il sacerdote dolce" was, in effect, a religious rock star.

The program was unabashedly modeled after "Life Is Worth Living," an enormously popular television show in America in the 1950s that starred Bishop Fulton J. Sheen. In fact, not the least reason Father Giancarlo was selected for the Italian version was because he bore a striking resemblance to the bishop.

Even the day and time were similar. The American program put Bishop Sheen in competition with Milton Berle and Frank Sinatra, but people watched the bishop anyway. In Italy, the station reported that the show had almost as many viewers as when *Gli Azzurri* was playing a soccer match, and it widely advertised videotape copies of his program.

The station—and the church—couldn't have been more pleased.

Nowhere was the program more popular than in the cramped living room shared by two former nuns in an old palazzo near the Basilica of Santa Croce in Florence. Every Tuesday night, Anna Sporenza and Leonora Acara brought in bowls of Tuscan bean soup and took a break from managing *Casa di Maria,* the home for unmarried girls who were about to have babies.

"I live for this all week," Leonora always said as she turned on the small black-and-white television set. "I don't know what I would do without Father Giancarlo. He makes everything we do worthwhile, doesn't he?"

Anna had to agree. "He's a blessing," she often said.

Leonora was surprised, then, when Anna was not sitting next to her ten minutes before Father Giancarlo's program on the second Tuesday of April in 1990.

"Anna," she called. "It's almost time."

Leonora helped herself to more soup and called again. "Anna, the soup's getting cold and Father Giancarlo is almost on."

Leonora had finished her dinner and still Anna had not appeared. Except for the time when Leonora was called to her father's funeral and Anna went to a reunion of former nuns who had left the Abbey of Santa Margarita di Cortona, neither had missed one of Father Giancarlo's programs for more than seven years, almost since the very beginning.

"Anna," she called again. "The game show is ending."

On the screen, women with long hair and short dresses held up the winning numbers of whatever game was being played. Anna and Leonora could never figure out what the game was and didn't care.

"She must be with Anastasia," Leonora thought. "There must be some emergency."

Still, three volunteers had been on hand with the young woman when Leonora had left fifteen minutes ago.

"It's starting!"

The screen went dark and then the words: "Living Life Day by Day with Father Giancarlo Moretti."

Anna suddenly appeared, sank into the armchair and picked up the bowl of soup. "Thank goodness, I made it. Anastasia was having problems. She's all right now."

The screen focused on the set, an upholstered couch and chair, a small table with a statue of the Virgin Mary and a crucifix on the wall. Father Giancarlo entered from the right and strode to the camera.

"Good evening. I'm Father Giancarlo Moretti and I want to thank you again for inviting me into your homes."

"We want to have you here!" Leonora said.

"Shhhh."

"Hasn't this been a wonderful day!"

"Yes!" Leonora answered.

"Yes, April in Italy. What could be better than that? Except maybe May, June, July—well, you know what I mean. But let's celebrate, and what better way to celebrate than with this quote from Saint Paul: "We are fools for Christ's sake, but ye are wise in Christ; we are weak, but ye are strong; ye are honorable, but we are despised."

"Fools for Christ? I've never heard that," Leonora said.

"Leonora…"

"Now," the priest said, "what does it mean to be a fool? Let's translate that as being a clown."

He took a red crayon from his pocket and drew two red circles on his cheeks and chin. He pulled out a red clown's nose and pushed it onto his own. Finally, he folded a red napkin into a clown's hat and put it on his head. Anna and Leonora laughed so hard they could hardly hear the priest say, "Perhaps we can all be fools for Christ?"

Still wearing his clown nose, Father Giancarlo said that we might appear to be fools because of our commitment to Christ. It isn't always popular to believe in Jesus, and we who do believe might appear to be fools. He went on to illustrate that with other examples, and soon the half hour was up.

"Thank you again for joining me in this conversation. Let's talk again next week. God bless you!"

He smiled and exited, and closing credits appeared. Anna turned off the television set.

"Well, that will give us something to think about in the next week."

"Isn't he amazing?" Leonora said. "I wonder what he's really like, I mean apart from the television programs."

"He doesn't seem to reveal much in all those newspaper interviews."

"I wish I could meet him," Leonora said.

"Really? Why? He's just a priest with a television program, isn't he?"

"Oh, Anna, you know you'd love to meet him and talk to him. Maybe someday you will."

"I doubt it. Well, I'd better get back to Anastasia."

ONE OF ANNA SPORENZA'S earliest memories was the doll she carried around from morning to night. It had a porcelain head and a soft body. Its hair was tangled and stains covered its cheeks. Her mother had made an outfit for the doll that was supposed to represent a girl in a dancing troupe—white blouse, red skirt with red suspenders. It didn't have any shoes.

Anna called her doll Michelina.

She remembered when her mother gave her doll. For nine years, Anna had been the youngest girl in the family. Her older sister, Lucia, was fifteen, her older brother Roberto was eleven and her younger brother, Adolfo, was seven. Her mother and father doted on the little girl, dressing her up in pretty pink dresses and parading her around the village of Sant'Antonio in the evening ritual of the *passeggiata*.

"Isn't she the cutest thing?" people invariably said.

Then her mother became pregnant and then, worse, had another girl. Anna was furious. She threw tantrums. She wailed on her bed. Finally, her mother gave her a doll so that she, too, could have a baby.

She was carrying Michelina on that terrible day in June 1944 when everyone in Sant'Antonio was ordered to evacuate. The Germans were going to set up headquarters in the village because they wanted to secure the bridge against the Allies.

With her father off to war and never heard from, Anna joined her mother, her sister, her brothers and baby Carlotta as they trudged up the treacherous hill to an abandoned farmhouse.

"It's all right, Michelina. It's all right," she kept saying. She kissed the top of its frizzy hair and hugged her tight.

There were other people in the farmhouse, Anna remembered. They slept in rooms on the first and second floor. Her family was given the vacant third floor and her mother hung up sheets to give privacy. Carlotta got sick and her mother spent much of her time with her. Anna sometimes played peek-a-boo with the little baby but mostly lay on her bed or looked out the window, always clutching Michelina.

Then Carlotta died. She died! Anna went up to the drawer that was the baby's coffin and looked at her little sister. She put Michelina next to her. Michelina was almost as big as Carlotta.

After that, without Michelina, Anna sat in a corner most days. Sometimes she drew pictures of a doll that looked like the doll. When the family and all the others were allowed to go back to Sant'Antonio, her mother gave her another doll. Anna played with it sometimes, but she thought she was getting too old to play with dolls. She was ten.

Everyone was busy in Sant'Antonio after the war. They had to rebuild their houses, and their lives. Gina, her mother, devoted her life caring for her husband, Pietro, who had returned from the war broken in mind and body. Lucia suffered the pains of the pregnancy she had begun with a boy she had met at the farmhouse and finally delivered a baby, Dino. Roberto and Adolfo became teenagers and did what teenage boys do.

Anna remembered the exact day, a terribly hot August day, when she decided to leave. It was four years after the war and she was fourteen years old. Almost everyone in Sant'Antonio remained inside, hiding from the relentless sun. Upstairs, Anna's mother and father were in their stifling bedroom, and her mother was attempting to calm her husband. Pietro kept yelling and screaming.

"They're coming! They're coming! Get down!" he kept shouting. He pushed his wife to the floor.

"No, no, Pietro. No one's here. It's all right." She took him by the arm and led him to the bed.

"Nonononono..."

"It's all right, Pietro. It's all right."

Anna covered her ears.

Downstairs, Anna's brothers were engaged in one of their frequent loud wrestling matches, one of them pounding the other before the other got on top.

"Be quiet!" her mother kept shouting from upstairs. "Your father needs his rest!"

"We're being quiet," one or the other yelled back. "We're just playing."

The brothers continued to wrestle.

Across the hall, Anna's sister Lucia lay on her bed, hugging her boyfriend Paolo and giggling. Paolo had become a frequent visitor, sometimes staying late into the night before Anna's mother told him to go home.

"Mama," Lucia would say, "we were just talking. Paolo was telling me stories about Dino."

Dino, Anna knew, was the father of Little Dino, who was born just after Dino was killed in a firefight outside the farmhouse where the family had been trapped during the war. Paolo had been his best friend.

Everyone expected Anna to care for four-year-old Dino. He wasn't much trouble, mostly wanting to sit at a table and draw pictures, but he had to be watched all the time, and she felt overwhelmed. She couldn't leave him. She couldn't play with her friends. In fact, she didn't have any friends.

Her father's screams, her brothers' yelling, the strange noises from Lucia's bedroom, and taking care of Little Dino. Every day, the same thing. It was driving her crazy. She had to get away, find some quiet.

It was then that she thought about what a priest had said in his sermon last Sunday. It was the feast of Saint Clare of Assisi and, in between warning about missing Mass and failing to contribute to the church, the priest described this wonderful woman who left her family and became one of the most important saints in heaven.

Anna made up her mind right then. She didn't want to be an important saint in heaven. She only wanted to get away, to find some peace and quiet.

After all, she didn't mind going to church. She rather liked looking at all the paintings and statues and listening to the organ music. She even liked to say the rosary sometimes. She would become a nun. One of those nuns who never left the convent.

The cloistered routine of life for Sister Anna della Croce in the Abbey of Santa Margarita di Cortona was comforting at first. Rising at 4 o'clock and going to the chapel for Lauds, then private adoration of the Holy Eucharist, followed by Mass.

The rest of the day was scheduled to the minute, something she always liked, even as a young postulant. Prayer, work, meals, more work, more prayer. Even the work was enjoyable, with the nuns lined up in the huge kitchen making Communion wafers that were sold to churches throughout the region.

At night, the nuns had an hour of "recreation," and indeed a few of the younger ones played table tennis, but most knit or sewed. Anna liked to read books from the selection the governing sisters had reviewed. There was no television set, but a radio could be turned to classical music.

At 7:30 p.m., the nuns gathered in the chapel again for nightly prayers and the rosary, and at 8:30, everyone went to the long dormitory on the top floor of the abbey. By 9 o'clock everyone was asleep.

Then Vatican II changed so many things in the church. Many of the nuns who had gone into the convent to escape from something, just as Anna had, now found that they wanted something more. They wanted to contribute, to help people. So, after three decades in the convent, Anna left.

In Florence, she reunited with her brothers, Adolfo and Roberto, both working in an organization that helped poor people repair their homes, even build new ones. And then Dino, now thirty-one, suggested that she manage a new nursery above a soup kitchen at the Basilica of Santa Croce. It was called *Figli di dio*, "God's Babies," and it was run by a Franciscan priest, Father Lorenzo.

Volunteers helped with the staffing, but Anna was eternally grateful when another former nun, Leonora Acara, knocked on the door one day and asked, "May I help?" It soon became clear that there was another need. Pregnant young girls needed a place to stay before, during and after they had their babies. With Father Lorenzo's help, an old palazzo in the back of Santa Croce was purchased. Adolfo, Roberto and Dino tore down walls and put up others, painted and scraped and made the place a welcome home. With the help of Anna and Leonora, up to twenty young women could stay there, have their babies and get steered to establishing their lives again.

Occasionally, Anna missed the convent life, but it was easy at *Casa di Maria* to keep busy. She could forget that even with all the people around her, she often got very lonely.

IF ANNA SPORENZA REMEMBERED the doll from her childhood, Giancarlo Moretti remembered his dog. A brown fluffy ball of fur, Primo had been found at the side of the road with his left leg broken and his left eye badly damaged. Giancarlo's father brought him home and laid him in a makeshift bed in front of the fireplace. The boy brought him milk and bits of wild boar or chicken twice a day.

Eventually, the leg healed, though there was always a slight limp, and his left eye looked in the opposite direction from the right.

Primo followed Giancarlo everywhere, sat under his chair at the table waiting for scraps, and slept on the corner of his bed. He answered the boy's roughhousing with friendly licks and a tail that wouldn't stop wagging.

Until he was old enough to go to school, Giancarlo and Primo ran through the hills near their home in the rugged Garfagnana region north of Lucca. Without any brothers or sisters, and with no other children in the village, Primo was his only friend.

Giancarlo was twelve years old when the Germans swept through the Garfagnana during World War II. Everyone in Montagna Sole said their village was too small and too isolated for the Germans to find it, and they were right. But Giancarlo's father knew he couldn't stay at home.

A man of few words, he told his wife, "I'm joining the partisans."

"Nooo!" she cried. "Don't go!"

"I have to go."

"Please, Papa!" Giancarlo grabbed his arm.

His father went into the hills anyway and never returned. Long after the war, a fellow partisan told his mother that her husband died in an ambush only five miles away and his body was buried right there. His mother didn't want to go and look.

When he was fifteen, Bianca came into Giancarlo's life. Her family had moved to Montagna Sole and of course someone had to help her get acquainted. They went on bike rides. He showed her the little river that ran through the outskirts of town and the lake where they could swim. When she took off her dress to reveal her bathing suit, he looked away. And then he looked back. He was pleased that she was impressed when he held his breath underwater for ten minutes.

Afterwards, the ravine was a good place where they could get to know each other even better. Giancarlo always remembered that summer as the time he became a man.

After Bianca drifted off with Ferdinando, Giancarlo found solace with Antoinetta and then Victoria and then Rosetta.

He had no plans after high school, but one night his mother brought the parish priest home. Giancarlo should have had an inkling of what was going to happen. His mother had been devastated by the loss of her husband, and except for going to church and shopping, she never went out and spent most of her time praying in her darkened bedroom. Giancarlo didn't know how to help her.

After the priest left, his mother sat down with her son at the kitchen table. Her eyes were filled with tears.

"Gianni, I have such wonderful news. Father Federico has arranged for you to enter the seminary. Gianni, you can become a priest! Oh, thank you, God. I have been praying for this ever since…since your father…"

"But…"

"I know you're surprised, Gianni. Maybe I should have talked about this with you before. But I wasn't sure if Father Federico could manage to get you in. Not every boy gets in, you know. This has been very special."

"But, Mother…"

"I'm so proud of you, Gianni."

As he had feared, Giancarlo found the seminary extremely difficult. He had never been away from home before. He had a hard time making friends and he missed his mother. And Primo. And Bianca and Antoinetta and Victoria and Rosetta.

Although he had never been an exceptional student, he managed to get through the history and theology and philosophy classes, but his favorite turned out to be homiletics. While other students considered sermons as "preaching," he thought of them more like conversations. He would get up in front of the class and talk about the stories in the life of Christ and try to apply them to daily living. His professor was impressed.

"Giancarlo," Father Antonio told him one day, "this is what people in your parish will want to hear. Not so much talk about hell and fire and brimstone. Giancarlo, you are bringing humility to the priesthood, something that is so badly needed. I think you're going to have a very bright future, maybe even a famous one."

The seminarians were required to make a retreat before ordination. "Our last chance to escape before it's too late," they joked.

Giancarlo wasn't so sure it was a joke. Aware of the warnings about developing "particular friendships," he worried that the priesthood would be a lonely place. He didn't know if he was ready. How could he help people who were so much older, so much more experienced, than he was? Especially, he didn't know if he could stand a life without a Bianca or an Antoinetta or…

But he had gone this far, and every time he had doubts, he thought about his mother, who hugged him and cried every time he went home for a visit.

She took the bus to the cathedral for his ordination and smiled all the way through the long ceremony, as well as his first Mass the next day.

"I'm so proud of you," she kept saying.

The new Father Giancarlo Moretti found his first parish, as an assistant pastor in a remote Tuscan village, in disarray. The pastor was a serious alcoholic and sometimes couldn't even say the Mass on Sundays, let alone weekdays. Unable to cope with this, the housekeeper had quit. The first thing Father Giancarlo did was call home.

"Mother, I need your help. Can you come and be my housekeeper?"

In the first weeks, the new priest took charge. He talked to the diocesan people and found a rehabilitation home for the pastor, who went off surprisingly willingly. Although he was technically still an assistant pastor of the church, Father Giancarlo set up a schedule for Masses, baptisms, confirmations and weddings. He went to the school and arranged to teach Catechism to each of the seven grades. He rejuvenated the long-dormant Altar Society, the Christian Mothers Society, the Catholic Youth Club and the Men's First Friday Club. He organized a boys soccer team and served as referee.

Parishioners couldn't get over him. He was invited to homes for dinner. Father Gianni—for that was the name he wanted to be called—enjoyed this at first. Then something strange happened. When he returned to the rectory, he felt more alone than he had before.

"Did you enjoy yourself?" his mother would ask.

"It was all right."

"They're such a nice family, aren't they?"

"Yes."

"They have a lot of children, don't they?"

"Yes."

"Was it fun to watch them play?"

"Mother, I'm tired. I think I'll go to bed."

Father Gianni learned to pour himself into his work. Masses, parish organizations, the school.

"Why do you have to keep so busy?" his mother would ask.

"I need to, Mother. I need to."

As Father Giancarlo's reputation as a kind and gentle pastor, not to mention a great administrator, grew, he was transferred to a bigger parish. Then another one even larger. And then a third in the heart of Florence.

He found that the parishioners there, especially the women, wanted to have a more active role in the church than he'd been used to. In his second week, Signora Maria Alfonsi asked to come to see him since she was the treasurer of the Christian Mothers Society.

Father Giancarlo expected an elderly, or at least middle-aged, woman. Signora Alfonsi was no more than thirty-five, with short blond hair. She wore no makeup, and her face glowed.

"Welcome, Father! We are so pleased that you have joined us."

Her hand seemed to remain on his for an extraordinarily long time. He noted that her eyes were green. Antoinetta had green eyes. So did Rosetta.

He invited her into the parlor, where his mother brought them tea and looked disapprovingly at the visitor.

They talked about the Christian Mothers Society and the parish and the neighborhood.

"And your family?" he asked.

"My son, Giorgio, is twelve and my daughter, Lucia, is ten. My mother lives with us and she takes care of them."

"And your husband?"

"He's away a lot."

He didn't understand why she didn't say more and why she looked straight into his eyes.

He could smell a light sweet fragrance that he didn't recognize, and when she leaned down over his desk he could see a gentle cleavage. He lost track of what they were talking about and knew he had to end it.

"Well," she said, "I'll go then. I'm sure we'll see each other again."

"Yes…yes," he said.

"No…no," he thought.

That night, he couldn't figure out why he kept thinking about her. He had certainly worked with other beautiful women before. Perhaps he'd been attracted to one or two, but there was nothing beyond simple conversations.

"I'm forty-four," he thought. "What's going on?"

He needed air.

"Mother," he called. "I'm going for a run."

In the past year, he found that running helped to clear his mind and keep his waist trim. With his cap down and in his running shirt and shorts, no one recognized the priest as he ran through the tourists on Ponte Vecchio, up to Fort Belvedere, across on San Leonardo, left at Viale Galileo, over to the Church of San Minato and back to Ponte Vecchio. He was back home in a half hour, too tired to think.

A week later, he was late for a meeting of the Christian Mothers Society and found that the only seat at the front table was next to Signora Alfonsi.

"Nice to see you again, Father," she said, reaching for his hand.

"Yes." He pulled his hand away.

"I really need to talk to you about our finances."

"Um, yes."

"Maybe on Friday?"

"I'll have my secretary call."

Father Giancarlo had his secretary tell Signora Alfonsi that she really had to talk to the church administrator.

"I can't get involved. I can't get involved."

Yet he did. He found that he had to go over the finances even after the administrator had looked at them. That required lunch at a nearby trattoria. He wore his Roman collar and easily greeted parishioners who stopped by their table. That was followed by dinner at a popular restaurant where he didn't wear his Roman collar. Followed by four dinners in increasingly secluded restaurants.

Followed by nights in even more secluded villas.

When he thought back on those three months, he realized how incredibly stupid he had been. He could have been seen and reported to the bishop at any time. There was, after all, a self-appointed watchdog group called Florentines for Morality that was on the lookout for such wayward priests.

Fortunately, both Father Giancarlo Moretti and Signora Maria Alfonsi realized that they had little in common and no future together. The little fling was just that. Anyway, Signora Alfonsi and her family moved to Milan.

There were three other near-relationships over the years, but none as intimate. Father Giancarlo increased his run from three miles to five to ten to twenty, and he ran four or five times a week.

"It clears my head," he told people who asked.

It also stopped him from thinking, he realized.

He got a dog, Secondo, to replace the long departed but never forgotten Primo. He spent more time on his homilies, and soon even people beyond his parish came to his Masses just to hear him.

One Sunday after he had been at the church for five years, he noticed that a man he had never seen before was taking notes. The man was back the next Sunday, and on the following Sunday he had a tape recorder.

"Mother," he said after Mass, "did you think there was anything objectionable in what I said? I think I'm in trouble."

"Trouble?"

"Mother, I've heard that the bishop is clamping down on priests who say things that aren't quite what the church teaches. I know of one priest who dared to talk about the ordination of women and they transferred him to a retirement home."

"Gianni, you didn't say anything anywhere like that at all. I'm sure this is nothing to worry about."

The following week, he was called in to see the bishop, who pointed to a chair across from his desk.

"I'll come right to the point," the bishop said. "You know, Giancarlo, there are so many terrible things happening in this world. Divorces, children not obeying their parents, teenagers taking dangerous drugs. Abortions! Priests and nuns leaving their holy orders!"

Father Giancarlo felt sweat developing on his forehead but was afraid to take out a handkerchief to wipe it off.

"It's terrible," the bishop continued. "People don't come to church anymore. Our churches are half empty, and those who do come are mostly women."

"Excellency," Father Giancarlo said, "I have really tried to be faithful to the church's teachings in what I say. I go over and over my sermons. Every word. If you think there is something offensive…"

"Offensive! No, on the contrary, Giancarlo, your sermons are a breath of fresh air in this diocese. I've heard from so many people, and my communications director confirmed that. And when I listened to the tape recorder, I was convinced, too."

This time Father Giancarlo did pull out his handkerchief to wipe his forehead. "Well, thank you. Thank you, your Excellency."

"And so, Giancarlo, I want you to take on a new assignment. We want to reach out to every person under our jurisdiction and even beyond. Men, women, children. We have tried to do that, but always in the traditional ways. Church bulletins, announcements from the pulpit, our weekly newspaper. Now we want to use a method that everyone else has found so useful. Television!"

"Television?"

"Yes, television. Giancarlo, we would like you to have a weekly television program in which you would simply give the kind of sermons you have been used to giving at your parish. We would like this to be very informal. We would create a simple set somewhere in this palazzo, but instead of standing in the pulpit, which would be too formal, you would walk around or sit in a chair and just talk."

"Just talk?"

"Exactly. Just say what you say in your sermons, because they are from your heart, and we think people will listen."

"Excellency, I hesitate to ask this, but do you think people will actually sit in their living rooms and listen to a priest talk? Especially since there are so many other programs on television, game shows, movies, westerns?"

The bishop then recounted the story of how Bishop Sheen's program had been so popular in America.

"I'm not a bishop, Excellency."

"Giancarlo, I'll be frank. We want a personable, good-looking priest to be the face of the diocese, not some old fogy like…well, we won't mention names. You are just the man to do this."

Seven years later, "Living Your Life Day by Day" was one of the most popular programs on Italian television, and Father Giancarlo had something else to occupy his mind.

ANNA HAD MARKED THE DATE on her calendar, the third Saturday in April, but every time she looked at it she had mixed feelings. The woman she had known as Sister Fabiola had written to suggest that she and another former nun at the Abbey of Santa Margarita di Cortona have lunch together. "Wouldn't it be great to see each other again?" Fabiola had written.

Anna wasn't quite sure. While it would be nice to see the two women again, she knew that after fourteen years, their lives had changed so much that they would have little in common. Anna knew that Fabiola had married a former priest three years after leaving the convent. As for Maddelena, she had been in the convent for only a year so Anna didn't know her well. Maddelena had also married and, she'd heard, had children.

"Should I go?" she asked Leonora.

"Of course! Why wouldn't you?"

"It's just…well, I don't know."

"You're afraid you're going to hear them talk about being married and having kids and wonder what your life might have been like?"

"Yes."

On Friday, Anna finally decided. She was going. It was her Saturday off anyway, and Leonora was perfectly capable of handling the various problems of the young women at *Casa di Maria.*

The trattoria was near Santa Maria Novella and Anna enjoyed the walk on the sunny day. She recognized Fabiola immediately.

"You haven't changed a bit," they both cried after a long hug.

"Oh, I have, too," Fabiola said.

"Well, I have," Anna said. "I've gained weight, my hair is entirely gray now, I have to wear glasses all the time."

"Well, your work must keep you young."

"It does. It does. Is Maddelena coming?"

"She called. She'll be a little late."

Anna described working at *Casa di Maria*. She said she often worked twelve hours or more a day and was grateful for Leonora and an army of volunteers to help.

"Oh, Anna. That sounds so hard. How can you do it? In the convent, we only had to worry about making Communion wafers."

"And you?" Anna asked.

"Oh, Anna," Fabiola said, "I am so happy. You don't know how happy I am. Anna, Luca and I were made for each other. After ten years, we are still so much in love. We like all the same things, even food! We like going to plays and the opera here. Last year we went on a cruise to the Greek islands. He's just wonderful, Anna. I hope you'll meet him soon."

"I'm glad, Fabiola."

"I know how people talked when we got married. I know they said that Luca left the priesthood because of me, but he didn't. He really didn't. He was thinking about it long before we met."

Maddelena arrived then, not looking a day, well, a year, older than when she left the convent. Her hair was now in a ponytail and she had gained just a little weight.

Hugs and kisses all around.

"Sorry I'm late. Matteo was late coming back from soccer practice with Filippo, Silvia had to go to her dance class, Tonio couldn't be found and Pero had to be changed. Oh, there's always something going on in our house."

"Oh, Maddelena, that's sounds so wonderful," Fabiola said.

"Yes," Anna said.

She couldn't stop thinking about handling four children, but she was distracted by the young family at the next table. Even though it was Saturday, the father wore a sport coat and tie, the mother a pretty pink dress. Their son, about eight, also wore a tie and his sister a frilly white dress. They were all laughing and talking and then a waiter brought a cupcake with a candle in it and put it in front of the girl. They all joined hands and sang "Happy Birthday."

Anna thought it was the most beautiful thing she'd ever seen.

Their own waiter, who had been hovering, took their orders, and for the rest of the meal Fabiola and Maddelena talked about their husbands and their lives and how happy and content they were now. Anna's mind wandered.

Fabiola interrupted her daydream. "Aren't you happier now, too, Anna?"

"Yes. Yes, of course." She fiddled with her knife, then her fork, then her napkin.

"Anna," Maddelena said, "if you met the right man, do you think you'd get married?"

"Married? Me? Good lord, I'm fifty-seven years old!"

"Well, I'm fifty-eight," Fabiola said. "But I don't feel fifty-eight. Luca makes me feel, well, OK, fifty!"

No one wanted dessert, and when Fabiola suggested they meet again, they all agreed, knowing fully well that it might never happen.

When Anna returned home, Leonora wanted to know all about it.

"Did you enjoy yourself?"

"It was all right."

"It must have been nice to see them again."

"Yes."

"And one of them has children?"

"Yes. Four."

"Four! How wonderful! Well, you have a lot of babies to take care of here."

"Leonora, I'm tired. I think I'll take a nap."

In her fitful sleep, Anna dreamed of four children at a birthday party, holding hands and singing.

FATHER GIANCARLO had long wanted to have his old friend Father Lorenzo from the Basilica of Santa Croce as one of the monthly guests on his program. They'd run across each other many times over the years and Father Giancarlo had even been a member of a men's cooking class with him. By the time everything could be arranged, Father Lorenzo was working at the soup kitchen only part time and was involved in other parish activities.

Still, the priest had founded the *cucina popolare* and was actually a legend around Florence, especially after his work at the soup kitchen during the devastating flood of the Arno in 1966.

Father Lorenzo reluctantly agreed to appear on the program in May, "but only to talk about the other people and the volunteers."

Anna and Leonora were more excited than he was about a television appearance.

"I think you should get a haircut," Anna said when they stopped at the soup kitchen. "It's getting long in the back."

"As opposed to the bald spot on the top of my head," Father Lorenzo said.

"That's just your tonsure showing."

"And," Leonora said, "couldn't you ask for a new robe? That one is getting so shabby. The elbows are almost worn through."

"I'll keep my arms down. Nobody is going to notice me with the handsome Father Giancarlo on the screen."

The interview went fine, of course. Father Giancarlo spent a lot of time asking about the soup kitchen's work, and Father Lorenzo said that not only did people die during the flood and so many valuable pieces of art were ruined, but also that many Florentines lost their homes and their jobs. And there were still problems.

"There seems to be a perception that everyone here is wealthy," he said. "That's the face that Florence likes to present to tourists. But there is still a great need for volunteers to help the poor, and for donations."

A telephone number flashed on the screen.

Anna and Leonora applauded when the program ended. "He did very well," Anna said, "and maybe they'll get more donations now."

Leaving the set, Father Giancarlo thought that the least he could do for Father Lorenzo was to offer him a drink. They sank back in the leather armchairs in Father Giancarlo's office off the makeshift studio in the palazzo.

"Thank you for coming, Lorenzo. That was great." He opened a bottle of grappa and a box of Toscana cigars.

"My pleasure. It's nice to have some exposure for what we've been doing. And you, Gianni? How have you been? You look a little tired."

"Well, I still have all the parish stuff besides this television gig. You know, meetings, meetings, meetings. Plus the school. Plus the kids' soccer team."

"Ever get away?"

"Hmmm. I went to Rome three years ago. Conference on television ministry."

"Sounds really great."

"Well, I didn't go to some of the sessions."

"Good for you."

Father Giancarlo got up to take off his Roman collar. "Lorenzo, how old are you now?"

"Fifty-nine. That's my actual age. Don't ask me how old I feel."

"And I'm fifty-six."

"We should be up for old-age benefits pretty soon, right?"

"Such as they are."

Noisy Vespas rattled on the street outside as the two old friends contemplated getting old.

"Lorenzo, can I ask you something?"

"Of course."

"Have you—you don't have to answer this if you don't want to—have you ever, well, strayed?"

Father Lorenzo laughed. "Oh, my, you're asking me that? Hmmm. Well, Gianni, as a matter of fact…"

"You did? You really did? Lorenzo, I'm shocked. Shocked. Shocked."

"Oh, I know it's hard to believe. Holy priest that I am. Model of virtue. But let me tell you about something that happened to me, well, about sixteen years ago. I met this beautiful woman at a party in Siena in honor of my mother."

"Your mother the feminist leader."

"Yes. Well, this woman, Victoria, sat at my table and we got to talking. Gianni, she was gorgeous! American. Red hair, upturned nose, eyes that crinkled when she smiled, and she smiled a lot. She owned a jewelry shop in Rimini. Well, she was so interested in me. I mean, she kept asking me all kinds of questions about my life."

"And you, of course, told her all about your work in the soup kitchen."

"No! That's the thing. I couldn't—well, I didn't anyway—even tell her I was a priest. I didn't have my collar on, so she wouldn't have known."

"And she didn't guess? Lorenzo, come on."

"Well, if she did, she didn't let on. Anyway, I was so infatuated with her that I made up a lame excuse to go see her in Rimini."

"Rimini! The hot sun. The golden sands. A beautiful woman. A handsome man. Oh, wait, the handsome man's a priest."

"I'm ignoring you. Well, I was there for three days. We spent time on the beach, walked a lot, had dinner, went to a movie. Gianni, I even danced."

"Now I know you're making this up."

"I did! Well, at the end of the three days, I told her the truth. She said she suspected all along. I came back to Florence. I had a very long confession with my superior, a great guy, and I've never seen Victoria again."

"OK, let's get this straight. You didn't actually…you didn't…"

"No, Gianni, we didn't. Almost! But we didn't."

"Wow. What a story. Have another cigar."

The smoke in the room was getting thicker, the noise in the street was getting quieter.

"Lorenzo, do you ever think about her, Victoria?"

"Oh, I suppose once in a while. But I'm sure I'll never see her again. I don't even know where she is. She's probably not in Rimini anymore."

"See! You have thought about her!"

"Well, OK, maybe once or twice. All right, Gianni, I've made my confession. What about you?"

Father Giancarlo told his fellow priest about his brief affair with Signora Maria Alfonsi, "but that was the only time, really."

"And that was years ago?"

"Yes."

"Other opportunities?"

"A few, I guess. But, no, I haven't. But lately, it's just…"

"Just?"

"Just that I've been feeling so lonely lately. I know, I know, the loneliness of the priesthood. How many books have been written about that? I could write one myself. I guess that's why I keep so busy, so that I don't have to think about it."

"Have any priest friends?"

"Oh, a few. But the older I get, the less I want to be with them. There were four of us. We got together to play poker, sometimes we went to a soccer game. But two of them started to drink. I mean really drink. And they all groused so much. Complain, complain, complain. It was painful to be around them. So I don't see them much anymore."

"We Franciscans have each other, I guess."

"You're lucky. Sometimes, Lorenzo, I just wish I had a friend, yes, a woman friend, that I could sit down and talk to. Maybe not anything more than that."

"But maybe more?"

"I'd have to see."

"You know, Gianni, I bet every priest in the world has felt the same way we do. And there's not much we can do about it."

"I guess not."

"It's getting late. Way, way past my bedtime, Gianni. Thanks for having me on the program, and let's talk more sometime, OK? Sometime soon."

They shook hands at the doorway.

"Good to see you, Lorenzo."

"Take good care, Gianni."

"Thanks for listening, Lorenzo."

"Oh, by the way, Gianni, if you want another guest on your program. There's a woman who does fantastic work for us. She's a former nun, actually. Her name is Anna. Anna Sporenza. Give her a call."

BOTH THE DIOCESE and the television station kept transcripts of all of "Living Life Day by Day," and the following excerpt was available for June 19, 1990:

ANNOUNCER: Good evening and welcome to another visit with Father Giancarlo Moretti and "Living Life Day by Day."

(Father Giancarlo and Anna Sporenza are seated in armchairs under the crucifix.)

FATHER GIANCARLO MORETTI: Good evening, viewers, and welcome to another of our weekly conversations. I hope you've had a good day. I did. And one of the reasons was because I was looking forward to talking to tonight's special guest. For many years, Anna Sporenza was a cloistered nun, but now she manages a wonderful place for up to twenty teenage girls who are expecting babies. It's called *Casa di Maria,* and it is near the Basilica of Santa Croce. She helps the girls before, during and after the babies' births, and we must be grateful for everything she does. Thank you for all your good work, Anna. May I call you Anna?

ANNA SPORENZA: Of course.

FGM: Can you tell us how you became involved in all of this? Was *Casa di Maria* always this big?

AS: No, no. It wasn't.

FGM: So you started off slow.

AS: Yes.

FGM: And gradually welcomed more girls.

AS: Yes.

FGM: Anna, I know the bright lights here make people nervous, but don't be. Please?

AS: All right.

FGM: Instead of giving all this history, maybe you can just tell us about a typical day.

AS: Well, there really isn't a typical day. They're all different.

FGM: Well, maybe you could explain *Casa di Maria.*

AS: We established the *Casa* to take care of young women who were about to have babies and had nowhere else to go. Often, their parents have thrown them out of the house and their boyfriends have abandoned them.

FGM: I don't know if this is relevant, but I've read recently that the number of teenage pregnancies has been increasing in Florence.

AS: We've seen that. Girls as young as fifteen. Father, it would break your heart to see these girls. There really needs to be more education about how to prevent these pregnancies.

FGM: Yes, there certainly are ways.

AS: These girls want their babies so much, but there is no place for them to stay until the babies are born. No one seems to care. No one but us.

FGM: Perhaps you could give us an example, not by name, of course.

AS: Well, last year, there was a girl, only sixteen years old. She became pregnant and her parents were furious. They kept yelling and yelling at her. The poor girl dropped out of school and stayed in her room all the time. She was afraid to go out of her room! She wouldn't eat and of course that wasn't good for the baby. Somehow, a friend told her about *Casa di Maria* and she came to us. A few months later she had a healthy baby boy. Her parents were so excited that they welcomed her back home. Now they're happy grandparents.

FGM: That's a wonderful story, Anna. Now before we go into another subject, I want to open this conversation up to our viewers. As you know, we accept calls on our telephone here and...

(A number flashes on the screen and the phone rings.)

FGM: Well, here's one already. You're on the air, Caller. Would you identify yourself?

CALLER: Yes. This is Franco and I live over near San Maria Novella. I just want to make sure I understand what this is all about. Here's this woman who abandoned her vows as a sister and now she helps young women who have committed sins and she wants us to believe she's doing a good thing?

FGM: Franco, I'm afraid you're not understanding this right. Anna is helping many young women who have nowhere else to go when they are about to have babies. Is that right, Anna?

AS: Yes, that's exactly right.

CALLER: But what I said is true, isn't it, whatever your name is? Isn't it?

AS: My name is Anna Sporenza. Anna, as in the mother of Mary. I wonder if I could ask you a question, sir. What do you think the alternatives for these women would be? Would you rather that these women have their babies aborted? Well, would you? I'm waiting.

CALLER: Well...

AS: Since these women have nowhere else to go, would you rather that they live on the street? Become beggars? Have their little babies in alleyways? Well, would you? I'm waiting.

CALLER: Well...

AS: I'm so glad that you have all the answers, sir. That you are able to see things in black and white. That you have no mercy for poor unfortunate human beings. That you don't realize that one of these young women could be living next door to you, or maybe she is the daughter of your brother or sister or maybe, sir, just maybe she could be your own daughter. You, of course, wouldn't throw your daughter out because she was going to have a baby. No, of course you wouldn't. I just want to say…

FGM: Anna…

AS: Let me be, Father. I am so tired of people making judgments. I wish that people would come down off their pedestals…

FGM: Anna…

AS: …and have some sympathy and understanding for those less fortunate than they are and…

FGM: Anna…

AS: Well, Caller, how do you answer this? Would you answer me, Caller? Caller? Well, I guess you don't have any answers after all.

FGM: Well, I see that our time is up for tonight. Thank you, Anna Sporenza, for being such a powerful guest tonight, and thank you viewers for joining us again tonight. I hope you'll join us again next week.

(The closing credits.)

ANNA WAS STILL SHAKING when Father Giancarlo guided her into his office off the studio and into one of the leather armchairs.

"Are you OK, Anna?"

"I will be. Just let me sit for a while."

"OK. I'll be right back." The priest went into the adjoining room, took off his Roman collar and pulled on a light blue sweater.

"Grappa?" he asked when he returned. He brought out a bottle from the cabinet behind his desk.

"No, too strong for me, but thanks."

"Mind if I have one? I think I need it. How about some port?"

"That would be lovely."

He brought out another bottle and poured Anna a glass. There was no sound except for the Vespas on the street outside.

"Father, I'm sorry I caused that scene," Anna finally said. "I don't know what came over me."

"Anna, first, call me Gianni. Everyone does. Second, good Lord, there's no need to apologize. You were quite wonderful."

"I must have sounded like some crazy lady."

"Anna, Anna. No. Nothing like that. I'm sorry now that I didn't come to your defense and shout at that guy, too. The blasted bigot. Shithead."

"Father! Gianni!"

"Sorry. That just came out. I don't usually talk like that, especially in front of a woman I respect so much. Forgive me."

"Nothing to forgive."

"You know, I guess I didn't say anything because I was just so awed and inspired by your passion. You really love these women, don't you?"

"If you saw these women—girls, actually—every day, you'd be passionate about defending them, too. I get so angry when someone attacks them. Well, you saw that."

"You were wonderful. I'm sure the viewers were convinced."

"I hope so. Except for Signor Caller, of course."

"Shithead."

They both laughed. And smiled at each other.

"I wish I could be passionate about something," the priest said quietly.

"Gianni, aren't you? Surely in your work in the parish, in your television programs...there must be so many things for you to get excited about."

"Anna, I've been a priest for thirty-two years. I've had the television program for more than seven years. Anna, I feel like I've seen it all, I've done it all."

"You're not bored, are you?"

"No, not bored. Well, as I was telling Lorenzo—your friend Father Lorenzo—I get lonely. At night, in the rectory. My mother is there, she's my housekeeper, but as you can imagine my mother isn't exactly the best company."

"Lots of work to keep you occupied, but then you realize you're pretty alone?"

"Yes."

"Really? You feel that way, too? At night, after the girls are sleeping and the place is quiet, I have the same feeling. My friend Leonora isn't exactly the best company either."

The priest got up to pour another grappa for himself and more port for Anna. They sat in silence for a long time, not even listening to the sounds outside.

"You know," Father Giancarlo said. "This is really rather ludicrous. Here we are, in our fifties—if I may be so bold to guess that?"

"Fifty-seven."

"And I'm fifty-six. Anyway, here we are in our fifties, we have successful lives, we do good work, people admire us…"

"Admire! Gianni, you're a huge television star! People adore you!"

"Yeah, sure. And here we are complaining about being lonely. It's laughable."

"You're right. Other people would give anything to have what we have."

"We should be grateful."

"Yes.

Anna picked up her pocketbook. "Well, it's late, and I need to get home."

"Where's your car?"

"Car? I don't own a car. I walked. It was such a beautiful night."

"Well, you're not going to walk home alone. I'll walk you."

Anna's protests were ignored, and they walked down from the center of Florence to the Arno. A cool breeze drifted over the river as it shimmered in the moonlight, and the only people around were young lovers holding hands.

"Beautiful night," Father Giancarlo said.

"Yes."

"Cold?"

"Just a little." She hadn't brought a sweater along and had borrowed Leonora's best linen dress for the television appearance.

"Here, let me." He took off his jacket and put it on her shoulders. Then, unexpectedly, he put his arm around her waist.

"We'll keep each other warm," he said.

By the time they reached the National Central Library, the breeze had gotten stronger and they had to walk faster. By the time they reached the palazzo that housed *Casa di Maria*, they were almost running. And laughing.

"I'm almost out of breath," Anna said as they stood at the doorway.

"Take a minute."

He kept his arm around her and she wondered why she didn't resist.

"I've enjoyed tonight, Anna. You have no idea. Thank you for being on my program, but thank you even more for listening to me."

"I am grateful that you told me these things, Gianni. I really am."

"Let's talk again soon, OK?"

"Yes."

He took his jacket from her shoulders and put it on. In the awkward moments that followed, both felt as if they were teenagers on a first date. Anna finally resolved the question.

"Good night, Gianni." She kissed him on both cheeks and he suddenly hugged her close. He kissed her gently on the lips. She kissed him back harder. They could both feel how excited he had become.

"Anna," he whispered.

"Gianni."

They kissed again, long.

"No, I can't," she said.

"You're right."

Reluctantly, he ended the embrace and turned and went down the steps. When he looked back to wave she was still standing there. Suddenly, he bounded back up the stairs and they kissed again.

"Good night, Anna. I'll call you."

TWO DAYS LATER, Anna was surprised to receive a call from the Office of Social Justice for the diocese. She wasn't home, but there was a message on her machine. "We saw you on the program the other night. Please come to our office on Friday at 2 o'clock."

"Oh, God. Now I'm in trouble."

"Anna," Leonora said, "what kind of trouble could you be in? You didn't say anything wrong. You just said things you believe in. OK, maybe a little too strongly, but nothing the church would object to."

"I don't know. There might have been something."

"Anna, *Casa di Maria* is under the Franciscans. It's not under the diocese so even if they did object to something, they couldn't do anything about it."

"Leonora, the church would always find a way."

She called Father Giancarlo. "Gianni, I just got a call from the diocese and..."

"I did, too. Meeting Friday at 2."

"Am I—are we—in trouble?"

"No, no. Well, I don't think so. Let's see."

The Office of Social Justice was in yet another palazzo of the diocese. Since it was one of the smaller departments, it occupied three cramped rooms on the third floor. Anna and Father Giancarlo were surprised to be greeted by a young woman not even thirty who introduced herself as Margherita Petrini.

"Yes," she said, "I know it's hard to believe, but I'm the director of this office. Well, I'm also the secretary and social worker and...I'm the staff, in other words. Thank you for coming."

They sat on folding chairs next to Signorina Petrini's desk.

"I called you both because I saw your program the other night, Father. Nobody misses it, as you know."

"Thanks."

"And I want to thank you for what you said."

Anna and Father Giancarlo exchanged looks of relief.

"Here's why I called you here today. My superiors and I have been talking about how we can help women, young and old, like those at *Casa di Maria* who are about to have babies and have nowhere to go. We've been mulling this over for many months, and frankly, we are at a loss for ideas. We just have no experience in these matters. So it was such a relief to know that there is such a successful place here, and we'd like to use it as a model for what we would want to do."

"That's wonderful," Father Giancarlo said.

"Yes," Anna said. "Is there any way we can help?"

"As a matter of fact, there is. That's why I asked you to come here today. I wonder if you would spend some time and suggest to us how the diocese could establish such a place. We would provide you with the information for four areas to study: possible facilities, finances, resources and the problems of liabilities. If you could put your heads together and come up with some sort of master plan, we'd be most grateful."

"I think it's great that you're considering this," Father Giancarlo said. "Yes, of course, we would like to get together and think this out."

"I'd be most happy," Anna said. "It would be good to have another place in Florence. *Casa* can't handle any more. I think we could develop a plan."

"Anna," Father Giancarlo said, "we could meet in my office maybe a couple of times a week. Would that be all right?"

"I could arrange that."

Signorina Petrini raised her hand. "Actually, we were thinking of something a little more intense than that. We've found that if people get together for two or three days, maybe even a week, and spend the entire day on a project, the results are much better than if they work on something sporadically, piecemeal, as it were."

"Well, I guess, we could spend a few days in my office, Anna?"

"That would be fine."

Signorina Petrini raised her hand again. "I have an even better plan. We have a retreat house about eight miles north of here. It's an old monastery that we've converted, Villa San Martino. It's very quiet and secluded. Next week, the place is empty except for the cook, so you'd have the place to yourself. Perhaps for four or five days. Nice spaces to work in, with all the meals provided, of course. You'd have your own rooms, which are simple but very nice. We would pay you each a stipend, of course, and I think it will be generous."

Anna gripped her handbag. She felt her head spinning. "Stay there? Just the two of us?"

"Well, you'd be working, so you would need the peace and quiet. I know, Signorina Sporenza, that you could do this alone, but I thought that since Father Giancarlo has expressed such an interest in what you do, that he could offer his own experiences in running parishes. And besides, you might be a little frightened all alone. Right?"

"No," Anna said. "I'm not frightened alone. Never."

"But, well..." Father Giancarlo said, "there's my television program."

"Right," Signorina Petrini said, "I thought about that. But aren't they taped? Couldn't you show an old one just for one week? I think you've done that before."

"I guess so, but..."

"And," Anna said, "I don't know if I could get away for that long."

"It would just be for a few days," Signorina Petrini said. "There are others who could run things, aren't there?"

"Well, I guess so."

"The stipend, as I said, would be very generous. I'm sure the *Casa* could use the money?"

"It can always use money. Desperately. It's just that…well, I just don't think I can."

"Oh," Signorina Petrini said, "that's so sad. I had been so certain you would be able to help us to assist all those poor women and girls who have no place else to go. Just as you said the other night, Signorina. You were so passionate about wanting to help them."

Father Giancarlo felt perspiration forming on his forehead and he unconsciously began to twist a handkerchief. Anna opened her handbag for her own handkerchief.

"Well," Signorina Petrini said, "I guess we don't have to establish a place like this for all those poor girls and women. After all, we've never had one before and somehow all these poor girls and women have managed to have their little babies."

"It's just that…" Anna said.

"Yes, it's just…" Father Giancarlo said.

"Is there a problem with the stipend? I can certainly ask that it be increased."

"No, no," Anna said. "We aren't thinking about the money."

"Oh, I know," Signorina Petrini said. "You're worried about what people might think, a handsome priest and an attractive woman spending a week together in a secluded villa. Is that the problem?"

"No!"

"No! Nothing like that."

"Good, because I know you are two honest and sincere people and, well, you're not exactly teenagers anymore, are you?"

"No, we're not!" Anna said.

"No, hardly!" Father Giancarlo said.

"Well, then, would you agree to do this?"

Anna and Father Giancarlo were afraid to look at each other.

"OK, we'll do it," she said.

"Yes," he said.

IF ANNA HAD MOVED any farther away from Father Giancarlo as he was driving, she would have fallen out of the Fiat Tipo. He had picked her up at 8 o'clock on Monday morning and except for a "*buongiorno*" they had not spoken a word during the drive through the outskirts of Florence and into the verdant hills to the north.

Anna looked out the window, not seeing anything, while the priest stared straight ahead as he concentrated on his driving. The backseat was filled with boxes containing scores of file folders, their work for the next several days.

Neither could forget what happened on the steps of the *Casa di Maria,* and neither wanted to talk about it. What would happen when they were alone for days?

At Villa San Martino, they were greeted by a stone-faced woman in a green housedress who identified herself as Signora Valenti.

"I am the cook and the housekeeper. In other words, I am the entire staff this week. Follow me."

She led them to the second floor, which in its previous life must have been the monks' dormitory.

"Take these two rooms," she said. "Lunch is at 1 o'clock. Dinner is at 7. I don't do laundry."

"Nice to be greeted so warmly," Father Giancarlo whispered when Signora Valenti had departed. It was his first real sentence of the day.

Anna smiled but did not reply.

The rooms were adjoining and identical: a bed, a desk, a chair.

Without asking, Anna picked the one on the left and Father Giancarlo took his suitcase into the one on the right.

"Well, let's see what the place looks like," he said.

They found a maze of rooms on the first floor, some with expansive views of the countryside, others only a little larger than closets. The chapel, preserved from the building's eighteenth-century beginnings, was at one end. The dining room was in the middle, with a wood-paneled library on one side and an airy solarium on the other. Both had long tables equipped with typewriters.

They lugged in the boxes from the car and decided that they would split duties. Anna would go over the reports about facilities and resources;

Father Giancarlo would focus on finances and liabilities. She would work in the solarium, he in the library.

After a lunch of Tuscan soup and *panini,* with a conversation that was at best awkward, they went to their two workplaces and opened their files.

And so the task began. Work in the afternoon, have dinner, more work at night, bedtime.

Tuesday, the same routine.

Wednesday, the same routine.

Their silence didn't lessen the tension and, in fact, it only increased.

By Thursday afternoon, both Anna and Father Giancarlo had completed their work. Now they had to combine their efforts and, obviously, had to work together. The library was chosen. Anna brought in her stacks of papers and they sat across from each other at the table.

As if giving a report to a group of bankers, she proceeded to read out loud her proposal to convert an old palazzo near the Church of San Marco as the best alternative of those suggested by the diocese. She gave seven reasons in detail. Discussing resources, she proposed that a separate foundation be established apart from the diocese so that management would be independent. She outlined the benefits.

Father Giancarlo then discussed finances and presented a budget that called for private donations to supplement diocesan contributions. The budget would adequately take care of both staffing and maintenance. Aware of the liabilities that might threaten such an institution, he had researched Italian laws and outlined preventive measures.

All they needed to do now was put their typewritten reports together in a binder.

"If you stand next to me, it will be easier," Father Giancarlo said.

Anna was more than three feet away at the start but gradually moved closer. Occasionally, their arms touched, and both jumped back. At one point, Anna reached for a page at the same time as he did, and she scratched the back of his hand.

"I'm sorry!"

"It's all right."

"It's bleeding!"

He wrapped his handkerchief around it. "There. It stopped. It's fine."

Then he dropped a paper clip and they both bent down to fetch it and their foreheads clashed.

"Ouch!"

"Ouch!"

Father Giancarlo laughed. Anna did something she hadn't done since she was a child. She giggled.

When they had put all three hundred and twenty-two pages into the three-ring binder, they congratulated themselves with smiles and a very small hug.

"Let's look at it one more time," Father Giancarlo said.

They went through it page by page.

"Oh my goodness," Anna said, "where is page one hundred and eighty?"

They looked.

"Here it is," he said, "behind two hundred and forty-four. And two hundred and sixty is behind two hundred and eighty-five."

For some reason, this seemed hilarious.

Laughing uproariously, they put the pages where they belonged and collapsed on the leather sofa opposite the table.

"Well, that's that," Anna said.

"Yes."

"And we can go home tomorrow."

"Yes."

"And go back to our lives."

"Yes."

Anna started to weep. "Gianni, I just wish things were different."

He put his arm around her and held her close.

"Anna, can I tell you something? After I left you on the doorstep that night, I couldn't stop thinking about you. I couldn't sleep that Friday night. I was supposed to referee a football game Saturday morning and I made terrible calls. I couldn't concentrate hearing confessions Saturday afternoon. I suppose Signora Pocatelli wondered why she was supposed to say ten rosaries when she usually gets only one. I barely made it through Mass on Sunday. Anna, I couldn't wait to see you again when we got the call to go to the diocesan office."

"Gianni, it was the same with me. Only when I'm upset, I get nasty. I'm sure Leonora wondered why I yelled at poor Anastasia when she wouldn't hurry, or when the deliveryman put the packages in the wrong place. I was on edge all weekend after that call because I was thinking about you."

"So where does that leave us?"

"I don't know, Gianni."

"I don't either."

"I suppose," Anna said, "we could go upstairs and continue what we started the other night."

"Are you serious?"

"No! I was just acting like a teenager. But then, as Signorina Petrini so delicately reminded us, we're not teenagers anymore."

"No, I'm afraid we're not."

"You know, that was the first time I was kissed by a man. And you know something else? I liked it."

"But you don't want more?"

"Gianni, I have a way of life that would be hard to change. This is who I am. I don't think I could be anyone else. But let me tell you one thing. If I were able to love someone, truly love someone and commit myself to that person for the rest of my life, it would be you. You are so kind and generous and thoughtful. I'll always be grateful for the time we've had together. Yes, and for those minutes on the steps of *Casa di Maria*. I'll never forget that. I'm going to return to my life knowing that someone could care for me, even want me. I never thought anyone would."

"Anna, for the first time in my life, I feel the same. I'm grateful that you came into my life, especially when I most needed someone like you. You are quite wonderful, you know. And I too will go back to try to be a good priest, but I'll know that someone could love me as I am. And, you know, I'll remember that kiss always, too. But let's not end it, all right? Can we still be friends? I need a friend, Anna. I badly need a friend to talk to."

"Gianni, I need a friend, too."

"I need you, Anna."

"And I need you, Gianni."

They hugged and, yes, they kissed.

Driving home the next day, they told stories about their childhoods and their friends. He talked about life in the seminary and she about life in the convent. He told funny stories about his parishioners and she described the joy she felt holding babies. They laughed. They cried a little. They even told jokes. And when he said good-bye at the door of the *Casa di Maria,* they embraced and made plans to see each other very soon.

His Mother's Son

Siena

AFTER HEARING ONLY RARELY from his mother for years, Father Lorenzo had become increasingly concerned, and bothered, by the frequency of her calls now. He could expect a call every week, sometimes two or three.

Starting in January 1992, while he was occupied with problems at the soup kitchen, she began with complaints about how he never called or came to visit her.

"Lorenzo, I've been sitting by this phone, waiting, waiting, waiting."

"Mother, this has been a very busy time at Santa Croce," Father Lorenzo said. "Four of our volunteers have gotten sick, there's a record cold in Florence now and some people are without heat, one of the major industries has laid off workers so the soup kitchen is overflowing and…"

"Excuses, excuses, excuses. And what about your mother? Can you just forget about her?"

"Mother, I called you on Christmas Eve and again on Christmas day. Also on New Year's and on Epiphany. Don't you remember?"

"How long did we talk? Five minutes? That's all the time you could give your poor old mother? When are you going to come to see me?"

"I'm really busy, Mother."

"I thought you were only part time there now."

"Part time at the soup kitchen, but I'm still a priest at Santa Croce. Masses, confessions, meetings."

"I get so lonesome here."

"I'm sorry about that." *(You didn't seem to miss me all those years after I entered the order. You never called me then, and you cut me off when I did call. You didn't want anything to do with me.)*

"When can you come, Lorenzo?"

"I'll see if I can in a month or two."

Father Lorenzo hung up. *(I'm not going to feel guilty. I'm not going to feel guilty.)*

The calls continued like that. In February, her complaints were about her doctor.

"Lorenzo, why don't you talk to Michetti? He doesn't listen to me."

"What should I talk about, Mother?"

"He keeps telling me I have to lose some weight. How can I lose some weight? I've got to eat, don't I?"

"You've put on a few pounds, Mother. More than a few pounds. And that's not good for your heart."

"He wants me to eat a lot of vegetables. Carrots! Broccoli! Asparagus even! You know how I hate vegetables. He wants me to eat fish. I hate fish! He doesn't want me to eat meat. Meat has proteins, doesn't it? Why can't I eat meat?"

"Too much meat isn't good for your heart, Mother."

"And he gives me all these medicines! How can I take so many? You know I always hated taking pills. Sometimes I just don't take them."

"Mother, you have to take your medicines. Do I have to ask Isabella again to tell you to take them? The poor girl, I've asked her so many times."

"Yes, she tells me. Nag, nag, nag. Lorenzo, when are you going to come to see me?"

"I can't now, Mother. I'm really busy."

Father Lorenzo hung up. *(I'm not going to feel guilty. I'm not going to feel guilty.)*

Around the first of March, the complaints were about Lorenzo's brother.

"Lorenzo, Giorgio never comes up to talk to me. I haven't seen him in weeks. He just lives downstairs and he never comes to see me."

"I suppose he's busy." *(Yeah, busy all right, with that new woman in Rome. It's easy to get lost in that palazzo, and Giorgio knows how to do it. But he's probably never home anyway. I don't know how Maria Elena has stood it all these years. For the sake of the kids, I guess.)*

"I have only two sons. One of them is a banker who lives just downstairs and never comes to see me, the other one is a priest who never comes to see me. I wish I had a daughter. A daughter would pay attention to me."

"I don't live that close, Mother. I can't just drop everything and come to see you."

"You live, what, ten minutes away?"

"Mother, I'm in Florence. You're in Siena. That's almost two hours on the bus."

"I don't know why you never bought a car."

"Mother, Franciscans don't own cars."

"And what's your excuse now for not coming to see me?"

"It's Lent, Mother. I can't get away now."

"Excuses, excuses, excuses. Well, anyway, talk to your brother. Tell him to come to see me."

Father Lorenzo hung up. *(I'm not going to feel guilty. I'm not going to feel guilty.)*

He put in a call to his brother. The maid answered. "He's in Rome. On business."

(Of course he's in Rome. On business. Right.)

In April, the complaint was about a pain in her left side.

"Lorenzo, it's terrible."

"How terrible, Mother?"

"Every once in a while I get this pain."

"How often?"

"Maybe every other day."

"Just every other day? When?"

"After I eat."

"What have you been eating, Mother?"

"You know how I hate vegetables."

"Mother, you have to eat what the doctor says you should eat. And you shouldn't eat what he says you shouldn't."

"The doctor, the doctor. What does Michetti know? He killed my brother, you know."

"Mother, your brother was ninety years old. He died of old age."

"Michetti killed him."

"I'll call Doctor Michetti about your pain, Mother."

"When are you going to come to see me?"

"It's right after Easter, Mother. I can't come now."

"Excuses, excuses, excuses."

Father Lorenzo hung up. *(I'm not going to feel guilty. I'm not going to feel guilty.)*

He called Doctor Michetti.

"Lorenzo, I've been treating your mother for forty years. She's getting old. She's eighty-three now and of course there are changes. Physically, I worry about her heart. She has to lose some weight. It's not good for her. And she has to eat better. And she has to exercise more. She should at least walk up and down the stairs of the palazzo. She just sits in that chair all the time and watches television. It's not good."

"And besides that?" Father Lorenzo asked.

"And besides that, it's her mind. Obviously, there have been changes. Her memory isn't what it used to be, but beyond that there's been a change in personality, as you've noticed. She's angry because she doesn't have control of things anymore. She wants more attention now because she's afraid of what's happening to her, and she's taking that out on you."

"And what should I do?"

"Try to be patient. And don't feel guilty, Lorenzo. Don't feel guilty."

In June, the complaint was about her legs.

"Lorenzo, I can hardly move."

"Mother, are you trying to walk?"

"It hurts."

"I know it hurts a little, but you have to strengthen your legs. You need to get a little exercise. Doctor Michetti says so."

"Michetti, Michetti. He killed my brother."

"Mother, try walking up and down the stairs twice a day."

"I can't walk those stairs! What are you telling me?"

"You used to. You used to walk up to that third floor all the time. And you were never out of breath. You even ran up faster than me and Giorgio when we were kids."

"Not any more."

"Try, Mother, try. Maybe when you're down on the second floor you can see Giorgio."

"Giorgio! I don't know where he is. He never comes to see me. And I can't walk up and down those stairs. I'm eighty-three years old. And I don't want to eat what Michetti tells me to eat. And I don't want to take those awful pills. Oh, Lorenzo, when are you coming to see me?"

"I'll try to come soon."

Father Lorenzo hung up. *(I'm not going to feel guilty. I'm not going to feel guilty.)*

FATHER LORENZO DID FEEL GUILTY, of course, and he didn't know why he didn't go to Siena more often. He could have arranged the time off, and buses ran from Florence every couple of hours. He could even go in the morning and return at night.

The last time was five years ago, in 1987. The terrible strain of dealing with the hysteria caused by the serial killer called the "Monster of Florence" almost caused the priest to have a breakdown. He had comforted dozens of people who were sure the monster would strike someone in their families and, even though he was exhausted, he slept very little at night. The final straw was when he heard that Dateline NBC was making a documentary on the case and wanted to interview him. He didn't answer his phone calls.

"Father, you have to get away from Florence," his friend Dino Sporenza had said. "You're not going to be any help to anyone in your condition. Why don't you go to Siena? I know you always like just sitting in the Campo and watching people."

"And then I'd have to see my mother."

"I think you can stand your mother for a few days."

Three days later, after checking in with those he had helped most closely, he had taken a bus to Siena and his mother's palazzo. He slept in his old room and spent the days wandering the city, going to bookstores, praying at the Basilica of San Francisco, and enjoying watching people and eating chocolate gelato in the Campo. In the evenings, with Isabella silently serving the meal, he sat at one end of the long table in the ornate dining room, his mother at the other. Even then she could barely say a sentence that did not contain a complaint. Father Lorenzo tuned her out.

When he returned to Florence, he didn't feel all that rested.

Before that, he had gone to Siena in 1983 for a peace and justice conference that his superiors thought he should attend. It was held in a conference center near the House of Saint Catherine and, after three days, he felt himself nodding off during speech after speech. But the entire experience was enough to invigorate him, and he returned to Florence even more determined to help the poor.

He did see his mother at that time. Briefly. Although he had called to tell her he was coming, she was rushing out for a meeting of other feminists concerned about threats to Italy's law permitting abortions.

"So sorry," she said. "This meeting just came up and I have to attend. Have you eaten? Tell Isabella to fix you something. Call me!"

Mink coat almost flying off her shoulders, she was out the door.

In 1981, he had returned for the funeral Mass for his uncle Luca, his father's brother, who had died at the age of eighty-four.

"Michetti killed him," his mother said when she called Father Lorenzo.

His mother insisted that the funeral, like that of his grandmother, be held in the Duomo. She also insisted that the cardinal celebrate the Mass, and Father Lorenzo was lost in the dozens of priests and altar boys parading after the casket.

At the reception after the Mass, his mother commented, as she always did, on how she hated his Franciscan robes and urged him to change. "Ask Giorgio if you can wear one of his suits." He did not.

And then there was 1974. That was when his mother received the Clara Maffei Award for her work in getting the divorce law passed. It was an elegant affair at Palazzo Franconi, and speaker after speaker praised the efforts of Signora Renata Salvetti. His mother, seated at the head table, gloried in all the attention.

It was at that dinner that he met…that he met…he didn't want to think about it. Although it was eighteen years ago, he knew he would never forget her red hair, her upturned nose, her tanned arms, her perfect teeth and her wide smile.

He shuddered. Eighteen years. Sometimes it seemed like yesterday. Too often it seemed like yesterday.

He put the telephone back on its place on the desk and hurried out the door. It was his night to serve at the *cucina popolare*, the soup kitchen off Piazza Santa Croce that had been an institution in Florence for decades.

New clients came, old ones died or, if they were lucky, found jobs and didn't need the nightly bowl of hearty Tuscan soup.

Lines had already formed, and all the tables were filled with boisterous people talking and yelling back and forth to one another. Father Lorenzo quieted them down and began the evening with a prayer of thanksgiving for the food they were about to eat and the blessings God had given them. Then he was again coaxed into singing his signature song, "It's Been a Hard Day's Night," as he served. The patrons clinked their glasses, cheered and hooted.

Volunteers had changed, too, over the years, and tonight, Father Lorenzo was working with Pietro Rossi. Years ago, as a young boy, Pietro was brought to the soup kitchen by his mother Caterina. Now that her son had his degree in engineering from the University of Pisa and had a good job, Caterina didn't need to come to the *cucina popolare* any more. But Pietro tried to repay the soup kitchen for all the meals he and his mother had received by volunteering at least four times a week.

"How's your mother, Pietro?" the priest asked as he lifted a kettle of soup onto the table.

"Fine, just fine. Her legs bother her a little, but she still manages to climb those three flights of stairs every morning and night."

"Yes. I wish all mothers would do that."

"Father?"

"Oh, nothing. I was just thinking to myself."

He wondered what would happen to his mother. She had changed so dramatically in the last few years. Once a strong-willed energetic woman who could rouse the passions of other women when she talked about feminist issues facing Italy, she was now weak in body and spirit, trying desperately to hold on to the past and very angry that she couldn't. Father Lorenzo tried to be patient and understanding, but that was often difficult, and then the waves of guilt came over him.

As usual, he didn't return home until after midnight and was surprised to hear the phone ringing.

"Lorenzo? It's Doctor Michetti. I think you should come here."

FATHER LORENZO was on the first bus to Siena the following morning. He didn't understand why there were so many people at that hour and finally found a seat next to a young man with shaggy brown hair that fell down his back from his cowboy hat.

"Why is everyone going to Siena?" he asked.

"The Palio, of course. Didn't you know?"

If Father Lorenzo had paid attention to such things, he would have known that the first of Siena's famous summer horse races, preceded by days of parades and pageantry—not to mention exuberant eating and drinking that filled the hilly streets—would be held in another week, on July 3.

"Everybody knows that," his companion added, making the priest feel even more clueless.

"What *contrada* is expected to win?" he asked, trying to sound interested.

"Eagle, of course. Everybody knows that."

"Oh. Really? That's my *contrada.*"

"You're kidding. You belong to Eagle? No shit."

In his young and boozy days, Lorenzo Salvetti and his friends, all from the Eagle *contrada,* looked forward to the Palios, run in July and August, all year. They'd gather in the Piazza del Campo for the pretrials days before, set up the tables for the nightly banquets, serve the wine and meals, take girls out afterwards, and get there early to mix with the crowds on the day of the races.

Although the races themselves took only ninety seconds, with the horses running around the piazza three times, they were fiercely competitive. Eagle's special enemy was the Panther *contrada*, and Father Lorenzo remembered the couple of fistfights he won.

He hadn't been to a Palio since moving to Florence almost forty years ago.

"Maybe I'll have time to get to it this year," he said.

"Get to it? Get to it?" his companion said. "My God, what could be more important?"

"Well, I can think of a few things."

He took out a book so that there would be no further conversation and tried not to think about what Doctor Michetti had said.

The bus rumbled into Chianti country, Father Lorenzo's favorite region in all of Italy. He wished he could see the countryside better, with its rows of cypresses, ruined castles on mountaintops and small stone houses along little rivers. But his young companion was seated next to the window and dozing now, his large cowboy hat obstructing much of the view.

He recognized Tavarnelle and Barbarino when the bus went by, and soon they had stopped at Poggibonsi. Ah, the memories of Poggibonsi, as sweet as they were forty-five years ago. It was there that he got to know Maria-Teresa, his blond classmate, on a class trip to the village. Then, sixteen years old, he got to know her even better in a hidden bedroom in his palazzo in Siena. It was the first experiment for both of them, and they were thrilled.

Father Lorenzo smiled.

When the bus stopped at Colle, Father Lorenzo remembered his relationship with Patrizia, who was eight years older and taught him some new ways of doing things. Then there were Francesca and Daniella and Leila and so many others. He was young and handsome and reasonably wealthy and who was to care what he did?

"I can't believe I did all that," he mumbled. "I don't know how I became a priest."

He may have thought he was talking to himself, but his companion stirred.

"You're a priest? Why aren't you wearing your outfit?"

"I don't usually wear my robes when I go to Siena."

"Why? Planning to do a little hanky-panky? That's why you might not get to the Palio?" He elbowed the priest in the side. Father Lorenzo edged away.

"No, I'm not planning to do a little hanky-panky. I'm going to see my mother."

No need to go into detail.

"And you? You're going to the Palio, I suppose?"

"My buddies and I have been planning this all year. They're from Eagle, too. There's a party every night. There are a lot of things to do besides the horse race, if you know what I mean."

"I think I know what you mean. Be careful."

"I'm always careful, Father. You should have seen the babe this last time. She had…"

"It's all right. It's all right. I don't need details. Well, if you'll excuse me, I want to finish this chapter before we get there."

Father Lorenzo opened his book again, though his companion's adventures only made him think more about those he'd had. He knew that instead of that he should be thinking of the path he'd taken to the priesthood and then the life he'd led.

The young man put out his hand when they stepped down from the bus after it arrived at Piazza Antonio Gramsci in Siena. "Well, nice to talk to you. My name is Matteo. Matteo Norelli."

"I'm Lorenzo Salvetti. That's Father Lorenzo Salvetti, of course."

"Of course. OK. See you around, Lorenzo. Come to the dinners at Eagle. They're going to win!"

Even this early in the morning the celebrations were well underway, or perhaps they were just continuing from last night. Father Lorenzo made his way through the throngs from the bus stop and down Via dei Montanini Banchi and then around the Campo and on to Via del Casato. Everywhere people waved the yellow Eagle flag, embossed with a black eagle with two heads and holding a scepter, a sword and an imperial globe in its claws. Some women wore the flags as scarves.

He was soon in front of Palazzo Murano, which some people called a fortress but he knew as home. Looking strained and sleepless, Isabella answered the bell and ushered him into the vaulted entrance.

"Doctor Michetti is with her. Go on up."

He climbed the three flights and found his brother outside his mother's bedroom, holding some sort of black bulky instrument to his ear. He seemed to be talking into it.

"It's my new mobile phone," Giorgio said after he pushed a button and put the thing in his pocket. "Now I can call anyone anywhere anytime."

"Just what the world needs," Father Lorenzo said. "How's Mother?"

"Glad you came, Lorenzo. Go in to see her."

Doctor Michetti was taking his mother's pulse and shook his head when he finished.

"Not good. She was doing all right, but yesterday she had an attack. Then she fell. Her leg is bruised, but not broken."

"Stop talking about me like I wasn't here!" his mother tried her best to shout but began to cough.

Father Lorenzo hardly recognized his mother. Her face was flushed, her hair, always neatly coifed, flowed out on the pillow. Her thin hands held a satin sheet to her neck. Only her eyes were as piercing as always. He kissed her forehead.

"Lorenzo. You came. Finally."

"I'm here, Mother. How are you feeling?" He held her cold hand.

"Feeling? How do you think I'm feeling? I'm dying."

"Well…"

"It's true. Ask Michetti here. He's killing me, too."

Doctor Michetti ignored the comment and put a thermometer in her mouth. He shook his head again when he removed it.

"See? Ask him how long I have."

"Her heart is not good, Lorenzo, and we're doing everything we can. She needs to rest and not have any stress."

"Stress? How can I not have stress when that son of mine is out in the hall figuring how much money he'll get when I'm gone."

"Mother…"

"It's true. Well, he'll find out, and soon enough, too. And won't he be surprised!"

She began to cough, and Doctor Michetti soothed her forehead.

"Now listen, Lorenzo, I want you to do something before I go."

"Of course, Mother."

"I want you to find someone and bring her here."

"Of course, Mother. Who?"

"I don't have long, so you had better hurry."

"Of course, Mother. Who do you want to see?"

She pointed a fleshy finger at Father Lorenzo's chest.

"Victoria. Victoria Stonehill."

SUDDENLY, THE MEMORIES that he had tried to suppress over the years came rushing back. How he had met Victoria Stonehill at that dinner in Siena honoring his mother's work in getting a divorce law passed in Italy. How she was one of the most beautiful women he had ever seen. How she seemed so interested in him, asking all sorts of questions about his personal life. How he found an excuse, rather lame, to see her in the beach town of Rimini, where she had a jewelry shop. How they spent days on the beach and nights at restaurants. How they walked around the city, and even, for God's sake, went dancing.

And after a few days they were dangerously close to continuing the story that he had begun with a girl in a hidden bedroom of his palazzo. But he was sixteen when he had been with Maria-Teresa and he was forty-three when he met Victoria Stonehill.

More to the point, he had become a priest.

Incredibly, he never told her he was a priest until their final day together, though she had her suspicions.

After a tearful parting, he remembered returning to Florence and meeting with his superior for a long confession. Father Alphonsus had put the episode in perspective, talking about how priests were men, after all, and that they could get lonely. Father Lorenzo listened, but every once in a while over the years, he still felt pangs of guilt. And he still thought about her.

As for Victoria, except for a brief note after he had returned to Florence, he had never heard from her again.

"Mother, Victoria Stonehill? Why would you want to see her? It's been years."

The old woman coughed. "She was very helpful to me when we had that campaign about divorce. In fact, she was the only one who stuck with me when we had all that opposition. The only one, Lorenzo."

"Of course, she was going through a divorce herself, remember?"

"Makes no difference. She helped me. I want to see her again. I want to thank her in a very special way. I never did, you know. She got all involved with you at that dinner and I hardly saw her again."

Father Lorenzo had never told his mother anything about the Rimini experience.

"Well, I'm not sure where to look. It's been eighteen years. She could be anywhere. I think she was going to get married. Maybe she moved away. She could have gone back to America."

"I don't think so. I don't think she liked America and I don't think she got along with her family."

"How do you know that?"

"I just do. Now go!"

"Go where?"

"Well, Rimini, you blockhead. That's where she was. You have to start there."

"And if she's not?"

"Then ask around and find out where she is! God, how did they ever let you become a priest? Do I have to get up from my deathbed to do this?"

She accentuated that threat with another round of coughing.

Father Lorenzo kissed his mother's forehead and said good-bye. He didn't want to dwell on the possibility that she would no longer be around in a few weeks so it wouldn't matter if he found Victoria Stonehill. And that raised the questions: Did he actually want to find Victoria Stonehill? Was he afraid that those old feelings would return?

But his mother told him to do it. On her deathbed. He had agreed. He had to look.

Giorgio was on his mobile phone again when he left the room. Father Lorenzo didn't even look at him. Exhausted, he went down the hall to his own room, sat in a chair and spent the rest of the day trying to avoid the thoughts that swirled through his head. He visited his mother twice again, in the afternoon and evening, but she was asleep both times. Then he crawled into his old bed and stared at the ceiling with its plastered stars and angels.

"Victoria Stonehill. I didn't think I'd ever see her again. Maybe I won't. I hope I don't. But then..."

Sleep mercifully stopped him from contemplating the alternative.

The train station in Siena was crowded the next morning, but almost everyone was arriving for the Palio. In contrast, the train to Rimini was almost empty and Father Lorenzo found a seat at the rear of one of the first cars. He realized immediately that he should have brought a book along for the four-hour trip.

Instead, he took a nap, trying not to think about his mother's condition or Victoria Stonehill.

Rimini in early July was just as he remembered, crowded with beachcombers. But there was something different. Rimini had become so infested with drug users that a rehabilitation center, San Patrignano, in nearby Botticella had treated thousands of people.

"The world has changed since I was here last," Father Lorenzo thought. "Let's hope I have, too."

Victoria had owned a jewelry shop on Corso d'Augusto, so he'd better start there. Beggars were still clustered around Arc d'Augusto, and the priest remembered a mother and her little boy who were so grateful for the coins he gave them. He dug into his pocket and found a few *lire* for a little girl.

He walked down Corso d'Augusto. It was different, not nearly as elegant.

"Maybe I'm on the wrong street."

He crossed and looked at every shop across the way. The place where *Gioielleria di Victoria* had been now had a new name: *Negozio di souvenir.*

"A souvenir shop instead of a jewelry shop? That can't be Victoria's. She would never sell anything so cheap."

Behind the counter, a scruffy man put down his cigar and *La Gazetta dello Sport.* "What are you looking for? I've got more stuff back here."

He pointed to a display of pornographic videotapes under the counter.

"No. Thanks anyway. Wasn't there a jewelry shop here?"

"Jewelry shop? Hell, I don't know. I've been here three years. Before that, there was nobody. The place was closed for ten, twelve years. Hell, I don't know. Why? You want to buy some jewelry? I've got these rings. Imported. Look. You'd think they were diamonds, wouldn't you? Look at the price. Would you believe it?"

"No, thanks, but I'm trying to find the woman who owned the jewelry shop."

"Hell, I don't know anything about a woman and a jewelry shop."

"Would anyone else on this street know?"

"You could try next door. That woman has been here for a hundred years."

Father Lorenzo remembered that the shop next door had been something like Victoria's, carrying expensive necklaces, earrings, watches, picture frames and other items way out of his priestly budget.

The woman dozing behind the counter looked familiar. He must have noticed her when he stopped at Victoria's shop.

"Victoria Stonehill?" she said when Father Lorenzo awakened her. "Oh my. She hasn't been here for years. Poor thing. She should never have married that man."

"She got married?"

"The guy who ran the beach."

"What happened?"

"He left her, of course. That's what men do."

He remembered how Victoria had been dating Fabiano, the handsome manager of the beach and seemed so much in love. "He's really wonderful," he remembered her saying. *Well, not so wonderful,* he thought.

"Do you know where she is?"

"Who knows? She just closed the shop one day and never came back."

"She didn't say where she might go?"

"I don't know. Somebody said she went back to America. I don't know."

FATHER LORENZO DOUBTED that Victoria had gone back to America. She had talked about growing up in New York and going to an expensive school, but she had come to Italy after college, stayed and gotten married. She seemed to love Italy so much. Obviously, he needed to find more people to talk to. Luckily, he had packed a fresh shirt, underwear and socks in his knapsack, and perhaps he should find a room for the night.

He could have looked anywhere, but somehow he was drawn to the decrepit *pensione* where he had stayed eighteen years ago. It was still there, more decaying than ever. The landlady, who had not aged gracefully, eyed him suspiciously.

"Didn't you stay here once before?" she asked. "Maybe eighteen, twenty years ago?"

"No, no, not me."

He wanted to pull back the words as soon as he said them. He had told so many lies the last time in Rimini. Was he starting again? There was no reason.

The landlady led him to the same upstairs room where he had stayed the last time, and he suspected it was the only room ever available here. The large painting of a buxom nude woman was still on the wall, and someone had written a vulgarity over the woman's pendulous breasts. Someone, probably the landlady, had tried to erase the words but the smear only made the comment worse.

He dropped his knapsack on the bed and fled. Next door, the bar had just reopened after the afternoon siesta. He ordered an apple pastry and a cappuccino, exactly the same as he had so long ago.

"Weren't you here before, a long time ago?" the ancient *barista* asked as he placed a napkin over the pastry.

"Me? No. You must be thinking of someone else."

Another lie. Why was he doing this?

He gulped down the coffee and was still munching the pastry as he left the shop.

The Maramare portion of the beach was so crowded he could hardly see the sand. He could smell the suntan oil, though, and the sweaty bodies. Threading his way through packs of screaming children, he arrived at the office, where girls in bikinis were folding towels.

"*Buongiorno.* I'm looking for a man named Fabiano. He used to be in charge here."

"No one by that name here," one of the girls said, still folding her towels.

"Is there anyone here who worked here for a long time, maybe eighteen years?"

"Eighteen years? I wasn't even born then!"

"I know. But do you know anyone who's been here that long?"

An elderly woman, flabby portions of her body spilling out of her swimsuit, pushed her way forward.

"You looking for Fabiano? Why? Does he owe you money, too?"

"No. It's not that. I heard he got married and I'm trying to find his wife."

"You mean Victoria?"

"Yes!"

Father Lorenzo's heart began to beat faster. He was close to finding her!

"If I were you I wouldn't try to find that bastard," the woman said.

"Why not?"

"Trouble. Oh, he put on a good front, but underneath…bastard."

"Are they still here? Fabiano and Victoria?"

The woman laughed. "Fabiano's been gone, oh, fifteen years. Every year somebody comes looking for him. Trying to get the money he owes them. Good luck! Last I heard he was in Greece."

"What about his wife? Victoria? Did she go with him?"

"Never! She would have run in the other direction."

"Someone said she might have gone back to America."

"I heard that, too. Who knows? Wanted to get as far from that bastard as possible, I suppose. Why? You a friend of hers?"

"No. No."

Another lie.

Father Lorenzo couldn't get away from the beach fast enough. He wandered back into Rimini and found himself at Piazza Tre Martiri. This, he remembered Victoria saying, was where everything in Rimini starts. Then he remembered how he told Victoria the silly story of how Saint Anthony preached to fish at Rimini, how she laughed at him and how embarrassed he became. Surely she must have known then, if at no other time, that he was a priest, but she didn't let on.

Oh, the lies he told her.

They had talked about the films Fellini had shot in Rimini and when they walked to Marecchia Park they saw an old man who reminded him of the elderly gentleman in De Sica's *Umberto D.* Somehow, he suddenly knew then that he had to tell her the truth about himself. It took him another day to do that.

"What was I thinking of? How could I even imagine that I could leave the priesthood and be with her? She was so beautiful, though."

Shaking his head, he almost knocked over a woman carrying grocery bags in both arms. She muttered loudly as she walked away.

Then he remembered something else. There was the place where they had dinner on that first night. She said it was her favorite *trattoria.* It was on Via…Via…Via Carlo Cattaneo! It was called…Lorenzo's. No. Leonardo's! No. Luigi's! Yes, Luigi's. He was sure of it. He found the street and, miraculously, the *trattoria* was still there.

Nothing had changed on the inside, either. Red velvet walls. Tuscan landscapes in ornate frames.

A young man guided him to a table in the rear and soon an elderly waiter was at his side.

"*Buonasera,* Signor. Welcome to Luigi's."

He was sure it was the same waiter.

"Buonasera. Grazie."

The waiter handed him a menu, stepped away and returned.

"Excuse me," he said, "but I believe I remember you coming here many years ago? Am I correct?"

"Yes!" There wasn't any point in lying anymore. "I had dinner here one evening with a friend. A woman."

"Of course! I remember. It was Signora Stonehill, am I correct?"

"That's amazing. How did you remember that?"

The waiter bowed slightly. "A good waiter always remembers his customers."

"But it was so many years ago. Eighteen, in fact."

"Ah, but Signora Stonehill came here often in those days. Almost always she was alone. So I remember particularly the night you came. In fact, I remember that you had the lobster, *langousgine*."

"That's amazing!"

"And you wanted to have the house wine, but Signora Stonehill said no. She insisted on the *Brunello di Montalcino.*"

"I'm afraid we drank too much of it."

"Such a lovely woman, Signora Stonehill. I remember her well."

"Well, actually, that's why I'm here. My mother is very sick and would like to see Signora Stonehill again. I see that her jewelry shop is closed and I have heard that she might have gone back to America. Do you know if that is correct?"

The waiter looked around the room, which was virtually empty anyway, and moved closer to Father Lorenzo's table.

"A waiter must always be discreet, as you know."

"I respect that."

"I really don't know very much. I believe it was a few weeks after your visit that Signora Stonehill came here again. She was with a man one might call handsome, but he did not seem kind to her. He talked very loudly. But she seemed very attracted to him."

"Did she say his name?"

"I remember it well, because it seemed to roll off her tongue. Fabiano. Yes."

"And did they come here again?"

"Never. I heard she married him and one of the cooks said he heard Fabiano was not nice to her, but then you know how cooks like to gossip."

"Yes, I know."

"Many months later, I heard that dear Signora Stonehill had closed her shop and moved away. I don't know where, but I heard America. I wish I had more information, Signor. I am sorry for your mother."

"Thank you. You've been very helpful."

"And now, what would you like for dinner?"

"I'd like the *langousgine.*"

"And the wine?"

"The *Brunello di Montalcino.*"

"Very good, signor."

Although it was still steamy outside when he returned to his room in the *pensione*, the sheets on his bed seemed cold and clammy. With the moonlight streaming through the torn curtains, he could make out the painting of the buxom nude woman on the opposite wall.

"Poor Victoria. That guy, Fabiano, seemed nice enough when I met him. But you never know. The bastard! I wish she could have had some happiness. I have to find her."

He remembered how he kept repeating the same things over and over during his last visit to Rimini: "I've got responsibilities in Florence. I've got to run the soup kitchen. I'm forty-three years old. And I'm a priest."

"I'm a priest, I'm a priest, I'm a priest." He kept repeating the words until he finally fell into a fitful sleep.

WHEN HE RETURNED TO SIENA the following morning, he found his mother sitting up in bed while Isabella tried unsuccessfully to get her to sip some soup.

"Well," his mother said, "where is she? Did you bring her? Let me fix my hair first."

"How are you feeling, Mother? I'm glad you're eating something."

"Isabella made me this awful soup. Tastes like toilet water."

"Had Doctor Michetti been here yet?"

"The Doctor of Death comes in the afternoon. He's trying to kill me, you know."

"It's really lovely outside. How about if I open the curtains?" He did so, and the room was suddenly flooded with light.

"Shut the damn curtains! It's too bright in here."

He did so.

"So where is she? Where's Victoria Stonehill? Downstairs?"

Slowly and carefully, Father Lorenzo recounted the story of his trip to Rimini, how Victoria's jewelry shop was closed, how the woman next door thought she might have gone back to America and how others said the same thing. He didn't mention that he had dinner in a *trattoria* where he had dined with Victoria.

"People say that she married a very nasty guy who was mean to her and she wanted to get far away from him. They say they heard she went back to America."

"America? She was from New York, right?"

"Yes, she told me that."

"Well?"

"Well?"

"Well, have you looked there?"

"In America? Mother, I just found this out yesterday."

"Well, there are telephones, aren't there, Lorenzo? Have you tried calling? God, how did I raise such a stupid son?"

Father Lorenzo tried to control his rising anger. "Mother, may I remind you that New York is a very large city and Stonehill is a rather common name."

"Well, then start! Get your lazy brother to help you. He wants my money after I'm gone, he can start earning it now."

She started coughing so hard that she spit out what little soup she had eaten. Isabella patiently wiped her mouth and her lacy nightgown.

Seething, Father Lorenzo found his brother outside his apartment on the second floor, his telephone to his ear.

"Why do you always make your calls from the halls?" the priest asked when Giorgio quickly put the phone away.

"It's because…it's because the reception is better out here."

"Oh. Of course. Well, anyway, your mother wants you to do her a favor and she reminds you that she's dying and there's her will to consider."

Giorgio sighed. "Damn woman. What does she want now?"

Father Lorenzo explained the situation, interrupted frequently by Giorgio's curses.

"Don't you know someone in New York? Your bank has connections there, doesn't it?"

"Sure we have connections, but I don't deal with them. Hardly anyone does. I suppose I'd have to get Fogetto to try. He's the only one who knows someone there. But I don't think I can trust him with anything."

"Well, try, Giorgio. For once in your life, do something nice for our mother."

Father Lorenzo left the room while Giorgio was still muttering expletives.

For the next three days, the priest tried to hold off his mother's questions and commands by telling her that Giorgio was working very hard trying to find a trace of Victoria Stonehill in New York. He had, however, no idea what his brother was doing since Giorgio had gone off to Rome.

On the third night, Giorgio called. From all the background noise, he seemed to be in another hallway.

"Lorenzo," he said, "do you know how many damn Stonehills there are in New York?"

"I imagine a lot."

"Four times more than that. Fogetto's been calling and calling. The bank's phone bill has gone through the roof."

"Sorry about that."

"It's OK. We'll just charge it to expenses."

"Well, did he find her?"

"After about five million calls he got a lead. There's a woman on the upper East Side who may be her mother. But she got all upset when Fogetto tried to ask her if Victoria was her daughter."

"What did she say?"

"She kept saying 'no, no, she's dead, she's dead,' and then she started bawling. That's what Fogetto said."

Father Lorenzo felt a wave of relief go through him. "She's dead. She's dead. I won't be able to find her. It's over at last." Then he felt pangs of guilt and made the sign of the cross.

"OK, I'll tell Mother. She'll be upset, but this should put an end to this."

"Wait, there's more, Lorenzo. While this crazy woman was still crying, another woman got on the phone. She said she was the maid and she started asking Fogetto all kinds of questions."

"Like what?"

"Like who he was and why did he want to know and if he had seen Victoria Stonehill."

"So she must be still alive?"

"Or at least was when they had contact. The maid said they hadn't heard from Victoria for years and they always thought she was still in Italy."

"Did she say where?"

"No. It was the same story. She was last seen in Rimini."

"And that's it?"

"There's one more thing. This maid said that about fifteen years ago, they got a box sent from Italy with no return address. It was filled with expensive jewelry, rings, necklaces, bracelets, tiaras, everything."

"Just the jewelry?"

"There was a note inside. All it said was, 'Mama, I'm sorry.' It wasn't even signed, but it must have been Victoria."

"Poor woman."

"OK," Giorgio said. "That's all you want from me, right? I did what you wanted me to do."

"What Mother wanted you to do."

"Whoever."

"OK, thanks. And thank Fogetto."

Father Lorenzo put the phone back and lay on his bed. Outside, crowds from pre-Palio parties were in the streets, yelling and singing their *contradra* songs. He got up and closed the windows. Staring at the ceiling, he tried to reconstruct Victoria's years after he knew her. She married Fabiano. He was cruel to her. Maybe he even beat her. She had enough. She sold the jewelry store, packed up the jewelry and sent the stuff to her mother.

And then disappeared.

Except that she was still in Italy—if indeed she were alive. And what was she doing for money?

SIGNORA RENATA SALVETTI did not take the news well when Father Lorenzo reported to her bedroom the next day.

"So she's still in Italy? So you wasted all this time looking for her in America when you should have been looking for her here? What a nincompoop! You and your brother! Now I'm closer to death and you waste your time."

Father Lorenzo clenched his teeth and declined to tell his mother that it was she who ordered him to search for Victoria Stonehill in America. He went back to his room and picked up a book, trying to avoid the noisy celebrations outside.

In the afternoon, he accosted Doctor Michetti and told him about the fruitless search.

"She's really adamant that I find her, isn't she?"

"Lorenzo, you know your mother better than I do. Once she makes up her mind, there's no changing it. She's certain that you'll find this woman."

"And if I don't? Will she die angry with me? And I'll have to live with that?"

"Lorenzo, you know what I think? She's so stubborn I think she's going to refuse to die until you find Victoria Stonehill and bring her to her."

Thinking thoughts that were most unpriestly, Father Lorenzo stormed out of the room and ran down the three flights of steps and into the street. He was immediately engulfed in the crowds that were streaming up Via del Casato to the Campo for the Palio. Caught in the river of humanity, and not knowing where he was headed, he allowed himself to be swept along.

After a few streets, the crowds slowed, and he realized he was in front of the red façade of the Oratorio of Saint John the Baptist. He wondered what this had to do with the Palio when he heard a familiar voice.

"Lorenzo! Lorenzo! Over here!"

He struggled to find a body attached to the voice through the sea of men, women and children wearing the yellow Eagle scarves and finally saw a young man furiously waiving a cowboy hat.

"Over here! It's Matteo! Matteo Norelli! From the bus!"

Elbowing his way, Matteo was followed by two friends until they reached the priest's side.

"Hey, Lorenzo! Good to see you again. This is Gregorio and this is Nunzio. My buddies." He slapped the priest on the back.

"Good to see you again," Father Lorenzo said, cringing. "What are you doing here?"

"We came to see the horse blessed."

It was then that Father Lorenzo realized that a significant part of the Palio was the ritual of blessing the horses that would run. Each horse was brought into the *contrada's* own church for the ceremony. Having spent the last forty years helping the poor in Florence, the priest may have found the ceremony incongruous if not bizarre and sacrilegious, but, well, here he was in Siena and who was he to object to hundreds of years of tradition?

Inside the simple church, with its decorations of angel heads, they peered over scores of heads to see the horse carefully led into the chapel and up to one of three marble altars by two trainers. Black as pitch, the steed apparently wasn't accustomed to such sanctified chambers and charged its handlers left and right.

"A good sign," Matteo said. "He's anxious to run."

"His name is Galleggiante," Nunzio said. "That means Float."

"That's because he's so big," Matteo said. "He's going to win. I know it."

"There's a better sign," Gregorio said. "Our jockey is Andrea De Gortes."

"Yes!" Nunzio cried. "*Aceto!* Vinegar! He's the best."

"Vinegar?" Father Lorenzo asked.

"That's Andrea's nickname. Anyway, it's better than the name of the Panther's jockey, Sebastian Deledda. His nickname is *Legno.*"

"That means Wood," Matteo offered. He and his friends laughed.

The horse was now blessed and the priest commanded: "Go! And come back a winner."

Father Lorenzo wondered how, if every horse received the same command, God could decide which was the winner. He chose not to think about it for long.

"Let's go!" Gregorio cried. "We're going to miss the *corteo storico.*"

"Ah, yes," Father Lorenzo thought, "what would the Palio be without the *corteo storico*."

Ever since there was a Palio there was a triumphal march in the Piazza del Campo beforehand. With everyone in medieval dress, the number of participants totaled almost seven hundred, and since the marchers walked very slowly, the parade lasted up to four hours.

The crowds surged as they approached the Campo. Up Via del Capitano, on to Piazza Postierla, then Via San Pietro, then Via del Casato di Sopra and Via del Casato di Sotto. Men and women walked arm in arm, singing. Children dashed between legs, sometimes falling on their faces and getting up laughing.

At midafternoon, the sun beat down on the crowds and Father Lorenzo unbuttoned the top buttons of his shirt and wiped his forehead.

"Here, Lorenzo," Matteo said, "take my hat." He placed the cowboy hat on the priest's head. It was much too big, but Father Lorenzo was grateful.

The Campo had been transformed into a racetrack, with several inches of dirt laid around the perimeter and with padded crash barriers at the corners. The ubiquitous stalls selling *contrada* flags, necklaces, postcards, books and so many other souvenirs were at the sides, the vendors loudly hawking their goods. The crowds surged toward the middle, carrying Father Lorenzo and his new friends with them.

Then they waited. And waited. Oddly, no one seemed upset. This was just part of the Palio experience. They milled, they laughed, they sang, they hugged, they talked. Mostly, they talked.

With the first toll of the bell from the Torre del Mangia, *carabinieri* in their police uniforms entered on horseback, circling the Campo with, for some reason, swords drawn. Each *contrada* was then represented by a marching group in medieval costumes accompanied by flag throwers.

Then more: a horse accompanied by four of Siena's commanders; the musicians of the Palazzo; men carrying insignia representing the lands and castles of the ancient Sienese state; the captain of the people riding with a page and preceded by a standard bearer, three dagger-bearing pages with helmets and swords, followed by three *gonfaloniers* (a title from the Renaissance) and three centurions.

The parade concluded with an ox-drawn cart with the *drappellone,* the Palio banner. It was delivered to the reviewing stand, to be awarded the winner.

Father Lorenzo watched the flag throwers throwing their flags and the drummers drumming their drums and the marchers marching their marches until he became glassy-eyed. He tried not to think about his ailing mother, and felt a little guilty watching this glorious extravaganza while she lay in bed. Then he thought about how she had given him the impossible task of finding Victoria Stonehill. He would have liked to walk around, looking at the people and inspecting the souvenirs for sale, but he was wedged in so tightly he couldn't move.

The sun had faded now, and at 7:30 p.m. the horses lined up for the race. Matteo and his friends began shouting.

"Eagle is in seventh position!" Matteo yelled. "That's great!"

"But Panther is right next to him, in eighth," Gregorio added. "Trust me, there's going to be a fight."

It took more than an hour for the horses to line up because there were no starting compartments and they kept bumping into each other.

Each jockey then received a *nerbo,* the traditional riding crop made out of a calf's dried penis.

"Vinegar is going to beat Wood more than the horse," Nunzio predicted.

"They're starting!" Matteo shouted.

The din was unbearable.

"Look, Vinegar and Wood are beating each other! Hit him, Vinegar, hit him!"

Father Lorenzo had a hard time watching.

"Vinegar is trailing!"

He closed his eyes.

"Now he's gaining! Hit him again, Vinegar!"

He put his hands over his ears.

"He's in second place, right behind Wood!"

He opened his eyes again.

"Wood is falling behind!"

Now even Father Lorenzo was cheering. "Go, Vinegar! Go, Vinegar!"

"It's over! Vinegar won! Vinegar won! Eagle won! Eagle won!"

The race took less than ninety seconds. The Eagle *contrada* section erupted in cheers, with men and women rushing to the finish line and trying to reach, and touch, Vinegar and Float.

"OK, I've had enough," Father Lorenzo said. "Here's your hat, Matteo. Have fun. Be careful."

"See you around, Lorenzo," Matteo shouted as he and his friends joined the other Eagle members in pursuit of the glorious winner.

Father Lorenzo elbowed his way through the crowds, which were now thinning. He couldn't avoid thinking about his mother anymore.

"What am I going to tell her?" he thought. "There's no way out of this."

He passed one of the souvenir stalls and thought he might buy something for his mother. The choices were not good. He fingered a necklace and then a small jewelry box.

"Find anything here you like, Lorenzo?"

"I'm sorry, what?"

"I asked if you found anything you liked."

"Victoria? Victoria Stonehill? Is that you? Oh my God!"

HE COULDN'T STOP STARING at the woman. Her red hair was covered with a flimsy veil and she wore a worn red blouse and skirt. Her face was tanned, probably from spending so much time in the sun, and there was no doubt that she had lost weight. Her arms were thin and her breasts seemed shrunken under the cotton blouse. But he recognized her upturned nose and gleaming smile.

"You're surprised, aren't you, Lorenzo?" she said. "You didn't expect to find me selling souvenirs in the Campo, did you?"

"Victoria, I'm…I'm…"

"Try speechless."

"Well, yes."

"And you wonder why this woman who owned an elegant shop with fine jewelry in Rimini is now hawking cheap necklaces from China to unsuspecting tourists in Siena."

"Well, yes."

"Long story. But Lorenzo, how lovely to see you again!"

She put her hand on his arm, and soon they were in a long embrace.

"Victoria! I can't believe it."

"I can't either, Lorenzo."

The priest kissed the top of her head and held her closer. Of course, Matteo and his friends walked by at just that moment.

"Way to go, Lorenzo!" he shouted, giving him the thumbs-up. "Have fun!"

"Friends of yours?" Victoria asked.

"No! No! Not at all. Listen, we have to talk. Can we go to a *trattoria* or someplace?"

"I'll have to lock up first."

It took a while to put all the flags and trinkets and maps and calendars in their respective boxes and to shut the wooden doors on the souvenir stall. She made sure all the locks were locked. They walked two blocks before finding a *trattoria* that was open. It was also crowded with people wearing the yellow Eagle scarves and hooting and yelling. The celebrations had just begun.

A waiter, also wearing the yellow scarf, took their order—big bowls of Tuscan soup and a turkey and provolone *panino* for each of them.

"I'm starved," Victoria said.

"When was the last time you had a decent meal?"

"Let me think. Last Thursday?"

"Oh, Victoria."

"Lorenzo, please. Don't pity me. But first, you? You're not wearing your priestly collar. Does that mean…?

"No, no. I'm still very much a priest. I don't wear those things when I'm in Siena."

"Yes, I know. I'm glad you're still a priest, Lorenzo. I really am. All right, you want to know the story of how the *magna cum laude* graduate of Bryn Mawr has become a souvenir seller on the Campo."

She closed her eyes and began her story.

"As you know, when you left me in Rimini that day…"

"And I'm still so sorry that I led you on, that I didn't tell you I was a priest…"

"I understand. I understood then, and I understand now."

"Thank you."

"When you left me in Rimini that day, I knew that I would marry Fabiano. He looked like such a good man, a caring man. He even found employment for that beggar woman you met, remember? Anyway, Fabiano seemed so much in love with me. He sent me flowers every day. He kept asking me to marry him. So after my divorce was finally settled, I did. Just a simple ceremony in city hall."

She placed her knife beside her fork, then put it back again.

"We were happy at first, although he sometimes came home too late and drank too much with his friends."

"Victoria, you don't have to tell me everything."

"And then he started getting upset with me over little things, the way I cooked, the hours I spent at the shop. He wanted to know where I was every minute of the day."

She placed her fork beside her knife, then put it back.

"Then he suggested that he take over the ownership of the shop. He said he knew the laws and he could get a better tax break if the place was in his name. Well, I've never known anything about Italian tax laws. I always just gave the stuff to an accountant and signed the papers. So I thought if this would save money then I should do it. And I did."

She paused to take a long sip of water.

"Well, one day, we were having an argument. I don't even remember how it started. But I remember that he accused me of paying too much attention to one of the dealers, the one who sold me the emerald rings. I denied it, of course, and he slapped me. Right across the face. I was so stunned I didn't know what to do. Bernardo…"

"Your previous husband?"

"Yes. Bernardo might have had a mistress in every city in Italy, but he never hit me. That's about all I can say for him. I ran out the door and stayed with a friend for three days. Fabiano kept calling and asking me to forgive him and he sent me flowers, yellow roses, and of course I went back to him."

The waiter brought the soup and *panini*, said he hoped they'd enjoy them, and left. Victoria grabbed a spoon and began eating her soup.

"Well, this happened three times. Then I had enough. I knew I was going to apply for a divorce. After work one day I packed up a bunch of jewelry—rings, necklaces, watches—and sent them to my mother in New York. I just had a hunch that he might take them, and I thought they'd be safe with her. So I moved in with my friend. When I went back to the shop, the next day, I found the locks had been changed and I couldn't get in. And there was a big sign: 'Closed'."

"Oh, Victoria."

"Don't pity me, Lorenzo, You can guess what happened. The bastard took all the rest of the jewelry and left the country. Greece, I heard. A couple of years later, I heard that he sold the shop."

"You know, Victoria, there was a rumor that you had gone back to America, so my brother, who's a banker and has connections, had someone try to find you there. Obviously, they didn't find you, but they may have found your mother."

She gripped Father Lorenzo's arm. "My mother? My mother is still alive?"

"We're not sure. It seemed that she was. We really don't know any details. Except that a woman, probably the maid, said they'd received a box of jewelry from Italy but there wasn't any return address."

"I didn't have any address then but I wanted my mother to have those things. Well, I'm glad they got the jewelry."

They waited while the waiter refilled their water glasses.

"Did you stay in Rimini then?"

"No. I left. I knew a man who had a jewelry shop in Ferrara so I went there. After all, I had experience. Well, Rudolfo hired me and things were going all right for a while. He didn't pay well, but I managed. Then he accused me of taking two diamond necklaces because he couldn't find them. He fired me. I never did find out where the necklaces were.

"Well, I stayed in Ferrara for four more months but then the money ran out. I went to Venice, thinking that I could find a job there. I couldn't. I got desperate. I thought of going back to New York but I couldn't face my mother. She never wanted me to come to Italy in the first place."

She paused, and Father Lorenzo knew the next would be difficult.

"I went to Bologna," she said, "and met a guy who seemed sympathetic, and I moved in with him. Are you shocked, Lorenzo?"

"No."

"Disappointed?"

"Victoria, I would be the last person to judge what another person does."

She took a large bite of the *panino* and waited until she swallowed. "Mario was all right for a while but then he wanted me to do things that I wouldn't, couldn't do. I left. With hardly a *lira* to my name."

Briefly, her hands shook and Father Lorenzo held them. But she quickly gained control and put her hands in her lap.

"I won't tell you what happened in the next few years, Lorenzo. I lived in Modena and then Perugia. I was able to survive. But then I heard about this souvenir stand here that was for sale and I had a little money—just a little—so I bought it. I've been here for eight months. I've got a room over by Santa Maria dei Servi. In good weeks, I can pay the rent, in bad weeks, the landlady has to wait."

"Victoria, I can't believe that you've been through all this and you're still so…so strong."

"You don't know how scared I was sometimes. But yes, I've survived."

"And I can't believe that I've looked for you in Rimini and New York and you've been—what?—about six blocks from my palazzo."

"A coincidence, I guess."

"Victoria, my mother—you remember my mother?—is very ill and she would very much like to see you. The doctor says she doesn't have long."

"I'm so sorry. I always liked her. I found out about the palazzo where she lived and I thought of going over there several times, but I didn't want her to see me like this. She was always so good to me."

"And she says you were so good to her. That you were the only one who helped during that divorce mess. She says she wants to thank you."

"Me? Why would she want to thank me?"

"I don't know, Victoria. That's all she said."

They finished their *panini*. "I'm full," Vittoria said. "Thank you, Lorenzo."

She had her hands, worn and cracked, on the table. No jewelry except a small diamond on her engagement finger. The priest put his own hands on hers.

"Victoria, there's something I need to say. Many years have passed since we spent our few days together, and I've grown a lot older…"

"So have I, Lorenzo."

"…but I need to say that I am still attracted to you. You are a beautiful woman, inside and out. I'm a priest, but I still have feelings, even at my age, and if I gave myself a chance, I'd have more feelings about you. It's not possible. I wish it were."

She gripped his hands. "Thank you, Lorenzo. That's very kind."

"Victoria, how about if we went over to the palazzo now to see my mother?"

"I couldn't see her looking like this."

"I think Isabella, the maid, could help you freshen up, maybe even give you a dress to wear. She's about the same size."

Father Lorenzo left a generous tip and helped Victoria through the crowds and into the street. She squeezed his hand.

"If I haven't made it clear, Lorenzo, I'm very happy you found me."

"I am, too."

"I've thought about you a lot. I thought of you especially when I heard about that 'Monster of Florence' and all the people he was killing. I'm sure you were especially busy helping people at that time."

"We tried."

"Always the modest priest."

"We tried," he said again.

"And you've been all right?"

"Fine. I creak a little these days, but I'm sixty-one, you know."

"And I'm fifty-six. You know, Lorenzo, I thought I saw you earlier today in the Campo. There was a man dressed like you, but he had a silly cowboy hat on so I knew that it couldn't be you."

AFTER FIGHTING THE CROWDS, it was too late for Father Lorenzo and Victoria to see his mother when they arrived at Palazzo Murano. Isabella took charge of Victoria, drawing a bath and finding a nightgown. Victoria collapsed into the big soft bed in the guest room, and for the first time in years, slept through the night.

In his room, Father Lorenzo lay staring at the ceiling for a long time.

"This is a miracle, truly a miracle. How is it possible that I could find her just like that, in the Campo so close to here? It's not a coincidence. It's a miracle. No one, well, maybe a fiction writer, could make this up."

He folded his hands. "Thank you, God. I know you work miracles, some of them big, some of them small. This is a big one."

In the morning, he took Victoria to see his mother. She was barely conscious, but opened her eyes when she saw the woman at her bedside.

"Victoria?"

"Yes, Signora. I'm here."

"Come closer. Hold my hand."

Victoria sat on the edge of the bed.

"Lorenzo," his mother said, "I knew you would find her. You're a good son, Lorenzo. Now let us be."

The priest wiped tears from his eyes when he left the room. It was the nicest thing his mother had said to him since he was a boy.

Victoria didn't stay long in the room, and soon after Isabella came out to quietly announce, "She's gone."

That night, when Father Lorenzo and Giorgio and Victoria went through her papers in a drawer next to her bed, they were surprised to discover that Signora Renata Salvetti did not want her funeral in the Duomo, like Father Lorenzo's grandmother and uncle. Instead, she wanted the service in the Oratorio of Saint John the Baptist, the simple little church of the Eagle *contrada.*

"This is where they blessed the horse last week!" he told Giorgio. "I can't believe it."

She also ordered that the yellow Eagle scarf be tied around her neck.

"I never knew she even cared about the *contrada*," Giorgio said.

Under the papers they found a little book, a diary, that Signora Salvetti kept faithfully every day, just a sentence or two. Victoria began to read, skipping from one page to another.

Lorenzo was ordained today. I am so proud of him. He looks so handsome in his brown robes.

There has been a big flood in Florence and Lorenzo is helping so many people. He's a saint. I know it. He's a saint.

I wish Giorgio would pay more attention to his children. They are so beautiful.

Lorenzo called me today. That was the highlight of my day, no, my week, my month. Such a good boy.

Lorenzo told me how the people of Florence are so afraid of a killer there and he is trying to help them. This brought tears to my eyes.

Giorgio has become an important banker in Rome. I wish he would spend more time with his children, though.

I wish I could tell my sons how much I love them. Maybe it's because I was never loved by my parents so I can't express my emotions. So I drive myself with the feminist movement and pretend that my boys don't exist. I wish I could be different. I feel so bad sometimes.

There were many more entries, but Victoria put the book down. Father Lorenzo was sobbing.

"I wish she had told me all these things over the years," he said. "Things would have been so much different. I guess I never really knew her. I got so furious with her. Maybe I should have been more understanding. Maybe she just wanted us to love her more. She was really quite a remarkable woman."

"She did love you, Lorenzo."

"And I loved her. God, I wish things had been different."

"Well," Victoria said, "you got to see her a little at the end."

"It's kind of a miracle," Father Lorenzo said.

Borrowing vestments from the chapel, he said the funeral Mass alone. The only others in attendance were Giorgio and his wife and two children, Isabella, Victoria and Doctor Michetti. The simple casket was placed in the family vault in Misericordia Cemetery.

"Well, that's that," Giorgio said as the family drove back to the palazzo. "When will they read the will?"

"Giorgio," Father Lorenzo said, "could we leave a little time to think about our mother instead of what the inheritance is going to be?"

"Just want to take care of some bills, that's all," his brother said, pulling out his mobile telephone.

The reading of the will wasn't scheduled for two weeks. Father Lorenzo arranged to stay in Siena longer so that he and Isabella and Victoria could go through his mother's things. Her clothing and much of her furniture went to charity. Giorgio wanted to take her jewelry, but Isabella said they should wait to see what the will said about it.

Then there was the task of sorting out her office behind her bedroom. Signora Salvetti had been involved in feminist organizations and activities for decades and apparently kept every piece of paper she came across. There were file cabinets after file cabinets, all overflowing.

"This is incredible," Victoria said as she read the minutes of a meeting in which peaceful action was planned at a government office.

"Nobody is going to care about any of this in a few years," Giorgio said.

"You're wrong!" Victoria said in a pique of anger. "This is the history of the movement. People need to know. We have to save this."

She went back to sorting the papers.

The will was read in the dark and dank offices of a notary assigned to the task. A small man, he had trouble keeping his glasses on as he fiddled with the papers in front of him.

"Oh, here it is. Just a letter from Signora Salvetti. That's legal in Italy, you know."

He adjusted his glasses.

"Here's what it says.

"'To my dear maid and friend Isabella I bequeath one-twentieth of my estate and the invitation to remain in her apartment in Palazzo Murano for the rest of her days.'"

Isabella began to cry and Victoria put her arm around her.

"'To my beloved son Father Lorenzo I bequeath one-twentieth of my estate for the support of *cucina popolare* at the Church of Santa Croce in Florence.'"

"Oh, my, Mother, that's wonderful!" Father Lorenzo said. "Thank you!"

"'To my son Giorgio I bequeath one-fortieth of my estate and the requirement that he and his family find living quarters outside of Palazzo Murano within the next six months."

"Shit!" Giorgio yelled and stormed from the room.

"'To dear Victoria Stonehill I bequeath the remainder of my estate with the provision that she create a *Centro per gli Studi delle Donne*, a Center for Women's Studies, in Palazzo Murano. The Center will be a depository for information about the history of the women's movement in Italy and a place where women and men from throughout the world can understand and appreciate the efforts of valiant women who have fought for this cause. In addition, Victoria Stonehill is to have suitable accommodations in the palazzo.'"

Victoria gripped Father Lorenzo's arm. "Oh, Lorenzo, Lorenzo…"

"Don't say anything, Victoria. Just chalk it up as a miracle."

He stayed for three more days and then really had to get back to Florence. On the final afternoon, they sat on the floor of his mother's office, still sorting out minutes of meetings, receipts for travel, inaugural speeches, parliamentary proposals and so many other documents that described the history of a movement.

"You know, Lorenzo," Victoria said, "I keep thinking about those three days we spent in Rimini eighteen years ago..."

"I do, too."

"And I think they were the happiest days of my life. Really. You were so mysterious, and I found that so, well, interesting."

"You must have guessed that I was a priest before I told you."

"I suspected it, but I think I was trying to avoid thinking about it. I thought if you hadn't been a priest, then there might be a future for us, and I didn't want to think otherwise."

"I shouldn't have led you on. That was really cruel of me."

"No, not cruel. I think you were looking for something, too, and you thought maybe I was the answer."

He reached over to hold her hand. "You might have been, Victoria. If things had been different."

"Well, that's over with. We had our little adventure, didn't we?"

"Yes."

"It may have been a dream, but what I went through since then was a nightmare."

"I'm so sorry, Victoria. I wish I had known..."

"I've told you before, Lorenzo. Don't pity me. Things happened. I'm still here."

"You're a very strong woman, Victoria."

"I hope so." She looked around at the piles of papers, books and folders. "I'm going to need all the strength I have. But this is going to be good. I'm so happy I'll be able to do this."

After a tearful farewell and a promise to help in any way to set up the Center for Women's Studies, Father Lorenzo took the bus back to Florence the following morning. The bus wasn't as crowded this time, the celebrations for the Palio having mostly ended, and the priest found a seat near the front. He had just settled in when he heard his name.

"Hey, Lorenzo! Back here!"

He recognized the cowboy hat immediately.

"Come on back and sit with me!"

Father Lorenzo was pleased to see Matteo again, though he quickly tuned out the long accounts of his adventures after the race.

"But what about you?' Matteo said. "How's your mother?"

Matteo expressed his sympathy and listened to the abbreviated account of what the priest had been doing since the funeral.

"So now you're going back to Florence. Hey, are you in a church?"

"I'm at the Church of Santa Croce part time."

"Really? I love that church. All those tombs! Kind of eerie, you know, but they sure knew how to build tombs in those days, didn't they?"

"Yes."

"Part time? What else do you do?"

"I help out at the *cucina popolare*, the soup kitchen in connection with the church."

"Really? I've gone there a couple of times when I was, oh, between jobs."

"We're always glad to help anyone in need."

"It was great soup."

"We think so."

"You know, after I went there I was thinking that I should be a volunteer. Hey, I can ladle out soup just as well as anyone."

"I'm sure you can."

They were just approaching Florence when Matteo grabbed the priest's arm. "You know, I think I will."

"Will what?"

"Volunteer at the soup kitchen. Think they'd have me?"

"Of course they will!"

Father Lorenzo looked out at the approaching skyline of the city.

"Another miracle."

A Surprise on the Doorstep

Sant'Antonio

AFTER TWO WEEKS OF WORRYING, Amabilia finally decided to interrupt her husband. He was chuckling over another episode of *Casa Vianello* with, as usual, the aging Raimondo trying to read a newspaper and fighting with Sandra over a blanket in bed.

"Emilio," she said, "turn off that stupid program and listen to me."

"It's almost over."

She waited patiently until he clicked off the remote. They were still getting used to their new color television set, a gift for their fiftieth wedding anniversary from Signor Bernadetto Magnimassimo.

"Emilio, the Signor didn't finish his dinner again. Look."

She held out a plate that contained a half-eaten piece of chicken and a few Brussels sprouts.

"Maybe he didn't like it," Emilio said.

"He always likes my chicken. I know exactly how he wants it cooked and I always cook it the same way."

"And nobody likes Brussels sprouts except you."

"They're good for you."

"Amabilia, maybe he wasn't hungry."

"This isn't the first time. It happened Tuesday and last Friday and last Wednesday. I'm keeping track."

"Good Lord, Amabilia, let the poor man alone. If he doesn't want to eat, he doesn't want to eat. He's eighty-three years old. Let him do what he wants."

"Well, I know what's causing this."

"Of course you do."

"It was his fiftieth wedding anniversary two weeks ago."

"How do you know that?"

"Their wedding photo is on his dresser. I looked at the date on the back. He looks so happy in it. He must have been in his thirties. She looks barely twenty. And she's been gone now, oh, twenty-two years."

"Hasn't he gone through this before? On an anniversary?"

"It's worse this time. He just sits in that chair and stares at Stella's portrait. He doesn't even read books anymore, and he liked to read so much. He goes to bed early and doesn't get up early like he used to. And he doesn't sleep well. I know, because I hear him upstairs walking around his bedroom in the middle of the night, like he's pacing. Don't you hear him?"

"You know me, Amabilia, I could sleep through a train wreck."

Amabilia looked at the plate in her hands, sighed and rushed off to the kitchen. She tossed the leftover dinner into the trash and opened a drawer. On a calendar for 1994 she wrote in the space for May 22: "Didn't finish chicken or Brussels sprouts. Didn't want an orange for dessert."

"Well, I'm still going to make good meals for him. Holy Mary."

She and Emilio had worked for the Signor and his wife ever since they were newlyweds fifty years ago. She was to be the companion—the word "maid" wasn't to be used—for Stella, and Emilio was to be the chauffeur. Over the years and in many homes in many cities, their responsibilities changed. Amabilia now was the cook, baker and housekeeper, and Emilio was the driver, supervisor of the vineyards and sometimes a carpenter on the vast estate. People from the village contributed seasonal work.

Two weeks later, as they were sitting in their rocking chairs on the porch, Amabilia brought Emilio up to date.

"I looked at my calendar again today. The Signor hasn't finished his meals eight out of the last fourteen days, and sometimes he hardly eats anything."

"I don't know, Amabilia. Let's wait awhile longer and see if anything changes."

They waited a while. Two months later, nothing had changed, except for the worse. Amabilia wrote in her calendar almost every day. The Signor was now keeping to himself even more. He spent the days in his old blue chair in the living room, his nights in his bedroom. Amabilia noticed that the handkerchiefs he put in the laundry were wet.

Amabilia and Emilio tried to get him to go down to Sant'Antonio for the *passeggiata*. Before, the three of them always walked together in this evening ritual, chatting to the villagers as they walked around the new piazza. Now, the Signor said he was too tired.

"You go," he said.

"We don't want to go without you!" Amabilia said. They didn't.

One day, Stefano Frazzetti, the mayor, arrived just as Amabilia was finishing making a batch of biscotti.

"Here," Amabilia said, "fresh from the oven."

"I can never get enough of these," Stefano said. "They're wonderful. Here, I brought this newspaper article for Signor Magnimassimo to read. It's about Guido Cavalcanti. You know, the thirteenth-century poet the Signor likes so much."

Stefano found the old man in his chair in the living room.

"I thought you'd like to read this," Stefano said. "There's a new study about his work that's going to be published."

"How interesting. Could you put the article on the table there. I'll read it later."

Amabilia intercepted Stefano as he was leaving.

"Signor Frazzetti, I'm so worried. The Signor doesn't seem interested in anything anymore. Now not even your poet."

"I noticed that, too, the last times I was here. He's changed. Maybe he should see a doctor?"

She tried the next day.

"Signor," she said, "we've been thinking. We wonder if it's time for your checkup. It's been a couple of years, we think."

"No, no," Bernadetto Magnimassimo said. "I'm just fine. Don't worry about me. But thank you for your concern."

He closed his eyes.

"Emilio," Amabilia said when they returned to the kitchen, "let's go to Lucca and see Doctor Marino ourselves.

"All right, but I don't think his doctor will be able to tell us anything without examining the Signor."

"Well, he might be able to help us somehow."

DOCTOR CLAUDIO MARINO'S office was on the third floor of an eighteenth-century palazzo near the Basilica of San Frediano in Lucca. It still had the fresco of medieval warriors in the waiting room.

"Buongiorno." The doctor had met Amabilia and Emilio numerous times when they accompanied Bernadetto Magnimassimo for various checkups. The Signor had never had serious complaints.

Nervously, the couple described their worries about their employer, with Amabilia doing most of the talking. She told of how the Signor wasn't eating well, how he sat in his chair all day staring at the portrait of his wife, how he paced the floor at night, how he didn't want to participate in the *passeggiata* in Sant'Antonio, how he wasn't even interested in his favorite poet.

"I'm sure," she said, "this all started when he realized it was his fiftieth wedding anniversary."

When she had finished, Doctor Marino paged through Bernadetto's thick file and took notes. He took off his glasses and smoothed his white hair back.

"Well, you know I really shouldn't be talking to you about a patient. Privacy and confidentiality and all that, you know. But I see your concern and I have to say I'm concerned, too.

"Signor Magnimassimo has been my patient now for about fifteen years. He came to me soon after he bought that old monastery on the hill overlooking Sant'Antonio. I am very familiar with his medical history. When he first visited me he asked that all his records be transferred here. A few times I've had to contact his previous physicians for explanations.

"I do know a lot about his personal life, too, as I'm sure you do. I know that he made millions of dollars in the shipping industry and that he lived in various places in Italy."

"Yes," Amabilia said. "We were with him in Milan and Turin and Livorno...Where else, Emilio?"

"Rome for eight years," Emilio said. "Naples, too."

"And, of course, Capri," Amabilia said.

"Yes, all those places."

"He had a wonderful life," Doctor Marino continued, "but as you know, everything fell apart when his wife died. Stella was everything to him."

"And that's when we left Capri and moved here," Amabilia said.

"And when he came to see me. He came because he was having a problem with his arm, nothing serious, but when we talked I could see that he was very depressed. Extremely depressed."

"Yes, we knew that," Amabilia said.

"He tried to keep busy with all the work needed to convert the monastery into a sort of museum for his paintings. But when that was done, he got depressed again. He just needed something to do, something to keep him interested."

"I remember he didn't eat well then either," Amabilia said.

"And that's when that marvelous thing happened. The people of Sant'Antonio wanted to build a new piazza, and Signor Magnimassimo took charge. He paid for everything! Not that he couldn't afford it. He still had his millions. And then he built this wonderful little museum for his paintings in the piazza. It is a gem. I went on a tour there a few years ago. Even I could appreciate it."

"It's beautiful," Emilio said. "I know the Signor loves to visit it. Or at least did until recently. He hasn't been there in a long time."

"Well, that's why I'm telling you all this," Doctor Marino said. "When Signor Magnimassimo's wife died and he got depressed, he moved to Sant'Antonio and bought the monastery and kept busy restoring it. But when that work was finished he got depressed again. And then he had the piazza project so that kept him busy and he felt better. But now? What does he have? I'm not a psychiatrist, only a family doctor, but I firmly believe from what you've told me that without having something to interest him, he gets depressed. And it probably gets worse on his wedding anniversary."

"Can you help him?" Amabilia asked.

"I suppose I could prescribe some antidepressants, but sometimes they don't work and sometimes they have bad side effects."

"Can you give us a prescription for him?"

"No, he'd have to come in and I'd have to examine him first. I can't prescribe without seeing him."

"I don't think he'll come in," Emilio said.

"So there's nothing we can do?" Amabilia asked.

"Well, is there anything you can get him interested in? Anything?"

"He's not interested in poetry any more, and he doesn't look at his paintings."

"Except for the one of his wife," Emilio said.

"Does he watch television?"

"No. Hates it. So do I," Amabilia said. "And he doesn't read anymore."

They all thought for a while.

"Well, I just wonder," Doctor Marino said, "and this is just off the top of my head, but do you think he'd like a dog? A dog would be a nice companion, would sit with him, and dogs give a lot of affection. My wife and I have had one dog or another all the time we've been married. They have been such great companions."

"A dog!" Emilio said. "That's a great idea."

"I'm not so sure," Amabilia said. "He's never said anything about a dog. But I'll ask him."

That night, as Amabilia took away his half-eaten dinner, she broached the subject. "Signor, wouldn't it be nice to have a dog around here? Sometimes it gets a little lonely, don't you think? If we had a poodle or an Irish setter or a spaniel or…"

"A dog?"

"Yes, Signor, a dog. Wouldn't you like one? A dog would sit by your side when you're sitting in your chair and keep you company, and you could go outside and play catch with it. Give you a little exercise."

"Amabilia, Stella hated dogs, so we never had one. I can't imagine what I'd do with one. We had a cat for a while. Stella loved it. Little Franca. She'd sleep under the covers at the bottom of our bed."

"Under the covers, Signor?"

"Yes, under the covers. No, I don't want a dog. But thank you for thinking about it. Now I think I'll retire a little early tonight."

Amabilia retreated to the kitchen and she and Emilio didn't discuss the issue again for a long time. They just worried.

One night in November they were bundled up in extra sweaters in front of the fireplace because the villa's erratic heating system had gone out again. It was about 9:30 when they heard a car approaching.

"Good heavens," Amabilia said, "who could be coming here at this hour?"

Headlights from the car illuminated the room. The car screeched to a halt, and a door opened and then slammed shut. The car drove away.

"What the…?" Emilio asked.

"Maybe they left something, whoever they were."

"We'd better look."

At first when they opened the heavy wooden door they couldn't see anything different out in the darkness. Then they looked down at the doorstep. There was something white and furry and it was very angry.

"Me—ow—ow!"

EMILIO STRUGGLED to hold the cat in his arms but it kept squirming and fighting and finally sank its teeth into his arm. Fortunately, Emilio had two sweaters on over his shirt so the teeth didn't penetrate, but it did bite his hand. The cat leaped out of his arms and ran under a cupboard.

"Come back!" he cried.

"Oh, my," Amabilia said, "who could leave a cat on a doorstep on this cold night?"

"People are getting crazier every day."

"Emilio, your hand is bleeding. Put a bandage on it."

"It's nothing."

"It's something. Put a bandage on it."

Amabilia took a broom and tried to get the cat to come out. It only slunk back farther against the wall. Emilio poked. Amabilia prodded.

"He'll come out eventually," Emilio said. "When he's hungry."

They waited until 11:15, well past their bedtime, and then put a plate with bits of chicken and a bowl of milk next to the cupboard.

"See you in the morning," Emilio told the cupboard.

About 2:30 a.m., Emilio, who rarely woke during the night, thought he heard a noise. He slipped quietly out of bed and into the kitchen. Switching on the light, he was sure he saw a tail disappear under the cupboard. The plate and bowl were untouched.

"OK, I won't bother you again," he said.

In the morning, there were still no signs that the cat had eaten anything or, in fact, had emerged from its hiding place. Amabilia began making breakfast for the Signor while Emilio poured his morning coffee.

"Well," she said, "we can't let the Signor see the cat. This will only remind him of his wife and we don't want that."

"He'll never see the cat if it doesn't come out from under there."

At that moment, the cat did. It slinked out from under the cupboard and made a mad dash for the bench under the window. It leaped on the bench and began pawing the window.

"Oh, he wants to get out," Emilio said. "He wants to go home. It's all right, Kitty. We're here. We won't hurt you."

He began petting the cat, which returned the favor by howling and hissing. Now that they could see it, the cat turned out to be of mixed colors. Basically pure white, its thick fur had brown and black markings on its face, ears and head, brown spots on its back and side and a black tail.

"Isn't he beautiful, Amabilia? I've never seen such a beautiful cat."

"It's a cat, Emilio. It's a cat."

Emilio tried to pick up the cat, but it screeched and lunged at his arm.

"Ouch!" This time, Emilio didn't have sweaters on and blood soaked through his sleeve.

"No, no, Kitty. I won't hurt you."

He tried again to grab the cat, but it howled again and ran headlong toward a chair, jumped up on the stove and then on top of the refrigerator.

"Come down, come down," Emilio pleaded.

Every time Emilio tried to grab the cat, it batted him away.

"OK, come down when you're ready." Emilio went into the bathroom to bandage his arm.

Hoping that the cat would remain on the refrigerator, Amabilia went through the swinging door to the dining room to serve the Signor his breakfast. Naturally, the cat jumped off the refrigerator, ran through her legs and stopped in front of Bernadetto Magnimassimo's chair.

"What in the world? What's this, Amabilia?"

"I'm so sorry, Signor. I didn't mean to let it out of the kitchen."

The cat began circling the Signor's chair, alternating sniffing and hissing.

Amabilia described how the cat arrived on their doorstep the night before and how it had been acting so crazy since coming out of hiding. The Signor looked puzzled, not upset, just surprised.

"A cat in our house, Amabilia?"

"Yes, sir."

"Pretty cat. Stella's was all gray."

"We'll get rid of it, sir."

"She loved that cat."

"Emilio will get rid of it, sir."

The cat which had sat stolidly through this, now looked up plaintively at the Signor.

"Oh, it looks hungry. Has it eaten anything?"

"No, sir. We tried, but it wouldn't come out to eat."

Bernadetto Magnimassimo looked at his breakfast plate. "Sometimes I fed Stella's cat bits from the table. Maybe you'd like a little scrambled egg, Kitty?"

"Cats don't eat scrambled eggs, Signor."

"Of course they do. Stella's cat loved scrambled eggs."

He placed a spoonful on his red cloth napkin and placed it on the floor. The cat quickly nibbled it up.

"No, no, Signor. Please. Don't feed it from the table. Should I get a dish?"

"It's all right. It's fine."

He spooned more scrambled eggs onto the napkin on the floor. The cat was obviously very hungry.

When the cat had finished, there were no more scrambled eggs for the Signor. "It's all right. I'll just have this toast. I wasn't hungry anyway."

The cat wiped its mouth with its paws and dashed into the living room. It climbed on top of the sofa, leaped to the top of a bookcase and glared down at Amabilia and the Signor.

"I think the cat is possessed, sir," she said. "Maybe we should call the priest."

"I think it's just frightened. Let it be."

Amabilia cleared the breakfast dishes and scurried into the kitchen, looking behind her to see if she was being followed. She noticed that the

Signor went to his favorite chair, but instead of staring at the portrait of his wife, folded his arms and looked at the cat. The cat stared back at him.

"Who's going to blink first, Kitty?" he asked.

The cat won. And then it curled up on the top of the bookcase and went to sleep.

That afternoon, Amabilia told the Signor that they really couldn't keep the cat any longer. They should take it to the veterinary clinic in Lucca and they would find a home for it.

"Good idea, Amabilia," the Signor said. "Maybe tomorrow."

"Well," Emilio said, "if the cat is going to stay here overnight we'd better give him a place to poop."

Emilio found a wooden box in the basement, filled it partly with sand and put it in an empty alcove near the rear door. Wearing gloves, he pulled the cat down from the bookcase and put it into the box. "This is where you go, Kitty."

The cat immediately jumped out and ran away. Two hours later, however, there was evidence that the cat had used the box.

That night, no one knew where the cat slept. It just disappeared. But in the morning it was under Amabilia's feet again as she took the Signor's breakfast tray to him.

"Oh, Kitty, here for more?" he asked. The cat got more scrambled eggs on a napkin.

"Sir, when do you want Emilio and me to take the cat to the veterinary clinic?" Amabilia asked. "We could go right now."

"Hmm. It's awfully cloudy, isn't it? It looks like it's going to rain."

It didn't rain, but it threatened, and then it was late afternoon.

"Maybe tomorrow," the Signor said.

The cat again disappeared. In a place that had once been a monastery, there were plenty of rooms to hide in. The living quarters stretched into what had been the monks' cells, rows and rows of them. Bernadetto Magnimassimo spent some time looking for it under the sofa, the bed, the cupboards. Nowhere. He went into the monks' wing and looked in every little room. Nowhere.

"It'll turn up, I'm sure."

The next day, a bitter cold wind swept over the hilltop, rattling the windows. The frightened cat hid under the sofa all day.

"Maybe tomorrow," the Signor said.

The next day was sunny and bright. "All right," he said, "I suppose it should be taken in to see if they'll take it."

Emilio found a cardboard box and, wearing gloves again, pushed the cat inside. He tied the box with a strong rope. "OK, Kitty, we're going for a ride."

Amabilia and Emilio were surprised when the Signor appeared at the door with his coat and hat on.

"Of course I'm going," he said.

THE VETERINARY CLINIC in Lucca was in a storefront a few blocks from Doctor Marino's office. Emilio carried the box containing the cat, which was howling, followed by Amabilia and the Signor. They were surprised to find a large white cat with black ears sleeping on the receptionist's desk.

"That's Toby, our resident cat," she said. "He won't bother you. I'll call the doctor."

Emilio was sure he heard hissing coming from the box.

Doctor Diana Bennati was small with short blond hair and small thin hands. She wore a cross on her white uniform.

"Nice Kitty," she said, opening the box. "Now let's take a look at you."

The cat didn't protest and, in fact, purred a little as she lifted it out of the box, looked it over and placed it gently on the steel table. The cat looked interested but made no sounds as the doctor smoothed its fur.

"What a beautiful kitty," she said. "How long have you had her?"

"Her?" Emilio said. "I thought this was a boy kitty."

"No, she is certainly a girl kitty," the doctor said.

"You didn't look very closely," Amabilia told Emilio.

Amabilia explained to the doctor how the cat turned up on their doorstep and that they didn't know who owned it.

"We really can't keep it," she said. "It's really wild. I think it's possessed."

Doctor Bennati called in her three technicians. All of them gushed and agreed that this was one of the most beautiful cats they'd ever seen.

"So we can leave it here?" Amabilia asked.

"No, no," the doctor said. "We are a veterinary clinic, but we can't really accept cats or dogs. All of us have our own cats. I have three myself."

"So we have to keep it?" the Signor said. Amabilia glared at him.

"Looks like it," the doctor said. "Someone obviously didn't want it and thought it would have a good home with you. Certainly that's better than just abandoning it on a highway or something. We've seen that much too often, and often the cats don't survive."

"Who would leave a cat on a doorstep?" Amabilia asked.

"Sometimes," the doctor said, "there are more angels in this world than we know of."

"Angels," Amabilia muttered under her breath. "More like devils."

Signor Magnimassimo asked about the cat's condition and the doctor lifted it onto a scale.

"Eight pounds, four ounces. That's good."

"How old do you think she is?" the Signor asked.

"I would say three or four years. She's got a long life ahead of her."

Amabilia grimaced.

The doctor brought out her stethoscope. The cat didn't object.

"Her heart and lungs sound excellent."

She brought out a rectal thermometer. The cat endured the procedure without a whimper.

"Her temperature is just fine. And she's obviously been well cared for. Look, her nails have even been trimmed."

The doctor pressed her hands on the cat's back and belly and looked into its mouth. The cat began to squirm.

"Well, we have a problem. See the lesions at the gum line of these teeth? That's called tooth resorption, and it's very common in cats. I've seen estimates that thirty, forty, even fifty percent of cats develop this condition. What happens is this: Cells called odontoclasts gradually destroy the tooth, first the root, then the hard tissue below the enamel and then the center of the tooth."

The Signor shuddered. "Oh, that sounds horrible."

"It is, and often the cat doesn't complain until someone touches the tooth, as I just did."

"How many teeth are affected?" Emilio asked.

The doctor got out a magnifying glass and looked into the cat's mouth again.

"I see four."

"And what can be done?" the Signor asked.

"The only thing that can be done is extraction."

The Signor gripped the edge of the steel table. "You'd pull out four of her teeth? The poor kitty."

"I'm afraid if we don't do this, the resorption will spread to other teeth. Eventually, the cat won't be able to eat and, well, you know what would eventually happen."

Signor Magnimassimo's face turned ashen and his hands trembled. Amabilia put her arm around him.

"When…when can we have this done?" he asked.

"The receptionist can schedule this. I'd recommend this be done as soon as possible. The cat will be asleep so she won't know what's happening, but we'll have to keep her overnight."

"Overnight?" he said.

"We want to make sure she's all right before we release her."

The surgery was scheduled for the following Thursday morning. No one spoke on the way back, though the cat continued to protest loudly.

When they returned home, the Signor gently lifted the cat out of the box. The cat meowed loudly but didn't try to attack.

"I think," the Signor said, "as long as we're going to keep her, we should give her a name."

Amabilia was afraid that he would say 'Stella'."

"Well," the Signor said, "she's so beautiful, so there's only one name. Bella."

"Perfect!" Emilio said. Amabilia managed a thin smile.

Bella seemed more mellow after the trip and went to sleep on the pillow on the sofa. She ate some bits of chicken that Amabilia put in a dish near the sofa, washed her face and curled up again. At night, the Signor picked up his favorite book of poetry by Guido Cavalcanti and was reading quietly when he felt something at his side. Purring loudly, Bella nestled against his leg.

"Oh, Bella, you know something terrible is going to happen to you, don't you? Don't be afraid. I'll be right there. And when you come home I'll get you some special treats."

Bella purred contentedly, allowed him to pet her, and then abruptly turned, bit his hand and ran away.

"Ouch! Why did you do that? I guess you're mad that you have to have teeth out. Well, I would be, too."

All three took Bella in for the surgery the following Thursday. The Signor held her tightly and kissed her head before turning her over to the receptionist. He asked to be allowed to stay during the procedure, but Doctor Bennati said no. He could call later in the day. He did. At 3, at 4, at 5. Everything went well, the cat was sleeping in the recovery room and there was no need to worry. At 6, the office was closed. He called the next morning at 9 and at 10, and at 11 they were allowed to come and pick Bella up.

Instead of putting her in the box, the Signor held her all the way home. The cat was obviously still drugged and, probably because her mouth still hurt, she didn't want to eat anything.

"It's OK, Bella. You'll be fine. Tonight you can sleep with me."

IT WAS A BIG BED, and the Signor took up only half of it, but somehow Bella demanded more space and he almost fell onto the floor. He kept putting her back on a little blanket at the corner of the bed, but she wanted to cuddle.

"OK, OK, you can stay here." She stretched from his armpit to his thigh, and it took a while before he went back to sleep.

In the morning, he felt a heavy weight on his chest and opened his eyes to see a furry face almost in his. Bella seemed more curious than anything, and began to knead his neck and chest.

"We've got to get those nails clipped more."

Bella proceeded to jump off the bed, onto the dresser top and over the window ledge, and then landed with a thump back on the bed.

"Bella, it's only 5:45. It's too early to play. But I suppose you want to get up."

Bella followed him into the bathroom, sat on the toilet seat and watched while he shaved and showered. She jumped on the bed and sat on his shirt when he tried to get dressed and played with his shoelaces when he tied them.

"You are so frisky! I've never seen a cat like you."

At breakfast, Amabilia brought in a small extra dish and placed it next to the Signor's chair before huffing away. She also brought extra scrambled eggs.

"Well," Bernadetto Magnimassimo said when he had finished his coffee and they had both eaten their scrambled eggs, "what shall we do today?"

But Bella was nowhere to be seen. She had again disappeared for the day.

Amabilia was surprised when she heard music coming from the living room in midmorning.

"My God, Emilio. He's playing the Victrola. *Madama Butterfly.* He hasn't played records in years."

"I've always loved Rossini."

"Puccini, Emilio, Puccini."

"Maybe we can get him to go to an opera in Lucca sometime."

When Bella emerged in the kitchen in the afternoon—out of nowhere; she was just suddenly there—Amabilia filled her bowl next to the refrigerator with more bits of chicken.

"You've got to have protein if you want to get big and strong," she said.

Emilio howled. "Amabilia, are you talking to the cat? Are you talking to the cat like it's a little girl?"

"No, no, I wasn't."

"Yes, you were! I heard you. You're starting to love Bella, aren't you?

"She's just a cat. That's all. Just a cat." Amabilia started to clean out the refrigerator. "Well, the Signor seems to like her a lot, and that's the important thing."

The Signor at that moment was tying little pieces of paper on a long string. When Bella had finished eating and had wiped her face with her paws, he stretched the string on the floor and started pulling one end. She grabbed the other. He started walking toward the monks' wing. She bounded after him. He started to run. She followed. All the way down to the end and then back again.

"Come on, Bella! Come on!"

When they returned to the living room, he collapsed in his chair. "You wore me out, Bella."

Amabilia, who had been watching the scene, was alarmed. "Sir, are you all right? That's too much for you. Rest for a while. Would you like a glass of water?"

"I'm fine, Amabilia. Just let me catch my breath."

Bella sat at his feet, apparently waiting to play some more.

"In a few minutes, Bella. Let an old man rest for a while."

Rebuffed, Bella found a swath of sunlight on the plush carpet, curled up and went to sleep.

"Isn't she cute, Amabilia? Look at the way she puts her paws over her eyes. She doesn't want to hear us."

"Yes, sir, she's very cute."

The next day, Bella again helped Bernadetto Magnimassimo shave, shower, get dressed and have breakfast. He then spent an hour with Guido Cavalcanti, enjoying each poem as if he'd read it for the first time. Bella slept at his side in the chair, and he thought he'd probably have to get a new one so that they both could fit.

After lunch he told Emilio: "Let's go to Pisa. I want to go to the pet store there."

"All the way to Pisa, sir?"

"I don't think there's one in Lucca. Is that OK?"

"Of course, sir."

Amabilia decided to go along, "just to see what they have." She and Emilio had never been in a pet store. Neither had Signor Magnimassimo, and he was acting like a little kid going to his first toy store.

"I wonder what they'll have. I bet things we haven't even thought of," he said as they went out the door. "Good-bye, Bella! We'll be back soon."

Because parking is always impossible in Pisa they had to walk eight blocks to the address the Signor had found in the telephone book. He led the way, walking so fast that Amabilia and Emilio had trouble keeping up.

The store turned out to be overwhelming. Rows and rows of food supplies, toys, beds, aquariums, bird feeders, clothing and more. Many of the aisles were for dogs, but there were also sections for birds, fish and even rabbits and ferrets.

"Oh, my," Amabilia said.

"Let's find the cat supplies," the Signor said.

Confronted by shelf after shelf of cat food, litter and toys, they realized they needed help, and a young woman in a green apron was eager to answer questions.

"Tell me about your cat," she said.

"She's beautiful," the Signor said. "She's mostly white but has some brown and black…"

"I'm sure she is, but how old is she?"

Told that Bella was three or four and weighed eight pounds, four ounces, the clerk suggested cans of regular cat food.

"She can't just eat scraps?" Amabilia said.

"In order to get the proper vitamins and minerals, it's best if cats have a balanced diet, and we've been very pleased with this manufacturer."

The Signor put two cases in the shopping cart.

"Now this is what we recommend for litter," the clerk said, lifting a twenty-five pound bag off the shelf as if it were a candy bar.

"I thought we'd just use sand," Emilio said. "We have lots of sand."

"It's best," the clerk said, "if cats can use something that will absorb their output."

"Output?" Emilio said. "I guess you could call it that."

The Signor put three bags of litter into the cart, which was now almost filled.

"What about toys?" he said. "I want to get her some toys."

The array was mystifying. Little plush mice with catnip, soft balls and hard balls, feathers on strings, plastic butterflies on wires, an infinite range of scratching pads and posts. The Signor dashed from shelf to shelf and soon the shopping cart was filled to overflowing. Emilio carried a four-foot scratching post and Amabilia struggled with a big plastic game with rolling balls.

On the way to checkout, they passed a row of little sweaters.

"They're for dogs," the clerk said.

"Can't they be for a cat?" the Signor asked.

"Well, I suppose so."

"Bella would look good in that beige one. With the little red ribbon. We'll take it."

Then they passed the display of dog leashes.

"Don't you have leashes for cats?"

"I'm afraid cats don't like to be on leashes. They're not obedient like dogs. They like to run around on their own."

"But they could be trained," the Signor said, "couldn't they?"

"I suppose so."

The Signor held a large cat carrier on his lap on the way home, where they were greeted by a very talkative cat who seemed upset that she had been left alone. The Signor, Amabilia and Emilio spread their purchases all over the living room floor, and Bella went crazy. She sniffed a catnip mouse and hit a plastic ball across the room. She tossed a feather into the air and sharpened her nails on the scratching pole. Then she found a piece of tissue paper that one of the toys had been wrapped in. She pounced on it again and again. She carried it in her teeth across the room and attacked it again. When it began to tear, she threw it into the air.

"She's having more fun with that piece of tissue paper than with all the toys you bought," Amabilia said. "And you spent thousands and thousands of *lire.*"

"As long as she's happy," the Signor said, with only a trace of disappointment in his voice.

At 8 o'clock that night, Bernadetto Magnimassimo came out of his room wearing his overcoat and a big furry hat and carrying Bella.

"Let's go down to the village for the *passeggiata.* I want to see the Christmas decorations."

Pleased, because they hadn't walked the *passeggiata* for months, Amabilia and Emilio put on their coats.

"Where do you want to leave Bella?" she asked.

"Well, she's coming with us. And Emilio, bring her leash."

The villagers had never seen such a sight. Tall, distinguished-looking Bernadetto Magnimassimo, eighty-three years old in his furry hat and long black coat, flanked by Amabilia and Emilio and being pulled around the piazza by a fluffy white cat wearing a beige sweater with a red ribbon.

A Monster Threatens

Sant'Antonio

IF HE HADN'T SLOWED DOWN when Marianna dropped her doll in the backseat, and if he hadn't braked to avoid a passing car, and if he had looked to the right instead of the left, then Mario would never have seen the sign.

And if he hadn't seen the sign maybe he could have just gone on living the way he always had for years, without a major worry in the world.

Thank goodness, he thought, at least Anita hadn't seen it. At least not yet. Or had she? He tried to find out.

"Anita," he asked when they were cleaning up after dinner that night, "did you notice anything different when you drove past Reboli to Lucca the other day?"

"Different? Not really. But I was paying so much attention to this driver ahead of me that I didn't look anywhere else. Honestly, Mario, he was swerving all over the place and then he'd go fast and then he'd go slow. I tried to go around him but I couldn't because all these other cars were in the way. Anyway, why do you ask?"

"Oh, nothing. Just wondering."

"And then there was this other guy right beside me for almost all the way. He kept switching lanes, too. I was gripping the wheel so hard my knuckles turned white. You men really should learn how to drive on the highways, Mario. It's dangerous. Women are much better drivers, you know. It's a proven fact."

"Yes, yes."

He didn't hear any more of his wife's lecture. "I think I'll read a story to Marianna before she goes to bed."

Early in the morning two days later, he drove the route from Sant'Antonio toward Reboli again. "Maybe I was seeing things."

He drove so slowly that cars behind him started braking, and more than one rear-ended another. One almost ran off the highway. As they passed his Fiat Panda, the other drivers blared their horns and shoved their arms out of the windows, clearly holding fingers to the air.

"What the hell are you doing?" one asked. "Learn how to drive!" yelled another. "Get off the highway!" a third screamed. This was from a woman with a small child in a seat harness next to her.

Mario ignored them. He knew he was approaching the place. He closed his eyes. "Please God, say that I was imagining it."

But there it was. Off the highway and at the entrance to Reboli, the big bright yellow sign glowed in the sunlight, its letters almost bigger than a man.

Coming Soon!
SUPERMARKET!

Mario felt beads of sweat forming on his forehead, his stomach started to churn and his hands clutched the steering wheel even tighter. He found the next exit, turned around and returned to Sant'Antonio without so much as another glance at the sign. He was already late in opening his *bottega* and he knew Signora Cardineli would be waiting as usual outside, not patiently.

"I thought you'd never get here," the old woman said as he unlocked the door. "I knew I forgot something yesterday. Milk. Milk for Alessia. She's been bothering me ever since I got up. She wants her milk, that's what she says, and she wants it now."

Mario fetched a half-pint of milk from the cooler. "Signora, why don't you get a pint or even a quart? Then you wouldn't run out for your cat."

"A bigger bottle? I can't afford that! I'm just an old widow, you know. And besides, it would spoil. Alessia eats only a little at a time."

"I was only trying to make a suggestion, Signora."

"Well, I don't need your suggestions! Keep them to yourself!"

Without even paying, she tucked the milk carton under her arm and stalked out the door.

"Good grief," Mario thought, "now I'm getting my good customers mad at me. I sure can't afford that. Not now."

Mario Leoni had taken over the *bottega* almost twenty years ago when his grandfather, the venerable Nino Leoni, died suddenly after a heart attack. Mario's father had been killed in the war and although Mario had graduated from the University of Pisa and would have liked a career as an engineer, he dutifully assumed the family responsibility.

He didn't mind that much. It put him closer to Anita Manconi, who had taken over the nearby butcher shop that had been owned by her grouchy late father, Guido. Mario and Anita had grown up together, had gone to school together in Reboli and had kept in touch when he was away at the university.

With the entire village watching carefully, Mario and Anita entered into a prolonged courtship, followed by marriage, followed ten years ago by the birth of little Marianna. She was the first child born in Sant'Antonio in thirty-five years and therefore immediately adopted by every villager.

Women found they had to visit the *bottega* and the butcher shop more frequently, hoping to see the child at one place or the other. Everyone in fact, spoiled her with candy and treats.

Anyway, there wasn't anywhere else in the village but Mario's *bottega* to shop for groceries, sundries, small gifts, wine and liquor, and, of course, lottery tickets. Across the new piazza, which had become so very popular in just a few years, Anita's shop not only provided steaks, pork chops, sausages, and chicken livers and breasts, but also rabbits, pheasants and wild boar.

"I'll tell you," Lucia Sporenza invariably told her husband after every shopping excursion, "Sant'Antonio is lucky to have two shops like Leoni's and Manconi's. Some other villages might have one shop or the other, but no village has two places like that. You can find everything."

"We're lucky to have Mario and Anita," Paolo would say. "They're such good kids."

No matter that both of them were almost forty years old.

Lucia recalled the time when she wanted to buy a box of Gianduirotto chocolates, the kind she had seen in a magazine, to give to her friends

Donna and Ezio for Christmas. Mario had only the more popular Perugina and Ferrero, but he offered to try to get what Lucia wanted.

"Can you imagine? He called Turin and they sent him a box right away, in plenty of time for Christmas."

That got Paolo to remember the time he made *pappardelle* with wild boar ragu from meat that Anita had carefully cubed. "That was eight years ago and I can still taste it," he said.

Ask anyone in Sant'Antonio and the verdict was unanimous. Leoni's *bottega* and Manconi's butcher shop had the finest supplies and the most careful and attentive service of any place for miles around. It would be unthinkable if the village were to lose these valuable assets.

"I wonder how long we'll be able to do this," Mario wondered as he locked the door to his shop on the day of his encounter with Signora Cardineli. "I'll have to tell Anita tonight. She needs to know."

MARIO WAITED UNTIL AFTER Marianna had gone through her nightly ritual. First he helped her with her homework, which was becoming more and more difficult for him to do. What kind of math were they teaching these days? Then a half hour of cartoons on television. Then fifteen minutes to let her lead Romeo up and down the stairs with a string. Then a half hour getting into her pajamas and washing her face and brushing her teeth. Then fifteen minutes of a bedtime story and making sure Romeo was nestled at her feet, purring as usual.

"Is it me, or do you think the older she gets the longer it takes her to go to bed?" Mario asked as he collapsed into his chair near the television set.

"She's learned that she can manipulate her father," Anita said. "She's got you wrapped around her little finger. And you know you love it."

"I still wish I had more time to read the paper at night."

He picked up *La gazzetta di Lucca* and glanced at the headlines on the first page, then turned to the second and third, all the while keeping an eye on Anita as she put away her apron and sat down to pick up the latest *TV Sorrisi e Canzoni.* She quickly threw it down.

"There's nothing good on television anymore," she said. "I don't know why we even get this guide. Sometimes I don't know why we even have a television set."

Mario nodded and pretended to be reading the latest soccer news. "Marianna would be very upset if we didn't."

"Mario," his wife said. "I've been meaning to talk to you about something."

"Oh, oh."

"Now just wait and hear me out. You know how we've had that cooler in the shop for at least twenty years?"

"It's not that old."

"Yes it is. I remember when Papa bought it. It's at least that old."

"But still good, right?"

"Well, not really. Yesterday, I brought out some pork chops for Signora Mandolini and I could swear they were going soft. I didn't say anything. I just went back in and found some on the bottom that were still hard. But then I threw the other ones out."

"Good pork chops?"

"Not good, Mario. Soft. I couldn't sell them, not like that."

"Did you have the temperature low enough?"

"Same as I always do. And then today I noticed that part of that wild boar we got from Santo Scarpelli was smelling bad."

"Wild boar always smells bad."

"Not like this. Mario, I think we need a new cooler. I know it's expensive, but we can't be selling customers bad meat."

"Couldn't we have it fixed? Didn't we just have the Franconi Brothers out from Lucca?"

"That was five months ago. Mario, it's twenty-five years old. These things wear out. Better we get a new one now rather than wait until something bad happens."

Mario put *La gazzetta di Lucca* down and stared at the blank television screen.

"I don't know, Anita."

"We can get a loan. We paid off the last one in plenty of time. The bank will give us one."

"I know."

"We really have to do it, Mario."

"I know. It's just...well, I just wonder if we should be investing a lot of money into the shop at this time."

"At this time? What's happening at this time?"

Mario walked to the window. The *passeggiata* had pretty much ended for the evening, with only Donna and Ezio making a final walk around the piazza. With Marianna needing so much attention, it had been days since Mario and Anita had joined the other villagers in the nightly custom.

"Mario?"

He turned around. "Anita, remember the other day when I asked you if you had noticed anything different around Reboli when you drove to Lucca?"

"Sure. And I said I didn't, except for all those lousy men drivers. What was I supposed to see?"

"You didn't see the sign?"

"I saw some signs. I don't remember any of them. I don't know why people put those signs up on that busy highway. Either nobody is looking at them or people look and get into accidents."

"There was a new one the other day. Just outside Reboli but you could see it from the highway."

"For what?"

Mario's voice was so soft he could barely hear it himself. "It said a supermarket was coming soon."

"A supermarket! Oh, Mario!"

Of all the words that had entered the Italian vocabulary in the last two decades, none was more famous—or infamous—than "supermarket." Begun by the industrial and financial group Montedison in the town of Castellanza in the Lombardi region, the supermarkets had spread quickly across Italy, especially in the North. Many were cooperatives, others were privately owned.

Ranging from 2,500 to 32,000 square feet, the stores could carry not only food but also such consumer goods as kitchen supplies.

For shoppers, these huge supermarkets offered cheaper prices on just about anything. For shop owners, they tolled death knells. Like everyone else, Mario and Anita had heard horror story after horror story of little shops being devoured by the big enterprises. Customers who had been faithful for years quickly abandoned the little shops if they could get a pint of milk for twenty *lire* cheaper. The centuries-old traditions of going to one little shop after another to purchase individual items was swiftly becoming as quaint as the kindly old Christmas witch *La Befana.*

"Oh, Mario!" Anita said again.

"I know."

"Did it say when it would open?"

"Just soon."

"We've got to do something."

"What? What can we do, Anita? We can't stop them from opening."

"I don't know. There must be something."

Anita and Mario had not been this afraid since Anita was pregnant with Marianna. Anita kept having pains. They went to the doctor. The doctor said everything was fine. She kept having pains. The doctor sent her to a hospital in Florence that had new ultrasound equipment. Anita and Mario could watch the odd movements on the screen that the doctor declared was their baby.

It was a girl.

Perfectly healthy.

They both cried.

Now they were almost in tears again.

"What if we lose all our customers to the supermarket, Mario? What will we do?"

"We won't."

"How do we know that?"

Both of them knew that they didn't know.

"Let's just wait," Mario said, "and see what our customers have to say."

THE TROUBLE WAS, the customers weren't saying anything. Not a word.

Maybe, Mario thought, the sign had been taken down and he and Anita had worried for nothing. But a quick trip to Lucca found the sign still glowing menacingly at Reboli.

He tried to get his customers to acknowledge it.

"Say, Signora Marina," he asked one of his regulars, "have you driven to Lucca lately?"

"Oh, yes, maybe every other day. Marco is always forgetting to get something so I have to go."

"It's a nice highway. There's a lot to see."

"It's OK. I just drive, I don't look."

Signora Marina seemed inordinately interested in the package of sunflower seeds she was holding.

"Well, I have to go now." She plunked some change on the counter and rushed out the door.

An hour later, Mario attempted to broach the subject with Signor Michellini. He knew that the electrician worked for a shop in Reboli and that it would be impossible for him not to see the sign.

"You must get tired driving all that way every day, Sergio," Mario said. "It must get boring."

"Oh, I keep the radio on. There's a station that plays American country songs. Vince Gill, Kenny Chesney. Great singers. Sometimes, you know, I sing along. Or try to."

"I suppose you look around at the scenery, too."

"Not so much."

"I always look at the billboards when I drive to Reboli. Some new ones keep cropping up."

"Yes, well, I don't pay much attention. Oh, look at the time. Good to talk to you, Mario. Got to go. Angela will be wondering why I'm taking so long. I'll look for those spices next time."

The door closed quickly behind him.

That night, Mario told Anita the obvious.

"People know, Anita. They know. They just don't want to talk about it to us."

"I guess they're afraid they'll hurt our feelings. They know what's going to happen."

"They're going to hurt our feelings a lot more when they don't come in our shops and go to that fuckin' supermarket instead."

"Mario! You never talk like that!"

"Sometimes, Anita, I need to talk like that."

For the next hour they tried to figure out who might possibly continue to be faithful customers even if they could pay less at the supermarket. They even made lists.

"Donna and Ezio. Lucia and Paolo," Anita said.

"They're our friends. I don't think they count."

"No one else?"

They thought. The names on the list of possible defectors grew so long they needed another piece of paper. Almost everyone in Sant'Antonio was on it. Signora Miniotti and Signora Bruni and Signorina Cesi and…so many others.

"What about," Mario said, "Serafina Marincola and Salvo? Little Pasquale comes in here every day to buy ten *lire* of candy."

"I can see why they'd want to shop there and save a little money," Anita said, "but they'd have to spend money on gas so maybe they wouldn't save much in the long run. Maybe we should have another list, those of 'possibles.' Mario, surely there are others who won't go to the supermarket."

"Well, there's always Signora Cardineli," he said. "She's so old and she doesn't drive anymore. She probably won't even know there is such a store."

They went through other names. Even though both shops had been fixtures in Sant'Antonio for almost a hundred years, the fact remained that they were still business establishments. People came to buy things they needed. They may have liked Mario and Anita, and they loved little Marianna, but money was money, and no one had enough.

Since all they knew about the impending disaster was a billboard on the highway, Mario and Anita decided they had to find out more. The logical source was Stefano Frazzetta. As mayor of the comune, he would have access to, or at least know where to find, the official documents that the supermarket chain must have filed in order to build its abomination.

Stefano said he would find out. Three days later, he came to Mario and Anita's home just after Marianna was down for the night.

The first thing he found out, Stefano said, was something he already suspected. The supermarket would not be in the Comune of Sant'Antonio but in the neighboring Comune of Sant'Anna. He had gone to the comune's offices and talked to the mayor.

"They've already bought the property. It's about forty acres just west of Reboli."

"So close to here," Mario said. "And forty acres! What the hell are they planning to build? A soccer stadium?"

"Apparently it's for parking."

"Sure," Anita said, "for the thousands of cars that will be coming from all over."

"And how are the cars going to get there?" Mario asked. "Fly?"

"They're planning," Stefano said, "to build access highways."

"Good God," Anita said. "They must have tons of money."

"What about the building?" Mario asked. "How big will that be?"

Stefano studied his notes. "Looks like about 7,500 square feet."

"My God!" Anita grabbed Mario's hands. "We don't have a chance. How can we compete with something like that?"

Stefano looked very grim. "I'm very sorry. Really. I've heard about these things, what can happen to places like yours."

Mario began pacing the floor of the kitchen, linoleum that badly needed replacing. "When are they planning this?"

"In about six months. That would be March or April next year."

"Well," Mario said, "they can't just do this, can they? They have to get permission, right?"

"Right," Stefano said. "They have the land but they can't build until they have a permit from the comune. They've applied for one. But here's the problem. Our comune doesn't have a voice in the matter. As I said, the supermarket would be in the Comune of Sant'Anna, so it's up to them whether to approve it or not."

"So what do we have to say about it? It's right next door!"

"We don't have a say."

"Nothing?"

"Well, I suppose someone could go to the hearing."

"There's a hearing?"

"A week from Thursday," Stefano said. "They didn't announce it, but Donato, the mayor over there, happened to mention it."

"Happened to?"

"I think there's something very strange about this," Stefano said. "First Donato didn't want to show me any of the applications. Said they were private. I said 'Private? These are public records.' So then he showed them to me, but very reluctantly. And the fact of the hearing just slipped out. I just wonder…"

"What?" Anita asked.

"I just wonder if the mayor and the commissioners are going to profit from this. A little money under the table? It wouldn't be the first time."

"This is such a load of crap!" Mario shouted.

Anita tried to calm her husband.

"Mario, let's just wait and see about that. Let's round up everyone we know and go to the hearing and tell them we don't want this store built."

"And what would your argument be?" Stefano asked.

"That...that...that this big conglomerate will drive little businesses out of, well, business. That the little shops have been important parts of the community for decades, even centuries. That the owners live here and are their neighbors. And little shopkeepers have to be protected. Isn't that enough?"

"I'm afraid it's not that simple," Stefano said.

"Why not?"

"Only people from that comune would be permitted to talk. You wouldn't be able to."

"You mean...you mean...," Mario shouted, "that even though we're only ten miles from this damn thing we don't have a voice on whether it will be built and we can't even say anything at the hearing? That's bullshit!"

"Mario!"

"I'm afraid," Stefano said, "that's the law."

"Fuck the law!"

BY MORNING, Mario had cooled down enough so that he was able to call Donna and Ezio and Lucia and Paolo and ask them to come over and talk about what had happened. And what was likely going to happen.

They sat around the little white tables in the back room of Leoni's, a place where generations of elderly men had played *briscola* and *scopa,* and listened grim-faced as Mario and Anita told them the story. Each of them had seen the billboard and all were, as Mario and Anita had assumed, afraid to ask about it. They knew all too well what fate was in store for Sant'Antonio's only two shops.

"I can't believe this," Paolo said.

"This is terrible. I don't know what to say." For once, Lucia was at a loss for words.

"What interests me," Ezio said, "is the way they're keeping this secret. The hearing is supposed to be in less than two weeks and nobody knows about it. I thought they were supposed to announce these things. Put up notices, send out letters. Even put a notice in the newspaper. Nobody knows anything about this except for that billboard. There's something very suspicious going on. You know what? I've never trusted those people running that comune. We had so much trouble with them when I was the principal there."

"We've got to do something!" Anita cried.

"What?" Paolo asked.

Mario poured more coffee.

"Well," Ezio said, "the best thing is to bring this out into the open. Let people know."

"And how," Donna asked, "would you do that?"

It didn't take Ezio long to come up with an answer.

"Giacomo! Giacomo Arigoni! Dino's friend."

Now about forty-five years old, Giacomo Arigoni had become so well known as an investigative reporter that he didn't write only for his own paper, *La Repubblica,* but also sold his work to other newspapers. He had exposed everything from Vatican intrigue to presidential political scheming. More than six feet tall and weighing almost three hundred pounds, he easily intimidated any reluctant source.

"Remember," Ezio said, "when Sant'Antonio was trying to raise money for the piazza and this guy came from Florence and tried to con us into letting him open a pizza place here?"

"And Dino," Lucia said, "contacted Giacomo and Giacomo knew that this guy was a mobster who was trying to use the pizza place as a front."

"So that was the end of that plan," Paolo said.

"I'm sure," Ezio said, "Giacomo would be interested in the story about a giant supermarket threatening small businesses. He could write it for *La gazzetta di Lucca*. Everybody around here reads that."

The next day, Ezio called Dino who called Giacomo who then called Mario. On Saturday morning, the journalist, smoking one Toscano cigar after another, sat across from Anita and Mario, who held Marianna on his lap. On his big feet he wore an improbable pair of red running shoes. He took out a small notebook and a tiny camera. Like any good journalist, Giacomo asked a lot of questions, but he took surprisingly few notes. He snapped a couple of photographs, thanked them and left.

"I hope he understood what this is about," Mario said. "He seemed more interested in us than in the supermarket."

"I'm sure he knows all about that," Anita said. "He probably doesn't have to take notes."

"But there isn't much time. Maybe they won't get it in the paper in time."

"Let's not worry, Mario. It's out of our hands."

There was nothing in Sunday's paper, but they realized it would have been too soon for Giacomo to write the story and for the paper to publish it. On Monday, Mario dashed to the little newsstand that was now in a corner of the new piazza.

"Oh, my God!"

The photograph occupied a good two-thirds of the front page. Anita was standing behind Mario who held Marianna who held Romeo the cat. Marianna looked as if she'd been crying.

Above the photo in large letters: "Giant Supermarket Threatens to Close Little Shops!"

"Well," Mario said, "I guess that gets right to the point. But why does Marianna look like she's crying?"

"Because," Anita said, "Romeo had just scratched her. Let's read the article."

Mario spread it out on the kitchen table.

Today there is much sadness in the quiet little village of Sant'Antonio. You may not have heard of this village, just west of Reboli, because it doesn't advertise itself very much. Many know it, however, because of its fine new piazza and its museum dedicated to the works of Sienese artists.

But today we must pay attention. For more than a hundred years there have been two shops, and only two shops, in this village dedicated to Italy's beloved saint. There's Leoni's, a splendid bottega *that was owned for many years by Nino Leoni and is now operated by his grandson Mario. And there's Manconi's, once owned by Guido Manconi but now by his daughter Anita.*

And here's the lovely part. Mario and Anita were childhood sweethearts. Of course, they lived just across the piazza, so why wouldn't they fall in love? And they married, and now they have a beautiful little girl, Marianna, who is ten years old.

A story with a happy ending, right?

Perhaps not.

Last month, a big billboard appeared on the highway from Sant'Antonio to Lucca. In giant letters, it said: "Coming Soon! SUPERMARKET!"

A supermarket! Can you believe this? We all know what happens when a giant supermarket opens. People look for bargains, for cheaper prices, and so they rush to these big stores without thinking of the consequences.

This giant supermarket will certainly threaten little shops like Leoni's and Manconi's, put them out of business forever with one quick blow.

We heard about all this, so we sat down with Mario and Anita and little Marianna the other day. Marianna was crying. Well, of course she was. She knew what was going to happen. She knew her Mama and Papa were unhappy. She didn't care about herself. Little Marianna never cares about herself. She just wants her Mama and Papa to be happy.

She showed us a drawing she had made of her cute little cat. His name is Romeo. The drawing was so good we think it could hang in the Sienese museum of art.

But if things happen as they are likely to happen, Marianna's Mama and Papa will be forced to close their shops. They may even have to move away, maybe to some big city where they will be very unhappy. Little Marianna will be unhappy. Maybe even Romeo will be unhappy.

Is there hope for Leoni's and Manconi's? Perhaps. On Thursday, 12 October, a hearing will be held at the Comune of Sant'Anna. The question will be whether this supermarket can be built on the land it has already purchased.

Unfortunately, people who do not live in the Comune of Sant'Anna will not be allowed to speak. Mario and Anita and Marianna live in the neighboring comune, Sant'Antonio. So they cannot speak at the hearing.

But other people can show up and make their presence and their opinions known.

Perhaps they will say they don't want the big supermarket to suffocate two little shops.

"I couldn't have said it better myself," Mario said as he folded the paper.

"It's good," Anita said, "but I wish they hadn't made it such a sob story. And I don't like it that there's so much about poor little Marianna and that her big picture is there."

"That's what newspapers do," Mario said. "They like to pull all the chains. But now everyone here will know what's going on and they'll go to the hearing. They may sit silently but they'll make their presence known, and that will be the end of that supermarket."

Naturally, *La gazzetta di Lucca* was soon spread and read all over Sant'Antonio. Out on the piazza, Signora Della Franca and Signora Marina whispered so loudly that even old Giovanni Bertollino, Nico Magnotti and Primo Scafidi, settled on their white plastic chairs, could hear them.

"I think it's just terrible," Signora Della Franca said. "Poor Mario and Anita."

"And poor Marianna," Signora Marina responded. "Such a lovely child."

"What will you do?" Signora Della Franca asked. "Will you go to that hearing?"

"I don't know. If we can't speak, there isn't much point to go, is there?"

STILL SMOKING HIS TOSCANOS, Giacomo Arigoni spread out over two chairs in the front row for the hearing. His big feet, still clad in red running shoes, stuck out in front of him. On this uncommonly warm October night he opened the top buttons of his shirt to reveal a gold chain on a hairy chest and fanned himself with his notebook.

Unlike Sant'Antonio, which didn't have a town hall and held its meetings in the church basement, the Sant'Anna comune enjoyed a magnificent former palace from the seventeenth century. Heavy chandeliers glittered in the hearing room, once the ballroom, and the walls glowed with gilt and gaudy frescoes. The metal folding chairs seemed extremely out of place.

Mario shook Giacomo's hand. "Thanks for coming. And thank you for the excellent article. Maybe the publicity will stop this thing."

"Only trying to write a good story," Giacomo said, flicking ashes on the parquet floor.

Mario was trailed by Anita and Marianna. Ezio, Donna, Paolo and Lucia arrived shortly after and sat in a row near the back. Mario looked around for any other familiar face.

"There's nobody here!" he whispered to Anita. "There's nobody from Sant'Antonio."

"Maybe they'll come a little later. It's still early."

"Just ten minutes before it's supposed to start."

"Well, they know they're not going to be allowed to speak anyway."

The room gradually filled. Mario and Anita recognized a few customers from Reboli and elsewhere in the comune of Sant'Anna but none from Sant'Antonio. Significantly, the customers walked right past them.

"No one will look at us," Mario said.

A short, pudgy man in an ill-fitting black suit took his place on another folding chair in the front row. Giacomo looked at him, smiled a knowing smile and wrote something in his notebook.

At 8:10, nine men entered from a doorway that was almost concealed in the frescoes on the rear wall and took their places at the long table in front, with the mayor, Salvatore Donato, in the middle. Clearing his throat, Donato introduced members of the *Consiglio Comunale,* the legislative body, and the *Giunta Comunale,* the executive body. Both, the mayor said, would have to approve the supermarket's plans.

"Welcome to our meeting," Donato said. "We are here to approve the plans of this big wonderful supermarket to build a beautiful new enterprise in our comune. It will bring in so much revenue that we will be able to do all sorts things for our residents. All of us will benefit."

All of the members of the *Consiglio Comunale* and the *Giunta Comunale* looked at the mayor as if he had let some cat out of the bag.

"What I meant to say," the mayor hastily added after clearing his throat, "is that all of you villagers will benefit. Now, if there are no questions, we will proceed with the vote. Signor Alfredi?"

"Wait!"

Giacomo stood up, strode to the table and, walking back and forth, faced the audience. The comune officials seemed to shrink in their chairs as they looked up at him.

"I have some questions."

"Wait!" Donato said. "Do you live in the Comune of Sant'Anna? If you do not, you are not permitted to ask questions here."

"I am a journalist! I can ask questions anywhere I want!"

The comune members quickly conferred among themselves and then Donato spoke. "Proceed."

Giacomo flicked more ashes from his cigar and strode back and forth in front of the table.

"My first question is this. Is it not true that everyone who shops at the supermarket must first rent a shopping cart and therefore must pay 1,936 *lire* for the so-called privilege of buying merchandise at the store?"

A murmur went through the crowd. This was something they didn't know. Shops in villages didn't require payments for shopping carts.

Donato cleared his throat again and pointed to the pudgy man in the front row. "Perhaps Signor Grazetti will honor us by answering that question. Signor Grazetti represents the magnificent supermarket."

Signor Grazetti stood up, but didn't face the audience, and he certainly didn't look at Giacomo. "Well, that is because we want to keep our prices as low as possible. Anyone who shops in our stores knows that our prices are so low that…"

"And isn't it true," Giacomo said, "that people who shop at your store not only must pay for their shopping carts but they must bring their own shopping bags or else they must pay—pay!—for one if they forget?"

A louder murmur filled the room.

Once again, Signor Grazetti rose to his feet. "Again, we want to keep our prices as low as possible. Anyone who…"

Giacomo interrupted. "And isn't it true, Signor Grazetti, that your poor customers, even elderly ladies with shaky hands, must place their fruits and vegetables on scales and weigh them? What if their eyesight is bad and they can't see the little numbers on the scale? What happens if the scales are wrong? And what happens if they drop an apple or an orange? Must they still purchase it?"

In the middle of the room, two elderly ladies with shaky hands began to furiously whisper to each other. "No!" "I can't do that!" "Oh, oh, oh!"

Signor Grazetti got up again. "As I said, we want to keep our prices as low as possible. Anyone who shops in our stores knows that our prices are so low that…"

Giacomo cut him off. "And isn't it true, Signor Grazetti, that everyone who shops in your store must bag their own groceries? Even elderly ladies and gentlemen who may have to put their canes and walkers aside in order to do that? Perhaps they'll even be in wheelchairs. They would have to learn how to place some heavy groceries in one bag, some in another, the eggs all by themselves, the frozen dinners in another bag. Where will they put their canes and walkers while they do all this? Will you have clerks there to help them? Will you give lessons to teach people how to do that?"

In the third row, a woman with a cane at her side and far too much rouge on her cheeks loudly told her husband, "I'm not going to bag my groceries. I never have, never will. That will be your job." The husband grimaced. "I'm not going to do it either."

Now almost everyone in the crowd was talking, drowning out Signor Grazetti's response. "Once more, we want to keep our prices…"

Things were clearly getting out of control. Mayor Donato pounded his gavel.

"And now," Giacomo said, "I have a question for the esteemed members of the *Consiglio Comunale* and the *Giunta Comunale.* Can you tell the people of your comune why a notice of this hearing was not posted on the comune's announcement board outside and why it was not published in *La gazzetta di Lucca,* both of which are required by law? Can you answer that, esteemed members of the *Consiglio Comunale* and the *Giunta Comunale?"*

The mayor cleared his throat. "Well, we've been very busy and…"

"And you forgot? You forgot to obey the law. I see. I wonder why that would happen."

The room apparently became even warmer, because the men at the front table loosened their ties and unbuttoned their collars.

"But," Giacomo said, "I have another question for the esteemed members of the *Consiglio Comunale* and the *Giunta Comunale.* Can you tell the people of your comune how exactly you personally will benefit from the construction of the supermarket in your village? Just some short answers, please."

The members of the esteemed bodies suddenly found papers to shuffle in front of them.

The mayor wiped his forehead. "Well, the entire village will benefit. Yes. Everyone. Now if there are no further questions…"

"Wait!" Giacomo was shouting now. "Why don't you ask if anyone in your comune has any questions?"

Donato cleared his throat. "Does anyone in the comune of Sant'Anna want to question this wonderful project?"

The residents seemed very interested in the design on the parquet floor but no one spoke.

"All right," the mayor said, "will the members of the *Consiglio Comunale* and the *Giunta Comunale* raise their hands if they approve of this magnificent addition to our village? All in favor, raise your hands."

All of the members, joined by the mayor, raised their hands, jumped up and rushed out the door in the frescoed wall.

At first, those in the audience sat dumbfounded. Slowly, mumbling, they got up to leave. No one looked at Mario and Anita, who were the last. Mario stopped Giacomo.

"Thanks for asking those questions. But I guess it didn't do any good. No one else asked any."

"Just doing my job. Good luck, Mario."

Mario took his daughter's hand. "Come along, Marianna. I hope you've learned how comunes operate around here."

On their way out the thick oak doors of the former palace, they saw only the back of a tall, elegantly dressed man who got into a red Lamborghini and was driven away.

ANITA RECOGNIZED THE VOICE IMMEDIATELY when she picked up the telephone.

"Signor Magnimassimo! It's good to hear from you! We thought we saw you at the hearing last night but you left so quickly."

"Yes, that was me. I didn't want to stay and talk. I was too upset."

"Oh, I'm so sorry, Signor Magnimassimo."

"Anita, please, I keep telling you to call me Bernadetto."

"I'm sorry...Bernadetto."

Anita carried the phone with its long cord to the kitchen counter so she could box a couple of wild boar salami that Santo Scarpelli had brought the night before. Anita had added Signor Scarpelli's salami to her regular supply of offerings a few years ago and the demand for the delicacy had grown.

"How are you, Bernadetto? Is there a reason you called today?"

There was a pause at the other end of the line. "Anita, I had Emilio drive me to that hearing last night because I wanted to hear what was planned for this supermarket. But, as I said, I was very upset afterwards.

That hearing was a sham, a farce! I was going to get up and say something, even if I wasn't supposed to. I should have gotten up anyway. Now I'm ashamed of myself for not doing so."

"I don't think you could have changed anything, Bernadetto."

"No, I suppose not, but at least I would have had the satisfaction of telling those bastards off. Sorry, Anita. I guess I'm still upset. But we have to do something, Anita! We have to!"

"That's what Mario and I have been saying all along. But what can we do? We don't live in that comune. We don't have a voice. And anyway, people seem to want it. You can't blame them for wanting to get things cheaper."

"We can't just sit by and let this happen, Anita. You know it's the future of your shop and Mario's. Listen. Would you be able to round up some people and come up here on Saturday afternoon and we can talk about this?"

"I guess so, if you think we could still do something. Who would you like to come?"

"Stefano, of course. As the mayor, but also as my good friend. Ezio. Donna, whoever else you want to come. And your husband! Can't forget him."

"OK, I'll round up some people."

"And bring Marianna! Every time I see her my day gets brighter."

A caravan of three cars wound up the treacherous hill to Bernadetto's estate on Saturday afternoon. Mario, Anita and Marianna were in the first; Ezio, Donna, Lucia and Paolo in the second, and the mayor, Stefano Frazzetta, with his partner, Gino Rubino, in the third. Every quarter of a mile, one of the cars had to veer off the road to make way for an oncoming car or truck. Needless to say, they were all frazzled when they arrived.

Emilio, who rarely showed any emotion, smiled broadly as he unlocked the iron gate so they could drive up to the entrance. Amabilia greeted them with hugs and kisses.

Having recently abandoned his three-piece suit and tie, Bernadetto stood in the living room wearing a yellow cotton polo shirt and blue slacks. A white sweater was draped over his shoulders. His cat, Bella, was at his side.

"Buongiorno! Buongiorno!" Even his voice had grown stronger. Marianna gave Bernadetto a hug before Amabilia slipped her a biscotti that had just come out of the oven and took her off to the kitchen.

Bernadetto was flanked by two men, both almost as tall as he was. Both wore pin-striped suits.

"You remember Armando, my legal counsel," Bernadetto said, "and this is Ferdinando, who handles all my money matters. Thank goodness for Ferdinando or I would be living in the slums of Naples."

Hands were shaken all around. Amabilia brought in two pots of coffee and three trays of biscotti, which were quickly devoured.

"Now, let's sit and discuss this problem that we have."

Even though eleven people were seated around the long table there was plenty of room for papers to be spread out. Bernadetto had thoughtfully provided notepads and pencils before each place.

"All right," he said, "let's see where we are. We know it's been shown that when a supermarket enters the territory, small shops are going to suffer and indeed many of them will go out of business. And so the supermarket that's planned for Sant'Anna is a direct threat to Mario's and Anita's shops. Is that right?"

"Unfortunately, yes," Mario said.

"We realize that," Anita said.

"But there's something I don't understand," Bernadetto said. "Obviously Sant'Antonio has had many new visitors in the last five years."

"Thanks to your Sienese Museum," Ezio said.

"And the wonderful new piazza," Donna added.

"And your wonderful restaurant, Donna," Bernadetto said. "I have been very grateful. But since there are all these people, why aren't Mario's and Anita's shops doing big business? Why couldn't they bear the brunt of whatever losses are due to the supermarket?"

"Let me try to answer that," Gino said.

As the mayor's partner, Gino usually remained in the background, letting Stefano take center stage. But now he had something to say.

"As you know," he said, "I run a tourist agency in Lucca and our tourist association is always studying the habits of tourists. We want to send them to the best places, of course, but we also want to know what they like and what they purchase. So we are constantly conducting surveys. Constantly.

We hand out questionnaires, do telephone surveys, sometimes even ask them in person.

"We're especially interested in what tourists do in small towns, and we've been doing this long enough to know that we've got a good handle on this. I know that when tourists come to a village like Sant'Antonio because of a special attraction, like the Sienese School Museum, they will want to stay at a nice hotel, which Signor Magnimassimo has kindly built..."

"Both hotels are booked months in advance," Ferdinando said.

"And they like to go out to a good restaurant, like Donna's *Cucina*..."

"I could fill it twice over every night," Donna said.

"...but they don't spend a lot of money at shops like Mario's and Anita's."

"Right," Mario agreed. "They might stop to buy a souvenir or a pack of cigarettes, but they don't have to buy produce. What would they do with a rutabaga or a dozen apples in their hotel room? So they don't really have much effect. In fact, Anita and I did our own survey last year and found just that."

"And they certainly don't need to buy meat," Anita added.

"So even the recent influx of tourists coming to see the museum would not be enough to sustain your businesses when the supermarket moves in?" Ferdinando asked.

"No, not at all," Mario said.

Gino raised his hand. "But let me throw this out. According to our surveys, tourists do like to find something unusual in the small towns and villages. In fact, they say they wouldn't leave without buying these goods."

"Like what?" Anita asked.

"Well, everyone knows about Montepulciano and its wines. People always take home wine from Montepulciano. In fact, that's why many tourists go to Montepulciano. That's been true for years. But there's also a shop in San Gimignano that sells homemade chocolates. San Gimignano's Own Chocolates, they call them. Now you know that tourists go to San Gimignano to see the towers, but this little shop has made itself a regular stop on any tour."

"Interesting," Mario said.

"And in Pienza—well, you know that people want to go to Pienza for the lovely piazza—there is a shop that sells homemade *panatone* that's become famous."

"I've heard of that," Lucia said. "Remember, Paolo, you told me about it."

"So," Paolo said, "what Sant'Antonio needs is a shop, maybe even more than one, that sells something very special."

"Exactly," Bernadetto said.

"Hmmm," Mario said.

REALIZING THAT THERE HAD BEEN NO SOUND in the dining room for at least fifteen minutes, Amabilia, with Bella at her heels, fluttered in with more coffee and three more trays of biscotti.

"Just out of the oven," she whispered. "Hope you like them."

The trays were soon emptied.

"Something special," Lucia said finally. "That's what we need."

"Something *very* special," Paolo said.

"Hmmm," Mario said again.

Paolo could be heard crunching his biscotti. Unlike everyone else, he didn't like to dunk a biscotti in his coffee.

"I don't suppose Donna's cookbook would be something very special," Lucia said.

"Well, it's special, of course," Ezio said, "but it's sold all over Italy, not to mention in the *cucina* here."

"What about a nice drawing of the church?" Lucia wondered.

"No, no, no."

"It was just a thought."

"We've found," Gino said, "that people like to take home something edible. The chocolates from San Gimignano, for example. Or the *panatone* from Pienza. It should be something that will keep until they get home, though, not something that will melt in their cars on the way."

Paolo found some crumbs on the biscotti tray and wiped them up with his fingers. "Man, Amabilia makes good biscotti."

"Surely we can find something special that we could offer," Stefano said. "Something that's made only in Sant'Antonio."

"Right," Mario and Anita said together.

"Wait!" Ezio said. "I've got an idea. How about pasta? We could make it and have it ready to cook and put it in packages."

"Maybe," Gino said. "But are you sure it would be unique to Sant'Antonio? People can buy packages of pasta almost anywhere."

"It would also be an awful lot of work," Donna said. "Making it, packaging it. And we'd have to offer different kinds—spaghetti, linguine, penne, fettuccine, shells—there must be hundreds of varieties."

"But there are machines now, Donna," Lucia said.

"Still too much work," Donna said.

"I guess that wasn't such a great idea," Ezio said.

After a long period of silence, in which most of those around the table doodled on scratch paper, Amabilia sensed a need and trotted in with more coffee and plates of biscotti. Hands immediately reached out.

"Amabilia," Donna said, "I've had a lot of biscotti in my lifetime, as you can probably guess, but I've never had any that tasted like yours. Can you tell me what you put in them?"

"Oh, I don't even have it written down. I learned from my mother, and she said she learned from her mother. I guess I should write it down. You know, Emilio and me, we don't have any children, so I guess the recipe will be lost. I hadn't thought of that."

"Well, when you do write it down, please give me a copy," Donna said.

"And me!" Lucia said.

"And me!" Anita said.

"And me!" Gino said. "You know that I do all the cooking at our house." He smiled at Stefano.

Shaking her head, Amabilia rushed out the door.

"I don't know what I'd do without Amabilia," Bernadetto said. "She's quite fantastic. The biscotti are only one of her specialties."

More silence, more doodling on scrap paper. Mario found himself drawing a biscotti first one, then another and another.

"What are you drawing, Mario?" Gino asked.

"What? Oh, I don't know, just drawing. Must be thinking about what she said. Wait! biscotti!"

"What?" Ezio and Donna asked together.

"Biscotti!" Mario shouted. "We could make biscotti. Well, Amabilia could make her biscotti, and we could sell it!"

"Yes!" Bernadetto said.

"Yes!" the others agreed.

"And we could call it Amabilia's Famous Biscotti!"

"Yes!"

Now everyone was talking at once. Amabilia couldn't do it alone; she would need help. How about Serafina Marincola? Since that incident with her son Pasquale a few years ago, which had brought out the tensions between people from the north and southerners like the Marincola family, the villagers had gone out of their way to treat the family better.

"With Pasquale in high school and Francisco and Clara both at the university, I'm sure she has the time," Lucia said. "And I know she could use the money."

"And Emilio could help with the packaging," Paolo said.

"Let me say something," Bernadetto said. "Whatever this costs, I will pay. No matter how much. If more people are needed, I will pay them."

"You've already done so much," Stefano said.

"Not enough. And you know I've got good investments. What's going to happen to it all? I don't have anyone to leave it to. Might as well spend it here and now and do some good."

It was left to Ezio to bring reality to the proposal.

"Umm, shouldn't we ask Amabilia if she even wants to do this? I mean, it's her recipe, and it's going to be a lot of work even if we did get help."

The others quickly realized they were being presumptuous and Bernadetto asked Amabilia to return. He explained how the group loved her biscotti and thought that making and packaging dozens and dozens of them would be good for Sant'Antonio. He said that she would only have to supervise, and that others would bake and do the packaging.

"I…I…I don't know what to say, Signor. I am so flattered, so excited. Of course! Anything you want me to do, Signor. Anything. *Grazie*, Signor, *grazie."*

"You'd think we were doing her a favor," Bernadetto said after Amabilia left the room. "I just wish she wouldn't bow and scrape so much."

Everyone seemed pleased and satisfied until Anita raised a question. "OK, the biscotti could be sold at Mario's *bottega,* that would be obvious, but what about my shop? I don't think people would expect to find biscotti in a meat market."

Heads nodded. Doodles were scratched. Perishable as it was, meat did not seem to be something that tourists could buy and take with them.

"There must be something that isn't so perishable," Paolo said. "Hmm. I guess I don't know what."

Mario slammed his hand on the table. "I know! Anita, you sell a lot of Santo Scarpelli's wild boar salami, right?"

"It's very popular."

"Well?"

"Of course! People would love that. And it would keep. Well, at least six weeks or so."

"Great idea," Bernadetto said.

"But," Anita said, "there's only one problem. Santo has been telling me for years that he needs better equipment. He said he needs a new grinder, a new mixer, a new sausage stuffer. He said it takes him three times as long as it used to because his equipment is so old. It keeps breaking down and then he has to fix the grinder or the stuffer while he's trying to make the sausage. My God, they got the mixer as a twenty-fifth wedding anniversary present, and that was, what, thirty years ago!"

"Well," Bernadetto said, "don't worry about that. We can get him new equipment in a couple of days, right, Ferdinando?"

"Of course." He began writing on his notepad.

"If we're going to do this," Anita said, "I think he's also going to need help. Santo isn't so young anymore, and his wife isn't much help. His kids are all gone."

"Dante! Beppe and Sophia's son!" Lucia said. "He just graduated from his school and they can't afford to send him to the university. I know he's looking for a job."

"Perfect," Anita said. "And there are other young people looking for work. Alfonso Buretti just told me. And there's Antonetta Fiscoli."

"I'll pay them, of course," Bernadetto said.

"Excuse me," Gino said, "but I've never even had wild boar salami. I don't particularly like wild boar..."

"What? What?" This seemed sacrilegious to some in the group.

"Well, I don't. So what's so special about wild boar salami?"

"Gino," Donna said patiently, "you have to try it. Wild boar meat is leaner and tangier than other meats. When you add such things as fresh figs, walnuts, pistachios and the right spices, there's no comparison to other salami. I've got several recipes in my cookbook with it."

"OK, OK, I'll try it," Gino said. "Anyway, it's got an exotic name so that should attract tourists."

"Umm," Ezio said, "aren't we presuming that Santo is willing to do this?"

"Again, you're right," Bernadetto said.

Anita volunteered to talk to Santo, but she was sure he would be so excited about getting new equipment, that he would be delighted to produce more wild boar salami.

"Well," Gino said, "our tourist association is ready to promote two things you can only get in Sant'Antonio, 'Amabilia's Famous Biscotti' and 'Santo's Own Wild Boar Salami.'"

Hands were shaken, hugs were hugged. "Let the supermarket try to compete with that!" Bernadetto said.

IN JANUARY, THREE MONTHS BEFORE the supermarket was scheduled to open, two similar billboards went up at the entrance to Reboli. One had a sketch of Amabilia, white hair in a knot on top of her head, eyeglasses down her nose. She wore a blue cotton dress and a red apron and held up two packages. In giant letters: "Amabilia's Famous Biscotti! Leoni's *Bottega,* Sant'Antonio." A sketch of Santo was on the other billboard. His head was bald but he had a handlebar mustache. He wore bib overalls over a plaid shirt and held up a salami in each hand, "Santo's Own Wild Boar Salami! Manconi's Meat Market, Sant'Antonio."

Gino's tourist association designed a flier that was distributed to groups, offices and businesses.

What to See and Do in Sant'Antonio:

- Visit the Sienese School Museum and marvel at the priceless paintings of Giovanni Signoretti, Francesco di Vannuccio, Luca di Tommè, Niccolò di Ser Sozzo and others, all donated from a private collection.

- Spend time in the piazza, restored to its original medieval glory with authentic bricks and facades. Meet the welcoming residents during the evening *passeggiata.*
- Dine at Donna's *Cucina*, owned and operated by the author of one of the most famous Italian cookbooks ever written. Reservations required!
- Have a cappuccino and hard roll in the morning at Paolo's *Bar.* You may even meet the cheerful Paolo.
- In June, attend the medieval festival in honor of the village's patron saint. The highlight is a joust between the two *contrade* of the village. Plenty of food, music, dancing and games. A treat for all ages.
- Stay at the five-star Hotel Stella or the Hotel Giovanni just outside the village, or in one of the rustic villas in the hills. One of them, The Cielo, has received much praise and reservations are strongly encouraged.
- Take home two of Sant'Antonio's signature specialties, "Amabilia's Famous Biscotti" from Leoni's *Bottega* and "Santo's Own Wild Boar Salami" from Manconi's Meat Market, both located right on the piazza.

"Wow," Stefano said after reading the list. "Makes me want to live there."

"A little hyperbole never hurts," Gino said. "How do you think we can get tourists anywhere? It's all marketing, Stefano, it's all marketing."

Mario called Giacomo, who returned to write a long story for *La gazzetta di Lucca* on how little Sant'Antonio was fighting back against the monster supermarket. The inevitable headline: "David vs. Goliath." That got the attention of a television station in Florence, which sent a crew to interview Mario, Anita, Stefano and others.

"It's nice to get this publicity," Mario said after watching the television segment, "but I wish they wouldn't make us out to be such, well, peasants. We might as well all be wearing bib overalls."

"And we don't even talk funny," Anita said.

Customers duly reported on the progress of the supermarket with "huge" being the most common description. There was no doubt that construction was providing jobs for a hard-pressed region, and that people looked forward to buying food and merchandise at lower prices.

Mario and Anita waited anxiously for the fallout.

In March, six weeks before the opening, the supermarket appeared to be right on schedule if not actually ahead of it. Because everyone wanted to see what the place looked like, traffic was so dense on the highway that police were installed for twenty-four hours a day. The access ramps were nearing completion.

When Mario arrived at his shop one morning, a middle-aged man and woman were waiting at the door.

"We didn't know when you'd open," the man said, "but we thought we'd take a chance."

"Our friends, the Petersons from Leeds, told us about the cookies, what did they call them, Harry?"

"Biscotti," the man said.

"Yes, the biscotti, and we wanted to get at least six packages to take with us. They said they were so delicious and we're going to give them away as gifts. We're leaving at noon from Florence and then we'll fly to Paris and then London. It's been such a wonderful trip. We came here yesterday and saw the lovely museum and we had the most marvelous dinner at that restaurant over there and we stayed last night at Hotel Stella, it was so elegant. I really think this has been the highlight of our entire trip to Italy and…"

"Doris," the man said, "the man has unlocked the door. Let's buy the biscotti."

And they did.

Putting the packages into a large brown bag, Mario thought that this was the third couple from England this week, and it was only Wednesday. And there had been four from Germany and two from Norway and three from Japan.

"Here, take these with you and tell your friends," he said as he put a half a dozen fliers in the bag. "Oh, and go across the piazza to the meat market. They have some very nice salami you'll want to take with you."

"Oh, thank you!" the woman said. "We will! *Buonanotte!*"

"She means *buongiorno. Buongiorno!*"

"Buongiorno!" Mario said, filling the cash register drawer.

As they did every night, Mario and Anita toted up the figures on how many tourists had stopped in their shops and how much they had spent, and they compared the numbers to figures from their regular customers. The tourist numbers showed a steady increase and the regular customers' figures remained steady. In other words, business for both shops was good.

"But wait until that thing over there opens," Mario said. "Then we'll see if Signora Della Franca and Signora Marina and Signora Mandolini and all the others are still going to come here.

Making the rounds in the piazza during the *passeggiata*, Signora Della Franca whispered to Signora Marina.

"Do you think you'll be going over to…you know?"

"Are you going?" Signora Marina responded.

"I asked you."

"I don't know. What are the other ladies saying?"

"They won't say anything."

On the day of the opening, Mario and Anita got up early.

"You didn't sleep, did you?" Anita said.

"No, neither did you."

"Awake all night."

They turned on the television, only to be greeted by a young woman with a microphone in front of the new supermarket. She was interviewing shoppers as they streamed into the store, some of them pushing and shoving and all of them appearing to be terribly excited.

"Well," Mario said. "So it's open. Let's get to work."

They saw Signora Della Franca's car drive past.

A couple from Munich arrived at Anita's shortly after she unlocked the door, having heard about Santo's Own Wild Boar Salami. At first, the man seemed intent on arguing that Black Forest Salami was the finest in the world and nothing made in Italy could possibly be better.

Anita went to the new cooler, installed just three weeks ago, and pulled out a sample sausage. She sliced two pieces for the visitors.

The man was reluctant. "Hmm…"

The woman was certain. "This is incredible!"

"Well, I suppose…"

"We'll take two," the woman said. "No, make that four. No six! Ralf, we have to take some home for our friends."

Anita found a big box for the plane.

A similar scene took place at Mario's, where an elderly woman from Barcelona, having heard about the biscotti, bought ten packages. "I don't know how I'll manage to carry all these, but I will!" she declared.

By the time Anita and Mario closed their shops to take the customary afternoon siesta, they had already sold more biscotti and salami than they did in an entire average day. And by the end of the day, they had both put "Sold Out" signs in their windows. They called Amabilia and Santo, who promised to replenish the supplies the next day.

But, except for Pasquale, who bought some candy, not a single customer from Sant'Antonio had shown up, not even Signora Cardineli, who had bought a half-pint of milk for Alessia the previous day.

"This is very strange," Mario said. "If this is how it's going to be, we might as well close down both shops and open one that sells only biscotti and salami."

SIGNORA MARINA WAS THE FIRST of the regular customers to return. It was the day after the opening of the supermarket and, like almost every other woman in Sant'Antonio, she had spent hours at the store.

She slipped into Mario's *bottega* as two tourists from Denmark were leaving, looked shyly at Mario, then hastily made a beeline toward the produce section. She took her time picking up a cabbage and a bunch of radishes and a firm ripe tomato. She stopped at the olive oil section, pretending to compare prices, and then put the bottle she always bought in her shopping cart. She then went through the gift aisle, examining a jack-in-the-box toy for children and patting a baby doll. She admired the display for Amabilia's Famous Biscotti and rearranged the packages to form a perfect triangle. She put one in her cart.

Lacking any other excuse to delay talking to Mario, she brought a loaf of bread, too.

"*Buongiorno,* Signora," he said as he rang up the sale.

"*Buongiorno,* Mario."

She was on her way out the door when she suddenly turned around. "Mario, you know I've been a customer here for many years, forty, forty-five, I think."

"Yes, well before my time here."

"I knew your grandfather well, rest his soul. I always liked to come here. And now I have to say..." she stopped to wipe tears from her wrinkled cheeks with a white lace handkerchief.

"Yes?"

"Mario, I just want to tell you this. I have to confess. Yesterday, I went to the supermarket. The new one in Reboli, you know?"

"Yes, I've heard of it."

"I didn't really want to, but you know, my pension doesn't go very far and I thought if I could save a few *lire*, then I'd better do it."

She paused for breath.

"So I went with Signora Miniotti and Signora Bruni and Signora Leci and Signorina Cesi. We were all packed into this little car and Signora Della Franca is such a terrible driver I was praying the rosary all the way. Well, first when we got there we had to drive around and around looking for a place to park. They have this great big parking lot but there were so many cars that we had to park, oh my, it seemed like miles away. We walked and walked and we were so out of breath when we finally got to the store.

"And then there were so many people in the store we could hardly move. Finally, we found the place where we had to rent a shopping cart. Imagine! Having to pay for a shopping cart! So then we started going through the aisles. Well, we couldn't find anything. We couldn't see the signs. And the people were all pushing and shoving. And then...and then...the worst thing."

She wiped her eyes again.

"What happened?"

"I lost all the others. They were right next to me, and then they weren't. I couldn't see them anywhere. I got so frightened! It was like I was in a terrible dream. Finally, I found the office and I went in. I said I couldn't find my friends. The man there wasn't very nice, but he said he would announce on the loudspeaker that an old lady was lost and in his office. Imagine! So finally the others came. I tell you, Mario, we got out of that store so fast. Well, as fast as we could because there were so many people. And then we had so much trouble finding the car again. Signora Della Franca drove so fast back here. I think she's still in bed."

"I'm so sorry, Signora. That sounds like a terrible experience."

"Well, Mario, you know what we talked about when we were coming back? Everybody complained about having to pay for the shopping cart and for shopping bags. Imagine! Shopping bags! Signorina Cesi said the apples seemed soft and she saw bruises on them. Signora Bruni said the vegetable prices didn't seem much lower than you have here. Signora Leci said she looked at the meat and saw that it was all wrapped up in plastic and she couldn't tell if it was good or not.

"So, anyway, by the time we got back home we were so tired. We all went right to bed, and I'm the first one up, and it's 11 o'clock."

"I'm so sorry, Signora."

"Well, we figured it out. Considering the cost of gas—I can't believe it went up again—we really didn't save any money. The trip just wasn't worth it. We all said we will never go to that store again. And we won't."

"I'm so sorry, Signora. But I'm glad you came here today."

"Mario, we're so glad you're here. Anita, too."

Fifty Years! Imagine!

Sant'Antonio

LIKE COUNTLESS other Italians, Lucia and Paolo settled down in front of their television set every Tuesday night. Although they had just eaten supper, they always brought treats to snack on. On this night, Paolo dug into a bag of Amabilia's Famous Biscotti that he bought at Leoni's *bottega.*

"I'm addicted to these," he told his wife.

"They're very fattening," said Lucia, who was peeling an apple. "Just have one."

"What?"

"I said," she said louder, "just have one. Paolo, you really need to get hearing aids."

"What?"

"I said.... Never mind."

"I was just teasing. But you talk too soft, Lucia. I can't hear you anymore."

"I talk like I always have. It's you. You can't hear anymore."

"What?"

"Shhh. The program's starting. Turn the sound up."

The variety show ended, and the announcer said, "Welcome to 'Living Life Day by Day' with Father Giancarlo Moretti."

The tall silver-haired priest, universally known as *"il sacerdote dolce,"* the Gentle Priest, strode onto the set, smiling broadly and stretching his arms out.

"*Buonasera!* Isn't this a great day to be alive in the Lord?"

Lucia and Paolo nodded.

For the next half hour they listened intently as the priest interpreted Jesus' parables for modern audiences, they laughed when he told jokes, some of them corny, and they smiled when he almost danced around the set.

"It's been wonderful talking to you," he said in closing. "Now live in God's peace. *Buonanotte!"*

"Isn't he great," Lucia said as she clicked off the TV before Paolo could turn on a comedy show. "I look forward to Tuesday nights so much."

"Wouldn't miss it," Paolo said.

"You know, when he was telling those jokes tonight, I kept thinking that he seems so much happier now."

"Happier? He just tells corny jokes."

"They're not corny. They're funny. Anyway, he seems more relaxed. He laughs more. When he first started the program, he seemed a little nervous sometimes. I think I saw him frowning every once in a while. But, oh, in recent years, he seems changed."

"Lucia, you see things that nobody else does."

"Well, I do. I always have. And I'm glad for him. Maybe something happened in his personal life. Maybe he's been assigned to a different church or something."

"He's still in Florence, isn't he?"

"I think so. He never talks about his personal life."

"Why would he?"

"I think people would be interested."

"I think people would be nosy."

"Oh, Paolo."

Lucia got up to straighten things in the kitchen, but soon returned.

"Paolo, do you know what three months from today is?"

"What?"

She talked louder. "Do you know what three months from today is?"

"Three months from today. Let's see. Today is March 21st, so June 21st, right? What do I win?"

"And what's the 21st of June?"

"Hmmm. First day of summer?"

"I guess so. What else?"

Paolo scratched his head. "Hmmm."

"Paolo, what happened on the 21st of June in 1945?

"1945. Well, the war was over, I know that. The partisans had big parties on that hill over there. We all got drunk for days. Except those who were hunting down Fascists. Lucky I wasn't one of them."

"And after that?"

"I was hungover?"

"No, after you sobered up."

Paolo pretended he was confused, but of course he knew the correct answer. "I know! I know! We got married!"

"Yes! Remember we had to get permission to get married right away? The priest didn't want to do it, but we told him about Dino so he agreed."

"We had to pay him."

"Daniela was my bridesmaid and little Anna was my flower girl. She was so cute. I wore a white dress. I didn't care what people thought. I forget who your best man was."

"It was Daniela's boyfriend at the time."

"She had so many. I can't remember which one."

"Did we have a reception? I can't remember."

"No," Lucia said, "we came here and my mother made a great dinner. My father stayed in his room. Out of his mind since the war."

"We didn't go on a honeymoon."

"We couldn't afford it. And what was the point? Dino was about eight months old then."

"Come sit here, Lucia."

She sat on the arm of his chair and tussled what remained of his curly hair, now mostly white.

Fifty years. They couldn't believe it.

"Want to celebrate?" Paolo asked.

"I don't think so. I really don't want to do anything special. I'll make a nice meal. No, not ravioli. That's all. So don't tell anyone, OK?"

"OK."

"Don't even tell Dino and Sofia, OK? They wouldn't know about the date. And they'd tell Tarik and he'd want to come and have a party."

"OK."

"Or Donna and Ezio, OK?"

"OK."

"Or anyone else in Sant'Antonio."

"OK."

"Don't tell anyone that our golden wedding anniversary is on June 21st, OK?"

Paolo rolled his eyes. "OK, Lucia, I won't tell anyone that our golden wedding anniversary is on June 21st."

"Good."

Lucia went into the kitchen, but stuck her head out to say again, "Paolo, remember our golden anniversary is on June 21st, so if you want to get me a little something, that's OK. But don't tell anyone, OK?"

He rolled his eyes again. "OK, Lucia, I won't tell anyone that our golden anniversary is on June 21st."

Paolo flipped on the television again and was engrossed in *La Ruota Della Fortuna,* trying to beat the contestants on this version of *Wheel of Fortune,* when Lucia came into the living room again.

"Paolo, I've changed my mind."

He turned the sound down. "What? I didn't hear you."

"I've changed my mind about what I said."

"Oh-oh."

"You know how some people have their marriages blessed on their golden anniversaries? A priest does it at a special Mass."

"And then they have a party. We've gone to four or five over the years."

"Yes. Remember the time that Andrea and Maria did that?"

"Sure," Paolo said. "They had a big party afterwards in the church hall and Andrea got so drunk that he hit Maria's brother and then all of Andrea's relatives starting fighting with Maria's relatives. Who could ever forget that? It was the biggest thing that ever happened in Sant'Antonio."

Lucia laughed. "And Maria wore her wedding dress! Imagine, her wedding dress! Which was about three sizes too small for her, and when they were dancing the whole back came apart and she had to have her sister pin it back together."

"Don't say any more. I'm laughing too hard."

After they wiped tears from their eyes, Lucia thought of another example.

"Remember that party for Giorgio and Francesca? That woman that Giorgio had an affair with? Gina was her name. She lived in Lucca. Everybody knew about it. I'm sure she wasn't invited, but she showed up anyway. She wore a bright red dress, I remember, and she wanted to dance with Giorgio. Francesca started kicking her and pulling her hair and then everyone got involved."

"And when it was over, Giorgio was nowhere to be seen," Paolo said.

"He went home."

They laughed, stopped, and laughed again.

"Lucia, do you really want to have our marriage blessed?"

"It would be nice. All our friends would be there. We don't have to have a party, you know. We could just have the Mass."

"Just a Mass would be nice," Paolo said.

"Yes."

"OK, just a Mass."

Lucia went into the kitchen again, but then returned. "Of course, a Mass would be special if we had a famous priest celebrate it."

"A famous priest?"

"Yes."

"We don't know any famous priests, Lucia."

"No, but we know about a famous priest, don't we?"

"Lucia, suddenly I can't hear you anymore."

"Oh, Paolo, you can too. Well, why not? Wouldn't it be great to have Father Giancarlo say the Mass?"

AFTER PAOLO REALIZED that his wife was serious, he knew he had to confront her with reality before things got too far.

"Lucia, what are you thinking? Why would Father Giancarlo—'*il sacerdote dolce*'—come from Florence to Sant'Antonio to say Mass for us on our anniversary when we don't know the man, when we have never even met the man?"

"Well, maybe he'd do it because he's a nice man."

"Lucia, he probably gets a million requests like this every week. I'm sure he has a policy of turning them down. He probably has a secretary who does nothing else but turn them down."

"It wouldn't hurt to ask, Paolo. After all, he might enjoy coming to a little village and meeting people who love his program."

"And he also might be too busy to come to this little village. He still has a parish, you know, and the television program every week, and I'm sure lots of other things to do."

"OK, OK. It was just an idea."

Lucia's shoulders slumped and she returned to the kitchen once more. Paolo followed her.

"Look," he said, "I'm sorry I said all that, but I just want you to understand. It's a very nice thought and, good God, it would be wonderful if it happened. I would love to meet him myself. But it's just not going to happen. I'm sure our own priest would be happy to say the Mass. Father Marcello's been here for years. He knows us. And he's not such a bad guy, if you forget about his sermons."

"His sermons are awful."

"I know, I know. But otherwise, he's all right. He doesn't ask for money too much. So let's just forget about Father Giancarlo, OK?"

"OK."

He gave her a little hug and went back and tried to watch *La Ruota Della Fortuna* again, but the program was over so he began flipping channels.

Lucia returned. "Paolo, we could ask Anna if she could ask Father Giancarlo."

Paolo turned off the television and stifled a sigh. "Anna?"

"My sister. Remember she was his guest on one of his shows. She talked about that place she runs for girls who have babies. *Casa di Maria.*"

"And she really told that guy off who called in and made rude remarks about the girls. She was great!"

"I called her after that and told her."

"Have you talked to her since?"

"No, I'm afraid not."

There were times when Lucia was sorry that she hadn't been close to her younger sister, or, for that matter, with her brothers Roberto and Alberto, but they had all moved to Florence and had their own lives. She particularly regretted not having more contact with Anna, who had spent years in a cloistered convent and had little communication with her family. Even when Anna left the convent and began working for *Casa di Maria* in Florence, she and Lucia rarely talked on the telephone. And Lucia and Paolo almost never traveled to Florence since Dino and Sofia and Tarik were frequent visitors.

"I wish we had been more in touch over the years," Lucia told Paolo, "but she's had her life and I've had mine. We're still friendly, but we're just not close."

"Then how," Paolo said, "could you call her and ask her to ask Father Giancarlo to do this? She was on the program years ago, and it was only that one time. I'm sure they haven't had any contact since then. Why would they? Anyway, he's probably forgotten that she was even on his program."

Lucia thought a little. "I guess you're right." She went back into the kitchen. Paolo watched another variety show for a while, then decided it was time to go to bed and went into the kitchen for a glass of water. He found Lucia making a phone call.

"Hello? Hello, Anna? It's Lucia."

Paolo looked on in amazement as Lucia waited for a response.

"Yes, Lucia. Your sister. No, nothing's wrong. Nobody died. In fact Paolo's right here. We're both just fine. And you?"

Lucia listened intently.

"That's wonderful. And your work at *Casa di Maria*?

Another pause.

"Oh, Anna, you're a saint. Truly you're a saint. I tell Paolo all the time that you're a saint."

Paolo nodded.

"Anna, I'm sorry to call so late, but I knew you'd be taking care of the girls during the day. You're a saint, Anna, a saint.

"The reason I'm calling? Well, I wonder if I can ask a favor. You see in three months, Paolo and I will celebrate our fiftieth wedding anniversary.... Yes. Fifty years, can you believe it? Remember you were the flower girl? You were so cute. Well, we were talking and we would like to have a Mass said and have our marriage blessed again. We were so young when we got married and it was all pretty quick, so we thought it would be nice to say our vows over again and have a priest bless us. Don't you think that's a good idea?"

Another pause.

"I knew you'd say that. And of course we want you to come! It wouldn't be the same if you didn't."

Pause.

"Well, maybe when the time comes you'll be able to get away. We can talk about that later. We hope so! We'd love to see you again. But the reason I'm calling tonight is because, well, I know this is an awfully strange question to be asking, but we know you were on Father Giancarlo's 'Living Life Day by Day' program a while ago and as I said when I called you after that, you were so great. We were just saying tonight how great you were, weren't we, Paolo? Paolo's right here and he's nodding."

Paolo nodded on cue.

"So the thought occurred to me, Anna, I was wondering how well you knew Father Giancarlo."

Pause.

"Anna?"

Pause.

"Anna, are you there? Paolo, I think we've been disconnected."

KNOWING THAT ANNA WAS OCCUPIED during the day, Lucia waited until the following evening to call again. Anna wasn't home.

"A woman named Leonora Acara answered the phone," she told Paolo. "She must work at *Casa di Maria,* too. She said Anna had gone out to dinner. I didn't think Anna ever went out to dinner. I didn't think she had any friends. All she does is work. I asked Leonora Acara who Anna went out to dinner with, and she sounded a little flustered and then she said she didn't know. Something strange, Paolo."

"Good grief, Lucia. You find something fishy in every little thing. Anna went out to dinner. Fine. She works hard, let her have some fun."

"Well, I left a message. I hope she'll call."

Two nights later, Lucia tried again. Anna, Leonora Acara said, was busy with one of the girls.

"I told her to call when she was free," Lucia told Paolo.

After another failed attempt, Lucia finally yielded to Paolo's requests to stop trying.

"Look," he said, "we'll go to see Father Marcello tomorrow and arrange the Mass and talk about renting the church hall. Sure, let's have a little party, too. Then we can make up a list of people to send invitations to. And you and Donna can talk about the food. Ezio and I will talk about the beer and wine. It'll be fun, Lucia."

"OK, OK. But can we wait a day or two?"

"Why?"

"Maybe Anna will call."

"Lucia, when you get something into your head, you don't let it go, do you?"

"No, I don't."

Paolo went to work in the garden that badly needed weeding and Lucia picked up some shirts to be mended. When he returned, Lucia had another idea.

"Paolo, I've been thinking."

"Not another plan."

"Paolo, you know that Dino is a good friend of Father Lorenzo, that priest who runs the soup kitchen at Santa Croce in Florence. Dino has been friends with him ever since the flood in Florence in 1966. And Dino still sees Father Lorenzo at the soup kitchen. I think he and Sofia still volunteer there sometime. Even Tarik. Dino talks about Father Lorenzo a lot."

"Yes, I know that."

"Well, remember that Father Lorenzo was on Father Giancarlo's program too? He talked about the soup kitchen and the other things they do at Santa Croce. It was just before Anna was on the program."

"I don't think I want to know where this is going."

"So Father Lorenzo must know Father Giancarlo. Maybe they're even good friends."

"What? I can't hear you."

"I'll talk louder."

"Lucia, there must be dozens and dozens of priests in Florence. Some of them probably have never met each other."

"Well, just suppose Father Lorenzo is a good friend of Father Giancarlo's, or at least knows him well. We could ask Dino if he would ask Father Lorenzo if he could ask Father Giancarlo."

"Well, 'we' won't ask Dino. You can, but I'm not. I'm getting a little tired of this, you know, Lucia? Can't we just celebrate like other people, without having a famous priest on hand? You've become obsessed with having Father Giancarlo say our anniversary Mass, and it's just not going to happen. 'Let's call Anna,' 'Let's call Dino.' Who are we going to call next? The pope? Lucia, you've got to give up on this idea, OK?"

"OK, OK. That's fine. It was just a thought. Here's your shirt. I have a little heartburn. I think I'll lie down for a while before supper."

Paolo picked up a copy of *La Repubblica,* but he was too upset to read it.

When Lucia didn't come down before supper, Paolo went upstairs.

"Lucia, what happened?"

Lucia had collapsed next to the bed, struggling to breathe.

"Lucia!"

"Call someone, Paolo," she gasped.

Paolo raced to the phone downstairs. The emergency number was on the list by the phone and, hands shaking, he dialed the wrong number three times, before he got it right, 118.

"It's my wife! We're in Sant'Antonio! 43 Via Santa Caterina. Come right away!"

Paolo ran back upstairs and struggled to get his wife onto the bed. She was moaning.

Then he ran back downstairs and called Ezio and Donna.

"Ezio! It's Lucia! Please come!"

Normally, a trip from the Cielo at the top of the hill to Sant'Antonio at the bottom took twenty minutes. Ezio and Donna were there in ten. Paolo was pacing the room. Lucia, sweating, lay shivering on the bed.

"I don't know what to do!" Paolo cried. "I don't know what to do!"

"Calm down," Ezio said. "The paramedics will be here any minute."

"Where are they?" Paolo cried. "Where are they? I called them fifteen minutes ago."

"They're coming from Lucca. It takes a while." Ezio held Paolo while Donna rushed a cold wet towel and a bottle of aspirin from the bathroom.

"Try to chew this aspirin, Lucia. That will help calm things down."

She wiped her friend's forehead with the towel and covered her with a blanket. "You'll be fine, Lucia. You'll be fine."

But when Donna looked at Ezio, her expression showed she wasn't at all certain of that.

A minute later, the paramedics arrived and took over. They checked Lucia's heart, temperature and other vitals and gently placed her on the gurney.

"No," one of them told Paolo, "I'm sorry, but you can't ride with us. We'll be at Hospital Campo di Marte. Follow us."

Ezio broke every speed limit following the ambulance to Lucca. Donna sat in the backseat with Paolo, holding his hand and trying to calm him down.

"She'll be fine, Paolo. She's in good hands. The doctors will take care of her. She'll be home in no time, just wait and see."

Paolo was blubbering. "We had an argument. I wasn't nice. I got upset. It's all my fault."

"No, no. I'm sure you were just talking. Don't blame yourself. Look, we're almost at the hospital."

"What am I going to do, Donna? What would I do without Lucia? She was so excited these last days. We were going to have our fiftieth wedding anniversary on June 21st. She wanted to celebrate it, have a Mass with a special blessing and have a party afterwards. We never had that when we got married. And now we won't be able to have it. We won't be able to have it."

Tears flowed down his rugged cheeks.

"Paolo, June 21st is three months away. Lucia will probably be perfectly fine by then."

"And you know what?" Paolo said. "She wanted to have Father Giancarlo Moretti say the Mass."

"Father Giancarlo? *'Il sacerdote dolce?'* The priest from 'Living Life Day by Day'"?

"Yes."

"Do you know him?"

"No, not at all."

"Then how was she going to arrange that?"

"She thought her sister Anna in Florence might be able to ask him but Anna never returned her phone calls."

AT THE HOSPITAL, Ezio and Donna had to hold Paolo back as he tried to follow Lucia's gurney into the emergency room. He wouldn't let go of one of the attendants and had to be forcibly pulled out of the room.

"I want to stay with her! It's my fault she's here!"

"Paolo, settle down," Ezio said. "They're taking good care of her now. You can't do anything."

"She wouldn't want you to get upset," Donna said.

"It's my fault, it's my fault."

"No, it's not, Paolo," Ezio said. "It's not going to do Lucia any good if you're moaning and groaning about this being your fault. It happened. It could have happened anytime. Let's see what the doctor has to say about what happened to Lucia."

They stayed in the waiting room for more than an hour, and Paolo alternately paced the hall outside the emergency room and sat with his head in his hands. Finally, a young doctor, half the age of any of them, came through the swinging doors and sat down with them.

"Hello, I'm Doctor Tomassini, I'm a cardiologist, and I've just examined your wife. She is resting comfortably now and you'll be able to see her in a few minutes. But let me say first that she had a heart attack. I could say that it was a mild heart attack, but a heart attack is a heart attack, and we have to take every one of them very seriously.

"Now I know that at your wife's age—she's 67, right?—things could become more complicated, but we've checked her records and her vitals are good and she seems to have been in very good health for years. Is that right?"

"Yes," Paolo said, "not even a cold."

"Good. So let me explain in very basic terms. I could be more specific if you want."

"No," Paolo said, "just tell us what happened."

"Well, during a heart attack, a clot forms in an artery that supplies blood to the heart. The portion of the heart muscle deprived of blood carrying oxygen begins to become damaged. This is called a myocardial infarction, and that's more commonly known as a heart attack.

"Now this is very treatable. What we are going to do first is take an x-ray to see the blockage in the heart's arteries. Then we will do a procedure called an angioplasty to open the artery."

Paolo began to shake, and Donna put her hand on his arm.

"Your wife will be awake during the procedure so that she can respond to any directions we might have. A nurse will administer a light sedation so that she is comfortable. Now what happens is this. First, we will apply a medicine to numb the skin in the groin area."

Paolo gripped the arms of his chair.

"The groin? You're going to start in the groin for a problem in her heart?"

"Yes. I will insert a needle in this area and thread a tiny plastic catheter with a balloon on its end over a guide wire. This will go from an artery in the groin and up into the blocked coronary artery. Once the balloon reaches the blockage, it is inflated. The clot and plaque are pushed out of the way and the artery is opened."

Paolo was almost in tears. Both Ezio and Donna held him.

"I know this sounds terribly complicated, but it really is not. I've done this procedure myself more than one hundred and forty times. All of the procedures have been successful and all of my patients have felt better afterwards. I'm sure your wife will be just fine. Do you have any questions?"

"Will this hurt?"

"As I said, she will have a mild sedation."

"When can she come home?"

"Normally, a patient is kept in the hospital for about five days, but that can vary. We really can't make promises at this time."

"Can I see her now?"

"Of course. Just follow me."

Ezio and Donna watched as the doctor led Paolo into the examining room. "Oh my God," Donna whispered. "Paolo suddenly looks so… so old."

"This has been a terrible shock."

At Lucia's bedside, Paolo tried hard to hold back his tears.

"I'm so sorry, Lucia, I'm so sorry."

"Don't be sorry, Paolo. It happened. I should have told you that I've been having these pains before this. It had nothing to do with you. Just getting old, I guess."

"No, no. You're not getting old. Look, we've got our wedding anniversary to look forward to. Won't that be a great occasion?"

"Sure. Of course. I know it will."

It was now night but the procedure was still scheduled, and Lucia was wheeled into the operating room. Ezio and Donna stretched out on the worn leather couches in the waiting room, trying to avoid watching the interminable variety shows on television. Paolo paced the halls again. They were the only ones there.

At 1:30 in the morning, Doctor Tomassini emerged, his mask on top of his head.

"I'm pleased to report that the procedure went very well. Your wife is sleeping now and she's very comfortable. I think you should go home and get some rest, too. Why don't you come back tomorrow afternoon?"

"Are you sure, Doctor?" Paolo asked.

"I'm sure. Don't worry."

"I can't see her now?"

"Not quite yet. Go home. Get some sleep."

Perhaps because they were exhausted, no one said a word all the way back to Sant'Antonio. Ezio and Donna offered to spend the rest of the night with Paolo, but he assured them he would be all right. They did accompany him into the house "just to make sure everything is in order."

Everything was.

Since an ambulance could hardly go unnoticed in Sant'Antonio, all of the villagers had known within an hour that Lucia had been taken to the hospital and that Paolo had driven there with Ezio and Donna. As a result, there were fourteen messages on Paolo's telephone. Signora Miniotti, Signora Bruni, Signorina Cesi, Signora Marincola, even old Signora Cardineli and many others had called to say that they would be more than willing to help with cooking, cleaning, whatever was needed. Father Marcello left a message saying he would pray for Lucia and offered to visit her at the hospital.

"I'm going to save all these," Paolo said to himself. "Lucia will want to hear them."

The last message was the longest.

"*Ciao,* Lucia. This is Anna. I am so sorry that we got disconnected that first night and I'm also sorry that I haven't gotten back to you before this.

When you called the second time I was at the home of one of our girls. Her baby is now a year old and they were having a birthday party. I was so excited to go. I'd never been invited to a birthday party for a one-year-old before. Little Santino is so cute! And you should see how his grandparents love him. They can't get enough of him. Anyway, it was such a lovely evening and I didn't get home until late. The other times you called there was one emergency after another with the girls and I didn't have a chance to call back. This place gets so busy sometimes and there's only me and Leonora Acara. But I'm calling now, and I want to congratulate you and Paolo on your anniversary. Of course, I remember the day. I wore a pink dress that had been yours years before and Mama shortened it. You and Paolo were so happy. Fifty years, I can't believe it. So please try to call again. I promise to return the call as soon as I can, but if it's not right away, it's not that I don't care or love you. Oh, and why did you want to know if I knew Father Giancarlo?"

PAOLO HAD A RESTLESS NIGHT, finally falling asleep at 5:30 in the morning. By then he was so exhausted that he slept until 10, awakening with a start. He jumped out of bed, pulled on the same shirt and pants he wore the day before and ran down to the kitchen. There was a new message on the phone. He had slept so soundly he hadn't heard it.

"Oh, no. It must be from the hospital. Something's happened."

He quickly pushed the button to hear the message. "Paolo, it's Ezio. Listen. We'll be happy to drive you to the hospital. Just let us know when you're ready."

Paolo smiled. Such good friends.

In the living room, he found Lucia's sewing box and a scarf she had mended by her chair. He wrapped the scarf around his neck and sat in his chair but didn't turn the television on. And he didn't raise the blinds. In the darkened room, he did something he hadn't done for years at home: He prayed.

Getting himself together, he went into the kitchen, pulled out a pan and went out into the chicken coop to pluck three fresh eggs from the nest. After lunch, he called Ezio.

They found Lucia sitting up in bed, her hair somewhat askew and her face pale, but she was smiling. Paolo kissed her forehead.

"I'm sorry, Lucia, I'm sorry."

"Paolo, please stop saying that. It happened, OK?"

"But I wasn't nice to you. You were just thinking of ideas and you were so excited, and I yelled at you."

"You didn't yell, Paolo. It was nothing. Forget it, OK?"

"OK, OK."

Lucia said she'd had chicken broth—kind of tasteless—and pudding—too sweet—for lunch.

"They also gave me tea. I never drink tea but this was pretty good. Cinnamon."

The four friends were watching daytime serials when Dino, Sofia and Tarik rushed in.

"Got here as soon as we could," Dino said, kissing his mother. "Traffic from Florence was terrible. Mama, how are you?"

"I'm fine, Dino, just fine."

"You don't look so fine."

"I am. Don't worry. Tarik, look at you. You've grown three inches since I saw you last. When was that? Last month? Come give your grandmother a kiss. Here, have some chocolate pudding. I couldn't eat it."

They were still talking when Doctor Tomassini came in, took various readings on the machines attached to Lucia and wrote in his notepad.

"Your wife is doing just fine," he told Paolo. "Just fine. We'll need to monitor her for a few days more, but everything is going well. I'll see you tomorrow."

Dino, Sofia and Tarik stayed for a few hours, though Lucia soon dozed off. Tarik sat in a corner reading a book.

"What's he reading, Sofia?" Lucia wondered when she awakened.

"Another vampire book. He reads one after another. I guess all twelve-year-old kids do now. Well, it's better than listening to those awful jokes he used to tell."

"Hey!" Tarik yelled from the corner. "Want to know why the superhero flushed the toilet?"

"No!" Sofia, Ezio, Paolo and even Lucia cried in unison.

"Well," Dino said, "we have to get back to Florence. I'll call you every day, Mama. Maybe twice a day."

He kissed her forehead.

"Drive carefully," Lucia said.

For the next two days, Paolo, Ezio and Donna spent hours with Lucia, at first in her room but more and more walking with her in the corridors and sitting out on the patio when it was sunny although, in late March, it was still chilly. She gained more strength every day, ate better and talked more. They thought that was a good sign.

At night, Paolo returned to an empty house. He appreciated the hot meals that Donna had sent over from her restaurant but couldn't finish everything. He turned on the television, but he wasn't interested even in the shows he rarely missed.

He hugged Lucia's pillow as he went to sleep.

On the third day, Lucia, Paolo, Ezio and Donna were alarmed when Father Marcello knocked on the door to Lucia's room. Priests, they thought, don't come to hospital rooms unless someone is dying.

"Ciao," he said cheerfully. "I just want to see how Lucia is doing, and if you'd like I could administer the sacrament of the sick."

Now that was even worse. It had been the experience of all of them that this sacrament was administered only when someone was at death's door, and Paolo stopped the priest and quickly objected.

"It's all right, Father. Lucia is doing really well. Can't you see? Look how good she looks. She'll be home in no time."

"That's fine, if you say so. But you know we don't call this sacrament by its old name, Extreme Unction or last rites, anymore. It's simply an anointing, and people like to have it. Perhaps I should ask Lucia?"

"Lucia?" Paolo called out. "Father Marcello is here. You're not up to seeing him, right? I'll tell him to come back some other time."

"Of course I'll see him, Paolo. Send him in."

Paolo allowed the priest to go to Lucia's bedside.

"Lucia, how are you? Everyone missed you at Mass Sunday."

"I'm doing just fine, Father. Thanks for coming."

"How's the food here?"

"It's OK. I like mine better."

"I'm sure that's true. Paolo said you'll be home soon."

"Yes, I can hardly wait."

"Well, as I told Paolo, I could administer the sacrament of the sick if you'd like. It's just something that might help you heal faster."

Lucia thought for a moment. "Well, sure. Won't hurt. Might help."

Father Marcello turned to the others. "Perhaps you'd like to leave us alone for a few minutes?"

Still suspicious of what the priest might be doing, the others left.

The priest first heard Lucia's confession, which was very short, then said prayers as he anointed her forehead and hands with oils, and then took out a host and gave her Communion. He let her pray for a few minutes before calling the others back into the room.

Paolo looked worried. "Are you OK, Lucia? Was that all right?"

"It was fine, Paolo. Why don't you thank Father Marcello."

After the priest left, the others still weren't sure if this was a good or bad thing, but Lucia didn't seem to mind.

On the fourth day, Doctor Tomassini had the news Lucia and Paolo had been waiting for: "You can go home tomorrow."

He had instructions, however. She needed rest, especially a good night's rest. But she also could use physical activity, such as walking. She should eat light meals, but good ones. She should avoid stress as much as possible. She might experience mild chest pains or pressures in her chest, but these should quickly go away. If there were severe chest pains, she should call emergency right away.

"We'll come to get you at 2 o'clock tomorrow," Paolo said as he kissed his wife good-bye.

As they were walking to the car, they passed the hospital's medical clinics. Paolo noticed a sign on a door: Audiology/Hearing Aids.

"Ezio, wait!" he called. "I'll meet you at the car."

BECAUSE PAOLO had not talked to anyone in Sant'Antonio, and Ezio and Donna hadn't either, the villagers presumed the worse. Lucia was dying. No question. That belief was confirmed when someone reported that Father Marcello had rushed to the hospital to administer the last rites.

"Poor Paolo," Signora Bruni whispered to Signorina Cesi. "Who will take care of him now?"

"We will all have to."

The villagers were surprised, then, when Ezio drove up to Paolo's house and not only Paolo but Lucia herself got out of the car and went inside. They watched through the curtains of their windows, noting that Lucia walked slowly and that Paolo and Ezio supported her arms as she went up the stairs.

Donna had stocked the refrigerator with various meats from Manconi's and the kitchen shelves with cans and supplies from Leoni's. Ezio had helped Paolo clean and straighten and do other odd chores around the house, so there really wasn't anything else to be done.

Lucia settled into her chair and Paolo let her listen to all the telephone messages, which had now grown to thirty-one, with several women in the village calling more than once.

"I guess I'll have to call them all to thank them," she said.

"No, no," Donna said. "You don't have to do that. They offered something, but you don't have to accept, and you don't even have to acknowledge anything. And don't worry, they'll be at your doorstep before you know it."

Lucia also listened to the long message from Anna. She was in tears when the recording was completed.

"I'll call her back tomorrow," Lucia said. "I should thank her for calling."

"Maybe we should just forget about celebrating the anniversary, Lucia," Paolo said. "You might not be up to it by then."

"Let's just wait, Paolo. Let's see how I feel. And we'll forget about Father Giancarlo. That was just a silly idea. You were right."

"I'm sorry, Lucia. It would have been great. We'll watch his program and think about him."

On the second night after she came home, Lucia insisted that they join other villagers in the traditional *passeggiata.* Paolo kept his arm firmly around her waist as they walked from their house to the piazza.

As they slowly made their way around the piazza, they were stopped every other minute by one or another villager who wanted to know how Lucia was feeling. Signorina Cesi, Signora Bruni and her husband, Signora Marincola and her whole family. All of them volunteered to make a meal or do some cleaning. Lucia thanked them, but assured each of them that she was just fine and could do her own chores.

They would have made their way faster around the piazza if Paolo had not regaled anyone who would listen about the "major operation" that Lucia had had, but mostly about the balloon that was in Lucia's heart. He got the name of the procedure and most of the details wrong, but he was certain about the balloon.

"Don't hug Lucia too hard or the balloon will pop!" he warned.

"Oh, Paolo," Lucia said. "It's not like that at all. Don't listen to him." She grabbed his hand and hurried him along.

They did spend some time with Signor Bernadetto Magnimassimo and his cook Amabilia and his driver Emilio.

"I love your biscotti," Paolo told Amabilia. "Lucia keeps telling me not to eat too many, but I can't stop!"

"Maybe just one or two," Amabilia said.

Meanwhile, Lucia admired the beautiful white cat with brown and black markings that Signor Magnimassimo held in his arms.

"Her name is Bella," he said. "Isn't she the most beautiful cat you've ever seen?"

"She is very cute," Lucia said, reaching out to pet the cat's head. She did not particularly like cats.

Bella hissed.

Lucia and Paolo returned to church for Mass the following Sunday, Paolo even joining her in her regular pew, in the third row on the right side, instead of staying with the men in the back. So many people buzzed around Lucia that Father Marcello had to delay the Mass for ten minutes.

Lucia got better every day, eating more and taking fewer naps. Four weeks after she came home, she needed to return to the hospital in Lucca for a checkup. They waited. And waited. Even for hospitals, this was an especially long wait, and Paolo, mumbling something about having to run an errand, left her in the waiting room. She was still reading a magazine when he returned.

"Where did you go?"

"Oh, ah, just had to check on something."

"In Lucca?"

"Yes."

"What?"

"Oh nothing. Oh, look, there's the doctor."

Doctor Tomassini spent a half hour with Lucia and then pronounced her in good health and making an excellent recovery. She didn't have to return for three months.

When they returned home, Paolo sat Lucia down.

"I have something for you to see."

He presented her with a small black box.

"What's this? Oh, Paolo, you didn't buy me a new wedding ring, did you?"

"Um, no. That's not it. This is something for both of us."

"A wedding ring for you, too?"

"Open the box, Lucia."

She did. "Oh, for goodness' sakes, Paolo. You actually bought hearing aids!"

They were small and flesh-colored and tingled when held.

"Put them on."

He struggled to hold the little things and get them into his ears.

"Now I don't hear anything. They must be broken. And they hurt. I'm going to take them back."

"Paolo, do you have them in the correct ears? There's one for the left and the other one is for the right, you know."

"Oh."

He switched.

"Now?"

"Yes! Hey, this is pretty damn good."

He walked around the room, trying to get a new sense of his surroundings. He opened and closed the front door, pulled out drawers and turned the water off and on in the sink.

"Lucia, that clock on the wall. It ticks!"

"Paolo, that clock has always ticked. You just didn't hear it."

Paolo then told the long story of how he went to the clinic and was tested.

"You should have seen the headphones they put on me. They were huge! And then they beeped things to see if I could hear them, and I didn't hear a lot of them, and there was this big computer screen and red and green lines kept going up and down and across. So then they said I needed hearing aids."

"As if I haven't been telling you that for years."

"So they had to make them so they'd fit in my ears and they put this warm mushy stuff in my ears and waited until it hardened. And then they told me to come back in four weeks to get them, so that's where I went today when you were waiting for the doctor."

"Paolo, I think this is the best present I ever had. You can say it was my anniversary present."

"Well, it was for me, too."

"For both of us."

"Look, there are these tiny batteries. You'll have to help me put them in, my fingers are too big."

"How much did they cost?"

"Nothing, of course. Italian health insurance. Same as your hospital bill."

Then something occurred to Paolo.

"You know, if I had been wearing hearing aids I would have heard you fall when you had the heart attack. Then I could have called somebody right away. You were just lying there. For hours. It's my fault."

"Paolo, stop that. It happened. And it wasn't for hours. Anyway, I'm better now."

"I'll always think it was my fault. Always."

"Stop."

When they walked to the piazza for the *passeggiata* that night, Paolo had a new story to regale anyone who would listen, especially about the mushy stuff that they put in his ears and about the teeny-tiny batteries that you could hardly see.

On May 21st, Paolo thought he'd better bring up the subject they'd been avoiding.

"Lucia, our anniversary is a month from today. Have you thought about it?"

"Paolo, I thought about it too much before. Now I can't think about it anymore. If you want to plan something, fine. But I don't want to be involved."

"OK. Why don't we just have a Mass and have Father Marcello say it."

"That would be very nice. He's been so kind to me."

"And then we could have a little reception afterwards in the church hall. Just a few friends. Donna could send over meals from her restaurant, Ezio and I can buy the liquor and maybe we can put some records on for music."

"That's even more than I would imagine, but it sounds wonderful. Just don't go through too much trouble. Keep it simple. And, please, if you invite people, make sure to tell them not to bring a gift. I'd be too embarrassed."

"OK, you just forget about it. You just get better. We'll take care of this."

"You know something, Paolo. This is why I love you."

"And I love you, too, Lucia. For fifty years!"

They had rarely said those words in all the years they'd been married.

Paolo called Ezio and Donna and together they worked out the details of the meal, the drinks and the reception.

"It's going to be fun," Ezio said.

"You've been wonderful," Donna told Paolo. "Lucia is going to love it."

Paolo called Father Marcello to make the arrangements, and for the rest of the day he thought about the plans. Maybe he could do something else. Something special for Lucia. At night, after making sure that Lucia was asleep, he went to the kitchen, closed the door, picked up the telephone and dialed.

"*Ciao,* Anna? This is Paolo. Listen, do you have time to talk about something?"

JUST AS LUCIA HAD INSISTED that Donna buy new dresses when she went on a tour to promote her cookbook a few years ago, Donna insisted that Lucia get a new outfit for her wedding anniversary.

"Just something simple," Donna said, "but you really need to have something new."

Lucia, now feeling completely recovered, reluctantly agreed. Donna drove her to Florence, where they went to shop after shop on Via Tornabuoni. Lucia tried on half a dozen dresses and finally found a light blue frock with a lacy neckline.

Donna herself kept browsing through the racks.

"Are you going to get one, too?"

"Didn't you know?" Donna said. "I'm going to be the maid of honor at the ceremony. Ezio is going to be Paolo's best man."

"I didn't know that. I told Paolo not to tell me anything, and I guess he didn't. All I know is that Father Marcello is going to say the Mass."

"It's going to be a beautiful ceremony," Donna said, selecting a dark green dress for herself.

On the day of the anniversary, Paolo slipped out of bed early and cracked some eggs and made a parsley omelet. Lucia didn't usually have a big breakfast, but this was a special day.

Still in her robe, Lucia was so excited she could eat only half of her breakfast.

"I don't think I'm going to be ready on time, Paolo."

"Lucia, we've got three hours."

"Three hours! I'll never be ready." She rushed upstairs without finishing her coffee.

Paolo had even bought a new suit for the occasion, something inevitable since his old suit dated back to the days of wide collars and padded shoulders.

"Anyway, it doesn't fit you anymore," Lucia said.

"Well, I haven't worn it since Signor Ceci's funeral ten years ago."

While he tried to tie his tie, Lucia nervously put on too much face powder.

"My God, I look like a ghost." She ran into the bathroom to wash the stuff off.

Fortunately, it was then that Ezio and Donna arrived to save the day. Ezio helped Paolo with his tie while Donna helped Lucia with her makeup and hair. She gently lifted the pretty new dress over Lucia's head.

"I look fat," Lucia said.

"You do not!" Paolo said. "You look wonderful."

After Lucia put on the rhinestone necklace she had worn at her wedding fifty years ago, they were ready.

"Wait," Ezio said. "I want to take a picture of you two."

Standing in the living room in front of old photographs of their parents, the happy couple held hands and smiled. They hadn't had their photo taken after their wedding, and had had few pictures taken since then.

Just in time for another, Dino, Sofia and Tarik burst through the door.

"Mama! Papa!" Dino said. "You look like something out of a magazine."

Dino and Sofia didn't look so bad either. Sofia wore a striking deep red suit, Dino wore a light summer suit and Tarik wore his first tie, which was obviously uncomfortable.

"Tarik," Lucia said. "Look at you. You've grown three inches since I saw you last."

More photos were taken.

Throngs of villagers were waiting outside the church when they arrived, and cars were still pulling up.

"There's Adolfo!" Dino cried. "And Roberto! My uncles really did make it. All the way from Florence."

"You're surprised?" Paolo said.

"You never know with those two."

Lucia and Paolo rushed up to greet the visitors.

"My brothers!" she cried, trying unsuccessfully not to wrinkle her dress. "Oh this is so wonderful! Paolo didn't tell me."

She hugged Adolfo and his wife, Mila, then turned to their children.

"Leonardo! Just look at you. You've grown six inches since I saw you last! Clara! You're so pretty. I bet all the boys go crazy."

Then it was Roberto's turn.

"Roberto, Roberto. More handsome than ever. But when are you going to marry Rosanna here? How long have you been together now?"

"Not long," her brother said. "I think ten years, right, Rosanna?"

"Fourteen years, three months and thirteen days," Rosanna said.

"But who's counting?" Roberto said. He gave her a hug.

"Well, you're not getting any younger, Roberto," Lucia said.

"I'm only sixty-two."

"Well, it's about time you got married. You and Rosanna have been living together long enough. How about it? Paolo and I have been married fifty years! Fifty years! Imagine!"

"I'm waiting for Anna to get married," Roberto said. "When she does, I will."

"Good heavens," Lucia said. "Anna was in the convent for years and years. She doesn't even know anybody. She won't get married! Who would she marry?"

"Maybe you should ask her," Adolfo said.

Lucia suddenly noticed a petite woman in a coral dress smiling and waiting.

"Oh my God! Anna?"

"Lucia!"

"Anna, you didn't tell me you were coming." Lucia was laughing and crying at the same time as she hugged her sister. "When I called you, you didn't even mention it."

"Paolo didn't want me to tell you. Oh, Lucia, you look so beautiful."

"No, you do. Anna, that dress is gorgeous."

"Well, I couldn't wear pink like the last time so this was the closest thing. I'm going to be your flower girl, you know."

"I didn't know. Paolo didn't tell me."

They would have talked more but Signora Francolini, who had been playing the church organ for thirty-eight years, struck up the wedding march on the creaky instrument. Father Marcello, standing at the doorway to the church, signaled that they should enter.

Anna entered first. She carried a small bouquet of forget-me-nots.

Donna and Ezio followed. Then Lucia, with a bouquet of white roses, and Paolo. Then Dino and Sofia, with Tarik in between. They could see the beaming faces of the villagers as they slowly walked down the aisle.

More family followed: Adolfo and Mila and Leonardo and Clara and Roberto and Rosanna.

At the altar, Lucia gave her bouquet to Anna, who stood to one side. Donna knelt next to Lucia and Ezio next to Paolo.

"Welcome!" Father Marcello beamed. "We are here today to celebrate the remarkable marriage of Lucia and Paolo. Fifty years! Truly, God has blessed you, and He has blessed all of us for knowing you."

Lucia began to cry and Paolo put his hand on hers.

"I'm pleased today," Father Marcello continued, "to be joined by a fellow priest in honoring this lovely couple. Please welcome him."

A tall, silver-haired priest walked quickly from the sacristy to the altar.

"Oh my God!" Lucia cried, so loud that she was heard in the back of the church. "It's him!"

"Don't have another heart attack, Lucia," Paolo said, only half humorously.

Everyone in the church gasped and some of them even clapped.

"How did you get him to come?" she whispered to her husband.

"Tell you later."

Father Giancarlo Moretti smiled at Lucia and Paolo but otherwise joined Father Marcello in the rituals of the Mass. Father Giancarlo said the homily, noting especially how Lucia and Anna were holed up in an old farmhouse during World War II, how Lucia took care of their baby sister and when the baby died, how Lucia put her precious doll in a makeshift casket.

"How would he know all this?" Lucia whispered to Paolo.

"Anna must have told him."

"When would she have told him?"

"Shhhh."

At the end, the words of the marriage ceremony were repeated. "Paolo, do you take Lucia...," "Lucia, do you take Paolo...." Although they both had rings from their original ceremony, Paolo nudged Ezio, who dug into his pocket and produced two new gold bands. Paolo rarely cried, but tears ran down his cheeks as he took the old ring from Lucia's finger and replaced it with the new band, and she did the same for him.

Father Giancarlo then told the couple, "And now you may kiss."

The crowd in the church erupted, and continued to applaud as Lucia and Paolo walked down the aisle to the entrance. Outside, everyone threw confetti at them.

Last to greet the couple outside of church were Father Marcello and Father Giancarlo. Father Marcello hugged Lucia and shook hands with Paolo, then stepped aside for the celebrity priest.

"I...I don't know what to say, Father," Lucia said. "I just...I couldn't imagine...I don't know how...We listen to your program all the time and..."

"Lucia, I feel so privileged to share this day with you," Father Giancarlo said. "When Anna told me..."

"Anna?"

"Yes, your sister Anna. I believe your husband asked her to ask me."

"Paolo?"

"Yes."

Lucia slapped her husband on the back. "Paolo! Why didn't you tell me?"

"You said you didn't want to know anything. So I didn't tell you."

"Oh, Paolo." She hugged him.

She turned back to the priest. "So you know Anna?" Her sister was standing nearby, smiling broadly.

"Oh, yes," Father Giancarlo said. "You know, in Florence everybody knows everybody."

Father Marcello led the way to the church hall, followed by the happy couple, Dino and Sofia and Tarik and Donna and Ezio, Lucia's brothers and all the rest. Father Giancarlo said he wanted to get something from his car and he and Anna slipped away.

The hall was already filled, and there were far more guests than Lucia had expected. Father Marcello sat at one end of the long table, covered with a white cloth and baskets of flowers. Dino, Sofia and Tarik, then Paolo and Lucia, then Donna and Ezio, then Anna and Father Giancarlo. He had exchanged his Roman collar for a black turtleneck sweater and looked even younger and more handsome.

Father Marcello said grace, and waitresses in white blouses and black skirts brought in tray after tray of *chicken cacciatore* and *veal marsala* plus lots of side dishes from Donna's restaurant.

Dino gave the toast, thanking his Mama and Papa for their love and support and patience through the years. He remembered the time he hid under a blanket in a car that was leaving to find a fugitive Fascist, the times they must have endured his various girlfriends, the worries they must have had during the flood in Florence and how they must have wondered if he'd ever settle down and get married.

"But here I am with Sofia and our son and life is wonderful, so thanks to you for everything, Mama and Papa!"

Anna surprised everyone by getting up and offering another toast. She congratulated Lucia and Paolo, said she regretted she hadn't been closer to her sister all these years and pledged to make up for it with frequent visits to Sant'Antonio. Kisses all around. And then people clanked their glasses and Paolo and Lucia were forced to kiss again and again.

When Father Giancarlo got up to offer another toast, the crowd grew silent, but his words were simple: "Here's to a wonderful couple. May God bless you for many years to come."

A three-tier wedding cake topped with a bride and groom was wheeled in, and of course Lucia had to feed Paolo the first piece before it was cut for everyone else. Since guests were asked not to bring gifts, they chose instead to bring greeting cards, which filled a nearby table.

Then the music started. Ezio had hooked up a sound system to play recordings of traditional Italian wedding songs, "Con te Partiro," "Mama," "Cela Luna," "Santa Lucia," and many more.

"These are songs for dancing," Donna told Lucia and Paolo. "Go."

Paolo, who hadn't danced since he was a teenager, let Lucia drag him to a small empty space in a corner of the room. Despite a few missteps, they managed to waltz their way through "That's Amore" and ended with a kiss.

Soon others followed them and the tiny space was crowded. A young girl, Anastasia, tapped Tarik on the shoulder and led him to the dance floor. He looked awkward at first, but then he loosened his tie and began twirling the girl in a most frenetic version of a polka.

"Isn't that cute?" Lucia said. "He's growing up so fast."

"Yes," Dino said, "and we finally got the last of the adoption papers, so it's official."

"Thank God," Sofia said.

It was while "Santa Lucia" was playing that Donna and Ezio noticed that Anna and Father Giancarlo were dancing especially close and that Anna rested her head on his shoulder.

"We'd better stop that before anyone sees it," Donna said. "We don't want a scandal in Sant'Antonio."

She tapped Father Giancarlo on the shoulder. "Excuse me. I've never danced with a priest before. May I have this opportunity?"

She led him away as Ezio pulled Anna off to another side.

Both Donna and Ezio had seen enough so they knew not to ask questions.

After the party, with the guests carrying their little tulle bags of almonds home as souvenirs, Lucia, Paolo, Donna, Ezio, all the relatives and Father Giancarlo crowded into the anniversary couple's home for a post-party.

"Paolo," Lucia whispered. "I didn't know about this. I should have cleaned the house better."

"The house is fine, Lucia. Just enjoy."

Lucia cornered Roberto and urged him again to make his relationship with Rosanna official.

"OK, maybe," he said.

"More than a maybe. Do it."

"Always the bossy sister."

After an hour of conversation, *limoncello* and *grappa,* Lucia went into the kitchen and found an excuse for Father Giancarlo to join her.

"Father, I don't know what to say. I still can't believe you're here."

"Well, here I am. And happy to be here. I understand you and Paolo are two of my greatest fans."

"We never miss your program. Both of us. We watch it every week."

"Thanks. I really don't get a lot of response from people so I don't know how my corny jokes go over."

"We love them. Paolo always laughs so hard."

"He seems like a good man, Lucia. I know he wanted to arrange all this for you."

"I'm lucky, Father. And I'm glad that you and Anna are friends. You just continued after she was on your program?"

"Yes."

"And you see her quite often?"

"Sometime."

"You must have gotten to know each other really well."

"Oh my, look at the time. We really have to get back to Florence. Traffic will be awful."

"OK, I understand. Well, I can't thank you enough for coming. This has been such a surprise."

She held out her hand, which Father Giancarlo took, but then he pulled her into his arms for a very long, very strong hug.

"Oh, Father."

Lucia and Paolo watched as Father Giancarlo and Anna drove off together.

"They seem to have a lot in common," Paolo said.

"Yes," Lucia said. "They must have a lot to talk about."

Cleaning up, Paolo asked Lucia, "Tired?"

"Yes, but a good tired, Paolo. This was a great day and you sure did a wonderful job. All those surprises. Anna. The reception. All that food. All those people. Dino and Sofia and Tarik. I can't believe Roberto and Rosanna and Adolfo and Mila came. My whole family."

"Aren't you forgetting someone?"

"I still can't believe he was here. This must be a dream and I'm going to wake up and it never happened."

"It wasn't a dream, Lucia. He was really here. And you know what? I have another surprise. Father Giancarlo told me at the reception that he wants to have us on his program."

"You're kidding."

"Nope. In the next month or so. Just the two of us talking about being married for fifty years."

"Oh, I couldn't go on television."

"Why not? It would be fun."

"Oh, I just couldn't."

"Why not, Lucia?"

"Paolo, I don't have anything to wear."

Also Under the Tuscan Sun

Cortona

YEARS LATER, Bruno Pezzino would still remember the exact time and place when he first heard about something that eventually would change his life and that of his beloved Cortona. It was Saturday, March 24, 1990, and he and his three old friends were at their usual tables outside Bar Sport facing Piazza Signorelli.

It had been another rough week. Again, Bruno had no customers for Pezzino Tours and he was worried. How long could he support his growing family if no tourists came and the business dried up? How long could the family afford to live in their sprawling apartment in the center of the city?

The Italian economy was bad enough, but tourists to Tuscany hadn't yet "discovered" Cortona. Close to the border of Umbria, it was off the beaten track, with only Arezzo as the nearest city.

Tourists always made Florence their base, exploring the treasures of the Renaissance and shopping in the expensive shops and markets. Then they might go to Pisa to have their photos taken with the Leaning Tower. Or to Lucca to walk on the walls that circled the city. Then to San Gemignano to see the medieval towers. Or to Montepulciano to buy wine. And to Chianti country to drink wine.

And that was only Tuscany. There were still so many other places to visit in Italy: Rome and Venice and Milan and Assisi and Naples and Capri and Sicily and on and on.

If they'd heard of it at all, and few tourists had, the medieval city of Cortona was a place "maybe we'll see some other time."

Perhaps, Bruno thought, spending time with his friends would help him forget his worries. Although it was still March on that Saturday, temperatures were already climbing as the four friends sipped their espressos and broke open their brioches while watching farmers selling vegetables in the market under the arches of the nineteenth-century theater across the way.

There was Tino Armenti, the oldest at eighty-five. Tino always seemed angry. If someone wished him a *"buongiorno"* he'd say: "What the hell is good about it?" If someone said the weather was warm, for Tino it was cold. If someone thought the tomato crop was coming in early, he complained that it was late. And on and on.

Tino's wife didn't want him around and loudly suggested that he get out of the house. He suggested that she mind her own business. She told him not to get angry. This made him even more angry and so he lowered himself into his wheelchair and bumped down the cobblestone street to Piazza Signorelli.

Sometimes Bruno lost his patience with Tino, too, but then he wondered how he himself would feel if he had lost his right foot, his right arm and his right eye to a hidden bomb during World War II. Tino had fought with the partisans in the battle for Monte Battaglia and, like other war veterans, he never talked about it.

Cesare La Rosa was seventy-six. He had farmed north of Cortona for many years but when his wife died three years ago his son and daughter-in-law insisted that he live with them. He resisted. He was perfectly fine living alone, and farming was the only thing he knew. But Francesco, the son, warned that if something happened to him, no one would know about it.

"What's going to happen?" Cesare asked.

"You never know," Francesco replied.

So Cesare moved into the apartment near the center of the city. It was a mistake. His daughter-in-law, Luisa, kept nagging him to straighten his room, clean up after he ate, dress better. Then there was the problem with the three children, all under ten, who seemed to run around and scream all day long. Cesare was glad to get away, even if only for a little while on a Saturday morning.

The fourth member of the group was Giuseppe Scotti. Unlike the others, who wore work clothes and heavy shoes, Giuseppe invariably had on a white shirt and a dark tie with a coat draped over his shoulders, even on hot summer days. When he took off his cap he revealed a bald head with a fringe of white hair. His blue eyes always seemed sad.

Giuseppe had been a schoolteacher for many years and had never married. He lived alone in a single room near San Benedetto and took his meals at a *trattoria* a block away. Every morning, he was the first to arrive at the church for Mass and the last to leave. After that, Giuseppe walked to the outskirts of Cortona, slowly pacing a mile and a half to a small shrine at the side of the road. He had built the shrine himself some fifty years ago. It was a white Virgin Mary against a blue background, reminiscent of a Della Robbia. Before arriving, he picked a spray of flowers, oleander perhaps, or Queen Anne's lace or fennel, and tied them with a weed. He placed these at the bottom of the shrine, paused for a moment, wiped his eyes with a white handkerchief, and walked back to town.

Every day for fifty years. Except for once, in the late 1960s, when he was hospitalized for three days after falling and breaking his left arm.

Bruno, Tino and Cesare knew all about the shrine and his daily walks, but they never—ever—talked about it. Giuseppe never talked much about his walks either. But then, he didn't speak much, just listened and occasionally smiled. Often, he looked off in the distance, his mind even farther away.

The conversation that Saturday morning, as it had for months, involved the World Cup championships that would be held in Italy from June 8 to July 8.

"I just heard they might not have the new stadium at Torino ready," Bruno said.

"Of course they won't have it ready!" Tino shouted. "Has there ever been anything in Italy built on time? *Boh!*"

"Well, they'll probably finish it," Bruno said.

"And what about that other new one in…where is it again?" Cesare asked.

"Bari," Bruno said.

"They won't finish it in time," Tino said. "It'll be a cold day in hell."

"Well, it will be worth it," Cesare said.

"At the way they're spending money?" Tino said. "They're already way over budget for all the ten stadiums. Who's going to pay for it?"

Cesare said he hoped he could watch the games on television but that the grandchildren made so much noise it would be difficult. Bruno wondered if Stefano Tacconi would be the goalie for Italy. Tino disagreed at length, giving fourteen reasons why someone else should be chosen, until finally Bruno decided it was time to go home.

As they were clearing their cups and paper napkins, Giuseppe spoke for the first time that morning.

"Oh, on my walk yesterday, I saw a sign that Bramasole was for sale."

"What's Bramasole?" Cesare asked.

"It's an old villa outside of Cortona," Bruno said.

"It's a heap!" Tino shouted. "Who would want to live there? Anybody would be crazy to buy that place. Insane!"

IF CESARE WAS IGNORANT ABOUT THE MATTER, most people in Cortona knew about Bramasole. Of all the old villas in and around the city, it was one of the largest. With a name combining *bramare* (to long for) and *sole* (sun), it stood three stories high at the end of a narrow street off a great walking boulevard south of the city. It was tall and square, the color of apricots, with a tile roof, faded green shutters and an iron balcony on the second level. Because it had been vacant for thirty years, the grounds were overgrown with blackberries and vines.

With so much else on his mind, Bruno thought only briefly about the sale of the villa that Saturday. He wondered, though, why anyone would want to buy a two-hundred-year-old building that certainly would need a great deal of work.

"Someone very rich," he thought. "But I hope they don't tear it down. It must have been beautiful once."

Bruno's wife, Veronica, was making his lunch when he returned home. She always tried not to bring up their financial worries, but a problem with the refrigerator could not be ignored any longer.

"The thermostat just won't work anymore, Bruno. We'll have to call someone."

"OK, OK, I'll do it Monday."

"We'll have enough to pay him, won't we?"

"If he doesn't charge too much."

"And we really should have that broken window in the living room repaired. There's such a draft."

"I think I know a carpenter who wouldn't charge much."

"Maybe he could do some plastering in the living room, too."

Veronica went back to making rice balls for dinner on Sunday. She'd already made fennel seed *foccacio,* six loaves of crusty bread, *bracioli* from sliced veal, and a couple of desserts. The rest could wait until after Mass on Sunday.

No matter what their financial hardships were, one thing the Pezzinos would not scrimp on was the Sunday dinner they had for their family. In 1990, the family spanned four generations. Veronica's father, Luigi, blind and bedridden, and her mother, Maria Elena, occupied a large room in the center of the apartment. Frequently in tears, Maria Elena came out only to get meals for her husband.

The oldest son, Rudolfo, his wife, Roberta, and their two-year-old son, Sergio, somehow fit into the next room. If they had another child, Rudolfo said, they would have to move, but Bruno and Victoria insisted that they could always make room.

The twins, Massimo and Michele, were now nineteen years old, out of school and working, but still sharing the same room they'd had since they were infants. Massimo sorted artifacts in the Etruscan Academy Museum, and Michele worked for a real estate agent, Anselmo Martini, in an office on Via Sacco e Vanzetti in the lower part of the city. Michele helped fix up properties when they were on the market. Massimo and Michele each had a girlfriend, both of whom, fortunately, were able to entertain the boys in their homes. It would have been awkward otherwise.

The youngest daughter, Luciana, was now ten, and her brother, Silvio, was nine. Both were demanding their own rooms, but there weren't any to spare.

Meanwhile, the oldest daughter, Analisa, and her husband, Pippino, had moved their own family into a big apartment right across the hall. Their three older children, Lorenzo, Luca and Franca, were joined last year by Carlo and Clarissa, another set of twins. The doors between the two apartments were always open so it didn't matter who ate where, or for that matter, who slept where.

Everyone always—always—sat down for Sunday dinner, even Maria Elena after she was certain that her husband was sleeping. Sometimes the group even expanded. Pippino's parents and younger brother often arrived bearing freshly made apple pies. Bruno's newly found cousin, Dino, and his wife, Sofia, often visited from Florence. Roberta's sister, a manicurist, was a frequent guest and often took care of female fingers afterward.

As always, with everyone talking at once, the din was overwhelming, and Veronica interrupted the conversation by placing two more platters of *bracioli* on the table.

"Mangia! Mangia!"

Everyone went around the table reporting on what had happened in the last week, their new purchases, the newly acquired skills of their precious children, the adventures that Massimo and Michele recently had. The twins were still excited about their jobs.

"It's like I discover something new at the museum every day—every minute!" Massimo said. "I mean, I could look at that Etruscan bronze chandelier all day and still find something new about it. And then on Thursday I was cataloging items from the Roman villa of Ossaia that date from the First Imperial Period to the Fifth Century. There's this big earthenware jug called a *gliararium*. You won't believe this, but it's where dormice were raised to be eaten."

"Oh, yuck," Luciana cried. "Mama, make him stop."

"Massimo," Veronica said, "we're still eating. Michele, tell us about what you're doing."

"Nothing nearly so interesting," Michele said. "I just keep the records of where Signor Martini takes clients. He's been busy. Just yesterday he took a couple to a bunch of old farmhouses, but some of them were falling down, so the people weren't interested. Then he took them to one with a tower that was built centuries and centuries ago. He said the woman who owned it doubled the price when she thought this couple was interested.

"And then he told me this funny story about how they went to one farmhouse where there were chickens running all over but they couldn't go inside because there was a black snake coiled up at the door."

"Mama!" Luciana cried, "make Michele stop. Right now. You know how scared I am of snakes."

"Well, that's what Signor Martini told me," Michele said.

"Did he take this couple anywhere else?" Veronica asked.

"Yes, he did. He took them to Bramasole."

BRUNO SUDDENLY LOOKED INTERESTED. "I just heard from Giuseppe yesterday that there was a 'for sale' sign at Bramasole," he said. "I wondered if anyone was going to be interested in that old place. It's been empty for so long."

"Well," Michele said, "Signor Martini took these people there and when they got there, the woman liked it so much that right away she said, 'Perfect. I'll take it.' Then they went inside and Signor Martini pointed out the thick walls and the views in the valley of cypresses and green hills and other villas. He said they were especially impressed that there were two bathrooms that really worked. But there's dirt all over and a lot of work to be done. *'Molto lavoro,'* Signor Martini said. And that's just the inside. He said the work on the property might take months or years."

"I can't imagine," Veronica said, "anyone buying an old villa like that and fixing it up. Aren't there new places?"

"Of course there are," Bruno said. "But some foolish people think that old places are better. Just wait until the roof starts leaking and the plumbing stops."

"Michele," Massimo said, "do you know where these people are from?"

"Signor Martini said California."

"California!" Massimo said. "Why would somebody come all the way from California to buy an old villa for thousands and thousands of *lire* and then spend thousands and thousands more to fix it up? Insane!"

"That explains it," Rudolfo said. "I've always heard that everyone in California is crazy."

"And rich," Bruno added.

"Oh, and get this," Michele said. "Signor Martini said that the buyers teach at a university in California so they'd be here only during the summers."

"Now I know they're insane," Massimo said.

Someone asked Michele if he knew the buyers' names.

"Signor Martini said if they made a purchase it would be in one name. It's something like March or Hayes or Mayes. I've got it written down in the office. OK, now I remember the first name, though. It's Francis. Yeah, that's it, Francis. And the last name is Mayes."

"Well, if this Francis Mayes really does buy Bramasole," Massimo said, "we'll call him Francesco and make him feel at home."

"So are they going to buy it?" Bruno asked.

"No, once they found out the price, they said no and went home."

The conversation stopped while Veronica and Analisa brought in more plates and removed others and Luciana shooed the cat from under the table.

"Well," Rudolfo said, "maybe there will be other people interested in Bramasole. Who owns it?"

"Signor Martini said some people remembered an artist from Naples living there once," Michele said, "but until last year it had been owned by five old sisters from Perugia. Then a doctor from Arezzo, Doctor Carta, bought it."

"Doctor Carta?" Rudolfo said. "That rich guy that I see driving around in an Alfa 164?"

"That's him. I saw him the other day. My God, I've never seen such an expensive suit. It must have been an Armani."

"So he's selling this villa?"

"Well, Signor Martini thought he was going to, but he may be changing his mind. He may want a higher price."

"Everybody who sells a villa wants more than it's worth," Bruno said.

"Signor Martini said that Doctor Carta and his wife had intended to live there as a summer place, but then he inherited property on the coast so he was going to use that instead."

"Ah yes," Massimo said. "Those that have money get more money."

"And those who don't, lose theirs," Bruno said.

Veronica reached over to her husband's arm. "Don't be bitter, Bruno. You'll get more work."

"I don't see how."

After everyone was quite full, Maria Elena returned to take care of her husband, Analisa and Pippino took their children back across the hall, and the others scattered.

Helping his wife with the dishes, Bruno broached a subject he'd been thinking about.

"Veronica, maybe I should just give up the tour guide business. I didn't have any customers last week, only one the week before. People just don't want to come to Cortona."

"That's because they don't know how beautiful it is. Bruno, we'll manage. Really. Wait awhile and see how things go. OK?"

"I'll wait. I don't know how long a while is, though."

Bruno sat at the kitchen table and tried to revise the brochure about Cortona that he'd written seven or eight years ago.

Cortona was conquered by the Etruscans who called it Curtun, and parts of the Etruscan wall can still be seen today. As a Roman colony its name was Corito. Now it is known as a medieval city with steep narrow streets. The highest point of the city, almost 2,000 feet above sea level, offers a spectacular view of the surrounding valley and Lake Trasimeno.

You can see art and artifacts from the Etruscan period as well as items from the medieval and Renaissance eras in the Museo dell'Accademia Etrusca, located in the Palazzo Casali. The Diocesan Museum includes a beautiful panel painting of the Annunciation by Fra Angelico.

The heart of Cortona is the Piazza della Repubblica, with the Palazzo Comunale, or town hall, overlooking the square. Nearby is Piazza Signorelli, named for the famous Renaissance painter who was a native of Cortona.

Among the beautiful churches of Cortona are the Church of Santa Margherita, named for the city's patron saint; the Church of San Cristoforo; the Church of Sant'Agostino, and the Church of Santa Maria Nuova, built by Giorgio Vasari in 1554, as a domed church with a centralized Greek cross layout....

"Boring, boring," Bruno thought. "Who would want to visit Cortona after reading this?"

He put the paper and pencil away.

When he went back to the office on Monday, Bruno received a telephone call from Michele, who said he needed to make a small correction to what he had said on Sunday.

"Papa, I made a mistake. That person from California who had been interested in Bramasole? The name isn't Francis, a man. It's Frances, a woman."

"A woman was interested in buying Bramasole?"

"Yes, and Signor Martini told me she's a poet and a writer. And she's also a professor at a university in San Francisco. Can you imagine?"

"Sounds very impressive."

"Well, Signor Martini said it's still up in the air. I think they're dickering about the price now."

It was only weeks later when Michele called his father with news. "Papa, the deal is done. That American woman, Frances Mayes, bought Bramasole!"

He went on to explain that Signor Martini had taken Frances Mayes and her friend Ed to a notary in Arezzo to finalize the transaction. He said Doctor Carta had some last-minute reservations about the price and wanted to ask for more, but the *notario*, a Signora Maniucci, kept on signing papers anyway.

Signor Martini had said that, in typical Italian fashion, Carta said he would claim that he received a lower amount for the house. He said, "That is just the way it's done. No one is fool enough to declare the real value."

Hearing this, Bruno just nodded. He'd heard this kind of talk before.

When Bruno revealed this information to his friends the following Saturday as they enjoyed their espresso at their usual tables outside Bar Sport, Tino was the most surprised.

"A woman is buying Bramasole?"

"Why not?" Bruno said. "It's 1990, women can do anything."

"Boh!" Tino said.

"Boh!" Cesare agreed.

Giuseppe smiled.

Also, Bruno said, the woman is a poet and a writer and a teacher.

"Oh great," Tino said. "I imagine she won't even talk to one of us. We won't be good enough."

"Now, Tino," Bruno said, "don't make judgments already. You don't know anything about her. Maybe she'll write something about Bramasole. Even Cortona. I guess people do that. Maybe for a travel magazine or something. Maybe then Cortona will be on the map and I can get some business."

REPORTS ABOUT BRAMASOLE and those strange new occupants from America continued as spring turned into summer. Giuseppe said he'd seen many workmen going up and down the hill to the villa when he visited the little shrine at the entrance to the old house every day.

"Sometimes," he reported to his friends, "I see a woman in the window. She looks nice enough. I don't think she sees me. I leave my flowers anyway."

But Bramasole was forgotten when the most important event in Italy in 1990 began in June and ended in July: the World Cup. Italy was only the second country to host the event twice, the first being Mexico in 1986. When qualifications began in 1988, 116 national teams applied, with twenty-two finally approved, along with Italy as the host nation and Argentina, the defending champion.

It turned out to be the most watched World Cup in history, and even though Italy placed third, conversations dissecting the plays, the referees' calls and the games themselves went on for months. For once, Tino didn't argue, and Giuseppe actually spoke several times.

Clearly, the hero for many was Salvatore Schillaci.

"If I was pope, I'd make Schillaci a saint, right here and now," Tino said at one of their meetings in August. "Saint Salvatore!"

In Italy's first match against Austria, this twenty-six-year-old son of a poor family from Palermo came on as a substitute and scored the decisive goal as the match ended with a 1–0 win for Italy.

"Remember how he did that?" Tino shouted. "Incredible. I can still see it."

A few months later, they were arguing about the game against Czechoslovakia, in which Schillaci and Roberto Baggio each scored for a 2-0 victory.

"Baggio is good, but Schillaci is so much better," Cesare pronounced.

In the next two matches, Schillaci scored again, in the second round against Uruguay and in the quarterfinals against the Republic of Ireland.

"Twice!" Bruno said.

For the semifinal match against defending champion Argentina, Schillaci scored his fifth goal of the tournament.

"Five goals!" Tino declared. "Five goals!"

Then Italy was eliminated after a penalty shoot-out.

"I could have killed that referee!" Cesare said.

More than a year later, they were still talking about the matches, remembering that in the game against England for third place, Schillaci scored the winning goal in Italy's 2–1 victory, and he won the Golden Boot for the most goals in the World Cup, six.

"Incredible!" Bruno said. "Six! The Golden Boot!"

"Impossible!" Cesare said.

"It almost made losing worthwhile," Giuseppe said.

"No, no, no," Tino said.

This last time, their Saturday morning football recapitulation at their usual table was interrupted when their attention was drawn to two women buying vegetables at the farmers' market across Piazza Signorelli.

"Look at those girls," Cesare whispered. "What do they have on their heads?"

"They're scarves," Bruno said.

"Why do they have their heads covered on a hot day in July?" Tino asked.

"They're Muslims," Bruno said. "Haven't you ever seen a Muslim before?"

"I don't think so," Cesare said. "Where would I have seen one?"

"What are Muslims doing here?" Tino asked. "I thought they were only in Rome or Bologna or someplace. Now we're going to get Muslims in Cortona?"

Italy had established its first amnesty program for illegal aliens in the late 1980s, and as a result the number of foreign-born people in the country had increased dramatically. In 1985, the number of foreign-borns in Italy holding a residence permit was estimated at approximately 423,000. By 1991, that number had more than doubled, reaching 896,800.

"Did I tell you," Bruno said, "about how my cousin Dino in Florence is trying to adopt a little boy from Albania?"

"Really?" all three of his friends said.

"Yes. Well, Dino and Sofia are just starting the process of doing this, but remember that shipload of Albanians that landed at Bari in August?"

"And the government sent them all home," Tino said.

"Most of them," Bruno said. "Some escaped. But Dino and Sofia met this young couple who had a little boy with them. The boy was the girl's nephew and they had come to Italy to find another home for him."

"They wanted to give him up?" Cesare said. "No!"

"They did. But Dino and Sofia decided to adopt him."

"Say," Tino said, "I thought you said Dino and Sofia were kind of, well, old. They can still adopt?"

"They're in their forties. They can still do it. I hope it works out. They seem so happy about it. The boy's name is Tarik. Dino says he's eight years old and very smart."

"Tarik?" Tino said. "What kind of a name is that?"

"Well," Bruno said, "what kind of a name is Tino?"

"Never mind," Tino said. "I can remember when there were just people from Cortona here. Then we got all these people from Calabria. Then we got all these people from Albania. Now we're getting people from Poland and Hungary. I don't like it. I know I'm not supposed to say that, but I don't like it. Foreigners, that's what they are."

"Think of Cortona as being a little United Nations," Bruno said. "I think a lot of Poles went to Germany to find work but then there weren't any jobs there, so now they're coming here."

"Boh!" Tino said.

"I've seen some Polish workers going up to Bramasole," Giuseppe said.

"I've heard about them," Bruno said. "Michele told me that Frances Mayes wanted to have a long wall torn down, so Signor Martini sent over a contractor. The contractor hired three big Polish guys. I think their names are Stanislao, Cristoforo and Riccardo or something like that."

"I've seen them around," Cesare said. "Big guys. Don't speak Italian, but they seem nice enough."

"Father Fabio lets them live in a back room of the church," Bruno said. "He even provides three meals a day, but he won't let them work on Sunday. Anyway, Michele said they tore down the wall like nothing. Frances Mayes told Signore Martini they were carrying hundred-pound stones like watermelons. She was very happy. She said they were even singing while they were working."

"In Polish?"

"I guess so," Bruno said. "Well, after they tore down that wall, they built another. Just like that. Then they did a lot of work inside, washing down the walls. And you know what? They found a fresco on the walls!"

"I bet that was that painter from Naples," Cesare said.

"Or maybe someone famous!" Tino said. "Maybe Giotto?"

"The villa isn't that old," Bruno said. "Those Poles should be getting a lot more than they're being paid. But you know that that contractor isn't paying them a decent wage at all. It's more than they'd get at home, so they're happy."

"I bet I know that guy," Tino said. "It's just like him to rip off people who don't even speak Italian."

"Sounds like you're sympathetic to these Polish guys, Tino," Bruno said.

"I just don't like people being ripped off. I don't care where they're from."

"I wonder if Frances Mayes knows about this," Bruno said. "Well, it looks like they're fixing Bramasole up good."

IF 1990 AND 1991 WERE BAD for Pezzino Tours, business was worse in 1992 and didn't improve in 1993. On the average, Bruno had one or two tours a week. Usually, these were small groups, which let him use his smaller car, but didn't provide the daily income he needed. Not to mention that he didn't get many tips.

Veronica was pleased that he didn't talk about quitting the business anymore. At fifty-six, how could he find something else to do? Somehow, they would manage with their savings. She didn't tell her husband that their son Rudolfo and their son-in-law Pippino were quietly filling an envelope with *lire* in a kitchen drawer every week.

Not even the visit by Pope John Paul II, the "Polish pope," to Cortona in May 1993 helped to improve tourism. When the rest of the family urged Bruno to capitalize on the visit, Bruno pointed out that the pope would be in town only for an hour or so and probably at night since he had a big Eucharistic celebration in the stadium at Arezzo and other activities there earlier in the day.

"He's only going to be talking to people in front of the Church of Santa Margherita and then praying before her tomb in the church," Bruno said at one of the family dinners in April. "There won't be time for tours, too."

"Well," Veronica said, "I'm excited about the pope coming. He's never been in Cortona before. We'll have to get there early because I'm sure there's going to be a mob of people."

"We?" Michele asked. "We? Are we all going?"

"Of course we're all going," Veronica said. "What are you thinking?"

"But hardly anyone in this family even goes to Mass," Massimo said. "Well, you do. And Papa sometimes. And you drag Luciana and Silvio along."

"I don't drag them along," his mother said. "They want to go, right?"

"I only go to see Margherita's body in the tomb," Silvio said. "It's gross."

"Yuck," Luciana said. "I hate looking at dead bodies."

Of all the saints of the Catholic Church, Margherita of Cortona had one of the most interesting biographies. Born in 1247, she suffered under a cruel stepmother after her own mother died and her father remarried. As a teenager, she became promiscuous and ran away with a rich young man when she was seventeen. She lived in his castle near Montepulciano as his mistress for ten years and bore him a son.

When her lover was murdered, Margherita began a life of prayers and penance. She tried to return home, but her stepmother wouldn't accept her, so she took her son to the Franciscan friars of Cortona and he eventually became a friar, too. Margherita joined the Third Order of Saint Francis and somehow was able to establish a hospital in Cortona.

After her death, the Church of Santa Margherita was built in her honor and her body is preserved there. She was canonized in 1728.

"And did you know," Silvio said, "she ate only bread and vegetables."

"Yuck," Luciana said.

Silvio had more to say. "You know how the church says a saint is the patron saint of something? Well, I read a list of what Margherita is the patron saint of. Listen to this. She is the patron saint of people who are falsely accused, the homeless, the insane, orphans, midwives, single mothers, stepchildren, hoboes, tramps and reformed prostitutes. She must be very busy answering all those prayers."

"Hoboes, tramps and reformed prostitutes?" Massimo said. "Well, I guess they need a patron saint like anybody else. I don't know what a reformed prostitute is, though."

"All right," Bruno said, "let's change the subject. What's new at Bramasole, Michele?"

"Signor Martini says they're still doing a lot of work. Frances Mayes and her friend Ed go back to teaching in California and then come back here in the summer. I think those Polish guys are still doing work there."

"It still amazes me that they're doing all that work on that place," Bruno said. "It must be costing a fortune."

"Signor Martini says they are budgeting their money very well," Michele said. "And they've got good workers."

Bruno and his entire family did go to see the pope on May 23, climbing up the steep hill to the church with hundreds of other pilgrims. Michele found himself standing next to a small crowd of Polish workers who had come to cheer the first Polish pope in history. He looked up and saw the three Polish workers he had heard so much about, Stanislao, the oldest, then Cristoforo and Riccardo. They were neatly dressed in sport shirts and slacks, waving small Polish flags and shouting, *"Viva Papieza! Viva Papieza!"*

Michele got into the spirit of the evening and started shouting *"Viva Papieza!"* too.

The pope told the crowd that Santa Margherita was a model for marriage and the family because she loved the father of her baby and eventually began a new life in penance, prayer and the exercise of charity toward the poor. Then he went inside to pray before her silver casket and everybody went home.

When they arrived back at their apartment Bruno took out paper and pencil, and Veronica asked what he was doing.

"I think I should have a new brochure," he said. "I've been using that old one for years and it doesn't seem to be doing any good."

"What will you put in it?"

"I'm thinking of something like 'Cortona: The Home of Santa Margherita.' And then I can write about her life and the fact that she had a baby even though she wasn't married and that the church canonized her anyway. And then I'll have a photograph of her tomb and say something like 'Come to Cortona and see the body of a saint.'"

"Do you think people will come to Cortona because of that?"

"I don't know. Can't hurt to try, right?"

UNFORTUNATELY, the body of a saint wasn't much of a lure for tourists, and Bruno saw little change in his business in the next years. His friends noted that he seemed more and more depressed each time they met on Saturday mornings, and tried to cheer him up with little jokes. Even Giuseppe told stories about the Polish workers who were finishing up at Bramasole.

"Looks like it's done, as far as I can tell," he said. "I haven't seen the owners for a while, though. Must be back in California."

"Michele says Signor Martini says they really like the place, though," Bruno said. "They're going to spend a lot of time there."

Although his tourist business was still stagnant, one thing that cheered Bruno was a visit every other month from Dino, Sofia and Tarik. The boy was twelve now and about to start high school.

"He's so smart," Bruno told his friends one Saturday. "He's already said that he's going to go to the University of Pisa to study engineering. Dino and Sofia are so proud. They're all going to come for dinner tomorrow and Veronica is very excited."

When the visitors from Florence arrived and everyone finally finished exclaiming how much Tarik had grown, they all gathered around the big table. Veronica began, as usual, with a prayer for her family, naming every one of them individually.

"Well," Dino said as they settled down, "I have a surprise."

"What?" Michele asked.

"You're going to move to Cortona," Massimo said.

"No."

"You bought a Lamborghini," Michele said.

"No."

"You won the lottery," Silvio said.

"I wish," Dino said. "Just wait."

By 1 o'clock, all the dishes were on the table, the pasta, the roasted chicken, the *bracioli,* the crostini, the vegetables.

"I think it's all here," Veronica said. *"Mangia! Mangia!"*

"OK, Dino," Bruno said, "what's this exciting news that you've been keeping a secret?"

Dino pulled out the package he'd been sitting on and tore off the wrapping.

"Look! Frances Mayes has written a book. About Bramasole! About Cortona! About the people who live here!"

"Oh, my God!"

"I know you can't read English," Dino said, "and I don't read it very well either, but I was in a bookstore near the Duomo that sells English-language books. It's called the Paperback Exchange and it's really good. I've bought three or four books there over the years. It helps me improve my English.

"So I was in there the other day and I was looking around and suddenly I saw this book with a villa on the cover. And I thought, 'That looks sort of familiar.' Well, I looked closer and I knew it was Bramasole. And then I finally read the title. *Under the Tuscan Sun.* That's what this says. And there's a subtitle, *A Home in Italy.* And down here, 'By Frances Mayes.' Look, here's her picture on the back."

"That's her!" Michele shouted. "The woman who bought Bramasole. Signor Martini told me once that she was writing something about Bramasole, but I didn't think she would actually write a whole book."

"A whole book," Silvio said. "A whole book about Bramasole."

"And Cortona," Luciana said.

"Here, I'll pass it around,"

Carefully, the book was passed from hand to hand. Everyone touched the photo and traced their fingers on the letters. When it reached Maria Elena, she began to cry. "Oh, I wish Luigi could see this. I'm going to take it to him."

She carried the book to her husband in the bedroom. For once he was awake but of course he couldn't see anything. "Touch this, Luigi. It's a book about Cortona. All about Cortona. Imagine."

She put his hand on the book, and the old man's sightless eyes began to tear. Maria Elena kissed him on the forehead and brought the book back to the table, where it continued to make the rounds until it returned to Dino.

"Well, as I said, I don't read English very well," he said, "but I'll try to tell you some parts. Here in the preface she writes about how the book began just with her notes about flowers and projects and recipes. And then she writes about how restoring the house and the grounds and finding the links between food and culture helped her to learn another kind of life.

"Then she starts the book with how she signed the contract to buy Bramasole. Signor Martini is there..."

"Signor Martini is in the book?" Michele said. "He's going to be surprised."

"...and Doctor Carta. She quotes Carta as saying that he won't claim the full amount and he says, 'That is just the way it's done. No one is fool enough to declare the real value.'"

"That's exactly what Signor Martini said he said," Michele said.

"Then she says Cortona was the first town they'd ever stayed in and they kept coming back here. She talks about walking around town and the Bar Sport..."

"Bar Sport!" Bruno said. "I'll have to tell Giuseppe and Tino and Cesare."

"...and then she writes about visiting Bramasole and how Carta showed her the views and turned on a faucet to impress her with the fresh water. Let me find what she says. Oh, here it is. 'When I first saw Bramasole, I immediately wanted to hang my summer clothes in an *armadio* and arrange my books under one of those windows looking out over the valley.'

"Then she writes about the three Polish workers who were hired to help and how they lift big stones like watermelons. She says Riccardo is twenty-seven and Cristoforo is thirty and Stanislao is forty."

"They all look the same age to me," Bruno said.

"And she writes how they work from seven until noon and then they drive off in their Polski Fiat and come back at three o'clock for five more hours."

"My God," Sofia said. "I can't imagine Italians working like that."

"Frances Mayes obviously knows that the Poles are being paid less per hour than Italian workers," Dino said, "but she writes that they're pleased because before their factory in Poland closed they earned less than that in a day."

"They were still taken advantage of," Bruno said. "That's not fair. It's probably illegal, but who's going to say anything?"

"She writes about a lot of things," Dino continued. "How she shops at the market and takes walks around Cortona. She hires two carpenters, Marco and Rudolfo…"

"I know them!" Massimo said. "They did some work at the museum. They were very quiet."

"That's what Frances Mayes writes. She wanted a big table built for outside and they did that."

Bruno took the book from Dino's hands and paged through it. He tried to recognize a word here and there, but finally gave it back to Dino.

"Besides writing about Bramasole and Cortona," Dino said, "she also has some chapters that give recipes."

"In a book like that?" Analisa asked.

"Yes. Here's one for Baked Peppers with Ricotta and Basil. Here's one for Hazelnut Gelato. Here's one for Bruchette with Pecorino and Nuts."

"Dino," Veronica said, "do you think you could translate them for me? I could try them."

"I may get the ingredients wrong, but I'll try. But I've kept the best for last. Bruno, you know your friend Giuseppe?"

"Of course. Is he in there?"

"Not by name, but I'm sure she's writing about him. She calls him the man with the flowers. I'm going to go slow, but here's what she writes:

"A sprig of oleander, a handful of Queen Anne's and fennel bound with a stem, a full bouquet of dog roses, dandelion puffs, buttercups, and lavender bells—every day I look to see what he has propped up in the shrine at the bottom of my driveway."

"That's him!" Bruno said. "That's Giuseppe."

"She writes that sometimes she's working outside and sees him approaching:

"He pauses in the road and stares up at me. I wave but he does not wave back, just blank stares as though I, a foreigner, am a creature unaware of being looked at, a zoo animal."

"I'm sure," Bruno said, "that Giuseppe doesn't think she's a zoo animal. That's just the way he is."

"She writes that once she saw him in a park and she said something to him, but all he said was *'buongiorno.'* She says that he had taken off his cap and his bald head was 'as bright as a light bulb.'"

"It is, it's that bright," Bruno said. "But he hardly ever takes off his cap."

"Here's what I find most interesting," Dino said. "Let me find this here. She doesn't know who he is, but she imagines all sorts of things about him. She thinks he might be an angel because his coat hangs around his shoulders. I guess I don't understand that. Maybe she thinks the coat hides his wings, I don't know. But then she fantasizes that his mother was a great beauty who stepped out of carriages right where the shrine is, or that his father was cruel and forbade him to enter the house. Or that he visits the shrine to thank Jesus for saving his daughter from surgeons in Parma. She imagines all these things because she's so curious about him."

"Some imagination," Massimo said.

"She writes that she doesn't touch the flowers that he leaves and that she doesn't even dust off Mary's face in the shrine."

"Well," Bruno said, "if Frances Mayes knew why Giuseppe walks all that way every day to bring flowers to the shrine she'd have a better story."

"I've always wondered why he did that," Rudolfo said. "Why does he?"

"I don't think he wants people to know," Bruno said. "They might think he's crazy."

"No," Veronica said, "they wouldn't think he's crazy. They'd think he was a very fine gentleman. Tell them the story, Bruno."

"Well," Bruno said, "you shouldn't really repeat this, but here goes. From what I've heard, this happened a long time ago. There was a beautiful young girl, Felicità, and all the boys wanted to go out with her. She refused them all until she met Giuseppe. He was a couple of years older, and was a teacher in the school. She was just out of school and working in a card shop. Giuseppe and Felicità fell in love. Madly in love. They went out for almost a year, and one Sunday afternoon Giuseppe drove her out to the countryside near Arezzo. They had a picnic and Giuseppe took out a ring and proposed marriage. She accepted, and they were very happy. They had never been so happy.

"Well, they were anxious to tell their parents and were driving home when they were rounding that curve right in front of Bramasole. You know how dangerous it is there. Just like that, a big semi came out of nowhere from the other direction and slammed into them. Smashed the car to bits. Felicità was killed instantly. Giuseppe was thrown from the car but had only had a few bruises.

"He was so upset he couldn't teach for a year, just kept in his room and hardly spoke to anyone. One day he got the idea to build a little shrine at the curve right where the accident happened. He did that and started taking flowers there every day. He's done that every morning after Mass ever since, no matter if it's pouring rain or blazing sun or cold in winter. For fifty years. But he never talks about it."

"He always seems so sad," Michele said. "I don't think I've ever seen him smile."

"He has a few times," Bruno said, "but not very often. He'll go to his grave like that."

Suddenly, no one seemed interested in talking about *Under the Tuscan Sun* anymore. Dino put the book down.

"I'll leave this here in case anyone wants to look at it," he said. "Do you think somebody should tell Frances Mayes the real story of this old man?"

"No," Bruno said. "Giuseppe wouldn't want that."

SINCE FEW PEOPLE in Cortona could read English and since *Under the Tuscan Sun* hadn't been translated into Italian, the book became a topic of curiosity but not much conversation in Cortona.

"Did you hear about that book by that woman from Bramasole?" someone would ask. "I hear it's very good."

"I've heard about it, but I can't read it," was the usual answer.

That, however, was not true in America where, to the author's surprise, the book suddenly became a best-seller. It soared to the top of *The New York Times'* best-seller list and remained on the list for two-and-a-half years.

American readers were fascinated by the story of Bramasole and, by extension, about Cortona itself. They'd never heard of the city before, but it sounded like one untouched by tourists so they would be the first to discover it.

Bruno was surprised to get a phone call late one night.

"Hello. I'm calling from Chicago. Are you the man who has a tourist business in Cortona?"

"Yes."

"It sounds like an interesting place. We'll be in Florence in two months and we'd like to visit Cortona, too. How can I arrange a tour?"

That was just the first. It was followed by a call two days later from Philadelphia and by a third the following day from Houston. By the end of the week, Pezzino Tours had booked six excursions, a total of twenty-eight people, for the coming month.

"This is fantastic," Bruno beamed at dinner the following Sunday. "And it's all because of that book."

In the next weeks, Bruno took visitors from Cleveland, Des Moines, Kansas City and Seattle on tours of Cortona. At the end of each tour, the visitors wanted to see Bramasole. Bruno was hesitant. He wanted them to see the Etruscan museum, the churches—especially the Church of Santa Margherita with the body of the saint—and to just guide them around the beautiful city.

Reluctantly, he agreed to just walk a small group by the entrance to Bramasole, pointing out the little shrine that was so reverently described in the book.

"Can you tell us about the man who puts flowers at the shrine?" someone invariably would ask."

"No, I don't know much about it," he would say. "Now let's get back in the bus and continue our tour."

The tourists seemed satisfied. A few were astonished when Frances Mayes herself happened to be coming or going at the same time. They were even more amazed when she stopped to talk.

One cheeky visitor shouted, "How much did you pay for this?"

Frances Mayes smiled.

A few months later, in the group from Milwaukee, someone mentioned that he recognized the narrow street off Piazza Signorelli because he'd seen the photo "on line."

Bruno asked him what he meant. He said "the web."

Bruno didn't want to show any more of his ignorance, but he called Dino that night.

"He's talking about the World Wide Web," Dino said.

"What in the world is that?"

"It's something new," he said. "If you have a computer you can look things up and they appear on your screen. People put all sorts of things on it. Sometimes they do put photographs on, so somebody must have put up photos of Cortona and that's what this person saw."

"That's amazing," Bruno said. "I don't even have a computer."

"Well, you'll have to get one soon," Dino said, "or the world is going to pass you by. Maybe someday, if I can figure it out, I can put something on to advertise your tours. You can have your own page on the web."

"Dino, I can't even get used to this mobile phone."

"They're called cell phones now, Bruno. But here's one thing I'd suggest now. I'd change the name of your business. 'Pezzino Tours' doesn't tell anybody very much. How about 'Under the Tuscan Sun Tours'?"

"Really?"

"Why not? Why not capitalize on that name? People know it now. And it's not as if it was copyrighted. It's just a descriptive term. We all live in Tuscany and we're all under the sun."

Bruno tried the name out on his friends when they had coffee the following Saturday at Bar Sport.

"I don't know," Tino said. "Sounds kind of fancy. How about 'See Cortona.'"

"Not very descriptive," Bruno said.

Cesare and Giuseppe both liked the new name, though Giuseppe worried that people might want to see that old man who took flowers to the shrine every day.

"I promise you, Giuseppe," Bruno said, "I promise you I will never take anyone near Bramasole in the mornings when you're bringing the flowers. Never."

"OK. Thank you."

On about his sixth or seventh tour, Bruno was asked a question he'd never heard before.

"Bruno," a man from Pittsburgh said, "that story about fixing up Bramasole was very interesting. Are there other old villas around here for sale?"

It didn't take long for Bruno to think of at least three, the old Santucci mansion to the west, the Filippo villa to the south and the Montanini farm on the way to Arezzo.

Could Bruno take the man to one of them?

Bruno thought about it. No, real estate wasn't his field, and he didn't have a license. He called Michele. Would Signor Martini like to give a man from Pittsburgh a tour?

That was just the start. *Under the Tuscan Sun* soon became responsible for a wave of foreigners descending on Tuscany and elsewhere in Italy looking for old villas to rent or buy. Naturally, prices went up. Inevitably, many of the villas were in such terrible condition that some of the new owners gave up and went home.

And in a side development, there was a flood of books by the new owners writing about their own efforts at restoration and inhabitation. None of the books achieved fame like *Under the Tuscan Sun.*

One Sunday evening, as the 1990s neared an end, Bruno and Veronica enjoyed a quiet moment after the rest of the family had scattered and only the cat was left to keep them company.

"Just think of it, Veronica. In 1990 I was ready to quit because the tourism business was so bad. We might have had to give up this apartment."

"And now your tours are booked almost constantly. You've got two more tour guides to help out, and Massimo and Michele do some work on weekends. Even Cortona's population has grown now that people know about it."

"You know what, Veronica? I don't think I want any more business. I don't think I could handle it."

"You've got quite enough now, Bruno. Oh, do you know what I heard today? I heard they're going to make a movie of *Under the Tuscan Sun.*"

And Now, a Major Motion Picture

Sant'Antonio

ALTHOUGH HE WAS SEVENTY-THREE YEARS OLD, Ezio Maffini had never worn a tuxedo, had never thought of wearing a tuxedo, had never wanted to wear a tuxedo and, like countless men before him, was not happy about wearing one now.

"Stupid buttons," he muttered. "These pants fit in the store. Now they won't button. Donna, how am I supposed to go like this?"

"Oh, just take a deep breath and try again." Donna was looking in the mirror at her dressing table, trying to get her eyeliner even.

"I tried that. They still won't button."

"Well, then don't open your jacket."

"I can't go all night with my jacket buttoned."

"Of course you can. Anyway, your cummerbund will hide it."

"Fat chance."

"No pun intended, I hope."

He gave up on the pants and managed to attach the cuff links on his starched white shirt, but struggled with the studs on the front of it. Then he turned his attention to the tie. He looked at the directions the store had provided.

"Drape the tie around your neck, under your collar, and grasp the ends. The end on your right side should extend 1.5 inches lower than the end on your left side.

"OK, did that."

"Cross the longer end over the shorter end. You should cross the tie near your neck so the loop around your neck is just large enough to work with but not loose. You don't want your bow dangling in front of your chest."

"Well, no, we wouldn't want that, would we?"

"Pass the longer end up through the loop, forming a simple overhand knot."

"What the hell? This is crazy."

"Pull the dangling end to the left and then fold it back over itself to the right. Hold this fold, which will be the front loop of the completed tie, between your shirt's collar points."

"Fuck it! This is impossible! Donna!"

"Just a minute. I'm almost finished."

After Donna had tied her husband's bow tie—in seconds, it seemed—he made sure his zipper was zipped, tried to button the button on his pants again but failed, clipped on the cummerbund to hide the gap, put on his jacket and looked in the mirror. Like countless men before him, he uttered the immortal words: "I look like a penguin."

"You look very handsome," Donna said. "At least ten years younger. You should wear a tux all the time."

"Right. I'd look great repairing the shingles on the barn in a tux."

Donna herself looked resplendent in a long shimmering light blue gown held at the shoulders by tiny straps. There was just a suggestion of cleavage. Her blond hair, with only a few hints of gray, was clipped short.

"And you! And you, Donna, you look like you're eighteen." He tried to take her in his arms and kiss her but she gently pushed him away.

"Not now, Ezio. I've spent an hour on my makeup and an hour on my hair. There's one last thing."

She took a silver necklace from her jewelry box. It was a gift from Ezio on their fortieth wedding anniversary.

"No earrings?" he asked.

"You know I never wear earrings."

"Never?"

"No, not even to the premiere of a motion picture directed by the famous Salvatore Balconi with a screenplay adapted from a wonderful novel by the amazingly talented Ezio Maffini."

"OK, but everyone will be talking about how you're not wearing earrings."

Donna replaced a strand of hair that had fallen on Ezio's forehead. "Excited?"

"I could say no, but, yes, I am."

"I never thought we'd see this day. I'm so proud of you, Ezio!"

She leaned up to kiss him on the cheek.

When they went downstairs, Paolo and Lucia, who were going to drive with them to Florence, had just arrived. Lucia had insisted that she and Donna purchase new dresses for the occasion from a shop on Via Tornabuoni in Florence. She wore a long, rather bright fuchsia gown with a red scarf around her neck. Her gold necklace matched her gold earrings, which matched a bracelet on her right wrist.

Paolo wore the tux that he had rented from a shop in Florence with Ezio the day before.

"You look like a penguin," Ezio told Paolo.

"Like your brother."

"Remember that we have to get these back to the store by 1 o'clock tomorrow. I sure don't want to pay that penalty."

Although it was only 5 o'clock and the film wasn't scheduled to start until 9, Ezio was in a hurry to get started. They had time for only a quick drink and a toast from Donna. "To my husband, who started all this by writing the novel!"

They were in the car driving down the hill from the Cielo to the highway to Lucca when Lucia exclaimed, "I'm so excited! I don't think I've ever been so excited! There will be movie stars there, I'm sure, and photographers and even television. Do you think there will be a red carpet? Will we be stopped to answer questions? Oh, my hair looks just awful."

"Lucia," Paolo said, "the press isn't interested in us. Maybe in Ezio, but not us."

"Well," Lucia said, "we'll be following right behind and maybe someone will ask us questions."

As Ezio had feared, traffic outside of Florence was horrendous, and they were stalled twice for twenty minutes. When they finally got into the city there was nowhere at all to park.

"I would have thought," Paolo said, "the film people would have provided a parking place for you."

"I'm only the guy who wrote the novel," Ezio said.

They finally found a spot in the Oltrarno, which meant they had to cross the crowded Ponte Vecchio to get to the movie theater on the other side of the river. Which meant Lucia struggled to keep up in her high heels. Donna had wisely chosen flats.

"I knew I shouldn't have worn these," Lucia said. She was almost in tears. She finally took them off and carried them, immediately getting holes in the bottoms of her stockings.

After crossing the bridge, they walked up to Via Calimala, skirted Piazza della Repubblica and made their way up Via della Scala. The crowds became more dense as they neared the theater. And when they turned a corner, there it was. Spotlights lit the sky, a band was playing and, beyond the stretch limousines that lined the streets, hundreds of formally dressed patrons milled in the piazza.

They were, they knew, in front of one of the most famous, one of the most treasured, movie theaters in all of Italy. The Cinema Teatro Odeon was carved into a part of Palazzo Strozzino, which was built in 1462 and is still considered one of the great examples of Renaissance architecture. The theater itself was created in 1922 in an Art Deco style with sculptures, tapestries and a stained-glass cupola. Ezio and the others could see the three brightly lighted arches at the entrance in the distance.

On the marquee, in big lights: *Separazione. A Film by Salvatore Balconi.*

"Oh my! Oh my!" Lucia shouted over the din of the crowd. "I'm so excited."

Ezio went to the white tent where he was to receive his credentials.

"Ezio Maffini? Ezio Maffini?" the man behind the counter said as he thumbed through a card file. He was about twenty years old, had long hair and sported a rose tattoo on his wrist.

"It should be there," Ezio said. "I was told to come here. I wrote the novel on which the screenplay is based."

"Oh, well, you should have said that. You're in this box under the table."

Having secured four credentials, Ezio, Donna, Lucia and Paolo maneuvered their way through the crowds to the entrance of the theater.

"Look!" Lucia cried. "There really is a red carpet. I thought they made that up. Paolo, hold my arm. And stand up straight."

With Ezio and Donna leading, the foursome stepped gingerly onto the red carpet. Photographers lined both sides, television cameras were stationed along the way, and gushing reporters with microphones stopped the guests as they proceeded to the entrance.

"Look at all these people," Donna said. "Who are they?"

"I imagine some of them are the actors in the movie," Ezio said, "but I didn't realize there'd be so many. And then there are all the technical people."

"Excuse me," a young woman with long blond hair, a strapless red gown and too much makeup said as she pulled out a notebook and poked Ezio's arm. "Are you someone?"

"Um, well, I wrote the novel and they made a movie out of it."

"Oh, how exciting. What was the name of the novel?"

"*Il cielo.*"

"But isn't the name of the movie *Separazione?*"

"Yes. They changed it."

"Oh. So you wrote a novel and they made a movie but they changed the name."

"Yes."

"Well, thank you anyway."

"You're welcome."

Ezio and Donna proceeded slowly down the carpet, only to be stopped by a man about thirty years old with greasy hair slicked back. He shoved a microphone in Donna's face.

"I know you," he said. "You were in that film directed by Lucio Fulci. Brett Halsey was in it. You are…You are?"

"I'm nobody," Donna said. "This is my husband. He wrote the novel on which this film is based."

"Oh. Well thanks."

Behind them, another blonde with a microphone had stopped Lucia, who was delighted to answer her questions.

"No, not me, but I know the author of the novel on which the film is based. He's a real close friend, and so is his wife. We get together all the time. Wonderful people. And here is my husband, Paolo. He served in the war with Ezio, and…"

"Thanks so much."

"Let's try to get in there and find some seats," Ezio said.

With a little pushing, they arrived at the door, showed their credentials and found four seats together in the second to the last row. If the movie started on time, there was still almost an hour to wait.

"Think they sell popcorn here?" Paolo asked.

Lucia elbowed him in the ribs.

Donna opened her little silver beaded purse and took out a handkerchief. "I want to be ready for the sad parts," she said.

"There are going to be a lot," Ezio said.

"Do you think Salvatore Balconi will be here?"

"I don't know. Signora Franacini said it was doubtful. We'll see."

The crimson curtain was still closed and people were going up and down the aisles, spilling their drinks and shouting to each other. Ezio closed his eyes. He could hardly believe that he was here, that the journey—the word always used by pop psychologists these days—had taken him from the little room in the basement that he used for writing to his personal involvement in the film to the gorgeous Cinema Teatro Odeon in Florence. And in a few minutes—well, maybe an hour—he would be watching as the characters he created told, no, lived, his story. He didn't want to admit it, but he had never been so thrilled in his life—or so apprehensive.

He closed his eyes and remembered, if he didn't count the years and years of writing, how this "journey" had all began....

IT WAS ON AUGUST 11, 1990, WHEN EZIO ANNOUNCED, to the great relief of Paolo and Lucia, that he had finally finished writing his novel.

"Congratulations, Ezio!" Paolo said. "We thought you'd never finish it! Say, how long have you worked at this? Forty years?"

"Don't be mean," Lucia said. "You know it's only about thirty."

Coming to her husband's defense, Donna said, "Actually, it's only about twenty. A lot of authors spend much more time than that. Isn't that right, Ezio?"

"Well," Ezio said. "It was actually twenty-six."

"Oh."

They were sitting around in the farmhouse's living room on a bright Sunday afternoon. A warm breeze wafted through the open windows. In the distance, gunshots could be heard, a regular weekend occurrence this high in the hills as men aimed, mostly unsuccessfully, at birds. No one paid any attention.

On the coffee table in front of them lay the imposing manuscript for *Il cielo,* about two inches thick.

"Well," Paolo said, "now you can't use the excuse that you had to do some writing to get out of things."

"I didn't use it that much," Ezio said.

"What? You used it all the time."

They all knew it was true. When Ezio didn't want to go to a movie, or shopping in Lucca, or, yes, to Mass, he always said he was at a point in writing that he had to complete before doing anything else. Not that he went to Mass that often.

"I guess I'll have to find another excuse."

Donna brought out more lambrusco and they raised their glasses.

"To Ezio!"

"And to *Il cielo!"*

"You must be very proud," Lucia said. "And we're proud of you."

"Well, I couldn't have finished this without Donna's help. Nag, nag, nag. 'Why aren't you writing?' 'Go back to the typewriter.' 'Finish the chapter before we eat.' I think she was ready to starve me if I didn't finish."

Donna smiled indulgently. "I know I can be a nag, but if he wasn't trying to avoid writing he kept insisting on going over it over and over. I kept saying, 'Look, there's a point where you just have to say, 'that's it, and move on.' Finally, he did."

"Well," Ezio said, raising his glass to his wife, "one thing's for sure. You helped me more on my book than I did on yours."

"Oh, come on. Mine was different. I mean, it's a cookbook. I couldn't expect you to know recipes and ingredients. You helped with the introductions and the proofreading, and that was just fine."

Ezio shook his head. "Another thing that's for sure. My book won't be anywhere as popular as yours is."

Reprinted four times, Donna's cookbook, *Donna's Cucina*, had been such a success after it was published eight years ago that her publisher, Roma Editore, asked her to write a second volume. She had started on *Secrets of Tuscan Cooking,* but with all the tourists at the farmhouse during the summer and a hundred things to do in the off-season, including supervising the running of her restaurant in Sant'Antonio, she hadn't gotten very far. Sometimes, she felt that she really didn't want to write another cookbook. One was enough.

She and Ezio knew there was another reason, though. The first book had put such a strain on their marriage that she didn't want to risk going through that again. She kept putting off the people at Roma Editore and hoped they would eventually tell her to send the advance money back. She hadn't even cashed the check.

Ezio didn't discourage her from writing the new book. But he didn't encourage her, either. Anyway, he was pleased that she helped him so much with his book, reading everything he wrote each night and making valuable suggestions. He knew it was a better book because of what she'd done.

He always said *Il cielo* was "inspired by" rather than "based on" people and events he had experienced during World War II. He called it historical fiction, and was never quite sure if the emphasis should be placed on the first or second word.

It was the story of how, during their occupation of northern Italy during World War II, the Nazis had ordered a village, not unlike Sant'Antonio (Ezio called it San Bernadino) to be evacuated, allowing only the village priest to remain. The people fled into the hills, some living in huts, some in stables, some in abandoned farmhouses and some in the forests themselves.

Ezio's story focused on one of those farmhouses, which bore a remarkable similarity to his present home, the Cielo. A group of villagers holed up there for three months. There was a woman he called Franca, modeled after the Rosa he knew in the village, and her husband. There was another woman and her husband; Franca and the woman had fought decades earlier and hadn't spoken since. There were two elderly men, cousins, and two elderly sisters. There was a gentle and reticent former teacher who was a Dante scholar. There was a woman who turned out to be a Fascist. And there was a mother with five children, ranging from a baby to a girl of 16. That girl, Ezio knew, was inspired by his friend Lucia.

With the war coming closer and closer, with bombs dropping from the skies and with fighting resonating in the nearby hills, the terrified villagers were under intense pressure. Nerves frayed, arguments grew louder. Two little brothers ran away.

Then one day, the leader of a small band of partisans showed up at their door. Ezio named him Fabio, but he was clearly modeled after himself. Not even twenty years old, Ezio had been the leader of a partisan band during the war, and his memories informed the descriptions of hand-to-hand fighting, of placing bombs, of cutting wires.

But there were also romantic interludes. Fabio's lover, Angelina, lived in the nearby village of Sant'Anna di Stazzema. In this section Ezio abandoned fictitious names and events and gave the actual historical account. The real village of Sant'Anna di Stazzema was nearby and on August 12, 1944, Nazis descended on the frightened villagers and murdered about 540 of them in the space of four hours. It was the second-worst massacre in Italy during the war.

Ezio described the massacre in detail, and included Angelina among the victims. Broken by grief and guilt, Fabio vowed revenge.

Meanwhile, liberated at last, those in the farmhouse who survived the conflicts returned to their village to bury their dead and hope for an end to a war that had torn the nation apart.

"If you read the book," Ezio told Paolo and Lucia, "that is, if it's actually published, I hope you'll be able to recognize the courage of all these people. Those who were slaughtered in the massacre, but also those who managed to survive the conditions in the farmhouse. I've dedicated my book to them. The book isn't about me at all. I couldn't have written this without knowing them."

"It's a wonderful book," Donna said. "I'd say that even if I wasn't married to the author."

Paolo and Lucia said they couldn't wait to read it.

"If I'm not the handsome hero, you'll know about it," Paolo said.

"And if I'm not young and beautiful, well, obviously, this is pure fiction," Lucia said.

"Well," Ezio said, "nobody is going to read it if we don't find a publisher. And I know one thing. I don't want that publisher you had, Donna. At least I don't want that sleazy agent you had."

"Ezio," his wife said, "I've never told you this because I didn't think you wanted to hear his name again. But Antonio Palmeri was fired from

Roma Editore. Apparently he was making moves on all sorts of women authors, some even older than me. Can you believe it? So he's gone."

"Good. You're right. I never wanted to hear his name again."

"But there are other agents in the company, Ezio. Want me to call?"

"Let's wait a while."

Ezio knew the grim facts of publishing. It was becoming extremely difficult for an unknown author, especially a fiction writer, to find a publisher. For his only other book, *A Time to Remember,* a factual memoir about his experiences in the war, he hadn't been able to find a publisher so he found a small press in Florence and had a hundred copies printed. He gave one to his father, some to his students at school and some to libraries, but he knew that almost no one wanted to read about the war. And that was almost forty years ago. Who would want to read a story about the war now?

"Ezio," Donna kept telling him, "this is a good book, a fine book. It's a story that anyone can relate to—courage, resilience, hope. Those things are timeless. All it takes is for people to know about it."

"Well, I know one thing. I'm not going on book tours. I'm not doing interviews with reporters who get everything wrong. I'm not going on television."

"I understand," Donna said. She understood all too well because she was forced to do that for her cookbook and hated every minute of it.

FOR THE NEXT FEW MONTHS, Ezio attempted to find an agent. He found a list of those who dealt mainly with fiction, particularly World War II fiction, and wrote to twenty-four of them, enclosing the first three chapters. A few replied quickly: "We're sorry, but your manuscript does not fit our needs at this time. Good luck!"

"They didn't even look at the goddamn thing," he told Donna. "And they didn't return the chapters!"

One agent wanted to see the whole manuscript, so Ezio dutifully went to a copying store in Lucca and reproduced all 450 pages. He resented "all that *lire*" to copy and send it, and then never heard another word again. Two other agents expressed a little interest but suggested changes that Ezio was unwilling to make.

"Ezio," Donna said, "let me contact someone at Roma Editore. There's a nice person there I've been dealing with for *Secrets of Tuscan Cooking*, and maybe she'll forget that I've been so tardy."

Ezio reluctantly agreed. Right after Christmas, Donna wrote to Anna Menotti, a senior editor, who replied that she'd be happy to look at the manuscript but could make no promises.

Ezio went to the store in Lucca and made another copy.

"This is costing me more than I'll ever make on this book," he said. "If I make any money at all."

"Ezio, you know you probably won't make any money on this. You wrote it because you wanted to."

He had to agree. The story of the people in the farmhouse and Sant'Anna di Stazzema had remained in his head ever since the war and he knew he had to write it. As time went on, he tried to fictionalize it even more, but it was such a good story that he felt he was just writing his memories. The characters were so real to him that he also felt that he was just taking down what they were saying. Decades after the war, everything was like a motion picture playing in his head.

One Monday morning early in January 1991, Signorina Menotti called.

"Ezio, I finished *Il cielo* over the weekend. You know, I literally could not put it down, and I don't say that routinely. It's a wonderful novel, and so well written. I just talked to my editor and he agreed. Roma Editore would like to publish your book with our spring selections. Would that be all right?"

Of course it was all right. Ezio fumbled with the phone and called Donna. "They want to publish my book! This spring!"

"Oh, Ezio!"

Signorina Menotti said she would send the contract and then discussed the advance payment. She apologized for the amount, saying fiction wasn't selling well these days and even though Roma Editore was excited about the book, it couldn't promise a great deal of sales. Ezio said he understood, and was just pleased that the book would be published.

He and Donna celebrated that night with a late dinner on the patio in the moonlight and then a romantic time upstairs.

Ezio tried not to think about the book in the months that followed, but when the proofs arrived his hands were shaking so badly, he could hardly open the package. He read them three times and couldn't find anything to change. When the proof of the cover came, he was delighted with the typeface and an artist's sketch of a farmhouse in the hills. He and Donna kept fingering the words at the bottom: "A Novel by Ezio Maffini".

His photo on the back cover, a new one that Donna had insisted upon, showed a handsome man with thick hair that was only slightly graying, bright eyes and a firm nose and mouth.

"God, that man is gorgeous," Donna said. "I wish I'd married him."

"There's still a chance," Ezio said, pulling her close.

A box of the actual books arrived not long after and they drove down the hill to give one to Paolo and Lucia, who were so thrilled they passed it from hand to hand for a half hour.

"You know, Ezio," Paolo said, "I'm actually going to read this."

"I can't believe it," Lucia said. "What was the last book you read?"

"Hey, I read. Just can't remember them."

A week later, Lucia and Paolo told Ezio they had both read the book and were very excited.

"It's a wonderful story," Lucia said.

"Yes, Paolo said, "you may have changed the names, but it's pretty obvious you were writing about Rosa and Marco, and Annabella and Francesco..."

"And Maria and Dante," Donna added. "And Maddelena and her sister Renata."

"And Vito and his cousin Giacomo," Paolo said.

"And Gina!" Lucia said. "My mother! And my brothers and sisters! And me! Well, I was only sixteen years old."

"And me!" Paolo said. "I know you changed my name to Pino, but I recognized me. I like me!"

They celebrated with two bottles of wine from Montepulciano.

At first, people in Sant'Antonio seemed delighted that Ezio had written a novel. They had gotten used to Donna's cookbook, but here was a book that seemed to be set in their village, about people they knew.

But the people of Sant'Antonio were not generally readers. Mario and Anita bought a copy and loved it. They even had Ezio set up displays of the book in their shops, and a few copies were sold.

No one expected *Il cielo* to be a best seller, and it wasn't. As Ezio had predicted, people didn't want to read about the war. The book got a decent review in a small magazine devoted to new fiction: "The author writes with authority and the characters are so vivid and the story so real it could have happened."

"Could have happened? Could have happened?" Ezio shouted. "It happened!"

Signorina Menotti begged him to do a book tour. He declined. Perhaps some newspaper interviews? No. How about a short radio interview? Well, all right.

The radio interviewer obviously hadn't read the book and focused most of her questions on the process of getting the book published.

The book lay dormant for years. Occasionally, a visitor at the farmhouse would pick up a copy, prominently displayed on the mantel, read it and become so interested that he or she wanted to buy it. Ezio had a supply on hand.

After three years, Ezio and Donna didn't talk about *Il cielo* anymore, and Ezio tried not to think about it.

THEY WERE SURPRISED, THEN, when Signorina Menotti called excitedly on a Thursday afternoon in March 1994 just as Donna was beginning to prepare dinner.

"Donna!" Ezio exclaimed. "They're selling the film rights to RAI Cinema!"

"Really? That's incredible!"

"They're going to make a movie of my book!"

"Wait," Signorina Menotti said, "we're just selling the rights. Whether they make a movie or not is up to them."

"Oh."

Ezio had relinquished the film rights when he signed the contract for the book, so he wasn't going to make any money even if a film was made.

"If they make the film, they'll say it was based on your novel, that's all," Signorina Menotti said.

"Oh."

The news, however, was noted by *Segnocinema,* the popular magazine reporting on films. "RAI Cinema has optioned the rights to *Il cielo,* a war story by an unknown writer, Ezio Maffini."

For a while, Ezio picked up a copy of *Segnocinema* each time he went to Lucca, but then gave up trying to find any news about a possible film.

"It's not going to be made," he told Donna. "Let's forget about it."

And then came the fateful day when Signorina Menotti called again.

"Ezio! RAI Cinema is going to make the film! We're signing the papers on Thursday!"

More bottles of wine from Montepulciano with Lucia and Paolo.

Unlike their reaction to the book, the people of Sant'Antonio were thrilled when they heard that a movie would be made with Sant'Antonio as its setting. They couldn't believe that Ezio would not suddenly become rich because of it.

"You're not getting any money? Not one *lira*?" they asked.

It was difficult for them to understand that Ezio had given up all rights to the book.

"This is a dirty deal, Ezio," they said. "You should sue."

News about the film came sporadically from various cinematic publications after that. The big news, however, was splashed in every one of them: "Salvatore Balconi to Return to Films/Will Direct Movie about World War II".

"Salvatore Balconi! Amazing!" Ezio shouted to Donna when he read the headline.

"You're kidding. The real Salvatore Balconi? He hasn't directed a movie in years. I thought he was dead."

"Not dead, obviously, but he must be in his 80s."

Salvatore Balconi had been a major film director in the 1960s and 1970s, and was often declared to be the successor to the great pioneers of neorealist films, Vittorio De Sica, Roberto Rossellini, Luchino Visconti and others. Like them, he often shot on location with nonprofessional actors. And like their films, his were almost always in black and white.

He specialized in gritty films, often on the back streets of Naples or Turin. They dealt with gangs and corruption, fears and hatreds. His last film, *Silenzio, (Silence),* about a boy and his father living in a forest to avoid Mafia relatives, won Italy's most prestigious award, the David di

Donatello, the Hollywood Oscar for best foreign film as well as numerous international awards.

After Balconi had a stroke in 1981, he retired to his villa near San Gemignano. No one had seen him since, and everyone assumed he had finished his directing career. His films occasionally turned up in art festivals, but no one thought about him much any more.

Ezio knew about Balconi's films but didn't know anything about his life, so he went to the library in Lucca. He discovered that Balconi was born in 1915 near Castelforentino southwest of Florence. His parents were farmers who had nine other children. Salvatore dropped out of school after the third grade to work on the farm. He showed an early interest in film making and when he was twenty-four he managed to get a job as a technical assistant at Cinecittà, the large film studio established by Mussolini in Rome in 1937. After the war he started to make short films about animals, like his idol Rossellini. The films attracted more and more attention and he was able to get financial backing. Soon he made such widely praised films as *Povertà (Poverty), Tradimento (Betrayal)* and *Celebrazione (Celebration).* The last, one of his few films that ended on a happier note, was not well received.

"He certainly has had a fascinating career," Ezio said, "but I'm curious. I couldn't find anything about his experiences in the war. I wonder what he did."

"Odd," Donna said.

"Well, if there's anyone who can tell the story of the people in the farmhouse, it's Balconi."

"Remember that there's also the story of the partisans and the massacre."

"I know," Ezio said, "but I want the story to be about the farmhouse."

"You also remember that you gave up all the rights, so you don't have a voice in any of this."

"We'll just have to wait and see."

The next stories in *Segnocinema* were about the casting of Federico Stellini as Fabio the partisan and Maria Luccardi as Angelina, his lover in Sant'Anna di Stazzema.

"Who?" Donna said.

"That's strange," Ezio said. "Never heard of them."

Although not entirely unknown, neither Stellini nor Luccardi had been in major motion pictures, and the tabloids compared their casting to that by Franco Zeffirelli of Graham Faulkner and Judi Bowker in *Brother Sun, Sister Moon* in 1972.

"We wonder what Balconi is doing casting these two," one acerbic columnist wrote. "Few people want to see a film about the war and so two major stars would be needed to make this attractive. We can only hope Balconi knows what he is doing. He has not made a film in so long, and we understand that he may not be in the best of health. Certainly, he has an impressive career, but what can we expect from him now?"

Ezio cringed.

"It could also be argued," he told Donna, "that casting well-known actors would take the emphasis off the story. Balconi has never had major stars in his films. I think he knows exactly what he's doing."

A few months later, it was reported that the first filming would be about the massacre at Sant'Anna di Stazzema even though that occurred late in the story. The headquarters for the film would be in Pietrasanta, where an old marble factory would be converted. From there, crews would drive up the mountain to shoot at Sant'Anna and in various parts of the region for the scenes with the partisans.

Since Sant'Anna had been almost destroyed in the massacre, new houses and barns had to be built. Most were simply facades, but a sturdier one was constructed for Angelina. This would be where the lovers met.

The only building in the village left pretty much intact during the Nazi raid was the little white church. The filmmakers had to get permission to make some structural changes so that it looked damaged, but promised to return it to its good condition later.

The newspapers also reported that the film crew had rounded up local residents and others from the area to play villagers, Nazi soldiers and partisans. One newspaper had a feature story about two brothers, one playing a soldier and the other a partisan. They were photographed arm in arm in costume.

"It's curious that none of these stories mention that the film is based on a wonderful novel by Ezio Maffini," Donna said.

"It's more curious that they are doing the shooting about the massacre but they haven't said anything about shooting in a farmhouse. I just hope that's a major part of the story."

"Ezio, they can't leave that part out of the film! Can they?"

"They can do anything they want."

Then word came that the name of the film was changed. It was now *Separazione, Separation.*

"That's an odd title," Lucia said. "It doesn't mean anything."

"Balconi always has one-word titles," Ezio said.

Salvatore Balconi was not present in any of this, with an assistant director, Anton Silvestino, in charge and being quoted by the newspapers. The newspapers began to speculate that Balconi was so ill that he wouldn't take part in the direction at all, simply having his name attached to the film. Efforts to reach him at his villa were futile.

ON A MONDAY MORNING IN LATE FEBRUARY, Ezio was outside feeding the chickens and was terribly out of breath after he ran inside to answer the phone.

"Signor Maffini?" the voice at the other end asked.

"Yes."

"This is Signora Isabella Franacini. I am the personal secretary to Salvatore Balconi."

"Oh! Yes?"

"Signor Balconi would like to meet with you on Thursday next. Are you able to do that?"

"Sure! Yes! I mean, of course."

"All right. 2 o'clock in the afternoon. Here are the directions."

Ezio grabbed a pencil and wrote them down.

"Donna! Salvatore Balconi wants to see me!"

"Really? Why?"

"I have no idea. Perhaps about the rights? I don't have any rights anymore. I can't imagine what he might want."

It was bright and sunny on Thursday morning when Ezio kissed Donna and got into his Fiat Ritmo. He was immediately sorry he hadn't had the car washed before going to see the eminent Salvatore Balconi, but it was too late now. Maybe no one would notice the grime all over the bottom.

Ezio drove down to A11 and headed east to Pistoia, then Prato and around Florence. South to Tavanuzze, Iprunetta and San Casciano in Val di Pesa. He noticed a sign pointing west to Castelforentino and remembered that was where Balconi was born. Then south to Tavarnelle and Poggibonsi and finally San Gemignano.

Signora Franacini had told him to watch for a small shrine to the Virgin Mary on the left side of the highway about a mile from San Gemignano. Then he was to turn left and up the hillside. Ezio did. He glanced at his watch. 1:55 p.m.

"Good lord, I should have left earlier."

The villa looked like what one might expect: Built in the 1600s as a farmhouse, it stretched across the top of a hill with addition after addition over the centuries. Magnificent cypress trees were so thick that the red tile roofs could hardly be seen. Ezio drove into the circular driveway, got out of the car, brushed himself off, combed his hair and rang the buzzer.

A tall, thin woman, her hair in a bun on top of her head, her gray dress covered by a white apron, answered.

"Signor Maffini? I am Signora Franacini. Thank you for coming. Come in."

Entering from the bright sunlight, Ezio groped his way into the dark interior. He realized that all the drapes were pulled and that only a single wall sconce lit the vast entry hall.

"Please wait here."

She returned a few minutes later.

"Signor Balconi would like to meet with you on the terrace. Although we are in late February, the sun is bright there and he would like to get as much sunlight as possible. It makes him feel so much better."

She escorted him through one room, then another and another until they reached the rear of the house. Salvatore Balconi was seated in the sunlight in a corner, looking very small in a wheelchair on the palazzo tile. He was bundled in an overcoat and a thick woolen scarf, and he wore heavy shoes, the kind farmers wear. Apparently to absorb as much sunlight as possible, his bald head was bare, covered with brown spots.

Signora Franacini removed his dark glasses so that he could see Ezio better. His eyes were a soft watery blue. Holding out a thin, translucent hand, he said, "Thank you for coming, Signor Maffini. Please sit here on the bench next to me. I like to be in the sun now."

Ezio wondered why the voice sounded so mechanical, then realized that this renowned film director, whose voice gave the commands for so many award-winning films, was now reduced to using a machine, an electrolarynx.

"You will excuse my voice. I had the throat cancer four years ago."

He paused.

"At first I used paper and pencil or a blackboard, but that was so time consuming. I couldn't keep up if there were two or three people present."

He paused again, closed his eyes and then continued.

"But then the speech pathologist gave me this device. It took a long time to get used to, and I needed a lot of practice. But I'm used to it now."

After another long pause: "Again, I apologize for the sound of my voice. I know it is not natural."

"Please, Signor Balconi," Ezio said, "do not apologize. I am honored to have been invited to meet with you. It goes without saying that I have long admired your films so much and am so pleased that you are directing... will be directing...a film inspired by my little novel. And please, if this is difficult, maybe some other time?"

"The honor is mine, Signor Maffini. Please excuse me if I do not talk in long sentences."

Another pause.

"I don't have much time, as you can imagine."

He attempted a smile, but this was obviously painful.

At this point Signora Franacini arrived with a tray of hot tea and soft cookies.

"I knew it would be difficult for me to have a conversation with you," he began, but then he stopped for long moments. "So yesterday I dictated some comments and questions to Signora Franacini. She will read them to you and you can answer. She will take it all down."

"That would be fine," Ezio said.

Settling into a straight-back chair between Signor Balconi and Ezio, Signora Franacini said, "You should know that I have been with Signor

Balconi for many years, ever since *Povertà*. I am honored to act as his secretary."

Ezio could see the old director's eyes glisten.

"This," Signora Franacini said opening a long legal pad, "is what Signor Balconi would like to say." She began to read.

I thought I would never direct a film again. After my stroke and the throat cancer, I thought, well, that's the end of that. I had a good career and won many honors. I can look back with great pride. What would be the point of directing another film? I read some scripts, some books, but nothing interested me. Nothing!

Signora Franacini cleared her throat and continued.

But then I read this wonderful, truly inspired novel called Il cielo. *Someone sent it to me, I don't know who. I read it twice, a third time. I couldn't put it down. I loved the story, the characters. And I thought, why not? Why can't I make a movie from this book so people all over the world could see and hear this beautiful account of courage and freedom?*

The signora paused again, this time to adjust a hairpin.

And so I found the courage to make another film. I rounded up all my friends and workers from the old days. The directors, the technicians, the scriptwriters, the set designers and builders, the costume designers, the lighting people, everyone! And I appointed Signor Anton Silvestino, who had been my right-hand man in so many of my pictures, to be the acting director. I would give him my thoughts and he would give me daily reports. When the time came, he would show me the rushes.

Signora Franacini paused to sip her tea, which must have been very cold by now.

Signor Silvestino has directed the portions of the film that take place in Sant'Anna and with the partisans in the mountains, as well as with the Nazis in another part. I have seen the rushes and am very pleased. As you know, films are not always made in sequence. Now it is time to film the portions in the farmhouse.

Ezio could almost hear himself breathe a sigh of relief.

And that is why I have asked you here today. You wrote with such great passion about the people who were trapped there, and I want you to have a part in those sections of the film. What part, you ask? Well, I would like you to be our technical adviser, to make sure we are filming the people exactly as you have pictured them in your great book. We want you to be on hand during all the shooting. Will you be willing to do that? For compensation, of course.

Ezio said he would be pleased to be on hand and offer what little help he could. Signor Balconi put his hand on Ezio's arm. Ezio could barely feel it.

Signora Franacini turned three more pages.

Here are my questions. Would we be able to use the real farmhouse as the main part of the film?

Ezio hesitated, knowing that the farmhouse had been vastly remodeled when it became a bread-and-breakfast. He did some math and timetables in his head and then said, "I'm sure it could be put back the way it was."

Balconi smiled.

Signora Franacini whispered to Signor Balconi and then told Ezio that a crew would like to start work on the farmhouse in two weeks. Ezio agreed.

Would you know of anyone who would be likely actors in the scenes at the farmhouse in the film? I like to use local people as much as possible.

Ezio thought briefly about Lucia and Paolo, but decided against it. No, he didn't know anyone in Sant'Antonio, but he was certain people could be found in neighboring villages.

What about Sant'Antonio? Could that be used as the setting for the village?

Ezio realized that with the new piazza and other construction in the last ten years, Sant'Antonio did not look anything like it did during the war. Signora Franacini related this information to Signor Balconi, who asked if another village could be found. Ezio said that the village of Sant'Augustino nearby looked almost exactly like the old Sant'Antonio. Signor Balconi looked pleased.

What about the church?

That, Ezio said, hadn't changed in centuries.

Signor Balconi suddenly looked very tired, and whispered as best he could to Signora Franacini.

"He would like to stop now but to meet with you again. Perhaps Thursday next?"

"Of course."

She fussed with Balconi's scarf, put on his fedora, wheeled him around and pushed him into the house. Ezio followed and found his way to the car.

Back home, Ezio had a frantic conversation with Donna. Signor Balconi had asked him to help with the film! They were going to use the farmhouse! It had to be torn apart and put back to its original condition! But afterward they would restore it to what it is now!

"And they're coming in two weeks?" Donna asked.

"Yes."

"Oh, dear."

They figured that would be around the first of March. Demolition would take a week. Restoring the place to its wartime condition would take two or three.

"Let's say April 1," Ezio said.

Filming would probably take about a month. Or more.

"That brings us to May," he said. "And then they'll have to put the place back again. Maybe another two weeks. Mid-May, maybe June, by the time all that's done."

"And we're already booked with tourists for all of that time," Donna said. "I guess we'll just have to cancel them. Too bad. Well, we'll tell them to come next year."

Ezio and Donna then realized that they would have to move out while all this work was being done. They knew that Lucia and Paolo would pressure them into staying with them, but that was not an option.

"Can you imagine living with Lucia and Paolo for two or three months?" Donna said. "I mean, I love them dearly, but really..."

"You know what they say: 'Two Italian women should not be in the same kitchen at the same time.'"

Donna grimaced.

"Oh, and Signor Balconi would like to meet with me again next week."

CANCELING RESERVATIONS required personal, handwritten notes, and Donna took care of every one of them in three days. A few people called to inquire if they could come later in the summer, but Donna made no promises. As usual, the farmhouse was booked for the entire season.

She and Ezio spent the weekend packing up dishes, books, pictures, clothes and everything they could think of and took the boxes down to the basement. When the workers arrived Monday morning, the place looked denuded.

"I don't want to be here when they start tearing things apart," Donna said. "It's too sad."

"When we get back, it will all be the same," Ezio said. "Actually, this is going to be fun. Let's go."

They had made reservations for an open-ended stay at the Hotel Stella just outside the village. Knowing that the filming would bring in numerous workers, technicians, actors and others, the hotel told Donna and Ezio their stay would be on the house.

"The publicity we get from this will be priceless," the concierge said.

The hotel didn't just give them a free room, it gave them the Victor Emmanuel Suite, with a king-sized bed, a living room, a television room and a private spa.

"This is going to be the honeymoon we never had," Ezio said, dropping two well-worn suitcases on the plush carpeting.

On Monday, a dozen trucks wound their way to the top of the hill, unloaded what seemed like tons of equipment and proceeded to transform the old farmhouse into an even older farmhouse, one that looked like it had during World War II. It had been abandoned before that, so the crews tore away chunks of the tile roof, carved holes in the walls and removed not only the windows but also the window frames.

On Thursday, Ezio again visited Balconi, who had a list of questions about the people in the farmhouse.

Please tell me about Franca and her husband. Did she ever get rattled? Why did she have the argument with her friend so many years ago?

"Franca always seemed totally in control to others, but when she was alone or with her husband she showed her weaknesses and her vulnerability. Many years ago she and her friend argued over a boy, and the boy eventually married the friend. The two women hadn't spoken for years."

"Ah yes," Signora Franacini said, "the grudges that Italian women bear." She continued to read from her legal pad.

Tell me more about the other people in the farmhouse. How did they interact with one another?

Ezio went on at length about each of them.

Tell me more about the Dante scholar.

"He is one of the few characters based on someone I knew, a professor at the University of Pisa. Very kind, very generous and very modest, although he was more intelligent than any other professor I had there. He knew Dante from cover to cover."

"But he had a secret," Signor Balconi was able to say.

"Yes. As you know, that's revealed late in the book."

The meeting was not as long as the first, but Signora Franacini whispered to Ezio as he was leaving that Signor Balconi looked forward to meeting him again very soon.

"Your meetings have been so important to him. Can you meet again Thursday next?"

"Of course."

The following week at the Cielo, crews continued to re-create the older version of the farmhouse because Ezio and Donna had torn down walls to create one big room on the first floor. The workers built walls according to drawings Ezio had provided. Then they cracked all the interior walls and threw garbage and dirt all over the place.

"I sure wouldn't want to live here for three months," one of the crewmen said.

That is exactly what a group of Sant'Antonio residents did during the war, though, and their experiences were described in detail in Ezio's book. Now they would be shown dramatically in a film directed by the renowned Salvatore Balconi.

Once again, Ezio visited Balconi. This time, the old director wanted to know about the British soldier who had escaped from a prison camp and was taken in at the farmhouse despite the objection of one of the villagers.

But now, Signor Balconi seemed anxious, even agitated. Signora Franacini explained that he couldn't wait for the filming to start at the farmhouse, but that she wasn't sure if he would actually be well enough to be there.

"He's such a kind, dear old man," Ezio told Donna. "I wish we had met years ago. We might have been friends if we'd been able to communicate better."

It was almost time to film the first scenes at the farmhouse. Word spread through Sant'Antonio that crews and famous actors would soon fill the village. People buzzed about it at Mario's *bottega* and Anita's meat market. Sitting in their white plastic chairs in their customary places in the new piazza, Giovanni Bertollino, Nico Magnotti and Primo Scafidi were happy to spread every rumor they could. They reliably reported that Marcello Mastroianni would co-star not only with Sophia Loren but also with Gina Lollobrigida.

It was up to Anton Silvestino, appointed by Balconi as the director in charge, to dispel these rumors and take up the casting of locals. That took a few days, but eventually all roles were filled. A few were residents of Sant'Antonio—Signora Miniotti and Signora Bruni were cast as the elderly spinster sisters—but otherwise the performers were from Sant'Augustino, Reboli and villages as far away as Camaiore.

On a Monday morning, he gathered the group of amateur actors into the church hall to get them familiar with their roles and acquaint them with the story. Some appeared nervous, others proudly waited for their big moments.

"Now you know," Silvestino said, "that you are a group of relatives and neighbors who have been forced to live in the farmhouse because your village has been occupied by the Nazis. You have fled your homes with only the clothes on your backs. You are terrified. You could be killed. You don't know how long you're going to be away, but you fear that it might be weeks, months. And while you are there you will be hearing bombs and fighting. Can you understand all this?"

"Signor Silvestino," a woman from Camaiore asked, "will we be able to put on our own makeup? I would hate to have someone else do it and I'm perfectly able to do it myself."

"We'll see," Silvestino said, trying not to raise his voice. "Are there other questions?"

"Can I wear my own clothes?" a woman from Reboli wanted to know. "I have some that might look worn, but they're also attractive and I wouldn't want to look too shabby in the only film I'll ever make."

"The wardrobe department will provide all costumes, and I'm sure you'll look very nice in them."

"We wonder," a man from Sant'Augustino began, "when Signor Balconi will be arriving. This is supposed to be his film, and yet I don't think he's been seen since the filming began. Is he still the director?"

"Yes, yes, yes, of course," Silvestino said, trying not to look worried. "We are just taking care of the preliminaries. That's customary for any film. When we're ready to shoot, I'm sure Signor Balconi will be here."

Under his breath, Silvestino muttered, "I hope to God."

That night, Ezio tried calling the director, but there was no answer.

"I'm really worried about him," Ezio told Donna. "I don't think he's going to be able to do this, and he wanted to so much."

"I wonder if they'll take his name off the film."

"That would kill him."

At last it was time to shoot the first scene at the farmhouse. This was when the villagers arrived there after climbing the long and difficult hill on a hot summer day.

"Remember," Silvestino said, "you are sweating and tired and scared. You are very afraid. You don't know what's going to happen."

Most of the actors responded well. They said the few lines they had been given and looked appropriately terrified. The exception was a woman from Reboli, who started wailing.

"What in the world are you doing?" Silvestino said, stopping the filming. "You're ruining this."

"I was just showing how terrified I am," the woman responded.

"Well, be terrified quietly, please."

Ezio, who was watching all this from the adjoining room, shook his head. Silvestino prepared to resume shooting.

Then there was a voice just outside the room. "Wait! Let me handle this."

The voice was odd, as if from a recording. Everyone looked at the doorway. Somehow, unannounced, Salvatore Balconi had arrived in a special van and was transported to the scene in his wheelchair.

"It's him!" the villagers-turned-actors exclaimed.

If he didn't look like a different man, Balconi at least appeared to be much stronger than when Ezio had last seen him at the villa. Instead of an overcoat and heavy scarf, he wore a light blue jacket, its sleeves now much too long, a pink shirt and an orange ascot. Instead of a fedora, he had a blue beret on his head, and he had fine Italian shoes on his feet.

Smiling broadly, Signora Franacini wheeled him to the front of the set, and then retreated. Ezio couldn't believe what he'd just seen.

"He's feeling so much better," she whispered to Ezio. "I could tell day by day as he saw the rushes and as he talked to Signor Silvestino. He became more and more involved every day. This has given him a new life again. It's a miracle, really."

"Do you think he'll stay here long?"

"Probably not, but this is the first time he's been out of the villa in, oh, ages."

In the middle of the newly constructed living room, Balconi had gathered the neophyte actors around him. Haltingly, but with a voice as firm as he could make it, he talked gently to one and then another, asking not only about the parts they were playing but also about their personal lives, their interests, their loves. He tried to connect them personally to the characters, and suddenly the actors saw new depth in the roles they were playing.

Remarkably, he used his electrolarynx with more ability and he didn't have to pause for breath nearly as often.

"All right," he said, "are we ready now?"

The scene started again and rolled on without a stop for about seven minutes.

"Wonderful!" he said. "You were all terrific. Now let's try another."

This time the scene was between the two old cousins who were teasing the two elderly sisters. It was important not to overplay the scene, to make it light enough but not have the characters caricatures. After only two false starts, Signora Miniotti and Signora Bruni, playing the sisters, and the two men playing the cousins fell into the right rhythm of the piece.

"Excellent!' Balconi said. "Now let's try one more, and that will be it for the day."

This was the scene that showed, for the first time, that the little baby was ill.

"Now it's important," the director said, "that we don't bring too much pathos into this. We need to show that the baby is sick, but we can't let on too much because that will spoil what will come in the scenes ahead. Everything depends on pacing here. When we're further into the film we'll pick up the pacing and then things will happen very fast. For now, let's just go slow."

The actors took their cues. Ezio couldn't believe that Balconi was talking so much and not gasping for breath as he had on that day in February.

"Beautiful," Balconi said when the actors had completed the scene. "All right, I'll see you tomorrow."

Balconi took Ezio's hand as he was leaving. "This is going to be a wonderful motion picture, Ezio, and it's all because of you. I don't know how to thank you."

He kissed Ezio's hand.

Signora Franacini wheeled him back to the van and Ezio rushed back to the hotel to tell Donna.

The newspapers made much of Balconi's sudden involvement in the film, and every one of them requested an interview. Signora Franacini spurned all requests.

The next day, Balconi arrived a full hour before shooting was to begin. He conferred briefly with Signor Silvestino, but mostly wanted to talk to Ezio. What was it like when he visited the farmhouse? How fearful were the villagers? What about the woman who had Fascist sympathies? What about the two little boys? And the mother when her baby died?

Curiously, Balconi did not ask about Ezio's time as a partisan. Ezio also knew that Balconi was not present during the filming of the scenes with the partisan Fabio and his lover at Sant'Anna.

"Very strange," Ezio told Donna that night as they enjoyed another fantastic meal in the Hotel Stella restaurant.

The following day, Balconi shot the major scene when the trapped villagers argued about whether to allow an escaped British prisoner to stay at the farmhouse. This would put them in grave danger, and they were discussing the risks.

Balconi went through the thought processes for each of the characters, devoting much time to the Fascist sympathizer who argued against harboring the escapee. That scene played beautifully, and the next was when the young POW actually arrived. Except for the Nazis, this was the only non-Italian role in the film and Silvestino had to go to Florence to audition expatriates. He found a young man from Liverpool working as a waiter in a restaurant who was eager to show his acting talents, not to mention to make a little money.

The next day, the big scene was the carving of a pig that had been given to the refugees by a local farmer. The pig was donated by a local farmer, Santo Scarpelli, who also supplied the popular wild boar salami that was sold at Anita's meat market. The scene was supposed to provide a little levity in what was an entirely grim story, but Balconi did not want it too humorous. The people were still under grave threats, and that could not be forgotten.

When the new actors seemed queasy about cutting up the pig, Balconi hoisted himself out of his wheelchair and took knives and a hacksaw and began the procedure.

"I grew up on a farm, remember? We did this all the time. Now let's see. Let's start over here…" And he proceeded to make the first cuts. The actors soon began to become proficient in pig carving.

At first, Balconi would shoot three or four scenes in the morning, take a rest break of about two hours, then shoot two more scenes. As the days went on, this was far too rigorous a schedule. It was reduced to two or three scenes in the morning and one later in the day. Then only one scene a day.

"I'm very worried," Signora Franacini told Ezio. "I can see him getting more tired every day. He wanted to do this so very much that he forced himself at the beginning. But now he really should turn this all over to Signor Silvestino. But he won't. He insists on completing the film."

Ezio and Signora Franacini were sitting on the terrace above the farmhouse while everyone else was taking an afternoon break. Signor Balconi slept in an upstairs bedroom.

"I feel so bad," Ezio said. "Well, it's almost finished. There are only a few scenes left."

He hesitated, and then asked, "Signora Franacini, I've been wondering. Signor Balconi did not take part when scenes with the partisans were being filmed at Sant'Anna. In our conversations, such as they are, he seemed interested in all aspects of my life except for the time when I was a member of the Resistance during the war. Is there something about the war that he doesn't want to talk about, maybe even think about?"

Signora Franacini put down her teacup and stared toward the rolling green hills in the distance. A few puffy clouds floated overhead.

"Signor Maffini," she began, "have you ever heard of General Falcon?"

"General Falcon? Of course, I've heard of him. He was the leader of six bands of partisans in the battle for Monte Battaglia. There were only 250 partisans, along with three companies of United States soldiers, and they caught the Germans completely by surprise. They held it for five days and the Allies were able to advance throughout Italy. General Falcon was fearless. His group took so many chances, but they won. It was at a terrible cost to them, though. Many partisans were killed. Every schoolboy knows that story. Well, every schoolboy knows about General Falcon. What does this have to do with Signor Balconi?"

"You wonder why Signor Balconi doesn't like to talk about the partisans? Perhaps you should know that General Falcon and Signor Balconi are one and the same."

"Oh, my God!"

"As you know, it was a terrible battle. Among the partisans killed were Signor Balconi's father, a brother and two cousins. Signor Balconi used this code name Falcon, of course, like all partisans. He himself escaped with only minor injuries, and he came away with terrible feelings of guilt. And he never spoke about the battle or the partisans or the war again. That, Signor Maffini, is why he didn't take part in the filming of the sections about the partisans. Perhaps he has blotted it all from his mind. Or perhaps it is a terrible nightmare that he lives through constantly. We will never know."

Ezio thought about this for a long time. He knew that his own experiences as a partisan had marked him indelibly. He recalled how he was filled with remorse and anger and thoughts of revenge after his lover had been killed in the massacre. He still felt so many emotions about that time, and eventually tried not to think about it.

"But I wonder," he said, "why Signor Balconi wanted to make a film from my book. So much of it talks about partisans."

"I believe," she said, "that he now felt it was his duty to tell a story that would make people realize how valiant and courageous the partisans were. Yes, I believe that's why."

"But he didn't shoot the scenes of the partisans."

"No, that was too painful. He let Signor Silvestino do that, but he was very familiar with what was happening and he approved the rushes every night."

"But why did he want to shoot the scenes in the farmhouse? That must have been painful, too."

"You know," she said, "that during the Nazi occupation many people had fled their homes and stayed wherever they could."

"Yes, of course I know that."

"But you don't know that Signor Balconi's wife was among them."

"His wife? I didn't know he was ever married."

"His wife—her name was Florina—was much younger than he was. Only 20 years old when he went off to fight the war. They had a baby, little Giorgio. When the Nazis took over their village, everyone fled. Florina and Giorgio actually lived in an old barn with four or five other people. They were there about three weeks. Others gave them food. Then the Nazis found them. And shot them all."

"Oh, my God."

"When Signor Balconi returned, he learned about this. He had the bodies of his wife and little son moved from a cemetery near where they were killed and he built a large mausoleum for them in the family plot at Castelforentino. He built another large mausoleum for his mother and father and brother. Until he had the stroke, unless he was shooting a film somewhere, he visited that cemetery every day."

"The poor, poor man. How terrible."

"And so, Signor Maffini, that is why he wanted to be involved in the filming of the scenes at the farmhouse. He relates to those people. He wants to tell their story. Just like the other scenes are a tribute to the partisans, this is a tribute to his wife and son."

For a long time, Ezio watched an ant slowly crawl across the terrazzo. He had to let all this sink in.

The last scene Balconi filmed was of the villagers packing up and leaving the farmhouse after being freed by the Allies. It had been a bittersweet occasion for the villagers because two of their number had died during a gun battle outside and a baby had not survived an illness inside. Balconi directed the actors with great empathy and veracity.

"All right," he told them when the filming was finished, "I suppose I should say, 'It's a wrap,' but that's such a cliché. Instead, I can only say 'Thank you, thank you, thank you.'" He bowed his head and smiled briefly. Everyone else, the villagers and the entire crew, applauded. Tears streamed down many faces.

Ezio waited for him near the van. Signora Franacini stopped the wheelchair in front of him, and Signor Balconi held out his hand.

"I would like to talk more," he said, "but now I am too tired. Signora Franacini will call you, and you can come visit and we can talk. Would that be all right?"

"I would like that very much."

"In the meantime, my friend Ezio, *Grazie! Grazie mille!*"

Ezio watched as the van slowly made its way down the hill.

Three weeks later, workers had put the farmhouse back the way they had found it—the way Ezio and Donna had left it—and they moved back in.

"The hotel was great," Donna said, "but I'm very glad to be home. And very tired."

"Me, too."

"We don't have guests for another week. I'm going to sleep and sleep and sleep."

Ezio waited for a phone call from Signora Franacini. Two weeks. Three. Four. So he called.

"I'm afraid," she said, "Signor Balconi cannot talk to you now. Can you call again in another week?"

He did.

"He's sleeping. Another week?"

He called again.

This time, Signora Franacini had obviously been crying. "Oh, Signor Maffini, I can't talk." And she hung up.

Six months later, the premiere of *Separazione* was scheduled for the Cinema Teatro Odeon in Florence. Ezio received his embossed invitation in the mail and now he found himself in a red velvet seat waiting for the film to start. It had been such a long journey…

HE FELT DONNA POKING HIM GENTLY in his side. "Ezio! Have you been sleeping? At a time like this?"

"No. Just remembering."

"I think it's about to start."

When the lights dimmed, the audience quieted down at last and saw a small man emerge from the wings and stand under a spotlight in front of the crimson curtains.

"*Buonasera!* My name is Anton Silvestino and I have been proud to be a part of this story. Thank you for coming to the premiere of this wonderful film. Thank you very much."

With that, he left, and the audience murmured loudly. "What was that?" "Who is he?" "Where is Salvatore Balconi?" "Did he die?"

Then the curtains opened and faint music began. *Separazione. A film by Salvatore Balconi.*

High above a hill, the camera slowly, slowly descended in a grainy black-and-white film. Dark thick clouds swept over the eastern sky. The camera focused on a pastoral scene of sheep grazing, swung to a hilltop of stately cypress trees, then to a little highway shrine to the Virgin Mary, then to a cemetery with stark white monuments. Then the camera slowly went down on a village. The houses and streets looked completely empty.

"Look, that's Sant'Antonio," Lucia whispered to Paolo.

"No, it's Sant'Augustino standing in for Sant'Antonio. There isn't any piazza there, see?"

"Oh, yes."

In the distance, faint gunshots could be heard. Then the camera moved to a road leading from the village. First one person, then another and another, could be seen trudging up the hill. Slowly. Awkwardly. Some tripping and being helped by others. Some had packs on their backs. A few carried satchels.

They came into better view. Old women and men. Two boys running back and forth. A woman carrying a baby.

"Look, that's my mother!" Lucia said in a loud whisper. "And that girl must be me! Everyone is going up to the farmhouse."

"Shhhh," Donna said.

Ezio slid into his seat and put his hand over his eyes.

"What's the matter?" Donna asked.

"This is very hard to watch."

"Maybe it will get easier."

The farmhouse was now in view. It looked exactly as it did during the war. Ezio clutched Donna's hand.

The first man in the line tried to open the door. It wouldn't budge. Another man came up and together they put their shoulders against the door. It fell in with a crash. Dust rose.

Slowly, the villagers could be seen entering the farmhouse. The scene faded.

"I don't know if I can stand this," Ezio said.

Donna held his hand tighter.

The scene shifted to a road in the mountains. Two young men, wearing makeshift military uniforms, worked furiously stringing wires across the road. Woolen scarves concealed their faces.

"That's Dino and me!" Paolo whispered.

Suddenly they finished and ran into the woods. A truck with a swastika on its side approached around a bend and then disintegrated in a loud explosion.

"I'm getting sick," Ezio said.

"Hold on."

Not a word had been spoken in either of the scenes. Now the scene was in the small kitchen of a house in a village. A woman was feeding her infant son at the table, one spoon at a time. She was humming. The baby was smiling and the woman tussled his hair.

Ezio couldn't watch any more. "I'll be in the lobby." He crawled over Donna and Paolo and Lucia and made his way up the aisle, tripping once in the darkened theater. In the lobby, he found a gilt chair near the concessions counter and collapsed. He held his head in his hands.

That was where Donna found him more than two hours later as throngs of people exited the theater.

"Are you all right? Maybe I should have left, too."

"No, no. I wanted you to stay. I want you to tell me about it. But I couldn't. I just couldn't."

She found another chair and sat next to him. The lobby was now crowded with people, men in tuxes, women in long evening gowns. It could have been a gala fundraiser or the inauguration of a president.

But oddly, if they spoke at all, they whispered softly as they left the theater. The place was so quiet that when a woman dropped her purse on the thick carpet, everyone jumped.

Eventually, the crowds were gone, leaving only Ezio and Donna, who sat on one side of the lobby, and Paolo and Lucia on the other.

"I guess it's time to go home," Ezio said.

They walked, hand in hand, back to the car. As they crossed the Ponte Vecchio they stared down at the Arno. Reflecting the string of lights from the banks, it looked very peaceful.

The four were silent all the way home, and when they dropped off Paolo and Lucia, Ezio said only, "See you tomorrow."

"Yes," Paolo said.

"Soon," Lucia said.

Donna blew a kiss and Ezio started the car to make the drive up the hill and home.

"Let's wait," Ezio said when he took off the jacket and the cummerbund and the pants and the shirt and the blasted tie, "for you to tell me about the film. I don't think I can go through that now."

"You get a good night's sleep."

But Ezio did not sleep well that night, spending it mostly staring at the ceiling and reliving the few scenes he had seen. It was not until they were having lunch the next day that Ezio asked his wife to describe *Separazione.* She was careful in her description, not giving too many of the grim details but mainly reciting the basic story.

"Ezio, Salvatore Balconi has been very faithful to your story. A few characters have been eliminated and maybe some scenes, but it's all there. Really. It's your story on the screen."

"I'm pleased."

"It's a beautiful motion picture, Ezio. Salvatore Balconi can be very proud. And so can Ezio Maffini. By the way, the credits at the end had your name in pretty big type: '*Screenplay adapted from the novel* Il cielo *by Ezio Maffini.*'"

"Well, we'll see what happens. Why do you think people were so quiet after the film? I mean, nobody said anything. You'd think they'd say something, if they liked it, if they hated it."

"Ezio, why do you think none of us said anything in the car on the way home? We were all so affected. We were still in the movie. We didn't want to leave. That's because it's so powerful."

"Let's see what the critics say."

The reviews dribbled out in newspapers and magazines over the next days and weeks. Ezio couldn't believe it.

"Balconi's Masterpiece!" "Best Movie of the Year, Maybe Decade!" "Unforgettable!" "Will Surely Win the David di Donatello!" "Six Stars Out of Five!" "Everyone Must See This!"

"Well," Ezio said, putting down the latest review, "I guess they like it."

"Will you see it now?"

"I'm still not ready. Maybe I'll wait until it comes out on VHS."

"I don't think you can wait that long for a tape."

What Ezio couldn't wait for was some word about Balconi. He was now calling Signora Franacini almost every day, and every day, the response was always the same. "He's still the same. He's not able to see you."

"Just for a minute?"

"I'm afraid not."

"Could I just come over? Maybe he'd recognize me."

"No, I'm sure he wouldn't."

"So I shouldn't come?"

"Signor Maffini, I am sure Signor Balconi would not want you to see him like this. He's resting peacefully. The doctor is here every day, there are nurses here all the time. They are giving him more medication so I think…"

Her voice faltered, and it was a full minute before she could continue.

"Signor Maffini, you will be the first to know when…"

Her voice broke again.

"When the time comes, I'll call. Please. Thank you for calling."

It was only two days later when Signora Franacini called. Ezio told Donna and together they sat on the terrace, silently sipping tea.

The huge funeral was in Rome, attended by the president, prime minister, famous directors and actors, even a delegation from the Vatican. Everyone vied to be on television with their memories. Burial was next to his wife and son in the mausoleum at Castelforentino. Ezio thought of visiting the cemetery but decided it would bring little comfort. He did attend all four films when an art film theater in Florence had a Balconi festival featuring *Povertà, Tradimento, Celebrazione* and *Silenzio.*

"I just wish I could have talked to him again," he told Donna. "I wish I knew more about him during the war and what he went through. He suffered so much."

"Ezio, making the film must have been cathartic for him. He had been holding all his emotions in for so many years, and now he had a chance to release them. I'd like to think that when he had done that, his life was complete. He could join his wife and his little boy and his parents."

"Maybe my book had a role in all that."

"Of course it did. It started him on this, well, journey if you want to use that word."

"I'd rather not."

A month after the funeral, Signora Franacini called Ezio. "I'm sending you a package. Signor Balconi wanted you to have it. Thank you for being his friend."

The package arrived four days later. Inside, Ezio found a well-worn copy of *Il cielo* with a note:

"Caro *Ezio. I want you to know how much your book has meant to me, but more important, how much you have meant to me. You gave me the inspiration to complete this film. Some may regard it as my masterpiece. I regard it as a tribute to the courageous men and women you wrote about. Thank you for writing it. And thank you for being my friend.* Con gratitudine! *Salvatore*

It took Ezio about fifteen minutes before he could put down the note and look at the book. Its dust cover was torn and the corners of many pages had been turned down. Ezio sat in his favorite chair near the fireplace and turned the pages one by one. Sentences were underlined and exclamation points punctuated the margins. There was a handwritten note on every page, sometimes two or three.

Franca hides a young army escapee in her attic. *What a beautiful passage. I can just see that young man. And she is so brave.*

The village priest rebuffs the Nazis. *Yes, that's exactly right. I've known priests like that. There were so many courageous priests during the war.*

The partisans group on a hillside. *This reminds me of my friend Robin. I can still see him. I miss him every day.*

The kind teacher tries to instruct the villagers about Dante. *The language in this section is exquisite. I wish I had read more of Dante. I should try again now.*

The villagers must decide about taking in the POW. *Those poor people. What a decision to make. They're risking their lives.*

The little brothers want to get medicine for their sister. *I love the little boys. I wonder what will happen to them.*

Fabio's lover tries to escape. *She is so lovely. She reminds me of…*

The partisan wants to avenge the massacre. *This happened to me. It's like a different person now.*

The firefight outside the farmhouse. *A gruesome scene, well told. I can still see those battles.*

Page after page, note after note. Salvatore Balconi had obviously read every word, probably many times. The director, Ezio thought, might have given the world a masterpiece of storytelling, but he had given Ezio something personal, his love.

It was almost midnight when Ezio finished reading every page and gently closed the book. Donna was reading her own book on the other side of the fireplace.

"You're crying, aren't you?" she said.

"Can't help it."

"It's all right. Yes, Ezio, everything's all right."

Epilogue

WITH A NEW MILLENIUM, many of the villagers at Sant'Antonio and their relatives elsewhere in Tuscany have settled into quiet, comfortable lives. Some are looking for new adventures.

In Florence, Dino's uncles, Roberto and Adolfo, retired from *Gli Angeli della Casa,* and Roberto, in a small ceremony, finally married Rosanna in 2001. Dino and his son, Tarik, took over the home repair business and hired another manager. Tarik, who had shown exceptional prowess as a goalie on an amateur soccer team, was tempted to go professional but turned down an offer to join the *Fiorentino.* He would have been the first Albanian goalie on an Italian team.

Father Lorenzo retired from active ministry at Santa Croce and reduced his volunteer nights at the soup kitchen to twice a week. Once a month he took the bus to Siena to visit Victoria Stonehill, who took time off from an increasing amount of work at The Center for Women's Studies in Palazzo Murano.

"We're getting requests for information from all over the world," she told the priest one day. "We seem to have been a model for getting things done in the women's movement."

The relationship of another priest, Father Giancarlo, *"il sacerdote dolce,"* and Dino's aunt, Anna, was still a great mystery to the family. Anna only smiled and changed the subject when her sister, Lucia, asked about it.

"Did you watch Father Giancarlo's program the other night?" Lucia would ask and Anna would say. "Isn't he amazing? I was too busy with another girl's baby."

In Cortona, Dino's cousin Bruno had to hire two more assistants for his tourist business when the film of *Under the Tuscan Sun* was released in 2003. Although the film fictionalized Frances Mayes' account of remaking

Bramasole, its gorgeous views of the countryside made everyone want to experience Cortona for themselves.

In Sant'Antonio, Lucia and Paolo were enduring the usual complications of old age. Both had vision problems and severe arthritis; Lucia used a walker and Paolo a cane, but they still went to the piazza for the *passeggiata* almost every night. There was not a day when Lucia didn't talk about the celebration of their golden wedding anniversary.

"How can I thank you, Paolo?"

"How about a good dinner?"

Like many new things, the novelty of the supermarket at Reboli soon wore off and the villagers drove over there only to stock up on such things as paper towels and toilet paper. Otherwise, they continued to favor Mario's *bottega* and Anita's meat market for their daily needs. Both shops continued to attract tourists with Amabilia's Famous Biscotti and Santo's Own Wild Boar Salami.

Amabilia didn't make the cookies anymore, leaving Signora Marincola in charge. Since her husband Emilio's sudden death of a heart attack in 2002, Amabilia and Signor Bernadetto Magnimassimo were alone in the sprawling mansion on the hill, except, of course, for Bella. The cat was getting old, too, and played only sporadically with her favorite red ball. In the winter, she snuggled with the Signor under the blankets.

Signora Marincola's daughter, Clara, found herself on the cover of *Panorama* and interviewed by three television stations after her daring performance as a flag thrower in Lucca. *Sbandieratori* teams from Ferrara, Bracciano and Sansepolcro begged her to join, but she declined.

"They only want to exploit me, get some publicity as the only woman with all those men," Clara said. She enrolled at the University of Pisa to study business management. Her brother Francesco already had his engineering degree and was working for Ferrari in Modena. Their younger brother, Pasquale, was preparing to study art at the Accademia di Belle Arti in Florence.

At the Cielo, Ezio and Donna turned down an invitation to go to Hollywood for the Oscar presentations, preferring to watch the ceremonies on their new fifty-five-inch flat screen television. *Separazione* had already won the David di Donatello award for best picture in Italy and was considered a shoe-in for the Academy Award for best foreign picture.

The couple cheered when Anton Silvestino, who had assisted Salvatore Balconi in directing the film, accepted the award. Silvestino thanked all the actors, "especially the villagers who were new to this sort of thing," the crew, and, of course, Balconi, "one of Italy's great film directors who left us this great legacy."

Then Silvestino held the gold statuette in the air. "There's one more thing I'd like to say. Signor Balconi would want me to pay homage to the source of *Separazione,* the fine novel *Il cielo* by the wonderfully gifted writer and partisan hero, Ezio Maffini. Thank you, Ezio!"

"Oh my God," Donna whispered. "That's so incredible. Ezio, are you crying?"

"Yes."